Also by Lesley Eames

The Runaway Women in London
The Brighton Guest House Girls
The Orphan Twins
The Wartime Singers

***The Wartime Bookshop* series**
The Wartime Bookshop
Land Girls at the Wartime Bookshop
Christmas at the Wartime Bookshop
Evacuees at the Wartime Bookshop
A Foundling at the Wartime Bookshop

WEDDING BELLS AT THE WARTIME BOOKSHOP

Lesley Eames

PENGUIN BOOKS

TRANSWORLD PUBLISHERS

UK | USA | Canada | Ireland | Australia
India | New Zealand | South Africa

Transworld is part of the Penguin Random House group of companies
whose addresses can be found at global.penguinrandomhouse.com.

Penguin Random House UK, One Embassy Gardens, 8 Viaduct Gardens, London SW11 7BW

penguin.co.uk

Penguin
Random House
UK

First published in Great Britain in 2025 by Penguin Books
an imprint of Transworld Publishers

002

Typeset in Baskerville by Falcon Oast Graphic Art Ltd.
Printed and bound in Great Britain by Clays Ltd, Elcograf S.p.A.

The authorized representative in the EEA is Penguin Random House
Ireland, Morrison Chambers, 32 Nassau Street, Dublin D02 YH68

A CIP catalogue record for this book is available from the British Library

ISBN: 9781804993729

To my four precious angels – my beloved daughters,
Olivia and Isobel, and my utterly adorable
granddaughters, Charlotte and Anastasia.
Thank you so much for all the love and laughter.

Prologue

June 1942

The room is quiet except for the purposeful slice of scissors as they cut through newspaper. It's evening and the curtains are fully closed, not only because blackout rules insist that no light should escape but also to stop prying eyes from seeing what's afoot inside the room.

A table stands near the window, and on it small piles are arranged like anthills, each pile comprising individual letters cut from the newspaper. A pile for the letter A, a pile for the letter B . . . Not all letters have piles, though. X is unlikely to be needed and neither is Q. Probably some other letters won't be needed either – not tonight – but it doesn't hurt to put them by for future use. After all, this is the start of a campaign. All being well. Whether it works remains to be seen but, based on information received, there's hope. Definitely hope.

Enough cutting? For the moment. The newspaper is folded back up and the scissors set aside. Paper is fetched for the next stage in the process, together with a pot of glue and a pair of tweezers, but first a short break to put the kettle on and make tea. The tea is brewed and poured, the cup and saucer being carried back to the table so the next task can begin. A letter W is selected with the tweezers, dipped in glue and placed on the paper. A letter E follows, then an L and then another L. In less than ten minutes the task is finished. A moment is taken to study the result and this leads to a satisfied smile because it's perfect.

The paper needs to be left for a while so the glue can dry. It'll lose some of its impact if any of the letters are dislodged or smudged, and the intention is for the impact to be . . . powerful.

Meanwhile, there's an envelope to prepare. Glued-on letters can't be used because the envelope needs to pass through the postal system without raising eyebrows or suspicions. A typewriter would be helpful – nicely anonymous – but no typewriter is available, so the envelope will have to be written by hand – with the writing disguised.

A few trial runs are made by copying the shapes of letters in the newspaper on to a scrap of paper. Then it's time to write on the envelope. Slowly, carefully, the letters are added and a study of the finished result leads to another satisfied smile. There's an awkwardness to the envelope's appearance because the flow of regular handwriting is absent. But it should get the job done well enough, the name and address being crystal clear:

Mrs Naomi Harrington
Foxfield
Churchwood
Hertfordshire

CHAPTER ONE

Churchwood, Hertfordshire, England

Naomi

Naomi had no reason to suspect that the day was going to take a turn for the worse when she woke with the sun blazing in the sky and a happy mood glowing in her heart. She'd been floating on a cloud of relief ever since her divorce had come through the previous week. Not that she believed divorce should be celebrated, exactly. After all, it meant the failure of a marriage and Naomi took that seriously. But she'd married an arrogant man who'd treated her with coldness for more than a quarter of a century and betrayed her in the worst way possible, so who wouldn't be glad to be free of him at last, especially since happiness beckoned with a much nicer man?

There were other things to appreciate, too. The divorce meant that Foxfield, her home for most of her adult life, was hers now. It was the largest and loveliest house in Churchwood, set on the outskirts of the village in beautiful gardens. Built in early Victorian times with later additions, it was a rambling property with gables here and there and a pretty wooden porch embracing the front door.

Some of the money her former husband had fleeced from the inheritance she'd received from her father had also been returned. This had relieved her of her financial anxieties and meant she was now buying another property – a house she'd been renting as a temporary home for the bookshop she helped to organize. Established only two years ago in the Sunday School Hall, the Churchwood bookshop had soon become the hub of village life, offering a wide range of activities and social gatherings as well as books, not only to village residents but also to the patients and staff of Stratton House, a nearby military hospital. Keeping up the morale of injured servicemen and the people who looked after them was important.

Unfortunately, the Hall had been destroyed when an enemy aircraft had accidentally crashed into it. Naomi's purchase of the house meant the bookshop's temporary home could become permanent. She also had plans to replace the furniture and other equipment that had been lost in the crash, but that would take time. Until then, they were getting by with a mismatched collection of donated items and gradually replacing the books. Naomi's most recent purchases included two Agatha Christie mysteries, which were always popular.

Books were being donated by other people, too. On Saturday she'd been delighted to receive a package of books from a former hospital patient.

Dear Mrs Harrington,

I hope this letter finds you well. I also hope you'll be pleased to accept the enclosed books as a token of gratitude for all that the bookshop did for me during my time at Stratton House. The books I was able to borrow helped me through many a dark hour. I enjoyed the visits of bookshop volunteers, too, particularly Alice Irvine and Adam Potts. As for the concert the bookshop organized, it was a real boost to my spirits.

With every good wish,

Eric Morton, Sergeant.

*PS. I'm recovering well from my wounds now I'm conva-
lescing. It'll be back to the war for me soon, but I'll take many
happy memories of the bookshop with me.*

How gratifying it was to receive letters like this. Sergeant
Morton's books included Walter Scott's *Ivanhoe* and
John Buchan's *The Thirty-Nine Steps* and both were very
welcome.

Naomi intended to take all the new books to the bookshop
when she set out for it shortly. Just now, with breakfast over,
she was taking advantage of a few minutes of quiet – rare
in a house filled with the waifs and strays of wartime – to
retreat to her sitting room to make a note of the new books
in the bookshop register.

This sitting room was her favourite place in the house. It
wasn't as grand as the larger drawing room, the mahogany-
furnished dining room or even the study. But it was warm
and welcoming with a thickly piled blue carpet underfoot, heavy brocade curtains the colour of old gold at the
windows and matching sofas and armchairs.

Job done, she studied the rota of people who'd volunteered to help Jane Hunt, a local resident who'd been laid
low with a foot infection. Rotas like this had become bookshop business too and, once again, it was gratifying to see
so many names listed and to know that Jane was going to
be well looked after.

Community was always important but never more so
than in wartime, when the challenges were numerous –
absent loved ones, danger, rationing and food shortages . . .
But the bookshop seemed to be rising to the challenges
very well indeed.

Life seemed to be treating Naomi's fellow organizers

well, too. Alice Irvine, the original brains behind the bookshop, still had the worry of a husband serving overseas in the British army, but she was looking radiant in her second pregnancy – the first having ended tragically in miscarriage. Janet Collins and May Janicki also had family members in the army – Janet a son and May a husband – but, like Alice's Daniel, both men were uninjured and apparently coping well. Kate Fletcher had become Kate Kinsella and was blissfully happy in her marriage to RAF flight lieutenant Leo, who was currently training new pilots after being shot down and sustaining wounds from which he was recovering well. Adam Potts, the new young vicar, was proving a wonderful support to the bookshop and the village in general. Finally, there was Bert Makepiece, a down to earth and rather scruffy market gardener, who, amazingly, had turned out to be the love of Naomi's life.

Even Naomi's household seemed to be thriving. She'd taken in several families of evacuees from the East End of London not so long ago and, after some teething problems, the children had settled well. So had the women, who'd found work in aircraft construction in nearby Hatfield, with the exception of Ivy, a grandmother who kept an eye on the smaller children instead.

Naomi was particularly pleased for her housekeeper, Victoria, a pretty girl of only twenty-two who'd taken on two of the evacuee children who'd been orphaned. Victoria was in the early stages of a romance with an American sergeant, Paul Scarletti, of whom Naomi very much approved.

Then there was Suki, Naomi's little maid, who had a birthday today. Suki's pleasure in birthdays made them enjoyable for everyone. Naomi always put on a birthday tea for her.

After a lot of ups and downs, Naomi was pleased with life.

She glanced at the clock. It was almost time to set out. She began packing a bag with the books, rota and the notepad she always carried with her so she could jot down things she needed to remember.

A knock sounded on the sitting-room door and Victoria entered, looking lovely with her honey-coloured hair and kind green eyes. Naomi had insisted on first-name terms almost from the moment the girl had arrived six months earlier.

'The post is here,' Victoria said, presenting three envelopes on a silver tray.

Naomi took them with a smile, noticing that Victoria was blushing and swiftly diagnosing the reason. 'You've heard from Paul?'

Victoria's blush deepened endearingly. 'He's written to say he might be able to come to tea quite soon. Not next week but perhaps the week after.'

Paul Scarletti was based a few miles away. It was often difficult for him to get away but he always seemed keen to do his best. 'He'll be most welcome,' Naomi said. Entertaining was challenging given the wartime shortages but they'd manage to feed him somehow. With goodwill on all sides, they always did.

'Thank you,' Victoria said, and Naomi smiled as the admirable young woman withdrew.

Alone again, she looked at her letters. There was a bill, a list of new books from a bookstore in St Albans and – what was this? A personal letter, judging from the handwriting on the front. It was unfamiliar and rather odd handwriting, but Naomi imagined it concerned the bookshop in some way. Tearing the envelope open, she drew out a single sheet of notepaper – and gasped, recoiling in dismay at the words that spat contemptuously up at her.

WELL, AREN'T YOU A BOSSY WOMAN? IT'S TIME YOU STOPPED ORDERING PEOPLE ABOUT AND LET THEM GET ON WITH THEIR OWN LIVES. THEY'LL BE A LOT HAPPIER WITHOUT YOUR INTERFERENCE.

CHAPTER TWO

Suki

Suki washed up the breakfast dishes in the Foxfield kitchen with her usual efficiency but her mind was elsewhere – on the fact that today was her birthday. She'd always loved birthdays – other people's as well as her own – since they were cheerful occasions and it was wonderful to see the pleasure on people's faces when they received cards and gifts, however small. This birthday wasn't an ordinary one, though, and Suki's feelings about it were mixed.

It troubled her that turning eighteen would take her a step closer to being caught by the law that had been introduced last year making unmarried women and childless widows liable to be called up for war work. At present it only applied to women of twenty or above so Suki would still have two years before it affected her. But no one seemed to be predicting that peace would come soon – not even now the Americans were involved – and she was worried that the age limit might gradually be reduced to include women of nineteen or even eighteen. That would give her no time at all before the law required her to serve king and country.

Suki couldn't say that she loved her king, exactly. She was willing to allow that he might be a very nice man and a very good king, but he was a remote sort of figure who lived in a palace she'd never even seen, surrounded by jewels and red-coated guards. She *did* love her country, but more than her country in general, she loved this little pocket of it. Churchwood, and her life here. Suki couldn't imagine ever leaving it.

In any case, she believed she already was doing war work of a sort. She might be a housemaid but in working for Mrs Harrington – a job she'd held ever since leaving school at fourteen – she was looking after a woman who did so much to keep the village going through difficult times. After all, life on the home front wasn't easy, what with the rationing and the shortages and even more with the worry about those of its menfolk who were serving in the forces, not to mention the ever-present fear of an enemy invasion.

Mrs Harrington kept up village morale in so many ways. As well as being generally kind and generous, she was one of the chief organizers of the Churchwood bookshop. She'd also opened her home to evacuees from London – six women and ten children, including Victoria, the new housekeeper, and Arthur and Jenny, the two orphans Victoria had taken on. One of those women, Ivy, a grandmother who suffered from badly bowed legs caused by rickets, and her little granddaughter, Flower, slept in the village now, but they still came to Foxfield every day so Ivy could help with the younger children while their mothers were at work.

Officers in the army were allowed servants. Batmen, they were called, for some reason Suki didn't understand. Why shouldn't Mrs Harrington be allowed a servant, too, when the services of that servant left her free to do so much good? Suki feared the War Office wouldn't see it that way, though.

But the possibility of being required to undertake official war work in the not-so-distant future was only one aspect of this birthday. There was a second aspect that was much more exciting. Suki wouldn't officially be grown up until she reached twenty-one, but eighteen still felt like a turning point because surely it would mean that *he*'d stop seeing her as little more than a child – Suki was small and knew she looked young for her age – and realize she was now a woman instead. A woman he could come to love the way she loved him, which was—

She startled, blushing, as someone tapped on the kitchen window. It was Beth Ellis, a nurse at Stratton House Hospital. Suki had got to know her when Mrs Harrington and Victoria had taken in a foundling baby girl who had been left in the Foxfield porch. The baby had been happily reunited with her parents since then but, in helping to care for her for a while, Beth had become Suki's friend – much to Suki's surprise and delight. After all, Beth was several years older and a highly trained professional nurse. Suki had, in fact, felt rather awed by Beth when they'd first met, partly because of their different circumstances and partly because Beth's manner had seemed a little stiff. Distant, even. But she'd soon shown a warmer side of her personality and Suki believed her new friend couldn't be kinder.

She opened the door to her with a smile. 'Beth, it's lovely to see you.'

'I can't stay, but I wanted to wish you a happy birthday and give you these.' Beth handed over a card and a gift. 'They're nothing special since I haven't managed to get to the shops with the hospital being so short-staffed at the moment, but I hope you'll like them.'

Suki opened the envelope and found a pretty card inside. Then she opened the gift and saw a necklace of blue beads that she'd admired around Beth's neck one day. 'You can't give me this,' Suki cried, struck by the sacrifice. 'It suits you so well.'

'It'll suit you, too, and I want you to have it. In fact, I insist. But duty calls now, I'm afraid.'

'Have you come all this way just for me?' Suki asked. The walk to and from the hospital was long and Beth had obviously been rushing. Her pretty cheeks were pink, her brown curls a little dishevelled and her blue eyes sparkled from the exercise.

'I didn't want to miss wishing you a happy birthday,' Beth explained. 'It isn't as though I can come to your tea party this afternoon.'

How nice she was.

'Must dash now.' Beth stepped forward to kiss Suki's cheek and headed for the door. After a quick wave she was gone.

Suki placed the card and gift on the kitchen dresser and took up a tea cloth to dry the china she'd washed. She was lucky to have friends like Beth Ellis, though it was a pity Beth couldn't come to the party. On that thought, Suki's mind returned to *him*. Would he manage to come along? Oh, Suki hoped so!

CHAPTER THREE

Beth

Beth broke into a light run as she hastened along Brimbles Lane towards the hospital. It wasn't just because Matron was a stickler for punctuality, nor even because Beth took a pride in her work and always aimed to present herself for duty early. She had another reason for her eagerness today.

She was glad she'd made the effort to see Suki on her birthday, though. Mrs Harrington's maid was known in the village as 'sweet little Suki' and Beth was fond of her in the way of the younger sister she'd never had, Beth being an only child. But she also suspected that there was more to her friend than general niceness – a sharper brain and more spirit than met the eye. They were qualities Beth possessed, too. She'd needed them in order to become a nurse.

Beth's parents – good people – had always lived modest, everyday kind of lives, never moving from the neighbourhood in which they'd been brought up. They'd expected their only child to follow in their footsteps by marrying a local boy and living around the corner in a cosy little house which would be convenient for them getting together almost daily. Beth's ambition and achievements had baffled them – probably disappointed them a little, too, since they had taken her away from home – but they'd supported her despite their puzzlement and she loved them dearly for it.

Beth enjoyed her nursing work. Naturally, it took an emotional toll on her when patients suffered, but it rewarded her immensely to know she was using her skills to help them.

It remained to be seen what Suki made of herself, going forward. But watching her promised to be interesting.

Reaching the hospital – a beautiful stone mansion house that had been a private home years ago – Beth headed straight up to her little bedroom under the eaves. Some nurses had to share rooms but this one was too small for a second bed so she had it to herself.

Grabbing her washbag, she moved down the corridor to a bathroom where she washed quickly, and then returned to her room to change into her uniform, brushing her hair and pinning it back, then securing her cap on top. A glance at her watch showed she had a moment to spare and she used it to study her reflection in her mirror. She looked clean and neat, which should satisfy Matron. But what else did her reflection show her?

Beth knew there was nothing striking about her appearance. Like Suki, she was brown-haired and blue-eyed. Unlike dainty Suki, she was of average height and average build. No one would call Beth a beauty, but they often called her pretty and that was surely good enough.

She'd had her fill of men with dazzling good looks not so long ago when she'd lost her head over a handsome doctor. In hindsight it felt like an episode of temporary madness, but she was well and truly over it now and valued a man's true worth over and above his ranking as a fairytale character.

There was one man in particular whose worth she'd come to value most of all and the thought that she might see him in the hospital today sent a shiver of excitement over her.

She hastened downstairs and checked in with Matron before continuing on to Ward One. Smiles greeted her as she pushed through the door and one smile warmed her more than any other. The man who'd given it was too far away to exchange words but he waved and Beth waved back, anticipating speaking to him later with pleasure.

The man was Adam Potts, Churchwood's vicar, who visited the patients regularly. As well as bringing them books from the bookshop, he'd sit and listen to them, read to them, write letters for them, share jokes with them and, if they wanted, pray for them, too. He was also the man she was coming to love. At first glance he was hardly a romantic hero. He wasn't especially tall. He wasn't especially strong. And he certainly wasn't especially dapper when it came to clothes. He was often untidy, in fact, his thick shock of overlong brown hair being particularly untamed. As for transport, there was no sports car for Adam. He rode to and from the hospital, but instead of a fiery black stallion he had an ancient bicycle that often left him dripping wet from rain and tugging bicycle clips from his sodden, drooping trouser legs.

But he had the sweetest smile and the softest, kindest brown eyes Beth had ever seen. Adam took patients' troubles seriously and always had comforting words to say. But he also had a good sense of the ridiculous and wasn't above laughing at himself.

She heard him laughing now at something Private Jenks had said. 'William Jenks, you must be a menace to your mother's peace of mind,' Adam commented.

'Always was, always will be. Losing a foot isn't going to stop that.'

'She has my sympathy, but I expect she'll be pleased to know you're still the mischievous son she brought up.'

'That she will,' Private Jenks confirmed.

A doctor entered to make his rounds. 'Time for me to slip out,' Adam told the soldier and, getting up, he returned his chair to the stack of other visitor chairs at the far end of the ward.

He caught Beth's eye as he passed her on his way to the door. 'See you later,' he whispered, and he sent her a wink that warmed her through and through.

Beth was kept busy during his absence. As well as the doctor's rounds there were medications to supervise, patients to be got ready for theatre or surgery and a myriad other tasks that made up the day to be tackled from distributing cups of tea to changing the bedding of a patient who'd been sick. 'Sorry, Nurse,' Corporal Peterson said. 'I aimed for the bowl but somehow I missed.'

'It's nothing to worry about,' Beth assured him, always keen for patients to keep their dignity when they were at their most vulnerable.

She was carrying the soiled bedding to the laundry basket when Adam appeared in the corridor. His smile made her heart give a little fillip. 'How are you, Beth?' he asked. 'Overworked, I imagine.'

'We're still short-staffed,' Beth confirmed. One nurse had broken a leg falling off a bicycle. Another had developed glandular fever. And a third – poor Lucy Gibbs – had been granted compassionate leave because her fiancé had just lost his life after his ship was torpedoed in the Atlantic.

'Has anyone heard from Lucy recently?' Adam said.

'I had a short note thanking me for a card I sent,' Beth said. 'She's pretty cut up so I'm not sure when she'll return. Matron won't want to risk Lucy's grief upsetting the patients.'

16

'That's understandable.'

Matron emerged from her office and raised an eyebrow. 'I'm distracting Nurse Ellis,' Adam admitted, not hesitating to take the blame on himself. 'But I'll be on my way so I'll save you the need to give me a ticking off.'

He was joking, of course. He gave Beth another warming wink and then continued towards the ward.

'Sorry, Matron,' Beth said. 'I'll get rid of this bedding and return to work.'

'I'd never accuse *you* of slacking, Nurse Ellis,' Matron said. 'I want a word with you anyway.'

'Oh?'

'Take the bedding to the laundry basket and then come into my office.'

Beth hastened to do so.

'You'll be pleased to hear we've a new pair of hands coming to help,' Matron said.

'That *is* good news.'

'Nurse Whittaker is arriving today on a permanent posting. As someone who joined us only a couple of months ago, I'm sure your memory of the things it might be useful for a newcomer to know is fresher than that of our more established nurses, so I'd like you to give her a tour of the hospital.'

'I'll be glad to help,' Beth confirmed.

'Thank you.'

Beth left before Matron – never one for idle chit-chat – could chivvy her on her way.

Back in the ward, she noticed Private Hendricks trying to attract her attention and went to his bedside to ask how she might help.

'It's my leg, Nurse. It won't stop itching.'

'That often happens when a wound is healing,' Beth

17

explained, but she took a look anyway. There was no sign of infection and Private Hendricks's forehead was cool to the touch. 'Do you have anything to take your mind off the itching? A book, perhaps?'

'I've finished the one Alice brought from the bookshop but I can't change it because I don't think she's here.'

'I believe she may be in later.'

Adam glided up beside her. 'Did I hear you say you needed a book?' he asked the private.

'To take my mind off my itching,' the private explained.

'Itching, eh?' Adam was all sympathy. 'It can drive a man to distraction. Some of the other chaps might return books to me as I make my way around the wards and I'll be glad to save one for you. Meanwhile . . . how about I read a story out loud?'

'Suits me,' Private Hendricks said.

'Me too,' said Private Rugg, who occupied the next bed, and a few more nearby heads nodded.

'Don't forget us!' someone shouted from further down the ward.

'I'll be along to you lot shortly,' Adam called back.

'And I'll be sure to include you in the tea round,' Beth told him.

His grateful smile made her feel as though her veins were fizzing. He liked her as a person and he admired her as a nurse. Beth was sure about that. But how did he feel about her as a woman? Beth didn't yet know since he was friendly to everyone. But she hoped for a sign from him soon.

She walked away to continue with her other duties, thinking about Adam and also about the new nurse who was coming to Stratton House. Another friend in the making? Having been a little different from other girls at school, Beth hadn't formed the knack of making friends, but that was changing now she was in Churchwood. The village seemed to draw people into its warmth and Beth was rapidly shedding her reserve and opening up to friendships. The person she was most open to was Adam, of course, but she was sure she could make room for a new nurse to become a friend as well. Life was good!

CHAPTER FOUR

Ruby

Up in her bedroom at Brimbles Farm, Ruby Turner placed two shillings into a tin that had once held toffees. This was the fund she was saving for her wedding but it was woefully small.

As a land girl she was paid thirty-two shillings a week – a rise of four shillings from when she'd started – but twenty-one shillings were kept back for board and lodging for herself and Timmy. The remaining eleven shillings didn't go far. Not for two people, and especially not when one of them was a fast-growing boy of eight.

Her fiancé, Kenny, was also putting money into the tin but he, too, had little to spare. He might be the eldest son of the man who owned the farm where Ruby worked, but skinflint Ernie – called by his first name by all of his five children, perhaps because he was so lacking in parental affection – preferred to plough the money the farm made straight back into it. Not that he invested any of the money in the farmhouse where they all lived. It was a ramshackle old place, patched up here and there on the outside while on the inside there were bare floorboards, drab walls, an ancient stove from yesteryear and scuffed, mismatched furniture. Kenny didn't mind going without much cash to call his own, since he'd share in the inheritance of the farm when his father passed on, but it would be nice if he had a few more shillings to put into the tin.

The idea of asking mean old Ernie to contribute to the wedding costs was laughable and it wasn't as though Ruby's parents would help, either. She didn't expect it because, with her father working on the docks back in London and her mother keeping house, Ruby knew they hadn't much money to spare. But it was a pity they couldn't make up for it with enthusiasm and joy.

Ruby was their only child but had always been a disappointment to them. They'd criticized her love of pretty things for being vain and flighty and predicted that nothing good would come of it – a prediction they'd considered entirely justified when she'd fallen pregnant at just sixteen after a married man who'd employed her as a trainee hairdresser had taken advantage of her.

The pregnancy had shocked Ruby, too. Terrified her, in fact. But she'd loved Timmy on sight and wouldn't be without him now. Unfortunately, her parents had made no secret of their disgust for both their daughter and their grandson, and only to save face with the neighbours had they passed Timmy off as their own child.

That masquerade had at least spared Timmy from the cruelty that Ruby had seen inflicted on children born out of wedlock despite the fact that those children had had no say in the circumstances of their births. Vicious name-calling, snide looks . . .

Protecting Timmy had been the reason she'd volunteered as a land girl. At the outbreak of war Timmy had been evacuated to a farm in Bedfordshire, but he'd been miserable there. Desperate to help him, Ruby had hit upon the idea of becoming a land girl on a different farm in the hope that, in time, she'd be allowed to have the boy she called her little brother come to live with her. As plans went, it had been far-fetched and unlikely but, thanks to the kindness of Kate and Ruby's developing relationship with Kenny, it had succeeded.

Kate and Alice had soon guessed the truth about Ruby's relationship with Timmy, and Ruby had confessed it to a few carefully selected others – Kenny included – since they were kind and trustworthy. But to the rest of the world the masquerade had continued.

Change had come in the shape of a young girl who lived just outside Churchwood. Hannah Powell had also fallen pregnant at sixteen and even abandoned her daughter at Foxfield temporarily while hoping that Mattie, the man she loved, would return home from the war to marry her and put things right. Unfortunately, Hannah's secret had been exposed before that could happen, opening her up to the fury of her father and the disgust of much of the village.

Standing by and hiding behind her own secret while poor, defenceless Hannah was covered in disgrace had troubled Ruby's conscience. Besides, she'd come to realize that it was a strain for Timmy, too. It had made him careful when he should have been carefree, and she feared that it might make him feel he had something to be ashamed of when he was entirely innocent of any wrongdoing.

And so, with Timmy's blessing, she'd stood up in front of almost the entire village last month and announced that he was her son. She'd been touched by the love and understanding that many people – most people, in fact – had shown to her and also to Hannah. Happily, Hannah's Mattie had returned home on leave from the war and married her, and it was public knowledge that Ruby, too, was engaged to be married. But a few people still turned their noses up at them.

It seemed that those people included Ruby's own parents, judging from the letter her mother had sent in reply to the news of her engagement.

Dear Ruby,

Thank you for your letter. It's a pity you didn't marry eight years ago when you were cavorting with the father of the boy instead of bringing us so much shame, but we're relieved to hear that you're going to be marrying now, even if it's to a different man. Better late than never, as the saying goes. It'll be good for the boy to have a man to influence him, always assuming that the man you're marrying is respectable. We expect you'll want to keep the wedding quiet, given your unfortunate history, but we wish you well.

From your mother.

Ruby had read the letter several times since receiving it and had reached a number of conclusions:

1 She was still unforgiven for falling pregnant out of wedlock.
2 They were still calling darling Timmy 'the boy', as though he were a stranger's child instead of their grandson.
3 They thought a man in his life would be a good influence because they considered Ruby to be a bad influence.
4 The wedding might be a relief to them but they had little interest in it.

After all these years Ruby knew better than to be hurt by them, yet hurt she was. But she was used to making the best of bad situations. She'd needed a strong backbone to weather the storms life had blown her way and that backbone would hold her in good stead again.

Even so, she couldn't help a pang of regret passing through her. As a young girl she'd daydreamed about the sort of wedding she might have one day. She'd imagined a white dress for herself, pink dresses for her bridesmaids, masses of flowers and a three-tiered confection of a cake . . . Ah, well.

Closing the toffee tin and returning it to a drawer, she caught sight of movement out in the farmyard. Looking through the window, she saw Mr Baldry, the postman, approaching. Running downstairs, she opened the kitchen door to him and greeted him with a smile.

'Sorry I'm late,' he said. 'I got a puncture on the way.' He nodded down at his bicycle's front tyre.

'Not the first puncture you've had on Brimbles Lane,' Ruby suggested.

'Not the first. Unlikely to be the last,' he agreed.

From protruding rocks to potholes, there were numerous hazards along the lane that ran between Brimbles Farm and Churchwood. They made cycling to and from the village a painful affair of jolts, jars and rattling teeth. To Ruby, anyway. Kenny's sister, Kate, and Ruby's fellow land girl, Pearl, found it much easier, perhaps because they were both long-legged and athletic while Ruby was short and curvy. 'Do you need help mending the tyre?' she asked.

'Thanks, but I've patched it well enough for now.' He dug in his bag. 'Three letters for you lot today.'

He handed them over, declined a cup of tea on the grounds that he was already running late and went on his way.

Ruby looked down at the envelopes. None of them were addressed to her. The topmost one looked like a bill and was addressed to *Mr E. Fletcher, Esquire*. Ernie might be the owner of Brimbles Farm, but an esquire? The word implied respectability and even gallantry, neither of which described the sour-faced skinflint who employed Ruby.

The second letter was addressed to Kenny and was probably a catalogue of farming supplies. Kenny was second in command to Ernie when it came to farm matters but far better looking than his father. Tall, with a thick thatch of auburn hair and a muscled physique, he was a handsome man, though it had taken effort on Ruby's part to rouse him out of his customary moroseness. He had his gloomy moments still, but they were being increasingly outpaced by cheerfulness. His poor social skills were also improving, though he'd never be a charmer with words. Still, Ruby loved him and was grateful to him, too. Not every man would have taken her on given her history as an unmarried mother.

The third letter was addressed to *Miss G. Grimes*. In other words, to Ruby's fellow land girl, Pearl. The G stood for Gertrude but Pearl hated that name. 'Gertrude, Gertie, Gert . . . It's a horrible name however you say it,' Pearl had complained, when they'd met during their six weeks of training to become land girls. Days later, she'd been struck by an idea. 'I know!' she'd declared. 'We can be Ruby and Pearl!'

At almost six feet tall with a wiry build and hands and feet like enormous, clumsy shovels, there was little that was jewel-like about Pearl but she was a wonderful land girl, being strong and tireless. It was more than could be said of Ruby. She hated dirt and inclement weather.

Luckily, Kate, the only female member of the Fletcher family, had agreed that, despite land girls being employed to work only on farming, Ruby could swap some of her outdoor work for cooking, cleaning and the like. Domestic work suited Ruby much better and Kate insisted that she didn't mind spending more of her own time outdoors since she'd been working in the fields all her life.

Pearl's letter was from her mother, judging from the handwriting on the envelope. Pearl exchanged letters with her parents as infrequently as possible, always complaining that they didn't understand her and preferred her sister – a dainty, feminine girl, apparently, who loved smart clothes, cocktail parties and beauty parlours.

'I feel like a rhinoceros in their house and I get on their nerves terribly when I drop things or forget I'm wearing dirty shoes and tread mud into the carpet,' Pearl had said. 'They hate me wearing trousers, too. They think they're unladylike. They even sigh when I laugh because they say I sound like a braying donkey.'

But Pearl had never disgraced her family the way Ruby had disgraced hers and, while Pearl's parents clearly found her exasperating, there was no reason to think they didn't love her and wouldn't be delighted by the recent change in her circumstances, for Pearl, too, had become engaged. 'Surely they'll be pleased to hear that you're getting married,' Ruby had suggested, after weeks had passed and Pearl hadn't told her parents about it.

'You never know with my family,' Pearl had said gloomily.

Had she been thinking her fiancé wouldn't pass muster?

Fred was one of the twins who were the youngest of the Fletcher boys after first-born Kenny and second-in-line Vinnie. As farmers, all four brothers were exempt from military service since the country needed them to produce food, especially with imported food becoming scarcer due to the enemy sending so many merchant ships to the bottom of the ocean. But after an evening spent drinking heavily at the Wheatsheaf pub, Fred and his twin, Frank, had enlisted anyway, anticipating larks and adventure. Frank was still serving but Fred had returned home minus his legs and in a deep depression.

Pearl was no gentle ministering angel. She criticized Fred and bickered with him constantly, and he criticized and bickered right back. But somehow Pearl had managed to lift him out of his darkness, and in their own unconventional way they'd fallen in love.

Fred wasn't what many people would regard as a catch. Kenny was the best of the Fletcher boys, of course, being handsome, strong, hard-working and, in his own rough and ready way, loving, too. Poor Vinnie was the least handsome and the most gormless. Not as hard-working as Kenny, either, though he could work well enough when forced. The twins had been somewhere between the two older brothers – good-looking and strong if too inclined to lark about, but Fred's injuries and the pain that came with them had diminished him in size and looks and limited his capacity for work. He'd never had charm and now he had little chance of earning much money either. Would Pearl's parents judge him for that? Certainly, Mr and Mrs Grimes had done nothing to boost Pearl's confidence, but were they really as awful as she made out?

'At least getting married means you won't have to go back home to live when the war ends,' Ruby had finally said, and with that she'd struck a chord with Pearl at last.

'That's true. My parents must be dreading the thought of it.'

Relieved that one aspect of her marriage would please them even if she remained pessimistic about their response to everything else, Pearl had written to tell her parents about her engagement that same evening.

'Anything for me?'

Ruby looked up as Kenny entered the kitchen. He wrapped an arm around her and kissed her. Both kiss and hug felt wonderful. 'A bill for Ernie, a catalogue for you and a letter for Pearl from her mother. Probably about her engagement. Let's hope they approve.'

'Doesn't matter whether they approve or not. It's Pearl who's marrying Fred. Not them.'

Life could be simple to Kenny. He'd lost his mother when his sister, Kate, was small and had been brought up – or rather dragged up – by Ernie. Since Ernie approved of nothing except work, Kenny was used to his disapproval and couldn't have cared less about it. He didn't see why other people should care about parental disapproval either.

'I suspect it'll matter to Pearl,' Ruby said.

'Talking of weddings, I'm glad your parents won't interfere in ours,' Kenny said.

Ruby felt that pang again. No white dress. No bridesmaids. No flowers to speak of. No three-tiered confection of a cake . . . 'I still want our wedding to be nice, even if it has to be modest,' she told him.

'The less fuss, the better, as far as I'm concerned,' Kenny said. 'Walk down the aisle with lots of eyes on me? I'd rather we just turned up at one of those register offices and got the job done there. No fuss. Not much expense. And quick.' He kissed her again. 'Can't we set a date soon?'

'I'd like a few more shillings in the toffee tin first,' Ruby said. 'And I'd like the dust to settle a little more, too.'

In other words, she wanted the gossip about her being an unmarried mother to die down or at least lose some of its spice.

Kenny cared as little for public opinion as for parental disapproval. Feeling him slump beside her, she encouraged his spirits upwards again by saying, 'I put two shillings in the tin today. That's good, isn't it?'

He nodded, though it was clear that a simple trip to the register office would still have suited him better. 'I need to go to Pearson's,' he told her. Pearson's supplied the farm with much of its seed, fertilizer and tools.

Not long ago he'd have gone out with his hands filthy from the farm. Ruby was house-training him now, though, so he headed for the sink to wash his hands and dunk his head under the tap. Kissing her again in passing, he went out to the ancient truck and Ruby stood at the window, watching him start the engine by turning the crank handle with the fluid ease of a man to whom physical work came naturally. He climbed nimbly into the truck and waved. Ruby waved back and then moved away to place the envelopes on the kitchen table. One for Ernie, which he'd doubtless greet with a snarl; one for Kenny, which he'd open when he found time; and one for Pearl.

Ruby had never met Pearl's parents. No one at Brimbles Farm had met them yet. But Pearl had given the impression that they were more than comfortable financially. The thought made Ruby wonder what sort of wedding Pearl was likely to have.

CHAPTER FIVE

Naomi

The clock on Naomi's mantelpiece let out a sudden chime and roused her from the shock she'd been feeling ever since she'd opened that awful letter. For a while she'd been too distressed to do more than pace the room, returning to the letter again and again as she tried to make sense of it. But time was surging forward as time always does, even when a person would prefer it to tick by slowly. Naomi was due to open the bookshop.

On that thought, she felt another pang of dismay. Would the writer of the letter be there? Watching her? Judging her? Naomi's confidence shrivelled. She was a bookshop organizer. She *had* to give instructions sometimes, though she tried hard to frame them as requests. 'Janet, would you mind setting the books out?' she'd ask, or, 'Edna, if you wouldn't mind moving seats . . .'

Had Naomi perhaps overstepped the mark on occasion?

She was out of time for pondering the issue. If Naomi didn't leave soon, people would be waiting outside the bookshop, wondering what had happened to make her late.

Naomi recoiled from the idea of mentioning the letter to anyone. It had upset her and made her feel ashamed of being the target of so much malice. And the last thing she wanted was for anyone else to be upset on her behalf.

No, Naomi needed to think about the letter and gain some sort of perspective on it first. She finished packing her bag and went into the hall for her coat. Victoria looked out through the kitchen door, doubtless on her way to remind Naomi that she needed to set off.

'I forgot the time!' Naomi said, adding a small laugh which she hoped would come across as mild mockery of her foolishness.

She was relieved when Victoria nodded sympathetically, saying, 'Time runs away from us all sometimes.'

'Doesn't it just?'

Smiling, Naomi left the house, but as she made her way down the gravel drive towards the gateposts the smile fell from her lips and her thoughts returned to the letter. Could it have been meant as a prank, perhaps? An ill-judged joke or dare?

No. Naomi couldn't give much credence to that theory. The letter was just too spiteful. Too mean.

A moment of bad temper, then? Of hurt pride or wounded feelings? Sometimes the need to hit out could rise in a burst of frustration, and once it had exploded it would recede again. Perhaps even be regretted.

Again, Naomi found herself struggling to believe it. Producing the letter had been an elaborate, time-consuming business.

Was there a clue in the postmark? The letter had been posted in London but it didn't follow that the writer lived there or had even visited. They could simply have sent the letter to an acquaintance who could have posted it back to Churchwood to muddy the waters of suspicion.

But why choose Naomi as a target? Naomi wasn't aware of having said or done anything to offend anyone but perhaps she'd done so inadvertently. She might have failed to listen to the letter writer with proper attention or forgotten something important. Or she might have let her own words slip out thoughtlessly. If that were the case, Naomi would be only too pleased to apologize.

On the other hand, she might have been chosen as the target simply because she happened to be one of the village's more prominent residents. The thought of considering herself prominent made Naomi wince. It felt arrogant – full of self-importance – but there was no denying that she was known to everyone and heavily involved in the bookshop and most other community activities.

But perhaps she wasn't the only target. For all Naomi knew, her letter might be one of several that had been sent to residents of the village. Much as it pained her to think of anyone else receiving the jolt of a nasty letter, it would relieve her mind to know that she hadn't been singled out for malice.

She passed through the gateposts on to Churchwood Way, the main thoroughfare into the village. Walking past pretty houses and cottages, she realized she was cowering inside herself, wondering if the letter writer might be watching her from behind a curtain and perhaps even enjoying her discomfort. Revelling in it, in fact.

But enough of that. Until Naomi knew more about the letter – who'd sent it and why – she needed to keep her mind open and her emotions in check. She straightened her spine and walked on.

A tall, drooping figure appeared in the distance. It belonged to Marjorie Plym, who always roused mixed feelings in Naomi these days. Churchwood's worst gossip, Marjorie was more than a little silly and often tiresome, but she'd been a loyal friend to Naomi for many years.

She was moving at speed, cantering towards Naomi and looking agitated. Did that mean she'd received a nasty letter, too, and wished to talk about it?

'I'm glad I caught you,' Marjorie said breathlessly as she drew level. 'I need a word about something.'

So Marjorie *had* received a letter, too. Naomi was torn between sympathy for her old friend and relief that she herself wasn't the only target of the poison pen writer. 'I'm sorry you've—'

'*Idiot!*'

Startled, Naomi looked up to see old Jonah Kerrigan waving his walking stick at a motorcyclist who was racing through the village at a much faster speed than was safe. The rider was an American soldier, probably from the same base where Victoria's Paul Scarletti was stationed, though clearly not a sensible man like Paul since this wasn't the first time Naomi had seen him tearing along Churchwood Way.

'*Menace!*' Jonah added, though the motorcyclist was probably out of earshot now.

Concerned for the elderly man, Naomi moved towards him and Marjorie trailed after her, clearly impatient to talk about her own business.

'Did you see that?' Jonah demanded. 'The fool nearly ran me over. What's the world coming to when a man can't cross the road in his own village without being almost mown down by someone who should know better?'

'You're unhurt, though?' Naomi asked.

'No thanks to that clown. Those Americans should have stayed at home if they're going to behave like that.'

'The Americans are here to help win the war and not all of them are irresponsible,' Naomi pointed out gently. 'Some are extremely polite and considerate.' She had Paul Scarletti in mind.

'Humph!' Jonah said. 'That fool will kill someone if he doesn't learn to be more careful.'

'Let's hope not,' Naomi said, and deemed it wise to change the subject, though perhaps she'd mention the reckless motorcyclist to Paul when she next saw him. 'Are you coming along to the bookshop?'

'I'll be along shortly.'

'Then I'll have a cup of tea waiting to steady your nerves.'

'There's nothing wrong with my nerves. It's that idiot of a motorcyclist who—'

'I'm sure tea will be welcome anyway.'

'Maybe a biscuit, too?' Jonah asked, beginning to calm down. Jonah was fond of a biscuit.

'I'm sure that can be arranged.'

Nodding his satisfaction, Jonah walked on and Marjorie lost no time in saying, 'I want your opinion on something.'

'You've received a letter.'

Marjorie looked taken aback. 'How did you know?'

'Because I've also—' But, no. Belatedly, Naomi realized that Marjorie would be beyond agitated if she'd received a poison pen letter. She'd be hysterical. It was a good thing that Marjorie had been spared – so far, anyway – though it left Naomi wondering once again why she'd been picked on as a target for the letter writer's venom.

'Never mind,' she said now. 'Tell me about your letter.'

'It's from—'

Marjorie was interrupted again, this time by someone saying, 'Excuse me.'

Naomi looked round to see a young woman carrying a small suitcase as well as a handbag and gas mask. 'Looking for Stratton House?' Naomi asked and the young woman smiled in amusement.

'Either you're a very clever woman or I look like the

nurse I am,' she said. She was pretty with glossy dark hair and blue, confident eyes.

'We're a small community and don't have many visitors,' Naomi explained. 'Besides, with the military hospital almost on our doorstep . . .'

'And me being twenty-three and just the right age for nursing . . .'

'Precisely,' Naomi confirmed.

Churchwood was fond of the Stratton House nurses, including the most recent addition to their ranks, Beth Ellis, who'd been rather distant on her arrival but who'd gradually opened up to let her natural warmth shine through at both the hospital and in the village.

This newcomer looked to be a different sort of girl – one who was ready to grab at adventure with both hands – but, hopefully, they'd all come to care for her too.

Naomi pointed behind her. 'Take this road – Churchwood Way – and you'll come to a lane that runs between a cottage called The Linnets and a house called Foxfield. Turn into the lane and keep going. It's quite a long walk and the surface of the lane dwindles to little more than a rough path after a while, but you'll get there eventually.'

'I'm young and I'm fit and it's a fine day for walking,' the nurse said.

'It is indeed.' Early summer had turned the air soft and balmy. There was sunshine overhead and fresh green growth all around them.

Tucking her handbag under her arm, the nurse held out a hand. 'I'm Nancy Whittaker. If you're thinking there's something peculiar about the way I speak, it's because I'm from the north. Manchester, to be precise.'

Naomi shook Nancy's hand. 'I'm Naomi Harrington. I live at Foxfield, one of the houses I just mentioned.

This is Marjorie Plym, another Churchwood resident.'

Normally Marjorie would be the first to leap in and hog the attention of a stranger so she'd have something to report at the bookshop and in the village shops, but now she looked as though she couldn't wait to be rid of Nancy. Marjorie's letter really had to be momentous to break through her love of gossip.

Naomi dug her gently in the ribs to let her know that she was supposed to be taking part in an introduction.

'Oh! Sorry!' Marjorie's face turned puce – her usual colour when embarrassed – and she took Nancy's hand at last. 'Delighted to meet you, of course.'

'I hope we'll see something of you at our bookshop,' Naomi told the newcomer.

'Bookshop?'

'Yes, we sell books and lend them out, too, like an informal library. We have clubs and talks and social events as well. Ask at the hospital. Anyone there will tell you all about it.'

'I'll be sure to do just that,' Nancy said. 'And here was I thinking I'd landed in a quiet little place. It seems there's fun to be had here, after all. Duty calls now, but I hope to be back in the village soon.' She touched her temple as though saluting and walked away.

'About my letter,' Marjorie said. 'I really want—'

'I'm sorry to cut you off,' Naomi apologized, aware that Marjorie was being interrupted for the third time, 'but I need to open the bookshop. Let's talk there.'

She set off for the bookshop with as much speed as she could muster. Unlike young and fit Nancy Whittaker, Naomi was forty-seven and believed she resembled her pet bulldog, Basil, in being heavy of build with weighty jowls and short legs.

The bookshop's new home wasn't as large as the old Hall, but with a big room and kitchen downstairs, three bedrooms upstairs and a garden, it was serving them well, even if it was sometimes a crush.

Naomi unlocked the central door and stepped inside, glancing around the spacious downstairs room and relieved to see that Bert had set it up for today's session after his woodworking club last night. Chairs and tables were arranged here and there with one long table beneath a window holding the books. There were rugs on the floor for the children, with toys ready on each one. The walls were plain white-painted plaster, but Bert had made noticeboards for them and now bright colours burst out of children's drawings and paintings, seed catalogues for Dig for Victory gardens, fashion ideas . . .

'All right, Marjorie, you have my attention,' Naomi said.

Marjorie thrust a letter towards her. 'It came in this morning's post.'

The envelope was of good quality and addressed to Marjorie in the sort of rounded letters and numbers that suggested a female writer. Drawing out the letter, Naomi read the sender's address which appeared at the top: *6 Brooke Villas, Marcombe Parade, Bournemouth.*

Dear Miss Plym,

I hope you'll forgive me for getting in touch when we're strangers to each other. I hope we won't stay strangers for long and that you'll soon welcome me as a member of your family.

Naomi looked up at that. 'I didn't realize you still had family living.'

'Neither did I. I assumed there must be distant cousins somewhere, but none that I'd ever met.'

Naomi returned her gaze to the letter.

*It appears we have a great-uncle in common. Sir John Riley.
My father was his nephew through his brother Hugh. Your
mother was his niece by his sister Caroline. These facts have
only recently come to my attention since our great-uncle fell ill.*

*I was delighted to hear of your existence, though. I'm a
widow with no other family and I believe you have no other
family either. I would very much like us to meet in the hope of
becoming friends and perhaps a support to each other since we're
both alone in the world. To this end I'd love to visit you, perhaps
staying with you for a few days. Do write back and let me know
if this will be convenient.*

With kindest regards,
Constance Pearce

'What do you think?' Marjorie asked.

'The important question is: what do *you* think, Marjorie?'

'I don't know. Constance sounds nice, doesn't she?'

'I've no reason to think she isn't nice,' Naomi said.

Marjorie stood fidgeting for a moment. Was some sort
of awkwardness brewing? 'I haven't actually had anyone
staying in my house for such a long time,' Marjorie said. 'In
fact, I don't think I've ever had anyone staying in my house.'

So that was it. She was hoping Naomi would offer
Constance Pearce a bed.

It was understandable in some ways. Like Victoria,
Marjorie had also known wealth as a child, having been
brought up in a large country house with servants and acres
of grounds. But, also like Victoria, the family fortunes had
dwindled. Since Marjorie had never come close to being
married or earning her own living, she was reduced to
eking out a meagre existence in a shabby little terraced

house, keeping a careful guard over every penny. The house hadn't been spruced up in decades. Outside, dull brown paint flaked away from windows and doors. Inside, carpets, curtains and furnishings were faded and lifeless. The only brightness came from a collection of cheap pottery souvenirs of other people's visits to the seaside. Naomi had bought some of them. Not because she liked them – she couldn't actually bear them – but in order to give Marjorie pleasure.

Naomi's house was much larger and furnished with elegance and comfort, but it was full of evacuees from London – women and children both. She still made room for occasional visitors but wasn't convinced Constance Pearce should be one of them.

'It might look odd if your cousin came and you didn't offer to put her up,' Naomi suggested. 'It could make her feel unwelcome.'

That aspect of the matter didn't appear to have occurred to Marjorie. She considered it now but still looked worried.

'Perhaps a better way forward would be to meet your cousin for tea or lunch before inviting her to stay,' Naomi said. 'If you find you rub along together well, an invitation to stay could follow. But if you find you don't get along, you can go your separate ways without being forced to spend days in each other's company.'

'Perhaps that would be better,' Marjorie agreed. 'But you're not suggesting I go to Bournemouth?' She made it sound as though she were being asked to trek through the Himalayas with a view to climbing Mount Everest.

'It might be a pleasant day out for you,' Naomi said. 'It must be a long time since you last left Churchwood.'

'Bournemouth is such a distance away, though. Why, it must be more than *fifty miles*!'

'There are trains,' Naomi pointed out gently. 'London is nearer if you'd prefer to meet in the middle.'

'*London!*' Marjorie made the place sound like a den of iniquity where women might be snatched from the street and smuggled overseas to please the men of mysterious, foreign countries. Even plain women of a certain age, like herself. 'I couldn't go on my own. Besides, I might be bombed. Lots of places have been bombed recently. Exeter, Norwich, York . . .'

'True, but we need to live our lives, Marjorie. We can't hide away.'

'I'd feel safer if I wasn't alone.'

As if Naomi could protect her from enemy action! Guessing what Marjorie would suggest next, Naomi tried to forestall it with, 'I'd be in the way if I accompanied you.'

But Marjorie wasn't to be deterred. 'You could leave me at the tea room and go shopping,' she proposed. 'You used to shop in London often. And stay there sometimes, too.'

Naomi had owned a flat in St John's Wood jointly with Alexander, but she'd signed it over to him in return for his signing Foxfield over to her.

Movement out in the street alerted Naomi to the fact that people were beginning to arrive for the bookshop session. 'Why don't you write to your cousin, suggesting a meeting in London, and then we'll see?' she advised Marjorie.

'All right, but I'm relying on your support.'

Lucky Naomi! She opened the door and, as the arrivals streamed through it, she wondered if any of them had received nasty letters. Or if one of them was the letter writer. Her stomach tightened into a knot.

CHAPTER SIX

Suki

It was torture not knowing if *he* was coming to her party today. She'd tried to find out by asking Mrs Harrington during breakfast, though she hadn't asked about him specifically, of course. Suki was keeping her love for him to herself for the moment. Instead, she'd asked a general question. 'Do you know who's coming to the party, Mrs Harrington?'

'Bert, of course,' Mrs Harrington had said.

Suki liked Bert a lot but he wasn't the man who made her heart beat faster. Bert was old – at least fifty, and maybe even sixty! – and engaged to Mrs Harrington. Something which pleased Suki, since Mrs Harrington deserved some happiness after being married to her first husband.

Suki had been more than a little afraid of Alexander Harrington. Tall and thin with eyes like cold blue ice, he'd given every sign of looking down on her and everyone else who wasn't rich and important. Worse, he'd been cruel to poor Mrs Harrington. Good riddance to the man.

Whoever would have guessed that he had a secret family, though? A family he'd kept hidden for years until Mrs Harrington had followed him into a hotel in London and seen them all sitting there. She'd been devastated at the time but she was free of the horrible man now. She'd be

41

far happier with nice Mr Makepiece despite him dressing like a scarecrow.

'Alice is coming, too, and bringing her father,' Mrs Harrington had added.

Suki liked Alice. She also liked Alice's father, a retired doctor who was always willing to help Churchwood people without charging a fee.

'Kate will probably be busy on the farm,' Mrs Harrington had continued. 'Pearl and Ruby, too. But Mrs Collins and Mrs Janicki are coming.'

Suki liked both of them and had got to know them quite well because they helped to organize the bookshop and often came to Foxfield to talk about it. Janet Collins was a warm and comforting grandmother. May Janicki was much younger – still in her twenties – a career woman in London before she and her husband had taken in his two nieces and a nephew, Jewish refugee children from Poland. May had moved to Churchwood to keep them safe while her husband served in the army. Sadly, the children's parents had remained in Poland and nothing had been heard from them in an age.

'Anyone else?' Suki had asked.

'Miss Plym. I'm sorry, Suki, but I couldn't say no.'

Suki could hardly relish the idea of Churchwood's biggest gossip and silliest woman coming to the party, but Mrs Harrington couldn't offend her old friend.

Anyone else?

'Yes, there's—'

But the door had opened and Victoria had popped her head around it. Suki liked and admired Victoria but just at that moment Suki had hoped she would state her business and disappear, leaving Mrs Harrington to finish what she'd been saying.

Sadly, it hadn't happened like that.

'There's a telephone call for you, Naomi,' Victoria had said, and Mrs Harrington had gone to take it.

Afterwards, she'd gone into her sitting room to prepare for the bookshop and Suki hadn't liked to disturb her.

Ah, well. Suki didn't have too much longer to wait for the party. Just a couple of hours. But oh, they were going to feel like days!

CHAPTER SEVEN

Ruby

The kitchen door opened and Pearl entered. 'I've cut myself,' she announced, holding up a finger which had a grubby, bloodstained handkerchief wrapped around it. 'It's nothing really, but Kate is insisting I wash it and cover it with a bandage.'

Kate had entered the kitchen, too.

'Quite right,' Ruby approved. 'I don't think that filthy handkerchief can be keeping out germs.'

She glanced at Kate who gave her a rueful look in return, clearly having made this point already.

Not trusting Pearl to make a good job of it alone, Kate supervised the finger washing while Ruby fetched the first aid box, taking out a tin of Germolene antiseptic cream and a finger bandage.

'At least try to keep the cut clean,' Ruby pleaded, when Pearl's finger had been dressed.

'Wear gloves,' Kate suggested.

But the likelihood was that Pearl would plunge her hands into dirt the moment she returned to work.

'A letter came for you,' Ruby told her. 'It's on the table.'

'Oh, heck.' Pearl's good mood leaked away as though it had been punctured like the postman's bicycle. 'It's from one of my parents, I suppose.'

'Your mother, I think.'

Pearl sat at the table, picked up the envelope and stared at it with gloomy reluctance to explore its contents. This was usual when letters came from her family, but surely this letter was bringing congratulations instead of criticism?

'Putting off the moment you read the letter won't change what's been written,' Ruby pointed out.

Pearl heaved a sigh and tore the envelope open, pulling out a note and reading it.

'Well?' Ruby asked.

'I should have known this would happen,' Pearl wailed.

'Known what would happen?' Ruby said.

'They want to get *involved*. In my wedding.'

'Involved how?' Ruby questioned.

'They say they're going to pay for it. That means they want to organize it. They're suggesting I go home on a visit soon so we can start making plans.'

'They can't be expecting to take over the arrangements if they want you to go home to help,' Kate reasoned.

'You don't know my parents,' Pearl said, dourly.

'Then write and tell them what sort of wedding you *do* want,' Kate advised. 'If you and Fred have decided on that yet?'

Pearl shrugged. 'We haven't decided on anything. We don't know the first thing about weddings.'

'Then maybe your parents can help you decide.'

'Humph,' Pearl said and, stuffing the letter into the pocket of her filthy breeches, she headed for the door to return to work.

'Don't you just despair of Pearl sometimes?' Kate said to Ruby.

'Mmm,' Ruby agreed.

Privately, she was thinking that Pearl was lucky in having

parents who were actually interested in her. In having options about the style of wedding she wanted, too. It remained to be seen what sort of wedding she'd settle on, but one thing was clear. With Mr and Mrs Grimes's money behind it, Pearl's wedding was likely to make Ruby's look paltry.

CHAPTER EIGHT

Naomi

'Bye!'

'Thanks!'

'See you soon!'

Naomi smiled and waved as the residents who'd attended the morning bookshop session began to file out happily. They'd had what they called a general session today. Books had been returned and other books borrowed. Stories had been read out and children had played on rugs as the grown-ups chatted cosily over cups of tea.

'Knitting club again tomorrow?' one woman asked.

'And sewing club on Friday,' Naomi confirmed.

'Is Bert still planning on running another woodworking session this week?' someone else wanted to know.

'He is. Christmas may be months away but we want to be sure every child has a toy. There are all the birthday gifts to think about, too.'

Every child in Churchwood received something from the bookshop on special occasions. With the children's club, Nearly School for the little ones who weren't quite old enough for school, and numerous other clubs and social events, the bookshop was always busy.

Alice glided up beside her as they began to tidy up. 'That went well.'

'Indeed,' Naomi agreed.

'It was nice of you to read out Walter Dale's letter.'

'It was only right, seeing as so many people helped with the flowers for Frances's funeral.'

They'd gathered at the bookshop with flowers brought from their gardens to decorate the coffin of long-time Churchwood resident Frances Dale, and the church where the funeral service had taken place. There'd been a collection in the bookshop to help with other funeral costs, too, since Frances's husband had little money. 'I can't take your charity!' Walter had protested.

'It isn't charity,' Naomi had assured him. 'It's a small token of appreciation for all Frances did to help Churchwood during her lifetime.'

Eventually, he'd taken the money with obvious gratitude and relief.

Naomi had been glad to share his thank-you letter. But no one had mentioned receiving a poison pen letter or given any other sign of having received one.

Kate arrived at that moment, a tall, slender young woman with striking auburn hair and a lovely face. 'I'm in a rush as usual,' she said, a common refrain from Kate since Brimbles Farm was always busy. 'But I wanted to give you this. It's a birthday gift for Suki. A wooden keepsake box. I got Fred to make it.'

Fred Fletcher was slowly building some sort of life for himself since he could no longer farm. He'd discovered an unexpected talent for woodworking and had even begun to sell his creations in a gift shop in St Albans.

The box was beautiful, the top and sides being carved with leaves and forest creatures, Suki's name appearing in the midst of them. 'Tell Fred she'll adore it,' Naomi said.

'I'll be glad to.'

Clearly, Kate knew nothing of any poison pen letters. She had a temper and would have been the first to give vent to fury if she'd received one or heard of anyone else receiving one. But Brimbles Farm was some way out of the village and tended to be a day or two behind on news.

The same couldn't be said of Adam Potts, the vicar, who walked in as Kate was leaving. He was often out and about in the village so would be sure to hear of any such letters, but there was nothing in his smile to suggest that he'd learned of anything untoward.

'Everything all right?' he asked.

'We've had a lovely letter from Walter Dale,' Alice told him. 'Naomi read it out to everyone.'

Adam nodded approvingly. 'I'll call in on him later. Make sure he's coping.'

'I met a new nurse on her way to the hospital earlier,' Naomi said, not wanting to appear out of sorts. 'She seemed like a nice girl. Interested in the bookshop, too.'

'I'll look forward to meeting her soon,' Adam said.

He helped them to finish clearing up, waved to Janet and May as they went off and then announced that he was leaving, too. 'I'll call on Walter now,' he said.

'Walking home?' Alice asked Naomi. Alice was still living at The Linnets, the picturesque cottage that was just across the lane from Foxfield, while her husband, Daniel, was serving in the army.

'I have a couple of errands to run first,' Naomi told her.

'Then I'll see you at Suki's tea. Is she excited?'

'You know Suki. She loves birthdays.'

Naomi locked the bookshop door, gave Alice a parting hug and then set off to the shops. The poison pen letter sat in her handbag and Naomi was as conscious of it as if it had pulsed with heat, like a rock fallen to Earth from some distant part of the galaxy.

She decided to call on Bert after she'd run her errands. Not to discuss the letter with him, since she didn't want him to be annoyed or anxious on her behalf, but just to have him beside her for a while. It would be comforting.

CHAPTER NINE

Beth

'I've asked Nurse Ellis to show you around,' Matron told the newcomer. 'She hasn't been with us for long so should be able to remember all the small details it will be useful for you to know.'

'Thank you, Matron,' Nurse Whittaker said.

'Off you go, then.' Matron clapped her hands to chivvy them along.

They left her office and Beth set off for the main entrance, which felt a good place to start the tour.

'Hard taskmaster, is she?' Nurse Whittaker asked, nodding back towards Matron's office.

'She's strict about punctuality, efficiency and that sort of thing but she also has a human side beneath the starch. She cares deeply about the patients and she cares about her nurses, too. In her bracing way she looks after us and brings out the best in us.'

'That's good to hear. I'm Nancy, by the way.'

'I'm Beth.'

'Are you happy here?'

Goodness, Nancy Whittaker was direct. 'I'm very happy here,' Beth said, glad she could be truthful. 'Most of the staff do an excellent job caring for the patients and they're friendly, too. I'm making some good friends among the nurses. I saw you talking to a couple of them in the nurses' quarters. Babs Carter and Pauline Evans?'

Nancy nodded. 'I thought I'd introduce myself.'

How confident she was!

Nancy must have guessed what Beth was thinking because she smiled wryly and said, 'I come from a large family. Four brothers! All older than me. It was hard being heard among all those boys so I soon learned to sharpen my elbows and barge my way into being noticed. To grab food, too, before my brothers scoffed the lot.'

'They didn't treat you badly?'

'Nothing like that. But four boys make for a lively existence and lots of fighting over who gets to the food first and even who uses the lavatory first.'

'I imagine they must.'

'You don't have brothers?'

'No sisters either.'

'That must have been . . . quiet.'

'It was.'

'I'd have liked a bit of peace and quiet sometimes when I was growing up. Still, where I come from – Manchester, up in the north – they make women tough.'

'Manchester is famed for cotton, isn't it?'

'We've lots of mills up there. My father works in one. His father worked in one before him. Even my mother worked with cotton before she married. She sewed it into tea towels, tray cloths and things like that. Sewing was a skill she put to good use since she made her own clothes and most of mine, too. As you can probably imagine, with five children in the family there wasn't much money around when I was growing up.'

'Your mother sounds a remarkable woman.'

'She was.'

The use of the past tense wasn't lost on Beth.

'She died a couple of years ago,' Nancy explained.

'I'm sorry.'

'I miss her. But she wouldn't want me to mope. She wanted me to fly high. She loved my brothers dearly but she was glad to have a girl for her fifth child. She told me she thought our relationship was special and it was she who chose my name. My brothers' names were all chosen by our grandparents on our father's side. They were strict churchgoers and strict everything else. They lived next door and to keep the peace my parents agreed to call the boys Matthew, Mark, Luke and John. They were known as the Gospel Boys in our street.'

'I don't think Nancy is a biblical name,' Beth ventured.

'It isn't. My mother was a sincere churchgoer herself but she said she'd done her bit to please my grandparents and now it was time to please herself. She called me Nancy because she thought it was both feminine and bold, and suited a girl she intended to bring up to live in the world on her own terms.'

'How did your grandparents feel about that?'

'They weren't pleased, apparently, but my mother stood strong. She insisted church should be about joy more than doom and gloom. I barely remember my grandparents, to be honest. They died when I was small.'

'You still have your father and brothers?'

'All of them, thankfully. So far, anyway.'

'They're involved in the war?' Beth guessed.

'My father is too old for service. Matthew, the eldest boy, is some sort of engineer. He works with submarines in Scotland but he fits them out and maintains them instead of being part of the crew. Naval bases are targets for enemy bombing but we're hoping he'll stay safe. Mark, the next eldest, is involved in the fighting. He's in the navy, crewing a destroyer. Luke and John are both in the army, Luke in the Far East and John in North Africa.'

'You must be anxious about them,' Beth said.

'All the time. But the more my brothers are at risk, the more I want to help the war effort and the men who are wounded in service.' She sounded as enthusiastic about that as about life in general.

They'd reached the main entrance where Beth introduced Nancy to Tom, the most senior of the porters who manned the desk in the hall. 'Tom is the man to come to if you want news of the war,' Beth said.

'I like to keep abreast of developments,' he confirmed.

He was a nice man and always kind to the nurses.

Beth continued the tour: visitors' waiting room, pharmacy, operating theatre, therapy rooms, prosthetics . . . 'We treat a variety of injuries here but the most common ones are limb wounds – or losses,' Beth explained.

She finished the tour of the general facilities and then said, 'I'll show you around the wards now.'

'I've told you about my family. Tell me about yours,' Nancy suggested.

'There isn't much to tell,' Beth said. 'I still have both parents, luckily. They live in Norwich where my father is a postman and my mother keeps house. There wasn't much money around when I was growing up, either, though we got by well enough.'

'Then we have something in common,' Nancy said. 'Some of the nurses here seem to come from well-to-do families. Did your mother want you to fly high in life the way my mother wanted it for me?'

It was a tricky question to answer, honesty doing battle with loyalty. 'My mother is a good woman,' Beth said, feeling protective. 'But I think – no, I *know* – she'd have preferred me to settle down close by instead of going off to become a nurse. She still hasn't quite given up on the idea of it. She saves things for my bottom drawer, which is sweet of her.'

'You've no intention of going back to Norwich, though,' Nancy guessed. 'You want to achieve things in your career.'

'I do,' Beth confirmed.

'Then we have that in common, too. Not that I think we should be all work and no play. Life and good health are precious, as we're reminded every day by what we see in our hospitals. I'm all for enjoying them every chance we get. We're a bit isolated out here in the Hertfordshire wilderness but I hear there's a bookshop in Churchwood that offers a lot more than books for sale.'

'It's the hub of the village,' Beth told her. 'Churchwood is another reason I'm happy here. I've made good friends in the village.'

'I plan to do the same.'

They reached the corridor that led to Ward One. 'Linen cupboard, sluice room . . .' Beth pointed out and then pushed open the doors to the ward itself.

'Goodness,' Nancy said, and no wonder.

In many ways the room was a typical ward with metal-framed beds facing inwards. But Stratton House was a mansion and its former glories showed in floor-to-ceiling windows, wood-panelled walls and an ornate ceiling with a series of chandeliers set down its length.

'What's this? Another angel come to minister to us?' one of the patients joked. Corporal Murray, who'd lost a lower leg.

'An angel who stands for no nonsense,' Nancy told him.

'But who still likes a laugh and a joke,' Corporal Murray suggested.

'You're not wrong,' Nancy said. 'I love to laugh and joke – as long as it doesn't bring the wrath of Matron or a doctor on my head.'

Corporal Murray nodded, grinning at the same time. 'Welcome to Stratton House, ministering angel. I think you're going to fit right in.'

Other patients welcomed Nancy and she took them all in her stride.

They moved on to Ward Two and Beth saw that Alice Irvine had arrived. She was writing a letter for a patient. 'Alice is one of those village friends I mentioned. She's the person who started the bookshop. I'll introduce you.'

As always, Alice was kind and sweet, though intelligence glowed in her blue eyes.

'I hear you're the brains behind the bookshop,' Nancy said.

'The original idea might have been mine but it would never have come about without a lot of help from other people. Naomi Harrington and Kate Kinsella, to name but two.'

'I've met Mrs Harrington,' Nancy said. 'I haven't met Kate Kinsella.'

'You may meet her when you walk into the village since her family's farm is along Brimbles Lane,' Alice told her. 'Two land girls work there as well. Ruby and Pearl. Both are characters in their different ways.'

'I'm looking forward to meeting them all. And coming to the bookshop, of course.'

'It's a long walk but worth it,' Alice said.

'Having been brought up with brothers I've learned how to battle for what I want, no matter what obstacles may get in my way,' Nancy said. 'A long walk won't hold me back.'

'Spoken like a true fighter,' Alice said.

'That's me,' Nancy said. She was smiling but there was a glow of determination in her eyes.

Alice laughed. 'I hope I never get into a fight with you, Nancy.'

And Beth laughed too. 'So do I, because I'm pretty sure I'd come off worst.'

CHAPTER TEN

Bert

'So,' Bert said, after Naomi had arrived at his market garden to find him working in a greenhouse and told him about her morning. 'The day's news is that Marjorie has a newly discovered cousin, there's a new nurse at the hospital and the morning session at the bookshop went well?'

'Quite a bumper day for news,' Naomi confirmed.

But Bert suspected he was hearing only a carefully edited version of the day. 'Hmm.' He dusted soil from his hands. 'I suggest we go indoors so I can put the kettle on. Then we can settle down for a proper chat. About the real reason you're here, I mean.'

He watched the false cheer fade from Naomi's face to expose vulnerability and dismay. 'I love you, woman,' he told her. 'I'm going to marry you. It would be a sad state of affairs if I didn't know when you were hurting.'

'Oh, Bert!' Naomi swallowed. 'I don't want to be a trouble to you. And I don't want you to think I'm a silly old woman.'

'Silly or not, you're *my* woman,' Bert pointed out. 'And I don't want to hear talk of you being old because you're younger than me. If you're old, I'm ancient, and I like to think I still have some life left in me.'

She smiled, which was the response he'd hoped for, though it tugged on his heart to see the effort it cost her. He wanted to hug her but his hands were still filthy so he kept them in the air and folded his arms around her shoulders, pressing a kiss to the top of her head – an easy matter considering she was a short little woman. 'Come on,' he said. 'Let's get that kettle on.'

They headed for Bert's house, entering by the door that led straight into the kitchen. It was pristinely clean because Bert had his pride, but when it came to furniture and furnishings this room – most of the house, in fact – had stood virtually unchanged for decades. The cream-painted cupboards were old and worn. So, too, were the stone flags that made up the floor. There was an old dresser which had belonged to his long-dead parents along with the old cream-and-green pottery that stood on its shelves. Bert had bought the table and chairs himself, as well as the armchairs that stood on each side of the hearth, but that had been almost thirty years ago and all had now settled into middle age along with Bert himself. There was nothing modern or stylish about the place. It wasn't even bright because the colours were subdued. But to Bert's way of thinking, it had a warm and welcoming air that wrapped a person in comfort the moment they entered.

'Before you ask, the answer is no. I don't need any help, thanks,' Bert told Naomi. 'Sit yourself down and say hello to Elizabeth.'

The aged cat was lying on the rag rug in front of the hearth. She raised her head and began to purr, probably because she knew from experience that Naomi would stroke her. Sure enough, Naomi sat in an armchair to do just that.

Bert lit the stove beneath the kettle and set about

preparing teapot, cups and saucers. He'd known Naomi for more than a quarter of a century but for most of that time they'd moved in different circles. Naomi had been a distant figure to him as she bustled about the village organizing people's lives or swished past him in a chauffeur-driven car before petrol rationing had brought driving for pleasure purposes to an end. Bert had been a scruffy down-to-earth market gardener who had no taste for finery and certainly no inclination to bow and scrape to people who considered themselves better than others. In Bert's world, everyone was equally important.

As the years passed, he'd come to suspect that Naomi's apparent confidence and bustle were a carefully constructed front designed to hide her insecurities and unhappiness in being married to a cold icicle of a man. And when he'd got to know her through the bookshop, his suspicions had been confirmed. In the eyes of the world Alexander Harrington was probably considered quite a catch. He was tall and trim. Handsome, too, with sharp blue eyes and exquisitely cut clothes. He also spoke in the crisp accent of the upper classes, an attribute that had doubtless helped him to rise in his profession as a stockbroker with offices in London.

That same world probably looked askance at big, shambling Bert Makepiece, who wasn't at all hand-some and who lived a modest life digging his hands into filthy earth. But that world could take a running jump. When it came to treating a woman with respect and love, Bert would knock Alexander Harrington into a turnip field.

Bert's love for Naomi wasn't the misty-eyed kind. He saw clearly that she wasn't handsome either, in the traditional sense. She was short and dumpy, and her bad feet gave her grief sometimes. But she was the kindest, most generous, most tender-hearted of women and he considered it a privilege to be loved by her in return. And if he failed to make her happy . . . Well, it wouldn't be for want of trying on his part. He adored her.

When the tea was ready he carried a cup to Naomi and settled in the other armchair with a cup for himself. They'd had many a heart-to-heart here in this cosy kitchen. 'Well?' he asked.

Naomi took an envelope from her bag and passed it to him. He studied the handwriting on the front. 'Bit odd,' he said, for it looked awkward, as though copied letter by careful letter from a book instead of being written with natural flow.

'It gets even odder,' Naomi told him.

He took out the note that was inside and felt his eyebrows shoot up to his hairline as he read the disgusting pasted-on words.

WELL, AREN'T YOU A BOSSY WOMAN? IT'S TIME YOU STOPPED ORDERING PEOPLE ABOUT AND LET THEM GET ON WITH THEIR OWN LIVES. THEY'LL BE A LOT HAPPIER WITHOUT YOUR INTERFERENCE.

Surprise was soon followed by concern – for Naomi.

'It came this morning,' Naomi said. 'I won't pretend it didn't shock me.'

In other words, it had wounded her.

'Who wouldn't be shocked? But what it says . . . You know it's nonsense?'

She nodded, but he saw the doubts flicker across her face. 'I *did* use to be bossy, Bert,' she said, the thought of it obviously causing her pain.

61

Bert was familiar with Naomi's history and how it had shaped her. An only child who'd lost her mother at a young age, she'd been brought up by a father who loved her but was blind to the fact that he was feeding her insecurities. Cedric Tuggs had made a modest fortune by peddling quack medicines under the name of Tuggs Tonics and wanted to show it off to the world. He'd insisted that his daughter was beautiful, though she knew full well that she wasn't. He'd also insisted that she dress flamboyantly, parading his wealth with large, clumsy jewellery and an excess of ribbons, bows and furbelows. 'Isn't she lovely?' he'd asked almost everyone they met, and Naomi had cringed in mortification.

In time he'd sold his business and made an ill-fated attempt to launch himself and his daughter into what he considered to be high society, only for that society to turn its nose up at them. The shudders and grimaces that met his crude efforts to ingratiate himself had made Naomi burn with humiliation, as had the comments she'd overheard.

'What a common little man . . .'

'He talks of nothing but money. Can you believe he actually asked what I'd paid for my suit and told me my tailor had fleeced me?'

'The man eats his peas off his knife, and as for his belching . . .'

The attentions of Alexander, a tall and debonair man who'd put on a superficial show of charm had come as a great relief to Naomi. After her father died unexpectedly – much mourned by her because she'd loved him dearly despite his flaws – she'd been delighted to become Mrs Harrington.

She'd believed it would relieve her loneliness but it had done no such thing. On the contrary, she'd felt lonelier than

62

ever because the charm had soon fallen away to reveal that Alexander's interest lay only in her money. With her confidence flayed raw, and deprived of the children for whom she yearned, she'd tried to make an alternative life for herself, compensating for her lack of self-worth with a show of pompous authority that saw her setting up as a sort of queen bee of Churchwood, holding court at Foxfield to a favoured few and treating lesser mortals like servants.

When Alice Lovell – now Alice Irvine – had arrived in the village just two years ago, a wind of change had accompanied her. Alice was generous and gentle but steadfast in the face of injustice and keen to do good. Refusing to join the Court of Naomi Harrington, she'd taken it upon herself to work with another young woman, the rebellious Kate Fletcher – now Kate Kinsella – to set up the bookshop and refused to surrender control to Naomi.

Feeling snubbed, Naomi had become involved only gradually. But she'd found she enjoyed working as an equal instead of a ruler and – even better – she'd found that people had started to like her for herself instead of tugging their forelocks to her as their self-appointed leader.

Looking back on that bossy self always made her wince because she'd changed so much since then. These days she had friends. Real friends who cared for her.

And yet someone had written that awful letter.

'Maybe you *were* bossy in the past,' Bert conceded. 'But not for a long time now.'

'It seems someone doesn't agree. I don't *mean* to boss people about at the bookshop but perhaps I do.'

'Does Alice boss people about at the bookshop?'

'Of course not.'

'She *persuades* instead,' Bert agreed. 'So do you, beloved. You're tact and sensitivity personified.'

Naomi looked unconvinced but made an obvious effort to shrug off any appearance of foolishness.

'You don't know if it's a personal attack yet,' Bert said. 'There may be dozens of these letters floating around the village, and just because no one who came to the bookshop mentioned having received one—'

'It doesn't follow that none have been received,' Naomi finished.

'After all, did you mention your letter?'

'No,' she admitted.

'Then other people might not have mentioned their letters, either. They might have been too embarrassed or angry. Or they might just have wanted time to think about them. I'll wager not everyone in the village went to the bookshop today, anyway. I'm one who didn't. Even if no one else has received a letter yet, they might receive one tomorrow or next week or next month.'

Naomi nodded. 'I don't wish a nasty letter on anyone, but it would relieve my mind to know that this . . . *attack* isn't personal. I've also wondered if it might be a prank or something written in the heat of the moment and perhaps already regretted.'

'It's important to keep an open mind,' Bert agreed. 'Of course, there's someone who might have a grievance against you that *is* personal.'

'Alexander?'

'You exposed him, beloved. As a liar, a cheat – and a bigamist.'

Alexander hadn't only married Naomi for money and deprived her of children, he'd also gone through a secret marriage ceremony with another woman and had two children with her.

'You divorced him on your terms,' Bert continued,

'forcing him to give back some of the money he'd fleeced from your inheritance. And then there's William.'

William was Alexander's seventeen-year-old son. An unhappy boy, he'd come to Churchwood to confront Naomi under the mistaken belief that she was the villain who was causing his father to shout a lot at home and tighten the family's belt financially. When he'd learned the truth he'd befriended Naomi instead. Bert and the village, too. Now he often spent weekends and part of his school holidays at Foxfield. He also wished to follow Bert into horticulture – much to the disgust of his snobbish father.

'Alexander hates me,' Naomi agreed. 'But I can't see him writing a poison pen letter.'

'You don't think he's vindictive enough?'

'I'm sure he's vindictive enough. But he also thinks highly of himself.'

'A poison pen letter is too lower class for him?'

'Yes. Maybe. Oh, I don't know. He could have written it precisely so he can punish me from afar without me suspecting him of being the sender because it seems out of character.'

'Exactly.' Bert paused again before adding, 'The icicle doesn't live alone, of course.'

Naomi looked even more surprised. 'You're thinking of William's mother?'

'She's worth considering. She may resent the money side of things, too, if it's meant some belt-tightening on her part. And she may be even more resentful of William's friendship with you.'

Naomi had only seen Amelia Ashmore once, on the day she'd discovered the icicle's secret family. She'd described her as a golden-haired, blue-eyed beauty – which Bert guessed had only added to Naomi's sense of rejection – but, based on things William had let drop from time to time, Bert had formed the impression that Alexander's lover was neither clever nor strong-minded, being prone to tears and quite unable to stand up to him.

'It doesn't take much intelligence to send a letter like this,' Bert pointed out.

'Perhaps not.'

'There's also William's sister to consider,' Bert suggested.

Again, Naomi had only seen Emily once.

'She's – what? Fifteen? Sixteen?' he asked. 'She may well share her mother's resentment of you and the drama of a letter like this might appeal to someone her age. I noticed the envelope was postmarked from London and she doesn't live far from there. She could have posted the letter during a shopping trip or while visiting friends.'

Naomi gave a helpless shrug. 'I don't know enough about her to judge.'

'The point is that there's no reason to assume that someone in Churchwood sent the letter.'

'I'd certainly prefer that the writer wasn't a local person,' Naomi said. 'Especially not someone I thought was a friend.'

'Do you plan to mention the letter to anyone else?'

'I don't wish to spread unease and suspicion around the village, so no. Not for the moment, though I'm going to stay alert to any hints or clues about who may have sent it. If I've offended someone without knowing it, I'd like the chance to put things right.'

Typical Naomi. She was always big-hearted. 'And William?' Bert asked. 'Will you mention it to him?'

'It's tricky, isn't it? It would relieve my mind to know that someone in his family sent the letter instead of someone in the village. But it would mortify poor William. Perhaps I won't mention it to him either.'

More Naomi behaviour, putting someone else first. Amelia Ashmore was welcome to her golden-haired beauty. Plain but utterly marvellous Naomi was worth ten of her. 'With luck, the letter writer will be satisfied with having just sent one letter, especially if they think it hasn't worked in upsetting you,' Bert said. 'Meanwhile, the person with the problem isn't you. It's the letter writer, whether they wrote it because they're mean and vicious, suffering from a temper tantrum or just young and misguided. You're everything that person isn't, Naomi. Kind and generous and wonderful. Lucky, too, considering you'll soon be married to the best-looking man in Hertfordshire.'

It was a joke, of course, and Bert was pleased when Naomi laughed. 'Shall we see what the next few days bring?' he suggested.

'Yes, let's.'

He could see it was going to be hard for her, but he could also see her straightening her shoulders and gathering her strength of mind. Naomi was sensitive. More sensitive than was good for her, perhaps. But she also had courage. 'That's my woman,' he said, and he swept her into his arms and kissed her, something that embarrassed and delighted her in equal measure.

She left soon afterwards, Bert kissing her again before waving her off.

A robin hopped on to the ground in front of him. A familiar friend. 'Come to say hello, have you?' Bert asked. 'Let's see what I can find for you.'

He returned to the kitchen for a small chunk of bread and broke off some crumbs which he held out in his palm. The robin flew up and perched on Bert's rough fingers to peck at the bread. 'Mark my words, little one. If this nasty letter business is the start of some sort of campaign against my beloved, the writer will have me to answer to. Anyone who hurts the woman I love hurts me as well. But I'm getting ahead of myself with that sort of thinking, so there's no need to tell your feathery friends that old Bert has turned into an ogre. Not yet, anyway.'

CHAPTER ELEVEN

Suki

A glance at the kitchen clock showed Suki that it was half past three. Not that this came as a surprise since she'd been looking at the clock at least once every five minutes and would have looked at it even more frequently had she not been trying hard to avoid behaving like a giddy child. After all, she was a young woman now. A young woman who was in love and who needed to show the world – and especially *him* – that she was both grown up and ready for romance.

'Would you mind peeling potatoes next?' Victoria asked, when Suki had finished drying dishes and putting them away. Victoria never barked orders. Like Mrs Harrington, she made them sound like polite requests so Suki always felt she was regarded as a person rather than a skivvy. Alexander Harrington had made her feel like a grub he'd found in his lettuce.

Suki set to work on the potatoes. With so many people living at Foxfield or eating there, preparing meals was a gargantuan task, and today they were getting ahead to make time for Suki's birthday tea.

'I expect your family will be delighted to see you later,' Victoria said.

After her birthday tea, Suki was allowed to go to her family's little cottage to spend the rest of the day there, even staying over if she liked. She was close to all members of her family – her mother, father and three younger sisters and brothers, particularly her sister Sally, who was just two years younger.

She chatted with Victoria as they prepared a giant stew for dinner later. At last Victoria smiled and said, 'You'd better run up and change.'

Suki wore traditional black and white when working but changed into a regular dress for her tea party. She only had two regular dresses since she gave much of her wages to her mother to help with the younger children, but May Janicki had helped Suki to make one of them – a dress in a pleasant shade of blue that matched her eyes – and it was this one that Suki changed into today. Smoothing down the skirt, she studied her reflection in the small mirror above her chest of drawers.

She knew that people often described her as a sweet girl. Suki had rather liked that description in the past since it seemed to suggest that she was a nice person whom they liked. But it was beginning to feel terribly unsophisticated. Never in a million years would Suki look glamorous like the film stars she sometimes saw pictured in magazines, but she wished she could look a little more grown up.

She unpinned her hair from the small bun she arranged low on her neck each morning, brushed it out and then lifted it this way and that way as she tried to copy some of the more fashionable hairstyles she'd seen in those magazines. None of them felt right, though, so she tried parting her hair at the side and letting a curtain of it fall over one of her eyes, the way a singer called Margueritte Moore had styled hers when she'd given a concert at the bookshop not long ago. The style had looked alluring on Margueritte. On Suki it looked stupid.

Sighing, she settled for her usual centre parting but instead of smoothing all her hair back from her face she pinned two wings of it over her temples and left the rest hanging free. It was light-brown hair so nothing special in Suki's opinion, but at least it was soft and shiny.

How did she look? Certainly not beautiful, but perhaps a little attractive?

The evacuee children were returning from school as Suki made her way back downstairs. Excitement was in the air since they knew there was a special tea today. Not that the food would be particularly special, given rationing and wartime shortages. And not that she expected much in the way of gifts for the same reason. But birthdays were fun.

'Remember, it's Suki who's the birthday girl today,' Victoria was telling the children. 'We want her to have a lovely time so let's all behave nicely, yes?'

'We will!' the children chorused. They were a lovely lot. A bit rough around the edges at times. Boisterous, too. But they were all good-natured.

One of them – Victoria's boy, Arthur, who was just eight but saw himself as responsible for looking after the others – was the first to notice Suki. 'Happy birthday!' he said. 'I know we wished you a happy birthday this morning but it was an ordinary day then and now it's going to become special.'

Suki smiled at him. He'd had a difficult time when he'd first come to Churchwood since his well-meant ways of trying to make the other children happy had led some people in the village to decide he was wild. He was settled now, though. 'Thank you, Arthur.'

'When are we having tea?' This was Lewis, another of the children.

Victoria rolled her eyes. 'Is that all you can think about? Food?'

71

'Food is important and my tummy likes it,' Lewis said, grinning.

'Shoes off and let's go into the drawing room,' Victoria instructed.

Mrs Harrington was already there. 'How pretty you look, Suki,' she said, kissing her.

Suki was pleased. But would *he* think she looked pretty, too? Was he even coming to her tea party?

'Look at this splendid spread Victoria has prepared,' Mrs Harrington continued, gesturing to the large serving plates that had been placed on side tables.

'It's wonderful!' Suki declared, because Victoria had indeed done her proud.

There were sandwiches – egg, cheese and some sort of paste. There were little rhubarb tarts as well, and in between them was a scattering of early strawberries, doubtless grown by Mr Makepiece. There were also biscuits, dotted with raisins which were a luxury now dried fruit was rationed. And there was a cake which Victoria had decorated with ribbon and spring flowers, sugar being in too short a supply for icing except on extra-special occasions. With so many people living at Foxfield, birthdays were frequent so icing was generally forgone.

'I'll fetch the teapots,' Victoria said, and Mrs Harrington followed her to help, Suki not being allowed to lift a finger as the birthday girl.

They returned with two large teapots just as a knock sounded on the door.

The caller was Alice Irvine, who was rapidly followed by other guests – Mr Makepiece, May Janicki, Mrs Collins and Miss Plym. Suki heard Marjorie talking in the hall. 'Does everyone know about my cousin's letter?' she asked Mrs Harrington.

'I believe they do. In any case, this is Suki's day.'

'Oh, of course. As if I'd try to draw the attention to myself!'

Hmm.

Suki smiled and welcomed each arrival, doing her best to hide the fact that there was one guest whom she particularly wanted to see – but who hadn't yet appeared. It would be a blow if he couldn't appear at all.

Teacups were handed round to the adults and small cups of milk were handed to the children. Suki guessed it had been watered down a little. A daily ration of half a pint of milk per child didn't go far.

'When is Suki going to open her cards and presents?' Jenny asked. She was Arthur's younger sister.

'Perhaps she'd like to open them now,' Victoria suggested.

It was the cue for the children to jump up and hand over cards they'd made themselves. Paper was in short supply, too, so several of the cards had been drawn on the backs of advertising leaflets and old letters. Suki didn't care about that. She was simply pleased to see how much effort had been made.

Jenny's card featured a strip of blue sky at the top and a strip of green grass at the bottom, with flowers rising out of the grass and a stick figure in the middle. *Happy birthday, Suki*, she'd written. *Love from Jenny x*.

'Arthur helped me with the writing,' Jenny said, always happy to share credit with the brother she adored.

'It's lovely,' Suki praised.

'Did you hear about the letter from my cousin?' Miss Plym whispered to Mrs Collins, only to subside in her chair as she encountered a warning look from Mrs Harrington.

More cards followed. Little Flower, the youngest of the children, had drawn a cat. Again, Arthur had helped. He took good care of both Flower and his sister. Others had drawn hearts, flowers, stars, a dog that looked more like a cow, and sweets. Barley sugars. Suki guessed that this last card was wishful thinking on the part of its sender, sweets not being rationed yet but hard to come by even so.

Once the children's cards were opened, Suki turned to the cards and gifts the adults were offering. Mrs Harrington gave her a small silver brooch in a swirling flower design. Suki was thrilled with it. Marjorie Plym gave her a pottery bird which was doubtless one of her own ornaments from home. Suki had been there a couple of times and been struck by the sheer number of them covering every surface. 'I hope you like it,' Miss Plym said.

'Of course I do,' Suki lied. The bird was misshapen and there was a thin crack along the tail, but she didn't doubt that it had been given in a spirit of generosity since Miss Plym loved her seaside souvenirs.

Victoria's gift caused quite a stir. It was a bar of Hershey's milk chocolate. Actual chocolate. The children's eyes widened.

'I thought you could take it home with you and share it with your family,' Victoria said, crushing the hopes of the children who were eyeing the chocolate with longing. 'It's all right,' she told them. 'I have another bar for you.'

She must have got them from Sergeant Scarletti, the American soldier who visited when he could get away from his base. Victoria had told the children that he was just a friend who was in need of company due to being thousands of miles from home, but Suki knew that it wasn't every-day friendship that was bringing the glow of pleasure to Victoria's face. The thought put Suki in mind of *him*. He still hadn't arrived.

Alice gave Suki soap, scented with lemon balm – a

miracle since soap was now rationed – while Janet gave a pair of lavender bags and May a purse she'd made out of fabric scraps, using blue for the purse itself and pink for decorative flowers. 'They're all lovely,' Suki declared, thanking them.

She was thrilled by the potted rose Bert gave her, too.

'Shall we make a start on the food?' Victoria asked, and the children welcomed this proposal with enthusiasm.

Just then, another knock sounded on the door and Suki's heart gave a little jump of anticipation. Would it be *him*?

'I'll answer it,' Mrs Harrington said, since Victoria was busy handing round small plates so the feast wouldn't spill on to the carpet.

Suki took a plate from Victoria but her fingers fluttered and she had to hold it tightly. Mrs Harrington had closed the door behind her, and while Suki could hear voices out in the hall they were too remote for the speakers to be identified.

Then the door opened and *he* walked in. 'Sorry I'm late,' he said.

'You're here now,' Suki said, jumping to her feet while also trying to hide just how very excited she was. 'That's what matters.'

'Happy birthday.' He presented her with a posy of flowers.

'How beautiful!' she said, guessing that he'd gone to the trouble of picking them from his garden.

Would he kiss her cheek? Suki waited, hiding a blush by inspecting the posy closely. But he never got the chance to kiss her because Flower, having no idea that she might be interfering with the course of true love, tugged on his jacket, wanting to show him the cat card she'd drawn for

Suki. Then Victoria handed him a cup of tea and the moment passed.

'You haven't missed the food,' Arthur told him.

'I'm relieved to hear it. I don't know about you, but lunch feels a long time ago to me, and my tummy is distinctly empty.'

'Mine too,' Arthur told him.

'Then let's tuck in,' Victoria said.

'The birthday girl first,' the new arrival suggested, and Victoria held the plate of sandwiches out to Suki who took two small quarters.

She looked up to see him smiling at her and her heart gave another little dance of joy. How kind his smile was. How kind *he* was.

Oh, he wasn't the sort of man she'd read about in the romance books that circulated around the village bookshop. He wasn't tall or broad-shouldered or particularly handsome, and he certainly wasn't rich.

But the man she'd come to know over the time he'd lived in Churchwood was the best of men. Patient, kind, caring . . . And with a good sense of humour, too. Adam Potts, the vicar of St Luke's.

Suki knew she had little experience of the world but it seemed to her that even a village like Churchwood produced men in considerable variety. There were cold-hearted men like Alexander Harrington, who'd spread a chill whenever he was home. There were bullies like Jed Powell, whose daughter, Hannah, had given birth in secret and temporarily left the child at Foxfield because she feared her father's reaction.

There were short-tempered men, too. Like old Humphrey Guscott. Suki wouldn't call him a bad person since she could understand that an aged and aching body might take a toll on smiles and sunniness, but even so . . .

Then there were the younger men. Many were absent from Churchwood and its surrounding villages because they were involved in the war in one way or another, but those who worked on local farms were exempt from war service. Suki hated the way they sometimes called out to her. One evening she'd made the mistake of taking a walk past the Wheatsheaf pub with her brothers and sisters, and a group of young men standing outside had called out and made suggestive noises to her. One had even run up and planted himself in front of her, saying, 'How about a kiss, darlin'?'

Suki had ducked around him and hastened on.

Of course, there were other men whom she liked. Older, steady, reliable men like Mr Makepiece, Dr Lovell and her own father. Younger men, like Alice Irvine's handsome soldier husband, Daniel, and Kate Kinsella's equally attractive flight lieutenant husband, Leo.

But only Adam made her heart beat faster. Only Adam made her think she might be ready to leave Mrs Harrington one day so she could love him as his wife and be by his side as he served Churchwood with tact and generosity of spirit.

She took a deep breath and said, 'Today isn't an ordinary birthday. It's my eighteenth.'

'Suki has become quite the grown-up,' Victoria told Adam.

'Indeed, she is,' Adam said, smiling again.

Did that mean he'd begun to see her differently, as a young woman who could become his sweetheart? Oh, how she hoped so!

Just then Jenny tugged on Adam's jacket and when he looked down she raised her arms to be lifted up. Then Flower wanted to be held as well, so he moved to a sofa and balanced a little girl on each knee. Other children swarmed around him. They all loved Adam, and the children's club he ran at the bookshop was immensely popular.

An idea struck Suki. She considered it for a moment and it took root as a good plan. She felt another little spurt of excitement at the thought of taking it forward.

'Have you heard about my cousin's letter?' Miss Plym whispered in her ear.

'Marjorie!' That was Mrs Harrington.

'I have heard, and I hope you become good friends,' Suki said, but Miss Plym was already slinking away, looking guilty at being caught out again.

Mrs Harrington and Victoria left the room to refill the teapots and Suki spoke to her other guests. Alice Irvine was looking radiant in her pregnancy and Suki hoped she'd have a happy outcome this time. Alice deserved it. May Janicki complimented Suki on her appearance. 'It isn't for me to praise your dress seeing as I helped you make it, but the colour suits you. So does the way you've arranged your hair,' she declared.

Compliments like that from tall, stylish May were worth having.

Mrs Collins asked after Suki's family. 'I'll be going home after this tea and spending the evening there,' Suki told her.

'I expect your mother wants to spoil you.'

Suki smiled. Her mother was a strict parent but also a loving one. 'She does.'

Adam was still occupied by the children but when Alice glided over to sit with them he extricated himself. 'Time for me to circulate,' he announced.

Suki determined to seize her moment but Miss Plym got to him first. 'You've heard about my new cousin?' she asked.

'Yes, you told me all about her,' Adam reminded her, but gently.

She'd probably told him the story of her cousin's letter several times.

'I've written back to suggest she meets me in London,' she said. 'I won't feel at ease in a big city all by myself, especially not with bombs falling, but I'm hoping Naomi will come with me.'

'Moral support,' Adam approved. 'How nice.'

Suki tried not to resent Miss Plym for hogging Adam's attention. There was usually little going on in the older woman's life so it was hardly surprising that a new-found relation was big news for her, giving her the chance to feel important and interesting for once. Even so . . .

When Mrs Harrington and Victoria returned, Miss Plym jumped away from Adam like a scalded cat, doubtless fearful of being chided for talking about her cousin again. But they'd brought with them the birthday cake they must have smuggled from the room before. Now it was ablaze with small candles. 'Happy Birthday' was sung and, blushing, Suki blew the candles out.

'Did you make a wish?' Arthur asked.

'I did,' Suki said.

'She can't tell you what it was or it won't come true,' Victoria told him, which was a relief since Suki wouldn't have confided to anyone that she'd wished for Adam to fall in love with her.

The cake was cut and small pieces handed round, leaving enough for the children's mothers to eat on their return from work.

'Time I was going,' Bert said then.

He pecked Suki's cheek and left the room with Mrs Harrington. They closed the door behind them, probably so they could kiss in private. They seemed very old for romance but Suki was glad for them both.

May, Alice and Mrs Collins made time-to-go murmurings, too. Miss Plym was likely to need turfing out because she was difficult to shift once she was inside Foxfield. Adam must have realized it, too, because, in a show of sacrificing himself for the common good, he said, 'May I walk you home, Marjorie? You'll be able to tell me more about your mysterious cousin.'

'How delightful!'

Suki admired his selflessness, but she was running out of time to make her move. She marched up to him, her heart making sharp little taps in her chest. 'Thank you for coming, Adam, and thank you for the flowers. They're lovely. I wonder . . . I've been thinking . . . Might I help with the children's club sometimes? Only when Mrs Harrington doesn't need me, of course.'

Helping at the children's club would throw herself into his company more often. He could get to know her better. See that she was no longer a child.

'That would be wonderful, Suki,' he said. 'All the village children seem to be coming along these days so the more helpers, the better. Be warned, though. It can become a little wild at times.' He smiled ruefully.

Suki smiled back, cherishing the moment – until Miss Plym called over to urge him to make haste. Ah, well. Suki would be with him again just as soon as she could manage it and she'd make sure she showed herself to be kind, sensitive, sensible . . . All the qualities a young clergyman needed in a sweetheart. In a wife, too. It might be much too soon to think seriously of marriage, but as a little daydream for the future it was rather pleasant.

CHAPTER TWELVE

Ruby

'Have you decided if you're going to visit your parents?' Kate asked Pearl. They were in the kitchen with Ruby.

The mere mention of her parents had Pearl looking hounded, rather like a defensive creature drawing in its neck. 'Heavens, Kate. I only received their letter yesterday.'

'It's just that it would be helpful to know if and when you're planning on taking a few days off to visit home, so we can think about how to arrange the work.'

'All right, then. I'm not going home,' Pearl said. 'Once my parents get me in their clutches . . .'

Kate sent Ruby an eye-roll and Ruby managed a smile. 'They can't do anything against your will,' Kate reminded Pearl. 'You're an adult.'

'Hmm,' Pearl said, sounding unconvinced.

'The sooner you let them know what you want for your wedding, the better,' Kate continued. 'It won't help to get their hopes up about their own ideas only to disappoint them, will it?'

'Why are you picking on me?' Pearl demanded. 'Ruby hasn't fixed her wedding yet, and she got engaged before me.'

'Ruby is saving up for her wedding,' Kate pointed out.

Ruby didn't have parents to please, either. Not parents that cared.

Oh, she was trying not to let it trouble her. She'd spent years under the cloud of her parents' disapproval so it was ridiculous to let their indifference bother her now. And there was nothing wrong with a small, modest wedding. All that mattered was that the bride and groom loved each other and wanted to spend the rest of their lives together. If their families and friends were happy for them, that was a bonus. Ruby loved Kenny and was sure that he loved her in return. She was also sure that, with the exception of her parents, everyone she knew would be delighted she was getting married. It really shouldn't matter if the reception took place in the Brimbles Farm barn and comprised just sandwiches and beer for a limited number of their friends. But somehow it *did* matter.

Kate had suggested that Naomi might be willing to host the reception at Foxfield, but Naomi already had her hands full with the evacuees and would have her own wedding to arrange soon. Kate had also suggested the bookshop as an alternative venue, but Kate had held her own wedding reception there and virtually the whole village had come along. 'We can tell people it's a private party so you don't get overwhelmed with well-wishers thinking it's a public event,' she'd said.

Ruby still feared that holding the reception in the village would lead to awkwardness over the number of guests they could invite. Bring-and-share parties were common in Churchwood but Ruby couldn't expect her guests to provide *all* the food and drink, and the few shillings in the toffee tin would barely supply the basics. No, a small gathering in the barn felt less awkward, even if it also felt . . . disappointing.

It wasn't just for herself that Ruby cared. It was also for darling Timmy. She was working hard to rid him of any sense of shame over his unorthodox birth but a hole-in-the-corner wedding for his mother would seem only to confirm that there was something almost reprehensible about it, as though it were being held out of the public eye because she and her son weren't quite respectable.

Ruby realized she'd drifted away into her own thoughts and had missed at least some of the conversation between Pearl and Kate. 'I know exactly what they'll do if I go home,' Pearl was saying. 'They'll drag me along to see the vicar of St Cuthbert's to arrange the ceremony there and then on to the golf club to arrange the reception.'

'St Cuthbert's is your parents' local church?' Ruby asked.

'Yes, they're well known there. Pillars of the community. And my father is a committee member of the golf club. They'll want to show off the fact that they've managed to produce a daughter someone wants to marry even if she is a hopeless carthorse. They'll want to show off the fact that they can afford to put on a good show, too. Masses of flowers, a stupid white dress with a veil I'll trip over, tables with cloths so white they make my eyes ache and set with all sorts of glasses and silverware . . . They're terrible snobs.'

'Then it's down to you to tell them you don't want that sort of wedding,' Kate said again. 'Or at least not that sort of wedding where they live.'

'Kate's right,' Ruby said, though the sort of wedding Pearl had described sounded perfect. 'It's your wedding and it should make you happy.'

Ruby meant it. She was fond of Pearl and hated the thought of her friend being made miserable. But another thought had crept into Ruby's mind, shamefully and treacherously. If Pearl's grand wedding were held out of sight of Churchwood, Ruby's meagre wedding wouldn't look half as paltry in contrast.

CHAPTER THIRTEEN

Beth

'Sorry, I'm dripping everywhere.'

Beth felt a ripple of pleasure at the sound of that voice. She turned, smiling. 'Hello, Adam. It's good of you to come when it's raining so heavily.'

'I don't mind a bit of rain.'

No one could enjoy getting drenched by it, though. Adam was soaked, his hair plastered to his head, and his clothes sodden. He was here because he didn't want to disappoint the patients.

'Let me fetch you a towel.'

'I don't want to be a bother.'

'It's no trouble.'

He followed her back down the corridor to the linen cupboard. Beth took a towel out, handed it to him and watched as he dried his face and then rubbed his hair. It was going to look a mess when it dried, but to Beth there was something refreshing and admirable in Adam's dishevelled lack of vanity. When he'd finished, she took the towel from him.

'Any news?' he asked.

'We've a new chap in Ward Two. Private Higgins. Spinal injuries. He's rather depressed.'

Adam nodded. 'I'll have a word.'

Adam's word wouldn't be of the bracing sort she'd heard

other men utter, whether they were doctors or visitors. 'Buck up, man!' or 'Plenty of chaps are worse off than you.'

Adam would allow the patient his emotions and offer himself as a listening ear, if wanted, or a player of games, if preferred. Like Alice Irvine, he'd also read patients' letters to them, write replies, chat about this and that . . .

He left her with a smile and walked on to Ward Two. Beth deposited the towel in the sluice room, consulted her watch and went to finish the task she'd begun before Adam's arrival: consulting the list of patients who'd be having therapy that day to ensure they were made ready in good time.

'Was that Mr Potts's voice I heard?' Matron asked.

'It was.'

Matron nodded approvingly. She was the sort of woman who'd tramp through gales and ice and snow to help patients and she had little time for those who wouldn't.

Beth took the therapy list back to Ward Two where Nancy was also on duty. Adam hadn't yet reached Private Higgins and Beth understood why. Making a beeline for the man would have singled him out, drawn attention to him and put him on the spot, when that might have been the last thing he wanted. By treating him as just one patient among many, Private Higgins could remain blended into the scenery until he felt ready to emerge from it.

Beth and Nancy were kept busy – when were they ever not busy? – but both were attending to Corporal Greenstreet when Adam reached Private Higgins's nearby bed. He spoke softly. 'Hello, I'm Adam Potts. I'm a visitor here. Please don't be put off by the clerical collar. I'm not here to shove religion down anyone's throat, though I'm happy to talk about it to anyone who might find it comforting or even just interesting. I'm here to chat, mostly. There

85

are playing cards here. Draughts, dominoes, chess and . . . oh, yes, there's a backgammon set, too. Just speak up if you ever want someone to play with.'

Private Higgins was lying down flat but he managed a nod and Adam stepped away. But then the soldier's conscience appeared to trouble him because he called out a belated 'Thank you!'

'My pleasure,' Adam told him.

Beth had seen Adam's gentle approach work wonders with patients. Hopefully, it would do the same for Private Higgins.

'That was well done,' Nancy whispered to Beth.

'It was,' Beth agreed.

Later that evening, both Beth and Nancy were in the attic room that had been designated as a sitting room for the nurses. 'I don't know about you, but I'll be glad to give my feet a rest,' Nancy said. 'I've been run off them all day.'

'Cocoa first,' Beth suggested.

'Definitely.'

Beth made cocoa for both of them and also for Babs Carter, who'd become a good friend of Beth's. They all leaned back in their chairs and took deep breaths. 'Nursing isn't for the faint-hearted, is it?' Babs said.

They talked about their respective days for a while. Then Nancy said, 'I heard someone mention that there's a fashion event at the village bookshop next Saturday. To be run by the woman with the Polish name.'

'May Janicki,' Babs confirmed. 'She's English but married to a Pole. She looks like a model in one of those glamorous magazines I can never afford but she's very down to earth and full of good tips on how to be stylish in wartime, especially on a tight budget.'

'Will you be going?' Nancy asked.

'Unless Matron changes the rotas, yes.'

'I'll come along with you, if that's all right?'

'The more the merrier. Are you coming, Beth?'

'I'd like to.'

'It'll be good to meet more local people,' Nancy said. 'I don't suppose our friendly vicar will be there, though?'

'Adam?' Babs asked, clearly surprised. 'He's very involved in the bookshop but I'm not sure he's interested in fashion. Adam is a darling, but no one would call him smart.'

'There are more important things for a man to be than smartly dressed,' Nancy said, and Beth was aware of a hollow feeling opening up inside her.

Nancy had spoken both warmly and thoughtfully. On first meeting her, Beth would have predicted that Nancy would be attracted to lively, good-looking men, but perhaps she'd had her fill of those. After all, she must have met many such men among the doctors and patients she'd encountered since beginning her nursing career. It wasn't surprising if, like Beth, she'd learned to value more important qualities.

It didn't follow that Nancy had a romantic interest in Adam, though. Everyone liked Churchwood's vicar, so it would be silly to jump to conclusions. Beth still felt relieved when Nancy changed the subject to stockings. 'I hear there's an American base not far from here. Maybe we could wangle our way to some nylons . . .'

Beth forced a smile, 'No nylons yet, unfortunately . . .'

CHAPTER FOURTEEN

Naomi

'Well?' Bert asked, when he called round to see Naomi on Sunday afternoon and they managed a private word in her sitting room.

'If you're asking whether I've received any more nasty letters, the answer is no.'

Naomi watched Bert breathe out slowly as though a weight were lifting from his shoulders. 'That's good to hear.'

'I haven't heard of anyone else receiving one either,' Naomi added.

Bert nodded. 'Here's hoping the letter writer has either had their fun or realized what a stupid and cruel mistake they made.'

Naomi shrugged. 'I suppose we might never know who sent the letter.'

'That troubles you?'

'It does,' Naomi admitted. 'Not knowing makes me suspect everyone. Well, not *everyone*. Not our closest friends, but everyone else. It also means I can't put things right with the letter writer because I don't know what I did wrong.'

'You did nothing wrong. That's my guess. In fact, it wouldn't surprise me if the letter was sent out of spite because you're well liked and the writer is jealous. Whatever the reason, think on this. Churchwood is our home. We

88

have our moments of strife here but generally speaking we're a warm-hearted, cosy sort of place. Do you really want one foolish letter to spoil your pleasure in living here? In our forthcoming marriage, too?'

Of course, she didn't.

'Rising above the letter is easier said than done, I know,' Bert conceded, 'but you're equal to it.'

Was she? Bert always had such faith in her. Naomi wished she had half as much faith in herself but for Bert's sake as well as her own she needed to summon some strength.

CHAPTER FIFTEEN

Suki

The question of what to wear to the children's club on Monday had slid in and out of Suki's mind as she went about her days. Having worn her best dress to her birthday tea, she considered wearing her second-best dress only to decide it would be unwise to risk it. From what she'd heard, the children's club often involved games like football and rounders, or rather messy crafts. Besides, wearing something practical might better show that she was ready to be Adam's helpmate in all that he – and the club – might require of her.

Now the day for the visit had come, she settled for an old flannel skirt and blouse but sighed when she studied her reflection in the hall mirror. Some young women like Victoria, Kate Kinsella and May Janicki looked wonderful in simple clothes like these, but they were tall and elegant. Alice Irvine was almost as short as Suki but she had an air of cleverness and courage that made people sit up and take notice of her whatever she wore. In contrast, Suki felt she must look like a schoolgirl.

For a moment she toyed with the idea of changing into her second-best dress anyway, but just then Mrs Harrington came into the hall and said, 'Off to the children's club? It's very good of you to help out.'

The comment reminded Suki that she was indeed going to help out and that even if she also had hopes of getting closer to the man for whom she harboured tender feelings, the last thing she wanted was for anyone else to suspect this. A plain skirt and blouse were therefore . . . oh, what was the word? Camouflage? Yes, that was it. Camouflage for her fast-beating heart.

Still not entirely reconciled to her appearance, she walked along to the bookshop. Today's session was for older children of seven and above who came straight from school. The bookshop windows had been thrown open and Suki could hear the chatter of voices inside. Should she knock on the door and wait for someone to answer? No, that would seem too formal and she'd feel a fool if no one heard and she was left on the doorstep, looking awkward. She gave the door a rap and then opened it cautiously.

'Suki!' Adam cried. 'Come in!'

The warm welcome made her sigh with relief. With excitement, too, for it promised much for this visit.

She stepped inside and closed the door behind her.

'Suki is here to help today,' Adam told the children. 'Isn't that kind of her?'

The children nodded eagerly, and just in case any of the others weren't already aware of it, Arthur announced, 'Suki lives at Foxfield with me,' as though that gave her a seal of approval.

They formed a circle for the first part of the session. The children sat on the floor but, thankfully, Adam got out chairs for Suki and himself. Scrambling to her feet wouldn't have created a sophisticated impression, and chairs singled them out as the grown-ups.

Adam asked the children for news and stories about their days.

'Mrs Gregson told me I did well in reading today.' That was Lewis, another of the evacuee children who lived at Foxfield. Mrs Gregson was his teacher.

'Excellent,' Adam said, smiling.

'I saw a green woodpecker,' another child said. Pam Cooper's boy.

'They're beautiful birds,' Adam agreed.

'I finished a jigsaw,' Arthur said. He'd helped his sister with it.

Adam nodded approvingly. 'Well done.'

More children piped up.

'I'm going to learn knitting from my mum . . .'

'I found a farthing in the gutter . . .'

'I'm going to make a cart from old pram wheels . . .'

Adam had something nice to say to all the children.

Everyone laughed sympathetically when a boy said, 'I dreamed I had a great big bar of chocolate. I was sad when I woke up and realized it wasn't true.'

Then a girl announced, 'Our dog has had puppies and I'm going to choose their names.'

The children called out suggestions from Sweetpea to Fangs but a vote settled on three names: Winston, after the prime minister; George, after the king; and Lady, because the little girl who owned the puppies liked that name best.

'Suki?' Adam asked then.

Startled, she stared at him.

'Any news?' he prompted.

'Oh!' For a moment her mind was blank. But then she remembered something. 'I had a birthday a few days ago.'

'Suki turned eighteen,' Adam informed the children.

He'd remembered! Was that because her age was significant to him? Because it changed the way he saw her? Oh, she hoped so!

'Who wants to play rounders?' Adam said then.

Hands went up like trees suddenly sprouting growth. 'Me!' the children cried.

They headed into the garden behind the bookshop and divided into two teams. Adam was on one team and Suki on the other. Was this another sign that he saw her as the second adult here today? His equal?

Suki's team batted first. She'd never been good at sport as a child and now she was torn between wanting to impress him with her skill and not wanting to exert herself so hard that she'd appear before him like a dishevelled hoyden. She hit the ball more by luck than judgement and was rewarded with a 'Good shot, Suki!' from Adam as well as cheers from her team.

Running as fast as she could, she reached second base where she waited for the next child to hit the ball, poised to run to the third and fourth bases if there was time. She completed her run at last, relieved that she'd performed satisfactorily.

When it was her team's turn to bowl and field, she left the bowling to the children and stood well back, preparing to catch the ball if it came in her direction and hoping she wouldn't make a hash of things by dropping it.

Some minutes passed before the ball headed towards her but it was high enough to go over her head so she needed to move back if she were to stand any chance of catching it. Keeping her eye on the ball, she stepped back again and again and again.

'Careful, Suki!' Adam cried. 'There's a—'

Too late. Suki had run out of garden. Stumbling over brambles, she tumbled into a ditch that was full of water and mud.

She gasped. Winced. And felt the sting of humiliation

93

as everyone came running to her aid. 'Are you all right?' Adam asked worriedly.

The answer was no, she wasn't all right. She'd torn a stocking. Her hands were scratched and her posterior was both wet and sore from the heavy landing. 'I'm fine,' she said, too mortified to admit to being hurt.

'Let me help you.' Adam picked his way through the brambles and reached down a hand to pull her up.

Suki had often dreamed of holding hands with Adam but she'd pictured it happening on long romantic walks when they'd admire the countryside and sunsets. She hadn't imagined a muddy heave upwards that necessitated Adam wiping his hands on a handkerchief plucked from his pocket afterwards while she wiped her hands on a hand-kerchief plucked from hers.

'Are you sure you're all right?' he asked.

'Quite sure, thank you.'

'I'm sorry about your skirt. Your stockings, too.'

'No matter,' Suki said, though she wanted to burst into tears. 'I'd better go home and clean up.'

'Of course. I'm sorry your first day ended like this, but I hope you'll come back another time.' Was Adam saying that to be kind, when he really thought she was more of a liability than an asset to the club? At this moment, she was too raw to think straight.

'Would you like us to walk with you?' Adam said. 'To be sure you arrive home safely?'

Because she couldn't be trusted to walk there by herself without getting into another scrape? A procession of children following her down Churchwood Way would turn her into an even bigger spectacle, drawing all eyes to her misfortune.

'There's no need for that,' she said, hesitating, before adding, 'I'm sorry I've made a mess of things.'

'Accidents happen,' Adam assured her, but this accident couldn't have happened in worse circumstances.

So much for impressing him. Suki hastened away, torturing herself with the notion that Adam must think her a fool.

CHAPTER SIXTEEN

Naomi

Naomi sighed when she left the grocer's shop, willing herself to relax a little. No one had given her a look that could be described as hostile, smug or even awkward, and no one had said anything at all to suggest that they'd even heard about the poison pen letter, let alone sent it. Facing people in the village and knowing the letter writer might be among them was still an ordeal, but Naomi really was trying hard to put the letter behind her. After all, it had arrived last Wednesday and now it was Tuesday, which meant that almost a week had passed with no more letters being received.

Seeing Edna Hall emerge from the post office, Naomi smiled and walked forward to tell her that the book she wanted – Margaret Mitchell's *Gone with the Wind* – was now available to borrow from the bookshop.

But Edna looked horrified to see her and scuttled away to dive into the cobbler's shop.

Naomi stared after her in surprise and dismay. Was Edna the author of the poison pen letter and afraid that Naomi had guessed her identity and planned to confront her? Surely not? Not *Edna*? Naomi had long considered her to be a friend. A dear friend after that awful time when, desperately lonely after the death of her husband, Edna had thought to end her time on earth prematurely. Naomi had been one of the people who'd rallied round to help. She hadn't been the only person, of course, but she'd certainly been one of—

'There you are, Naomi.'

Turning, she saw that Marjorie had approached. It took a moment for Naomi to drag her mind away from Edna – distress was rippling through her – but she finally managed to ask, 'What is it, Marjorie?'

She must have been frowning because Marjorie looked affronted. 'I beg your pardon if you've more important people to see,' she said, huffily.

Oh, heavens. Naomi breathed in deeply to steady herself. 'Not at all. You just caught me with my mind elsewhere.'

'Humph.'

Naomi sighed. And tried again. 'I apologize, Marjorie. I didn't mean to be short with you.'

'Well, all right,' Marjorie said, though her forgiveness seemed begrudging. 'I've received another letter.'

'From your cousin?'

'From Connie, yes. See for yourself.'

Naomi took the letter that was offered to her and drew it from its envelope.

Dear Marjorie (how warm that salutation feels! It's as though we're friends already),

I was so pleased to receive your letter. Your good sense in suggesting we meet for lunch or tea before spending a longer time together does you credit. However, my circumstances are rather challenging just now and I hope you won't mind if I throw myself on your mercy. My flat requires some plumbing work and it's likely to be messy. In fact, it's been suggested that I'll be considerably more comfortable if I move out for a few days. I could go to friends, of course. I've been assured by several friends that they'll be delighted to put me up. However, once I return home afterwards I may struggle to find the time to visit you. It may be that you won't mind this. A few months of delay may mean little to you, but they'll mean a lot to me since I'm so excited at the thought of meeting you.

It's been suggested that I quit my home temporarily on 17th June. Next week, in fact. Might I come to you then and trespass on your hospitality until the work is completed? I've no wish to be an inconvenience, though, so please don't hesitate to let me know if this proposal doesn't suit you. I want to begin our cousinship – our friendship – with goodwill on both sides and I don't wish to mar it with what you might consider to be an imposition.

Looking forward to hearing from you, dear cousin,
Constance

'What do you think?' Marjorie asked.

Naomi thought that Constance Pearce sounded a gushing sort of woman but there was no harm in that. 'I think it's entirely for you to decide if you want her to come to stay or not. I don't think you need feel any sort of obligation towards her. It isn't as though she'll be out on the streets while the plumbers are at work. She specifically points out that she has friends who'll be glad to put her up.'

'But she says she might not be able to see me for months if I don't agree.'

'Yes, I saw that. I suppose she must have other obligations or plans.'

Marjorie wrung her hands in anxious indecision. 'She may be disappointed if she comes to stay with me and my house doesn't offer the sort of comfort she's grown used to. After all, it doesn't offer the sort of comfort *I* was brought up to expect from my home.'

Poor Marjorie, brought up in luxury only to be cast down into relative penury when the money ran out. Naomi could understand her concern that Mrs Pearce's branch of the family might have retained some splendour and expect similar ease on Marjorie's side, but there was a simple way to deal with that.

'If she looks down on your way of living, surely she isn't the sort of woman you want to befriend?' Naomi asked.

'I suppose not,' Marjorie said, but with no discernible lightening of her anxiety.

Naomi felt some sympathy for her. Marjorie was only human, and it took a certain amount of inner strength to hold one's head up against disdain. Strength that Marjorie lacked.

'I haven't entertained in years,' she said, continuing to wring her hands.

'No one expects to be entertained on a grand scale in wartime,' Naomi pointed out, but the words did nothing to still the twisting hands.

Naomi heaved a private sigh. 'I'll help to ready your house for the visit, Marjorie.'

'Will you, Naomi? That would be marvellous.'

'I suggest you look over the linens in advance and let me know if you have any shortages so we can work out how to supply them. Then we can prepare your spare bedroom together. If I'm able, I'll happily lend anything you may need in the way of china and cutlery, too. And I'll provide flowers from my garden so everything looks bright and cheerful.'

'How wonderful,' Marjorie said, but a hopefulness in her mud-coloured eyes suggested she wanted still more from Naomi.

Hiding another sigh, Naomi said, 'You could bring your cousin to Foxfield for lunch or dinner one day, too.'

Marjorie's relief was palpable. She might not live in grandeur herself but she'd be glad to show Mrs Pearce that she was on excellent terms with the owner of the best house in the village.

'We can ask Victoria to advise you on other meals since you know she's clever at making the most of limited ingredients,' Naomi said. 'We can even ask her to make a batch of scones for you so you'll have something to offer your cousin for tea.'

'I'll write to Constance now,' Marjorie said. She turned away only to come to a halt, looking along Churchwood Way. 'There's Bert's truck. He must be in one of the shops.'

Naomi saw that Bert's truck had indeed drawn up on the opposite side of the road. It was old and had an engine that rattled and roared but she'd been too distracted to notice its arrival.

'How strange that he didn't come over to say hello,' Marjorie added.

It wasn't strange at all. Marjorie had many a person running for the hills to avoid her and while Bert was a decent man, he wasn't a saint.

Marjorie loped away and Naomi walked over to the truck. She coughed beside the open window and Bert sat up suddenly. 'Is it safe?' he asked.

'Were you hiding from Marjorie?'

'Guilty as charged, beloved. She's a good woman in many ways, but . . .' He shrugged.

Naomi couldn't argue with *but* . . .

Bert heaved himself out of the truck to wrap his arms around her and kiss her. 'How are you feeling?' he asked then.

Naomi's thoughts returned to Edna Hall scurrying into the cobbler's shop. But she wanted to think about that before she told even Bert about it, especially considering she also wanted to show him that she was trying to be strong.

'I'm . . . well,' Naomi told him.

'Hmm,' Bert said, clearly unconvinced. 'William is coming on Friday, isn't he?'

'He is.'

'Have you thought any more about mentioning the letter to him? Obviously, it's still bothering you.'

'I haven't decided yet.'

'Finding out his family is responsible would mean laying your doubts about Churchwood people to rest once and for all.'

'True.' But after seeing Edna Hall, Naomi now had good reasons for suspecting that William's mother and sister were innocent.

'I know you don't want to hurt William, but he's under no illusions about his family,' Bert pointed out.

'I'll think about telling him,' Naomi promised.

'Do that.'

Bert parted from her with a kiss and Naomi headed home. She tensed when she neared the cobbler's shop where Edna had fled. Would Edna avoid Naomi by turning her back on her or – worse – watch her pass with disgust or triumph on her face? The thought of either possibility made Naomi shudder, so she walked past while staring rigidly ahead. Even so, she imagined Edna watching her with dislike in her heart. Why, though? Naomi had done nothing to offend Edna as far as she could recall. But perhaps there hadn't been a specific incident that had triggered Edna's hostility. Perhaps Edna simply disliked Naomi as a person. Perhaps during all those times when they'd chatted and laughed together Edna had been secretly despising Naomi.

But it was one thing to dislike a person. It was quite another to send them a vicious letter deliberately to cause them grief. What was Naomi to do? Challenge Edna when the shock had eased a little and some strength had returned? How unpleasant that would be. How complicated, too, given the fact that, while most of the evacuee women and children lived at Foxfield, grandmother Ivy and her little granddaughter spent their nights at Edna's and came to Foxfield only in the daytime.

Another thought jumped into Naomi's mind. Could Ivy be the source of the ill will against Naomi? Had she complained to Edna that Naomi was bossy and perhaps had other faults, too?

Reaching the Foxfield gateposts, Naomi was overpowered by a reluctance to go further, knowing Ivy was inside the house. But Foxfield was her home so of course Naomi had to go on. She let herself into the house and heard voices in the drawing room. Victoria's voice. And Ivy's. Steeling herself, Naomi popped her head inside.

'Oh, good, you're back,' Victoria said. 'I was just about to put the kettle on for tea.'

'Lovely,' Naomi said. Then she took a deep breath and looked at Ivy.

Who smiled back at her. Was it a genuine smile or fake? Naomi's self-esteem felt so ravaged that she couldn't trust her judgement to tell the difference.

'Basil has been keeping me company,' Ivy said, patting the head of Naomi's ugly but much-loved bulldog.

'How nice,' Naomi said.

Had Basil turned against her, too? Maybe his judgement was as weak as Naomi's. Or maybe Ivy had done nothing at all to turn Edna against Naomi. Certainly, Ivy had always been warm in both her manner and in her words, expressing what appeared to be heartfelt gratitude to Naomi for the help and hospitality she'd given.

Naomi had always liked Ivy and admired her in return. After all, Ivy hadn't had an easy life. She'd never risen out of poverty in the east of London, not helped by the fact that her bowed legs made walking a slow and uncomfortable business for her.

Despite that misfortune she'd married, only to be widowed early, and her daughter – her only child – had turned out to be a flighty young woman who'd fallen pregnant and then abandoned her child to Ivy's mercy. Fortunately for little Flower, Ivy cared for her granddaughter wonderfully well.

But perhaps there was another side to Ivy. A side that she kept hidden from Naomi.

Perhaps this . . . Perhaps that . . . It occurred to Naomi that the turmoil she was feeling might be precisely what the letter writer intended and, if she wasn't careful, her suspicions might spoil the friendships she treasured so much. She really needed to get a grip on her emotions.

CHAPTER SEVENTEEN

Ruby

'I'm going into the village,' Ruby announced.

She was in the kitchen at Brimbles Farm with Pearl and also with Kate, who smiled and said, 'You make it sound as though you're going into battle.'

'That's because I am. In a manner of speaking. I have some shopping to do but I also hope to see the lovely Mrs Nugent.'

'Ah,' Kate said, understanding gleaming in her eyes.

Mrs Nugent was the woman who was leading the continued disapproval of Ruby now it was known that she was an unmarried mother. 'It's all very well, that Ruby Turner making out that a man took advantage of her,' Ruby had heard Mrs Nugent saying. 'How do we know she didn't encourage him? No smoke without fire. That's how I see it, especially with the way she goes around with that cheap-looking dyed hair and that red, pouting mouth.'

Ruby had a temper, which meant that her first impulse had long been to challenge anyone who upset her. But she was older and hopefully wiser now, and instead of the sort of confrontation that might keep a conflict smouldering, she'd decided on the subtler approach of showing her face to Mrs Nugent often, stimulating the old crone to keep gossiping about her in the hope that people would soon grow tired of listening to it. It would be fresh news no longer. Stale news, in fact. Boring.

'Kenny is giving me a lift since he needs to go back to Pearson's for something they didn't have in stock when he went there last week,' Ruby said now. 'He'll drop me in the village and I'll walk home afterwards. Pearl, have you written to your parents to tell them you won't be visiting?'

'Yes,' Pearl said, looking down at the floor and shuffling her large feet.

'You haven't posted your letter, though, have you? Pearl, you're hopeless. There's nothing to be gained by putting it off. In fact, you'll only annoy your parents all the more if you keep them waiting.'

Pearl shrugged miserably.

'Give the letter to me and I'll post it,' Ruby offered.

Pearl dragged the letter out of her breeches pocket. It was crumpled and there was a smear of mud on the envelope. Ruby doubted its condition would endear Pearl to her parents, but the important thing was to get the letter in the post so they weren't sitting at home festering over their daughter's neglect.

Slipping the letter into her bag, Ruby went out to join Kenny in the truck.

There was no sign of Mrs Nugent at the butcher's where Ruby bought sausages for a casserole since sausages weren't rationed yet, though who knew how long that would last. There was no sign of her in the baker's where Ruby bought bread. But as Ruby returned to the street she saw Alice by the pillar box outside the post office.

Alice was posting a letter. Ruby watched her kiss the envelope before she dropped it into the slot. Seeing Ruby, Alice blushed. 'It's a letter to Daniel.'

'So I assumed. How is he?'

Daniel had been involved in the war since the beginning. He'd had some tricky moments, too, having been one of thousands of servicemen involved in the evacuation from Dunkirk and, later, having been caught by the enemy before escaping. But he'd avoided serious injury. So far. Ruby felt a swell of sympathy for Alice and all the other wives and families who lived each day dreading bad news of their loved ones.

'He was fine the last time he wrote,' Alice said. 'Thank goodness.'

'Long may that continue,' Ruby answered. 'How are you keeping?'

Alice patted the curve of her middle beneath which her baby was growing. She'd had some challenges herself, having miscarried her first pregnancy. 'I'm keeping well and staying optimistic,' she said. 'I can feel little flutters and kicks, which I love.'

'I remember Timmy's flutters and kicks,' Ruby said. 'They're magical, aren't they?'

She took Pearl's letter from her bag.

'Oh dear!' Alice smiled at the muddy state of it. 'I assume that's one of Pearl's letters?'

'To her parents, yes. They want her to go home to plan her wedding but she's refusing to go. I'm not sure what she wants for her wedding yet.'

'What of your wedding plans, Ruby?'

Oh, heck. 'I'm still saving up as well as waiting for the gossip to settle,' she said.

'Is Mrs Nugent still being her charming self?' Alice asked.

'She's still giving me disapproving glowers, but I'm hoping that the more she sees me, the sooner she'll grow tired of glaring and the sooner people will stop listening to her.'

'Good for you.'

Alice walked on and Ruby gave Pearl's filthy letter one last glance before dropping it into the pillar box, wishing she could quell the hope that Mr and Mrs Grimes would manage to persuade Pearl to hold her wedding near their own home. It was a mean and selfish wish. Unfair, unkind and reprehensible in so many ways. And Ruby hated feeling like that.

So Pearl's grand wedding might cast Ruby's into the shade. So what? Why did she care so much?

It was true that as a young girl she'd loved pretty things and gazed in the shop windows of London's West End, fantasizing that one day the lovely dresses, shoes and hats might be hers. She still liked pretty things, hence her dyed hair and cosmetics. But not to the extent of feeling jealous when other people had them and she didn't.

Her engagement ring was an example of that. Kate's engagement ring was a flashing, brilliant emerald surrounded by diamonds, while Ruby's was an inexpensive little garnet set on a slender band. But Ruby treasured her modest ring and not for a moment had she begrudged Kate her magnificent one.

No. Ruby was clear about her priorities. Timmy and his welfare came first. Happiness with Kenny and the friendships she'd made in Churchwood came next.

Was it a case of her being perfectly willing to accept a humble life in general but wanting her wedding day – a day that was supposed to be special – to be as full of pomp and splendour as anyone else's?

Maybe so, but she needed to come to terms with her situation soon because Kenny wanted to marry as soon as possible and was growing impatient with her excuses for not fixing a date for the wedding. It wasn't only the money side of things that he didn't care about, he also couldn't understand her dilemma over whether to invite her parents. Not now everyone knew she was Timmy's mother so there was no secret for them to let slip. Ruby had explained her concern that exposing Timmy to their continuing disapproval might undo all she was doing to build his confidence in himself, but Kenny had a simple answer to that.

'If you don't like them and they don't like you, why bother inviting them?' he'd said. 'Or if you feel you must invite them, just ignore their sour faces. I certainly will.'

To Ruby, it was more of a dilemma because her parents had at least allowed her to keep Timmy, and now she was also contending with this strange resistance to being overshadowed by Pearl. She needed to make sense of it all before Kenny's patience ran out and he began to doubt that she really loved him.

CHAPTER EIGHTEEN

Naomi

'I'll go,' Naomi said when a knock sounded on the Foxfield door.

Victoria and Suki were busy in the kitchen and, despite wondering if Ivy were somehow involved in the poison pen letter, Naomi wished to spare the older woman's bowed legs. She'd been struggling to face her since witnessing Edna's odd behaviour yesterday. Though Ivy had been as warm and friendly as ever, Naomi couldn't help wondering if the warmth and friendliness were actually fake.

Bewilderment, suspicion and hurt had been circling Naomi's mind non-stop and depriving her of sleep – which was only making her even less able to think clearly.

She opened the door – and gasped.

'Morning,' the visitor said. Then she put her head on one side and regarded Naomi with a frown. 'Are you quite well, Naomi? You look terribly pale.'

Naomi floundered for an answer. 'I'm fine. I just wasn't expecting . . .'

'I'm only here to bring Ivy her wool,' Edna Hall said. 'I unravelled it from an old cardigan of mine so she could knit a jumper for Flower. I know she wanted to make a start on it today but it must have fallen out of her bag, since I found it under her chair.'

Naomi's mouth was open but she could feel it making odd shapes as she tried to decide what to say in return. Edna looked so normal. So untroubled.

'Oh, my goodness!' Edna said as though a thought had suddenly occurred to her. 'Did I offend you when I ran off yesterday? It was inexcusable, but when I saw Marjorie bearing down on you I'm afraid I couldn't face her telling me yet again about her cousin's letters. She must have told me a dozen times already.' Edna stepped forward and touched Naomi's arm. 'I'm sorry.'

Did that really explain Edna's behaviour? Looking into her old friend's worried face, Naomi decided that it did. 'You haven't offended me,' Naomi hastened to assure her. 'If I'm a little slow today, it's only because I'm tired.'

'No wonder, with all the good you do in this village. You need to look after yourself, Naomi.'

'Come in, Edna.'

Naomi led her into the drawing room where Ivy was sitting. 'Edna's here with some wool,' she said.

Leaving Edna and Ivy together, Naomi made an excuse about needing to make a telephone call and headed for her small sitting room where she flopped down in her favourite armchair. How easy it was to misinterpret people! At least Naomi had kept her suspicions about Edna to herself. That was something to appreciate. Should she now talk to William about the letter?

Naomi decided there was no need to make up her mind about it yet. Instead, she'd wait to see if the post brought any more nasty letters to her door. On that thought, she glanced at her watch and saw that the second post was due soon.

CHAPTER NINETEEN

Bert

One glance at Naomi's strained face was enough to tell Bert what had happened. 'You've had another of those disgusting letters?' It was Wednesday again. One week exactly since the first letter had arrived.

Naomi nodded and handed it over.

YOU LOVE THE SOUND OF YOUR OWN VOICE, DON'T YOU? TROUBLE IS NO ONE ELSE DOES.

Reading the cruel and spiteful words, Bert felt anger surge inside him. 'Right,' he said. 'I was prepared to make allowances for a moment of anger on the part of whoever wrote that first letter, but this nastiness has gone far enough. It isn't angry. It's cold and calculating, and something needs to be done about it. In my opinion, anyway. What do you think, beloved?' He gathered her into his arms and held her close, wishing he could do more to ease her distress.

'I'll speak to William,' Naomi said.

'He's still coming on Friday?'

'As far as I know.'

'Good. And if that doesn't help, I suggest we involve our friends.'

Naomi looked up at him. 'Which friends?'

'The usual people we turn to in a crisis. Alice, Kate, Adam, May, Janet . . .'

'The bookshop organizers.'

'Also Victoria, Suki and your evacuee women. Perhaps Beth up at the hospital, too. These people all think the world of you. I guarantee they won't only feel angry at the letters but also be at pains to point out that what's written in them is rubbish. So there's no need for you to feel embarrassed.'

'I don't want to upset our friends, though. Or be a bother to them.'

'You're always at the front of the line when it comes to helping them. They'll be only too keen to help you. If we all pull together, we may be able to work out who's sending the letters and put a stop to them.'

'I really would like to know who's sending them,' Naomi said.

'Then that's what we'll do. You're a wonderful woman, beloved. Keep that at the front of your mind.'

'I will,' she said, and he had no doubt that she'd try. Naomi's confidence had grown nicely over the last couple of years but Bert knew it could still be fragile at times. This was one of those times and it made his heart feel like spidery cracks were threatening to break it apart.

CHAPTER TWENTY

Naomi

William bounced into Foxfield with his customary enthusiasm, his long, spider-like limbs loose and not particularly well coordinated but full of eagerness. Having opened the door to him, Naomi found herself wrapped into a hug. 'How are you? How's everyone else? Is everything all right?' His tone held the brightness of someone who anticipated that everything was indeed all right.

'We're having our moments,' Naomi told him. 'But everyone is well and wanting to say hello.'

She could hear whispering behind the drawing-room door and guessed that the children were jockeying for position to be the first to see William and tell him about the small triumphs and challenges they'd experienced since his last visit two weeks ago. It wasn't just the children who'd be glad he was here again. William was a favourite with adults and children alike.

He must have heard the whispering too, because he grinned and said, 'I'll go and see the little blighters before they fall through the door.'

Throwing his bag into a corner, he opened the door and the children swarmed over him.

'Come and see my drawing . . .'

'I got ten out of ten in my spelling test . . .'

'Mrs Barlow in the village has got a new kitten . . .'

His homecoming followed the usual pattern – exchanges of news, expressions of admiration where admiration was due, expressions of sympathy where sympathy was needed, promises to play and plenty of eating and drinking because William was always hungry.

It was later when Naomi managed to get him to herself. 'Let's have a catch-up in the sitting room,' she invited.

They could be more private there.

'You asked if everything was all right earlier,' Naomi began, once they were settled.

William's smooth young forehead furrowed into a frown. 'Are you saying everything *isn't* all right?'

'I'm going to show you some letters, but I don't want you to think I'm making accusations,' Naomi said. 'I'm merely asking for your thoughts and feelings about them. Whatever those thoughts and feelings might be, I won't hold them against you.'

William's expression had turned wary. 'This sounds . . . ominous.'

She passed him the poison pen letters and watched outrage develop on his features as he read the first one.

WELL, AREN'T YOU A BOSSY WOMAN? IT'S TIME YOU STOPPED ORDERING PEOPLE ABOUT AND LET THEM GET ON WITH THEIR OWN LIVES. THEY'LL BE A LOT HAPPIER WITHOUT YOUR INTERFERENCE.

The outrage cranked up even higher when he read the second letter.

YOU LOVE THE SOUND OF YOUR OWN VOICE, DON'T YOU? TROUBLE IS NO ONE ELSE DOES.

114

'These letters . . . They're awful!' he said. 'They're nonsense, too.'

Naomi must have looked troubled still because his jaw suddenly dropped open and then flapped for a moment before he managed to ask, 'You don't think *I* sent them, do you?'

'Of course not. That thought never crossed my mind.'

'That's a relief! But what these letters say . . . You don't actually believe them?'

'No,' she said, though the truth was that she still felt terribly hurt and every day a little more of her confidence was seeping out of her.

'Good,' William said, 'because whoever wrote them was just being spiteful.' He paused then added, 'Do you know who did write them?'

'Not for certain.'

William nodded slowly but then his jaw dropped again as another thought occurred to him. 'You think it was my father?'

'Do *you* think it could have been your father?' Naomi questioned.

William gave a bewildered shrug. 'I don't know. It never occurred to me that he might . . .' He shook himself visibly as though to marshal his thoughts. 'My father is mean enough, I suppose. And he resents the fact that you got the better of him over money. Over me, too, though only because it hurts his pride for me to visit here. I doubt he actually misses me.'

'But?' Naomi prompted, sensing he wasn't convinced.

'I can't explain why I think this, but it just doesn't feel like the sort of thing he'd do. He stamps his feet and shouts about money   and he won't have your name mentioned in the house – but writing letters like these . . .'

115

Naomi gave them a name. 'Poison pen letters.'

William nodded. 'They don't feel like his way of going about things.'

He'd confirmed her own instincts, though it was a pity, since Naomi would have loved Alexander to be responsible. Still, Alexander wasn't William's only family member.

She waited for him to say more and, after a moment, his jaw dropped yet again.

'You suspect my *mother*?' he asked.

'I can't answer that question because I don't know your mother,' Naomi pointed out.

'She wouldn't write this. She couldn't,' William insisted, but was love for his mother blinding him to her darker side?

He wrestled with the idea of his mother as author a little longer. 'She wouldn't have the nerve for this sort of thing,' he said then.

'Do poison pen letters need a lot of nerve?' Naomi wondered. 'They're anonymous.' And people who hadn't the nerve for face-to-face confrontation might hide behind anonymity.

'My mother never hits back when she's upset. She just goes quiet and cries silently. No. I really can't believe these letters are her work.'

Naomi made no reply, and another minute or so passed before it occurred to William that there was a third suspect at home. 'My *sister*?'

'I'm not accusing her,' Naomi hastened to say, 'but it would be understandable if she harboured ill will towards me.' Even if that ill will was the fault of Alexander's lying and cheating.

William's forehead pleated again as he gave the possibility some thought. 'I'm not saying she *couldn't* have written

116

the letters,' he finally said. 'But I don't think she *did* write them. She's too wrapped up in her own life to be interested in mine just at the moment. She has a new friend at school who travelled the world before war broke out. Emily thinks she's exotic and talks about her all the time – when she isn't visiting her or inviting her to our house. The girl has a brother, too, and Emily seems equally smitten by him.'

He'd spoken of Alexander with conviction. He'd spoken of his mother and sister with rather less certainty, putting forward his reasons for why they were unlikely culprits as though trying to convince himself as much as Naomi. William didn't *want* them to be guilty, and who could blame him?

'Will you think about it some more? Over the weekend?' Naomi asked. William was an honest and fair-minded boy, and perhaps on reflection he'd come round to the idea that someone in his family just might be responsible. 'I don't want anyone to be punished or even have their identity exposed,' Naomi said, to help him along. 'I just want to understand why the letters were sent and know that there'll never be another.'

William nodded.

'I'm sorry if I've upset you,' Naomi added.

'You haven't,' William said, though Naomi suspected that wasn't true. 'I understand you need to find out who sent these horrid letters.'

She did. Not knowing the identity of the sender was robbing her of sleep and making an ordeal of every time she left the house – for the shops, for the bookshop and even for church.

'I'll give the letters some thought, and I'll let you know if I have any ideas,' William said.

'Thank you. Now, then' – Naomi forced a smile – 'I think there are some children who are hoping you'll read them a bedtime story . . .'

CHAPTER TWENTY-ONE

Suki

'When are you going back to the children's club?' Victoria asked.

She wasn't the first person to ask Suki that question. Naomi and others had asked it, too, and all of them had appeared to assume that she'd be returning, despite her mortifying accident.

'Poor you,' Victoria had said, the day Suki had returned home, wet and muddy from her fall into the ditch.

Sweeping Suki into the scullery, Victoria had helped her out of her filthy shoes and stockings, and then hurried her upstairs for a bath, running up to Suki's attic room for clean clothing which she'd left for her outside the bathroom door. 'I'll put the kettle on for tea,' she'd called.

Downstairs in the kitchen, she'd asked Suki what had happened and smiled with rueful sympathy when she heard the sorry story.

'I've never been more embarrassed,' Suki had admitted.

'We've all fallen over,' Victoria had told her. 'If you can remember, I only met Naomi and got this job here because Alec Mead's dog attacked my bicycle and sent me sprawling into a ditch. It left me covered in mud and goodness knows what else. In fact, you helped to clean my clothes.'

119

Suki had remembered. 'Yes, but . . .' Her words had trailed off since she hadn't wanted Victoria to know that the main reason for her mortification was the fact that she'd made such an idiot of herself in front of the man she was trying to impress.

'Is Suki all right?' she'd heard Arthur ask Victoria when he returned from children's club. 'She fell into a ditch and got wet.'

'So I understand. She has a few scratches and I imagine she'll wake up to some bruises, but she'll be fine.'

'We were playing rounders and she kept stepping backwards until . . .'

Arthur must have moved out of the hall because his voice had faded away, but when he saw Suki later he'd given her a smile. 'I'm glad you're all right,' he'd said.

Lewis had nodded agreement. 'So am I.'

Everyone had wanted to hear the story of Suki's accident but they'd all been sympathetic. Some of the evacuee women had even shared stories of their own mishaps to show fellow feeling.

Mags had told the story of leaping towards the boarding platform of a bus only for the bus to move away before she'd landed, leaving her face down in the gutter. Ivy had told her of getting into a chair in a cafe only for the chair to break under her. And Jessie had told how she'd fallen down some stairs at Oxford Circus underground station and landed with her dress up around her waist and her stockings and suspenders on display.

The thought of facing Adam again had still scalded Suki's cheeks. But gradually her thinking had cleared. Yes, she'd made a fool of herself, but she loved him. Rather desperately. Did she really want her pride to get in the way of seeing if he might come to love her, too? Of course, she didn't. She'd never have a chance of winning him round if she hid away from him.

Falling into the ditch had been a setback in demonstrating that she was a woman instead of a clumsy child, but the mature thing was surely to dust herself off and move forward with her head held high.

Her mother had an expression for how to tackle misfortune: 'If you fall off the horse, you have to get straight back on instead of wallowing in failure.'

'We haven't got a horse,' Suki had pointed out when she'd first heard the expression as a child, and her mother had laughed, saying, 'It's a figure of speech.'

Suki understood that now and, yes, she wanted to get back on the horse called Churchwood Children's Club. If anyone laughed about her fall into the ditch, then she'd laugh alongside them. In fact, the best thing might be to mention it herself and start the laughter going. That way, the incident could recede into the past, leaving the future wide open to possibilities. Yes, she decided, she'd return to the children's club just as soon as possible.

CHAPTER TWENTY-TWO

Bert

'I've thought about it all weekend,' William told Bert and Naomi on Sunday evening. 'But I really can't believe that anyone in my family – not my father, my mother or my sister – wrote those letters.'

Bert was disappointed. Naomi had a smile on her face but he was sure she was disappointed too, because it left the finger of suspicion pointing towards Churchwood.

'I'm sorry,' William said.

'There's no need to be sorry,' Naomi assured him. 'You've done nothing wrong.'

'Even so . . .'

'William, you haven't surprised me,' Naomi told him. 'My instincts have been telling me the same as yours.'

He nodded, then sighed and said, 'I wish I could do something to help.'

'It helps just knowing you wish us well,' Bert told him. William was a decent lad and Bert wanted to comfort him.

'You'll let me know if you find out who did write the letters?' William asked. He was returning to his boarding school in the morning.

'Of course,' Naomi said.

William went off to bed and Bert put his arm around Naomi. 'Let's call a meeting of our friends.'

Naomi nodded.

CHAPTER TWENTY-THREE

Naomi

All members of the bookshop organizing team had come and they sat in a semicircle in the Foxfield sitting room – Naomi, Bert, Alice, Adam, May, Janet and even Kate, who could rarely find time for bookshop meetings in the working day. 'I can't stay long,' she said, 'but when Alice said you'd called a meeting I sensed something serious was going on so here I am.'

'I'm grateful,' Naomi told her. 'I'm grateful to all of you. I only hope you won't think I'm making a fuss about nothing.'

'You're not,' Bert said firmly. 'You know I think it's nonsense, but it's upsetting you so it's serious. There are other people to think about, too.' Bert folded his arms across his substantial middle in a pose that always meant he was preparing for . . . Not a fight, exactly. It was more that he was readying himself to stand firm and see justice done.

Questions and murmurs began.

'What's nonsense?'

'I'm sorry to hear you're upset, Naomi.'

'What's going on?'

Bert gestured Naomi to continue. She handed the letters to Alice first, since she was nearest. Alice's pretty face flushed in outrage when she saw what had been written. 'This is terrible!' she cried.

She passed the letters to Adam whose eyebrows shot up before he passed them on to May. Moments later, everyone had read the letters and everyone looked appalled.

'They're ridiculous,' Alice said. 'Utterly unjustified and cruel.'

'If I could get my hands on whoever sent them . . .' Kate's temper was always quick to fire up.

'Have you any idea who the sender might be?' Adam asked.

'None at all,' Naomi told him. 'But I've obviously offended someone.' She attempted a smile but tears shimmered in her eyes.

Alice leaped up and folded her into a hug. Kate did the same. In fact, everyone got up to hug Naomi.

Victoria entered with a tea tray and nodded approvingly. 'I'm glad to see all your friends are firmly on your side, Naomi,' she said. Naomi had told her household about the letters that morning and been touched by their support.

Victoria looked around at the others. 'What those letters say is absurd, isn't it?'

Everyone agreed.

'I don't know whether the writer is disturbed or just plain vicious, but either way the accusation of bossiness is groundless,' Victoria continued. 'You're entitled to boss me about since you're my employer, Naomi. You're entitled to boss Suki about, too. But you never boss either of us. You treat us with respect and affection, and we love you for it.'

'It's sweet of you to say that, Victoria,' Naomi said.

'Not sweet. Honest. Everyone in this house – adults and children alike – thinks you're wonderful. So kind and generous! I won't keep you talking, though. You and your friends need to work out a way of getting to the bottom of this horrible mystery.'

With that, Victoria handed teacups around and left the room.

Bert reached out and squeezed Naomi's hand encouragingly before addressing the others.

'None of you have received a letter like this or heard of anyone else receiving one?'

No one had.

'It's possible that anyone who's received a letter is keeping it to themselves because they find it embarrassing or upsetting or both,' Alice pointed out. 'Were the letters sent through the post?'

'Postmarked London,' Naomi confirmed.

'Possibly sent from there to throw us off the scent of anyone living locally,' Bert added.

'I'd prefer to think that the letters are a prank by a child making mischief than that they were written by an adult, but I'm afraid that looks unlikely,' Alice said. 'For one thing, the sender would need to know someone in London who was willing to post them. And for another thing, there's the cost of the postage to consider. Churchwood children don't tend to have much in the way of pocket money.'

'Are you intending to tell all the village about the letters?' Kate asked Naomi.

'I'd rather avoid that, if possible. There'd be so much unpleasantness and suspicion. The whole village would be in a stir. Besides . . .' Naomi would feel appallingly embarrassed.

'I understand,' Kate said, and everyone else nodded.

'The first step is to keep your eyes and ears open,' Bert said. 'If you're willing.'

'We're willing,' Alice said, speaking for all of them.

It was agreed that Kate would involve Ruby and Pearl, and either Adam or Alice would involve Beth. Perhaps also her fellow nurses, Babs and Pauline.

'You see?' Bert said, when everyone had left. 'Churchwood loves you. Not as much as I love you, of course, but then I'm the lucky man who's going to marry you.'

He wrapped his large arms around her and kissed her.

It was wonderful indeed that her friends loved her but not everyone did. One person disliked her and, try as Naomi might to dismiss that person as a crank, the letters still hurt.

Would her friends manage to expose the identity of the sender? Did she even want to know who that person was? Naomi's feelings were mixed.

If the sender was a mere acquaintance – a troubled acquaintance – then perhaps she'd be able to gain some sort of perspective on the criticism and not feel so hurt. But if the sender was someone she'd considered a friend . . . Heavens, that would hurt terribly.

CHAPTER TWENTY-FOUR

Ruby

Ruby was in the outhouse feeding wet washing through the mangle when she glanced through the door she'd left open to let in light and fresh air and saw Kate returning from the bookshop team meeting. 'Kate!' she called.

Kate turned, saw her and came over.

'How was the meeting?' Ruby asked. 'Or is it a secret?'

'It's mostly secret but I'm going to share it with you and Pearl in case you can help.'

Interesting. 'Pearl is just bringing some veg in from the kitchen garden,' Ruby said. It wasn't far away. Just behind the barn, in fact.

Kate nodded. 'I'll go and fetch her. Can you come to the kitchen?'

'Of course.' The washing could wait.

Ruby slung a wet shirt over the mangle, dried her hands on her apron and headed for the kitchen.

Kate and Pearl joined her, Pearl looking as curious as Ruby felt.

'I need to ask for your discretion,' Kate said. 'It's about Naomi.'

She told them about the poison pen letters and Ruby saw her own outrage reflected in Kate's face. 'That's monstrous,' she said. 'How has Naomi taken it?'

'She's trying to be brave but she's desperately upset.'

That was Naomi all over.

'She doesn't want a fuss so only a few of us know about the letters at present,' Kate continued. 'Bert, of course, and the rest of the bookshop team. Beth at the hospital is going to be told, and now you.'

'How can we help?' Ruby asked.

'Firstly, by not inadvertently making Naomi uncomfortable by asking how she is in front of other people,' Kate said.

Ruby nodded. 'Of course. What else?'

'I assume neither of you knows who sent the letters or why?'

'I've no idea,' Ruby said.

'Neither have I,' Pearl said.

'I can't imagine she has any enemies apart from that horrible former husband,' Ruby added.

'No, but sometimes people can take offence at something we do or say even if causing offence wasn't our intention,' Kate answered.

That was true. Some people acted as though they'd borne grievances from the cradle.

'I take it we're to look out and listen for clues as to who might be to blame,' Ruby guessed.

'Exactly.'

'What sort of person would set out to hurt Naomi like that?' Pearl demanded.

'A nasty one,' Ruby told her.

'Or a jealous one,' Kate suggested, 'though jealousy is nasty, too.'

Ruby squirmed inside because *she* was a jealous person. Jealous of Pearl.

Kate and Pearl headed for the fields to work and Ruby returned to the laundry, squeezing and pummelling the washing with rage at the letter writer. And also at herself.

Jealousy was contemptible.

CHAPTER TWENTY-FIVE

Beth

More than a week had passed since Beth had seen Adam and Nancy together, though perhaps they'd been together when Beth wasn't on shift. As anticipated, Adam hadn't gone to the fashion event at the bookshop. Beth knew that because she'd gone along with Nancy. It had been a fun evening on which Nancy had sparkled, offering herself as May Janicki's model and making everyone smile with her enthusiasm. Beth wasn't proud of feeling glad that Adam hadn't been there to see Nancy on such lively form, but she couldn't seem to help it.

Nancy was already on the ward when Beth went on duty on Monday afternoon. Beth tensed when she realized Adam was there, too, and talking to the girl she'd come to consider her rival.

Beth was too far away to hear what they were saying, but she was horribly aware of how glossy Nancy's dark hair looked, despite most of it being hidden under her cap, and how her personality sparkled, too. There was something vivid about Nancy that would get her noticed anywhere.

Realizing Private Renshaw had raised his hand for her attention, Beth roused herself and went over to him. 'How can I help?'

'My bandages feel wet,' he told her.

Beth peeped under the blankets and saw that the bandage around his leg was indeed leaking fluid. 'I'll call the doctor,' she said.

'Thank you, Nurse.'

Beth set off to call the doctor, becoming aware that Adam had moved on to Corporal Anstey while Nancy stood beside Private Harris's bed. 'Maybe I will dance with you if there's another dance at the bookshop,' Nancy was telling the patient. 'It'll only be a dance, mind. Nothing more.'

'Does your heart belong to another?' Private Harris asked.

'Maybe it does,' she told him, and Beth wondered if Nancy had Adam in mind.

A wave of dismay passed through Beth but she continued on her way and fetched Dr Marwood who happened to be in the corridor outside the ward. 'I'll be along in just a moment,' he told her. 'I need a word with Matron first.'

She nodded her thanks and, as the doctor entered Matron's office, Adam emerged from the ward. 'Beth, I was hoping to catch you.'

'You were?' Pleasure warmed her.

But then she noticed that he looked troubled. 'I'm sorry to be the bearer of worrying information but it concerns Naomi. She's been receiving poison pen letters.'

Beth was appalled. 'That's terrible! Poor Naomi!'

'Indeed. Unsurprisingly, she's very upset, though she's putting on a brave face. She doesn't want the existence of the letters to be common knowledge in the village yet. Only a few of us know about them so far, the idea being to try to discover the identity of the sender and put a stop to them before unpleasantness spreads around Churchwood.'

'I won't mention them to anyone else,' Beth assured him.

'Thank you. We're also telling Babs and Pauline here

at the hospital, so if any of you have any ideas about the sender . . .?'

'We'll pass them on. Not that I've got any ideas at present.'

Dr Marwood stepped out of Matron's office and Adam changed the subject swiftly. 'That's me finished for today, though I expect you've hours of work ahead of you, Beth.'

'You're going home to put your feet up?' she asked, and he laughed, knowing she was teasing.

'I may have finished for the day here at the hospital but I've parishioners to call on and then the children's club to run.'

'From what I hear, all of the children in Churchwood love the club,' she said.

'That's because Churchwood has wonderful children,' he answered. An idea seemed to strike him suddenly. 'Feel free to say no to this suggestion – I know how hard you work already – but it would be lovely if you could find the time to come along to the club one day.'

'To help?'

'Only if you like.'

Beth did like. She liked the idea a lot. There really were some wonderful children in Churchwood and, besides, Adam's invitation surely meant that the idea of working closely with her, of getting to know her better, of sharing time with her appealed to him. Nancy might be the sort of person who brought sunshine into a room, but Beth had good qualities too and perhaps Adam had noticed them.

'I'd love to,' she told him, vowing to make her visit soon.

CHAPTER TWENTY-SIX

Naomi

'Heavens, Marjorie, didn't I ask you to check the linen last week?'

Naomi was holding up a sheet which the moths must have begun nibbling a long time ago.

'I counted it but I didn't think I needed to get it all out of the cupboard,' Marjorie told her. 'Anyway, it isn't my fault. The moths are to blame. This is why I wanted you to help me yesterday. So I could check things over. You've known all along that Constance is arriving tomorrow.'

'I was busy yesterday morning and Sergeant Scarletti came to tea in the afternoon.'

'The sergeant came to see Victoria,' Marjorie pointed out.

'But I was his hostess,' Naomi retorted. Even though she'd been in something of a state over the poison pen letters, she'd been delighted to welcome him and see the warmth that passed between him and Victoria.

'Anyway,' she continued, 'you didn't need me just to look at your supplies of bedding.'

Marjorie's face warned her that tears weren't far away and that would mean nothing got done for hours.

Naomi swallowed down her exasperation. 'I'm afraid I've no bedding to spare from Foxfield but I'm sure Alice will be willing to lend some. I'll call at The Linnets on my way home.' She didn't invite Marjorie to accompany her, having no wish to inflict Marjorie's company on Alice. Not while Marjorie was in such a tizzy.

'Will Alice bring it here?' Marjorie asked.

'I don't know who'll bring it, but someone will,' Naomi assured her.

They set to work with the cleaning and made the house look as well as its drab decorations and faded furnishings allowed. Windows were washed, floors swept, rugs beaten in the tiny backyard and furniture polished. Marjorie's kitchen cupboards were wiped, too, and china, glasses and cutlery were all washed until they gleamed. For a woman who'd been brought up by servants, Naomi was becoming quite domesticated.

She unfastened her apron and folded it. 'I need to get home now.'

'I could make tea,' Marjorie offered.

'Thank you, but I haven't time.'

'You haven't forgotten you're giving my cousin lunch tomorrow?'

They'd settled on lunch at Foxfield on the day of Mrs Pearce's arrival and Marjorie hadn't stopped reminding Naomi about it – another irritation Naomi tried to bear by accepting that her oldest friend in the village was genuinely nervous.

'No, I haven't forgotten,' Naomi assured her. 'Stop worrying, Marjorie. You're going to be fine. Look at it this way. If your cousin is a nice person, then you'll gain a new friend. If she isn't . . . why, you didn't even know she existed until recently, so you'll be no worse off than before.'

Had she bucked up Marjorie's spirits? Not by the anxious look on Marjorie's face. But Naomi really had to go. She put on her coat, said goodbye and headed outside.

'Naomi!' Marjorie called after her.

What now?

'You haven't forgotten that you're going to give me some greenery and flowers from your garden to make my cousin feel welcome?'

Oh, for pity's sake! 'No, Marjorie, but I'll get them to you in the morning so they stay fresh.'

With that Naomi quickened her pace so she could play deaf to any more reminders of her obligations.

She was anxious to be home because the second post should have arrived by now and she wanted to be sure that it didn't include another nasty letter. She had business at the butcher's first, though. 'I'm just wondering what your expectations are for meat supplies tomorrow?' she asked. 'I have Marjorie Plym's cousin for lunch.'

'I might manage some sausages or maybe some liver. Not everyone is fond of liver but beggars can't be choosers in wartime. Gone are the days of nice legs of lamb and fine cuts of beef being readily available. Of course, I've heard they're still available on the black market, but I know you've too much integrity for that, Naomi.'

'I have. I'll report back to Victoria since she'll be doing the cooking. I won't ask you to set anything aside for me because that wouldn't be fair on other customers, but I'm sure Victoria will be here bright and early to see what you can offer.'

'She's a good girl, that.'

'She certainly is.'

Naomi called at the grocer's, too, and managed to come away with a jar of meat paste for sandwiches.

At home at last, she glanced at the hall table where Suki and Victoria tended to leave any post that arrived for her while she was out. There was an envelope there and Naomi snatched it up, only to exhale slowly when she saw that the handwriting was nothing like that of the nasty letter writer. Nor had it been sent through the post. It had been dropped through the letterbox by hand.

'Oh!' Suki emerged from the kitchen, dustpan and brush in hand. 'Sorry. I didn't hear you come in.'

'No need to apologize.'

'I'm just going to sweep up some soil in the drawing room. Little Flower knocked a plant over.'

'Is she all right?'

'She's upset that she made a mess but she's fine and so is the plant. I'll bring you some tea afterwards.'

'That would be lovely, thank you.'

Naomi entered her sitting room, which had long been a sanctuary for her, firstly from Alexander and now from the general bustle of the house. She kicked off her shoes – her bad feet were aching – and sat down in her usual armchair to read the letter.

It was from the woman whose brother Joe had once owned the house that Naomi was buying for the bookshop. After Joe's death Ellen had inherited the house, fighting off a challenge from an imposter.

Just a quick line to thank you for calling in to help when I was unwell and to thank Bert too for the vegetables he provided. Churchwood people are unmatched when it comes to kindness and generosity . . .

That was true. Generally. But was there an exception? Someone who had bitterness and cruelty in their heart and had written those nasty letters to Naomi?

All Naomi's thoughts seemed to head straight to those letters. It was frustrating but she was powerless to stop them.

Suki knocked on the door and brought in tea.

'Thank you,' Naomi said, and made a sterling effort to move her mind past the letters for fear of obsessing about them to the exclusion of everything else. 'How are you, Suki?' she asked.

She'd heard about Suki's ill-fated visit to the children's club. Accidents happened to everyone, but Suki had appeared to find her fall into the muddy ditch particularly humiliating.

'I've cheered up a bit,' Suki told her. 'I've decided to return to the children's club soon.'

'That's good to hear, Suki.' Naomi was pleased. She was fond of Suki and hadn't liked to see her looking disheartened, despite the girl's best efforts to hide her feelings.

'May I ask if you've heard anything about the nasty letter writer?' Suki asked.

'Not yet,' Naomi admitted.

'Hopefully, you'll hear something soon.'

'Hopefully,' Naomi agreed.

Watching her young maid retreat from the room now, it occurred to Naomi that maybe she had something to learn from Suki. The girl was little more than a child yet here she was, working her way through her upset to go back out into the world. Naomi hadn't been hiding from the world, exactly, but she'd certainly been flinching from it every time she stepped through the door. She needed to be more positive.

She thought of all the people who were trying to find out who the letter writer might be: the bookshop team, Suki, Victoria, the evacuee women, Beth and her nursing friends . . . So many people. None of them had been able to help yet, but that might change at any moment.

CHAPTER TWENTY-SEVEN

Ruby

Despite the letter her mother had sent in response to Ruby's engagement, an idea had crept into Ruby's head. On first reading that letter and in the weeks since then, Ruby had been convinced that nothing had changed and her parents disapproved of her – and darling Timmy – as much as ever.

But what if things could be brought to change? After all, her parents hadn't seen Ruby for more than a year and they hadn't seen Timmy for more than two years. Letters had passed between them in that time but only a few, and they'd been short letters that had said little.

What if her parents were to meet Ruby and Timmy face to face again? Ruby might be able to convince them far more effectively than in a letter that she was settled and respectable now. That she was marrying a good man and that they were both working hard to help the war effort by putting food in servicemen's stomachs and on Britain's tables.

As for Timmy, surely they'd see what a wonderful boy he'd become. Cheerful, polite and nice in every possible way. The sort of boy even the most exacting grandparents could – and should – be proud of.

She wasn't expecting them to contribute towards the wedding costs. But if they could just wish her well . . .

Yet Ruby had been hurt by them often over the years. Perhaps it would be foolish to risk being hurt by them all over again.

CHAPTER TWENTY-EIGHT

Naomi

'I'm sorry there's so much work for you both today,' Naomi told Victoria and Suki.

'We'll manage,' Victoria insisted, and Suki nodded.

Naomi glanced at the clock. Marjorie was due to bring her cousin in half an hour but Naomi didn't trust her not to arrive earlier. 'I'll just run up and tidy myself,' she said.

Upstairs, Naomi felt the lure of her bed tempting her to put her feet up for a few minutes.

Resisting, she sat at her dressing table and teased a few stray hairs back into place, then dusted her nose with powder. How haggard she looked! Her hair was growing greyer by the day, or so it felt. Her cheeks were wan and there were deep wrinkles around her eyes and mouth. As for her sagging neck . . . Oh, dear!

But this lunch might be worth the effort if Marjorie's cousin proved to be a nice person. And who knew? Constance Pearce might even take Marjorie off Naomi's hands for the duration of her visit. What a bonus that would be!

Ten minutes before the agreed arrival time, the doorknocker sounded. Naomi had already returned downstairs to take a bottle of sherry into the sitting room. Calling, 'I'll get it!' she went to open the door.

Marjorie stood in the porch and she was . . . simpering. Yes, that was the word for it. She was simpering as though her cousin had been showering her with compliments from the moment she'd set foot in Churchwood, and now Marjorie was basking in the pleasure of being appreciated.

'Hello, Naomi,' she said.

Not a word of apology for being too early when Naomi could have been rushing around with no dress on as she prepared for the visit. Marjorie looked far too smug to give social niceties a thought.

Ah, well. Naomi breathed deeply and forced a smile. 'Welcome, Marjorie. And Mrs Pearce, of course.'

'Constance, please,' the other woman said. 'I hope I may call you Naomi, given that you're such a good friend of dear Marjorie's.'

'Of course,' Naomi said. 'Do come in.'

Constance Pearce was middle-aged and rather stout, though Naomi guessed a girdle was doing sterling work at holding her midriff in. Her clothes comprised a sage-green dress and matching jacket, and brown shoes that were comfortable more than stylish, doubtless necessitated by the breadth of Constance's feet, which were challenging the leather's ability to stretch. There was nothing about her outfit that suggested wealth but neither did she look as though she was struggling with her last farthing. Her face was full, with apple-shaped cheeks and blue eyes, and her hair was an unremarkable mid-brown. It could have been a wholesome-looking face, but was it? Naomi hadn't seen enough of its expression to judge yet.

'What a pleasant house you have here, Naomi,' Constance remarked after accepting the invitation to take the sofa in the sitting room and enjoy a glass of sherry.

'I'm fond of it,' Naomi said.

'Lovely gardens, too. Though I'm of the opinion that a small house can be cosy and comfortable. Like dear Marjorie's house. It was such a pleasure to be welcomed by my cousin.'

'I'm sure it was,' Naomi said, and Marjorie preened again like a best-in-class exhibit at a cat show.

Naomi passed sherry to Marjorie and Constance, and then took her own glass to her usual armchair. 'This is your first visit to Churchwood, I believe,' she said, to start the conversation rolling.

'It is, though I'd have visited long ago if I'd known that dear Marjorie was here.'

Dear Marjorie. Uttered several times in only a minute or two. It felt gushing to Naomi but perhaps it was simply Mrs Pearce's way. 'I understand you only recently learned of her existence.'

'That's right,' Constance confirmed. 'I was at my great-uncle's house when I first heard that I had a cousin. I don't mind telling you that I was as excited as a small child at Christmas.'

'I'm sure you must have been . . .' Naomi's words tailed off as, sitting facing the window, she caught sight of the postman coming up the drive with the second post of the day. It was Wednesday again. Both of the poison pen letters had arrived on Wednesdays.

'Naturally, I lost no time in writing to dear Marjorie.'

'Naturally,' Naomi echoed.

Mr Baldry had several envelopes in his hand. He dropped them through the letterbox and walked away. Moments later, Naomi heard Victoria move into the hall from the kitchen to pick them up.

'Just two weeks later and here I am!' Constance said. 'I

think that goes to show how keen I was to see Marjorie.'

'I'm sure,' Naomi said.

'Of course, I didn't know then if we could become friends, but the moment I met her today, all doubts just melted away because Marjorie welcomed me with such warmth and care.'

'Lovely,' Naomi said, and felt a surge of tension as Victoria knocked on the door and then entered. 'Lunch is ready to be served,' she announced.

'Thank you,' Naomi said.

Victoria wasn't meeting her gaze. Why not? A moment later, Naomi had her answer. As Victoria left the room she looked at Naomi with such regret that it was obvious another poison pen letter had come for her.

Naomi felt sick. Punched in the gut. Tears welled up in her eyes but she fought for self-control like someone scrambling to stop themselves from falling off a cliff. She worked some moisture into her mouth. 'Lunch. Shall we go through?' Her smile was stiff. It hurt her face. Hurt her throat. But she got to her feet and gestured her guests out of the sitting room and into the dining room.

The table was laid for just the three of them. They all took seats and Suki entered with the lunch – a vegetable flan sprinkled with a little precious cheese, a bowl of salad and some rolls of bread.

'How lovely,' Constance declared, but Naomi was looking at Suki. Clearly, she, too, knew of the letter because her expression was pure sympathy.

Suki left and Naomi roused herself to cut slices of flan and encourage her guests to partake of the salad bowl and bread.

'I must confess to being jealous of you, Naomi,' Constance said.

Naomi glanced around the spacious dining room. It was

certainly impressive with its polished mahogany furniture and view over the garden—

'No, no, you misunderstand me,' Constance corrected. 'This is a fine room in a beautiful house but my jealousy has nothing to do with material things. I'm not an avaricious woman who craves riches. But I *am* a woman with an affectionate heart who craves good company. I'm jealous because you've had more than twenty-five years of dear Marjorie's friendship while I've been out in the wilderness, so to speak.'

'She wishes she'd met me sooner,' Marjorie explained, though even in her distracted state Naomi had understood Constance's meaning.

'Not that I'm one to complain about it,' Constance added. 'What can't be cured must be endured, as the saying goes, and I'm a great believer in a forward-looking attitude. I may not have enjoyed twenty-five years of Marjorie's friendship in the past, but I'm looking forward to twenty-five years of it in the future.'

'How nice,' Naomi said, but she could bear the suspense no longer. 'Would you excuse me for a moment? I need to see to something in the kitchen . . .'

She got up and left the room, aware that her abrupt behaviour was leaving a stunned silence behind her but needing desperately to know if she was right about the letter.

She hastened into the kitchen.

'Where is it?' she asked. Naomi hadn't even glanced at the hall table where post was usually left for her. Victoria and Suki were too sensitive to have left anything so incendiary on show, especially when Marjorie was in the house.

Victoria drew an envelope from her apron pocket and handed it over, her green eyes solemn and tender.

'The envelope, the handwriting, the London post-mark . . . They're just the same as before,' Naomi declared.

'That's what we thought,' Victoria said. 'Perhaps it would be better to wait until your guests have gone before you open it.'

It was sound advice since the letter was certain to upset Naomi. But not knowing what it said was unbearable. Naomi tore open the envelope and pulled out the note.

WHAT PEOPLE SAY TO YOUR FACE ISN'T WHAT THEY SAY BEHIND YOUR BACK. CLUE: WHAT THEY SAY BEHIND YOUR BACK ISN'T NICE.

Naomi's hand went to her mouth in distress and she sank into a nearby chair.

'May we?' Victoria asked, and when Naomi nodded she took the note and shared it with Suki.

'It's horrid and it isn't true!' Suki insisted.

'Exactly right,' Victoria agreed. 'Naomi, this is the work of someone who's bitter and twisted inside. There isn't an ounce of truth in these words.'

But someone disliked Naomi intensely because it was clear now that the letters she'd received weren't merely part of a campaign to make mischief in the village but entirely personal.

'Why don't I go into the dining room and tell your guests that you've been taken ill?' Victoria offered. 'You're in no fit state to be entertaining.'

Naomi was tempted. Tears had fallen despite her efforts to keep them unshed and her mind was in a whirl. But she shook her head. A mysterious disappearance in the middle of lunch would be an exciting opportunity for Marjorie to spread gossip and speculation all over Churchwood.

Besides, tiresome as Marjorie was, Naomi was reluctant to let her down, especially in front of her guest.

'I'll be fine,' Naomi said. 'Just give me a moment to wash away these silly tears.'

'I'll fetch your face powder,' Suki offered, and left the kitchen to run upstairs.

Naomi washed her face and patted it dry on a towel Victoria handed her. Then she powdered her nose and around her eyes to hide some of the redness. Probably – no, certainly – she still looked tear-ravaged, but it was the best she could do.

Victoria patted her arm as Naomi headed for the door and Suki called out, 'You're kind and lovely, Mrs Harrington. Don't let anyone tell you different!'

How nice they were. But somewhere there lurked a person who hated her.

'I'm sorry about that,' Naomi said as she returned to the dining room, her lips parted in a facsimile of a smile. 'I'm finding myself prone to a little hay fever these days and I spent rather a long time in the garden this morning.' She gestured to her eyes to explain the fact that they must still be shimmering with tears.

'I didn't know you suffered from hay fever, Naomi,' Marjorie said.

'It's only a recent thing and just a minor inconvenience.'

Even so, the entire village would probably know that she'd been stricken with hay fever by the time the sun set.

Naomi ate a small chunk of flan – doubtless it was delicious but her appetite had fled – and, anxious to move the conversation along, said, 'I believe you live in Bournemouth, Constance. It must be pleasant living near the sea.'

'I'm very fond of Bournemouth but it lacks dear Marjorie,' Constance said. Was there an edge in her voice?

An edge that suggested Naomi had offended her with her strange behaviour?

'I'm sure Marjorie could visit you there,' Naomi said, ploughing onwards. 'Once the work to your home has been completed.'

'I'm very much hoping she *will* visit. It's so beneficial to health to take walks by the sea . . .'

'I visited Bournemouth as a child,' Naomi told her. 'I liked it very much.'

'It's good of you to say so,' Constance replied, with what Naomi suspected was sarcasm.

Goodness, this was difficult. Naomi realized that the reason she hadn't found Constance's appearance to be quite as wholesome as her apple cheeks suggested was because she was the sort of woman to hold a grudge. She hadn't met with the welcome she'd considered to be her due and her eyes were hard with resentment. Oh, dear!

Naomi tried hard to make up for her distraction but Constance seemed disinclined to forgive her. But, at last, the meal was over. Would Marjorie and her guest linger? It usually took time and effort to prise Marjorie out of Foxfield but perhaps the affronted Constance would show more inclination to move on with her day?

Victoria must have decided not to leave it to chance. 'Mr Makepiece called in with some vegetables for tonight's supper and asked me to remind you that he needs to have a word about bookshop business.'

'Thank you, Victoria,' Naomi told her gratefully.

Constance was more attuned to atmosphere than her cousin. A little too attuned, in fact, because her mouth tightened even more at the hint to leave. 'How kind of you to entertain us when you're so busy, Naomi,' she said coldly, as Victoria left.

'I wanted to meet you today,' Naomi assured her, but Constance was already getting up.

'Come along, Marjorie. Let's not make nuisances of ourselves. We can sit and take our ease at your dear little house.'

'If you really think so,' Marjorie said.

Naomi saw them to the door. 'I really hope to see you again while you're in Churchwood,' she told Constance, still trying to regain some ground with the woman.

'We wouldn't like to put you out,' Constance told her.

'You wouldn't be—'

'Any friend of Marjorie's is a friend of mine, of course, but please don't go to any inconvenience on our account. Goodbye, Naomi, and thank you for the delicious lunch.'

'It was my . . .'

Constance had already linked arms with Marjorie and turned away.

Naomi closed the door and returned to the dining room where Victoria and Suki had set to work to clear the table.

'I think I might have slighted Mrs Pearce,' she said, then turned to the open window, hearing voices outside.

Marjorie had stopped on the drive to take a stone from her shoe. She and her cousin were facing away from the house and probably hadn't realized that they could be overheard.

'It was very kind of Mrs Harrington to give me lunch,' Constance said.

'Naomi. She's happy to be called Naomi.'

'Oh, of course. I wouldn't expect formality from such an old friend of yours, Marjorie. It would be strange if she didn't want to be called Naomi by you, her most loyal of friends. It's strange, though. I find myself thinking of her as Mrs Harrington. Perhaps it's because she seemed so . . .

147

Oh, what's the right word? Distant. Yes, distant.' Naomi could hear the barb in Constance's voice.

'She's very busy.'

'I understand that, and it's to her credit that she does so much for your little bookshop. I just don't like to think of you being left behind and feeling lonely, Marjorie.'

'I'm not lonely, Constance.'

'Aren't you? I'm relieved to hear it. But I'm also even more glad that *I'm* here now to give you the company and attention you deserve.'

Marjorie replaced her shoe and the women walked on.

'Well!' Victoria said, twin spots of colour appearing on her cheeks. 'That wasn't very grateful of Mrs Pearce!'

'But true,' Naomi pointed out. 'I *was* distant.'

'You gave hospitality to two people when it wasn't convenient. That was incredibly kind of you.'

But Naomi knew she'd fallen well short of giving her usual friendly welcome. Had she embarrassed Marjorie? And was Marjorie really lonely? The possibilities grieved Naomi. It shouldn't have taken a stranger – newly arrived in Churchwood – to alert Naomi to the fact that Marjorie might genuinely be unhappy. Perhaps the writer of the poison pen letters was right and Naomi really wasn't a good person.

'I'm sorry if I made things worse by inventing that story about Bert wanting a word,' Victoria said.

'You did the right thing with that, my dear,' Naomi told her. 'We all know how hard it can be to get Marjorie to leave.'

'She's a limpet,' Victoria said. 'I shouldn't worry about Mrs Pearce. You can make things up with her another time if she did feel slighted.'

Because right now Naomi had more important things on her mind. That was what Victoria was thinking.

They all made their way into the kitchen where Naomi read the third poison pen letter again.

'Go and show it to Bert,' Victoria recommended, doubtless because he was the best person to put the letter into perspective. The best person to comfort her, too.

'He's coming to dinner later,' Naomi said.

'That's hours away.'

'But I can't leave all the clearing up to you and Suki.'

'Yes, you can,' Victoria and Suki chorused.

Naomi thought of the solace Bert's big, comfortable arms would bring when he held her. 'Well, if you're sure . . . I shan't be long.'

CHAPTER TWENTY-NINE

Bert

Bert was in one of his greenhouses when he noticed Naomi making her way towards him as fast as her short legs and bunions allowed. He stepped out to meet her. 'How was lunch with Marjorie's cousin?' he asked, suspecting from her face that it hadn't gone well.

'I'm afraid I offended her.'

'That doesn't sound like you, beloved.'

'I was . . . distracted.'

'Ah.' Another letter. 'Luckily, I'm about to go into the house to make tea.' The comfort drink.

Naomi smiled but it was a trembling, fragile thing.

How dare anyone upset this wonderful woman? Bert's anger was rising rapidly but he got on top of it to wrap an arm around Naomi as they headed for the house.

Inside, he lit the stove and set the kettle to boil. Then he passed a large tin to Naomi. 'There's some of my home-made cake in here. Why don't you cut a slice for each of us?'

Soon they were settled in armchairs by the hearth, Elizabeth on the rug between them. 'Let's have it, then,' Bert said.

Naomi handed over the third poison pen letter and Bert felt contempt for the writer sour his emotions.

WHAT PEOPLE SAY TO YOUR FACE ISN'T WHAT THEY SAY BEHIND YOUR BACK. CLUE: WHAT THEY SAY BEHIND YOUR BACK ISN'T NICE.

'More nonsense,' he said.

'But a personal attack. No one else has received a nasty letter as far as I know.'

'The envelope is postmarked London again. You're not aware of anyone who's been in London recently?'

'No one,' Naomi said. 'But if someone is going to the trouble of asking an accomplice to send the letters, it shows commitment. Deep feelings at work.'

'Deep, perhaps, but still nonsensical,' Bert insisted. 'None of our friends have any ideas about the sender's identity yet?'

'Unfortunately not. Every time one of them approaches me, I hope they'll have something to share, but all they tell me is that they're as mystified as ever.'

'They still might come upon a clue. Meanwhile, you need something nice to take your mind off the nastiness and I have the perfect thing.'

'Oh?'

'I think you should give your mind a happier direction by arranging our wedding to take place as soon as possible.'

Naomi burst into tears.

'I'm sorry!' she said, a few minutes later when she had herself back under control. 'What must you think of me, dissolving into tears at the very mention of our wedding? Please don't think it means I'm reluctant to marry you.'

'Reluctant to marry me?' Bert demanded in mock horror. 'How could I possibly think such a thing when we both know I'm the catch of the county?'

Naomi managed a smile, just as he'd hoped, though it was a wan sort of smile. 'I don't seem to be thinking very clearly at the moment,' she said.

'I suspect that's because you're not sleeping well.'

'I'm not,' Naomi admitted, 'no matter how often I tell myself that the person with the problem is the letter writer, not me. I want to marry you more than anything, Bert, but I want our wedding to be the most joyful day of my life. I don't want to be wondering if the writer of the letters is among the guests, watching me and wishing me ill.'

'I think we should call another meeting of the bookshop team.'

'To say what?'

'That keeping things quiet hasn't worked.'

'You think all the village should know about the letters now?'

Bert saw the dread on Naomi's face. It was one thing for her close friends to know about them since they were all rallying round. It was quite another for the whole of Churchwood to be told what was happening.

He imagined she was picturing the looks she'd receive. The pity. The curiosity. The whispers. And perhaps also the triumph of the letter writer.

'I can see you don't like the idea, but have you a better one?' Bert asked.

Naomi hadn't.

Getting up, he tugged her into his arms. 'Take heart, woman. Churchwood will be on your side.'

'At least one person won't be.'

'The letter writer may not be on your side, whether they live in Churchwood or somewhere else,' Bert conceded. 'But everyone else will be. You mark my words.'

'All right,' Naomi said. 'Let's call a meeting and ask for

opinions. But please don't think it means I'm agreeing to make the letters public. I'm not sure about that yet.'

'Deal,' Bert said, kissing her.

CHAPTER THIRTY

Beth

The day was fine and balmy as Beth set out for the children's club. Her heart felt light and bouncy, and, eager to be there, she walked at speed. But in her hopeful mood, she was still aware of the pleasantness of the walk through the woods and along Brimbles Lane.

She glanced towards Brimbles Farm as she passed it, thinking of the land girls who lived there and who were both engaged to be married. Beth didn't wish her hopes to run away with her but couldn't help thinking how nice it would be if she were to become engaged, too.

There was only one figure visible in a distant field. The owner of the farm, she thought. Beth had only met Ernie Fletcher once, though the word *met* was overstating it. She'd been walking to the village one day when he'd turned out of the farm entrance on a tractor. Ignoring her presence, he'd simply driven by, doing nothing to avoid a wheel smashing into a puddle and splashing her dress and stockings. He hadn't paused to apologize or even sent her a sorry look. He was one of life's grumpy people but happiness had come to Brimbles Farm despite him. Kate's marriage to Leo, the engagements of Ruby and Pearl . . .

Beth passed Foxfield, too, and felt a pang of distress at the thought of Naomi's suffering. Unfortunately, Beth had no idea who the writer of the poison pen letters might be.

Continuing onwards, she felt a little skip of excitement at the prospect of seeing Adam in just a few minutes. She'd told no one that she was coming to the club today. Back at the hospital, she'd murmured something about writing a letter before going up to her room and then creeping out again so she wouldn't be seen. Not that it mattered as far as most people were concerned, but Beth hadn't wanted Nancy to learn where she was going in case it gave her ideas about tagging along.

Beth wasn't proud of feeling that way, but was it really so terrible to want a chance for Adam to get to know her better before she was cast into the shade by Nancy's vivacity? Wasn't it just a case of levelling things up a little since Mother Nature had given Nancy so much sparkle?

Reaching the bookshop, Beth paused at the door and then took a deep breath and knocked. No one answered. She knocked again, though by then it had occurred to her that there was no sound coming from inside the bookshop. Was she mistaken in thinking that the club was meeting today? She'd be horribly disappointed if that was the case.

Beth tried the door handle, half expecting it to be locked. It wasn't. Opening the door, she stepped into an empty room but then voices reached her from the garden at the rear of the building. The kitchen door was open. Beth walked through it and saw that the children were playing cricket. The relief was immense.

'Beth!'

That was Victoria's Arthur. Other children turned to look at her. And so did Adam. Smiling warmly, he came towards her. 'I hope it's all right for me to be here?' she asked.

'All right? It's wonderful! Isn't it, everyone?'

Heads nodded and mouths grinned.

'Do you know how to play cricket?' Arthur asked her.

'No, but I'm willing to learn. If I won't be a nuisance?'

'We're one player short so we need you.'

It was lovely to be needed.

'You can be the adult on Lewis's team,' Adam said, and only then did Beth realize that there was another adult on the other team. Suki. Small in height and build, she'd blended into the children at first. 'Suki,' Beth said, smiling warmly at her friend. 'It's nice to see you.'

Suki nodded. 'You too, Beth.'

'It'll be fairer now there's an adult on both teams,' Arthur said.

'What about you, Adam?' Beth questioned, not wanting him to feel obliged to surrender his place to her.

'I'm the umpire.'

'Very well, then.'

The rules were explained to her briefly. 'I'm not sure I've got them quite clear in my mind but I'm happy to give the game a go,' she said.

She was in the team that was fielding – which gave her the chance to stand and observe for much of the time. Suki was called up to bat and Beth's heart went out to the girl as she missed the first two times the ball was bowled towards her. But at least it didn't hit the wicket behind her so she was still in the game. 'Come on, Suki, you can do it!' Arthur, her teammate, called as the bowler prepared to bowl again.

This time Suki hit the ball into the air.

'Catch it, Beth!' Lewis cried and, rousing herself, Beth caught it more by instinct than anything else.

'Sorry, Suki. That means you're out,' Arthur told the little maid.

Suki smiled but it was obvious that she was disappointed.

When the teams changed position and Beth was called on to bat, she too missed the ball the first time it was bowled towards her. Steadying herself, she willed herself to concentrate. When the ball headed towards her for the second time, she managed to hit it. And what a hit it was, soaring into the air.

'Cor!' Lewis cried.

'Catch it, someone!' Arthur yelled, but no one could.

'It's gone into the trees,' Lewis observed.

'Oh dear, I hope the ball isn't lost.' Beth was contrite.

'Don't be sorry,' Lewis told her. 'You got six points and that means we've won the match!'

There were cheers from the winners and congratulations from the losers, subdued but sporting. 'You played very well,' Suki told Beth.

Unfortunately, Beth couldn't return the compliment but settled for, 'Beginner's luck, that's all.'

Suki headed back into the bookshop, her shoulders drooping a little.

'What happens next?' Beth asked Adam.

'Refreshments. Such as they are. No oranges, I'm afraid. We can't get them with the war on. But watered-down milk and biscuits.'

'Better than nothing,' Beth said.

'Indeed. You're a natural at cricket, Beth.'

'I don't know about that.'

'I do.' Adam touched her shoulder as though to emphasize the point and Beth felt her heart dance a merry jig. 'Would you mind helping Suki in the kitchen?' he asked then.

'Of course.'

Beth moved inside. 'I'm here to help,' she told Suki.

'Perhaps you could put the biscuits on a plate? We allow one biscuit per child. They'd all like more but we don't have more to give.'

'I understand. The children's club . . . . It's a great thing for the village, isn't it?'

Suki nodded.

The children ran in then. 'Wash your hands before touching those biscuits,' Suki instructed, and they rushed to the sink.

'You're good with them,' Beth said.

'I suppose everyone is good at something.'

It pleased Beth to see the children looking happy as they settled down to making little models out of much-used plasticine. And it pleased her even more when the session came to an end and Adam glided to her side, saying, 'We appreciated your help today. I hope you'll come again another time?'

'Just as soon as I can,' Beth told him, and he gave her another of his sweet smiles. He also touched her hand and made her skin tingle.

'I'll say goodbye,' Suki said, and Beth thought she still looked a little depressed by her disappointing performance in the cricket. It was only a game, though. It was the taking part that mattered.

Beth walked with Suki and the evacuee children as far as Foxfield and then turned up Brimbles Lane towards the hospital. She thought back over the afternoon and felt warmth envelop her at the thought of Adam's smiles and the way he'd touched her. There'd been nothing intimate about it. His touch had merely been friendly and appreciative but still it had been . . . promising.

Approaching the hospital, she saw Tom the porter heading for the stable block where his accommodation was situated. He waved and Beth waved back. But then Nancy ran down the hospital steps. 'Tom, you left your cigarettes behind!'

'Did I?' Tom grinned. 'Then I'm lucky I've got you looking after me, Nurse Nancy.'

She handed over the cigarette case. 'Have a good evening.'

'I will.' He held up the silver-coloured case and shook it gently. 'Thanks to you.'

'Hello, Beth,' Nancy said. 'Been out?'

'Just into the village,' Beth said, which was the truth but not quite the whole truth.

Nancy nodded. 'Well, I'd better get inside. Babs Carter has a cup of cocoa waiting for me and I don't want it to go cold.'

She ran back towards the hospital and Tom chuckled. 'Brightens the place up, that one.'

'Yes,' Beth said. 'She does.'

But it was Beth whom Adam had invited to the children's club and she couldn't wait to go again.

CHAPTER THIRTY-ONE

Bert

Bert abandoned his market garden to stand at the bookshop door when it opened on Thursday. He greeted everyone with a pleasant 'Good morning!' but Naomi could see steeliness in his eyes as though he was subjecting everyone who passed to a private interrogation: 'Was it you?' or 'Perhaps you?'

Bert was greeted pleasantly in return: 'Nice to see you, Bert' and 'Taking a break from work?'

It wasn't often that he was at the bookshop during the daytime in summer unless he called in for a few minutes while passing.

'It's good to be here,' Bert answered.

He gave no hint that there might be trouble ahead. 'We'll let them get settled first,' he'd said.

In other words, he'd lull them into a false sense of security before lighting the fuse under the bomb.

He waited until everyone had a cup of tea in their hand so no one would be able to sidle out, pleading that they were expected elsewhere. Then he walked into the centre of the room and clapped his hands. Bert's hands were large. They made a lot of noise. Everyone stopped chattering and turned towards him.

'Thank you,' he said. 'I hope you're all enjoying the morning?'

160

'Yes, thanks!' someone called and there were nods and murmurs of agreement.

'I'm afraid I might be about to spoil that.'

He'd had everyone's full attention before but now it sharpened. Frowns appeared. Looks were exchanged – some puzzled, some questioning. No one looked guilty as far as Naomi could see, but she couldn't look at everyone at once and, besides, the letter writer might be skilled at putting on a false face to the world. After all, that person might have been walking and smiling among them for years.

'There's been some unpleasantness in the village,' Bert said.

The tension tightened even further. So did the puzzlement.

'It involves some letters,' Bert added.

Naomi scanned the room again, searching for that elusive guilt or some sign of personal alarm. Doubtless Bert and the rest of the bookshop team were doing the same thing. But to Naomi every face was registering only shock. Whether it was genuine shock was hard to fathom.

'What sort of letters?' Molly Lloyd called.

'Anonymous ones,' Bert told her. '*Nasty* ones.'

'Do you mean . . . Do you mean *poison pen* letters?' Jonah Kerrigan asked.

'That's exactly what I mean.'

The news was greeted with more shocked murmurs. Constance Pearce turned to her cousin. '*You* haven't received a poison pen letter, Marjorie?'

'No,' Marjorie said, bewildered.

'Thank goodness for that,' Constance said. 'Vile things, they are.'

Other people declared that they hadn't received any

nasty letters either. 'But who *has* received them?' Molly wanted to know.

Bert stayed silent for a moment. Naomi knew he was giving her a chance to decide whether to keep her identity as the victim quiet – or not. For a second or two she cowered in silence, but then she took a deep breath and with as steady a voice as she could manage said, 'I have.'

Molly's face was instantly sympathetic. 'I'm sorry to hear that, Naomi. Especially considering how much good you do in this village.'

Naomi felt tears welling. She blinked them back and swallowed against the needles in her throat. 'Thank you, Molly.'

'Molly is right!' Edna Hall declared. 'These letters . . . They're a disgrace!'

No one appeared to disagree.

'Who sent them?' was the next question, from Jonah Kerrigan again.

'That's what we need to find out,' Bert said.

'You're not suggesting one of us sent them?'

'I'm not suggesting anything. But we'd welcome help in exposing the letter writer's identity.'

'It wasn't me!' someone said. Naomi couldn't catch whom.

'Nor me!' said someone else.

Other people began to deny that they were guilty, too. They were defensive. Eager to declare their innocence. And some of them were looking around as though searching for signs of guilt in others.

Naomi got to her feet. 'Please! We've no wish to set neighbour against neighbour. This isn't the time for accusations and blame. We're not trying to start a war. We want help.'

The small crowd sobered instantly. 'Sorry, Naomi. Fighting among us isn't going to uncover the letter writer, is it?' Edna Hall said.

Naomi managed a small smile of thanks, but tears were welling in her eyes again.

'If any of you think you might be able to help, have a quiet word with one of us on the bookshop team,' Bert said. 'But please don't use this sorry situation as a chance for getting even over petty grievances or causing trouble for someone who may have annoyed you.' He paused before adding, 'I'm sorry I've taken up your time and put a damper on the morning but please, carry on as you were before.'

It was impossible, of course. Gradually people settled back into small groups but the conversations were clearly about the poison pen letters.

'You didn't mention that the letters were postmarked from London,' Naomi said quietly to Bert.

'I didn't mention it deliberately,' he explained. 'If the letter writer lets slip about the postmark – perhaps to divert suspicion from themselves – it'll expose the fact that they're involved. Besides, if we mention London, people might think the icicle may be responsible and, since you don't think that's the case, it would be better to keep minds focused locally.'

'Did you get any feeling for who might be responsible?'

'No, but it's early days.'

True, yet they might never learn who'd sent the letters.

'Look on the bright side,' Bert said. 'It would take a brave person to keep sending nasty letters now they know the whole village is aware of them.'

But then there might be no chance of unmasking the writer. Naomi still couldn't decide which would be better – or worse. To know the identity of the writer and have to live side by side with them in a small village, or to remain unaware and continue to suspect almost everyone.

Molly Lloyd came over to them and pressed Naomi's hand. 'I really am sorry for what you're going through,' she said. 'If I could get my hands on the culprit, I might wring their neck. I know violence is wrong but I'm not sure I could resist it.'

More people came up over the course of the next hour and Naomi was touched by the kind words they shared. But did one of them speak with a forked tongue because they were actually the writer?

Marjorie was among those who spoke to Naomi. She looked awkward, since a coolness had developed between them since yesterday's lunch at Foxfield and for once her love of gossip appeared to be in abeyance. 'I don't know who sent the letters, Naomi, but I wish they hadn't done it.'

'Thank you, Marjorie. I appreciate that.' Naomi meant it.

'It's a terrible thing to have happened,' Constance agreed, though Naomi suspected she was commiserating more for form's sake than from genuine sympathy. Clearly, she resented the way Naomi hadn't fussed over her yesterday and wasn't ready to forgive her despite hearing of her woes today. Perhaps she even thought Naomi deserved to be brought down a peg or two.

Naomi thanked her anyway, and they walked away, Constance saying to Marjorie, 'I thought this was supposed to be a nice little village. I'm surprised you can bear to live here with such unpleasantness going on.'

Bert looked at Naomi. 'We'll get back to normal eventually,' he predicted.

But would they?

Eventually, only the bookshop team remained. No one had asked for a quiet word with any of them, it seemed. 'But someone might come to us with information in private,' Alice said.

'That's right,' Bert agreed. 'They might not have felt comfortable about approaching one of us in front of everyone else.'

It was possible.

CHAPTER THIRTY-TWO

Suki

Suki's first visit to the children's club had been a disaster and the second visit hadn't gone well either. Oh, Suki hadn't met with an accident this time. She hadn't needed to scuttle off home to change out of wet, muddy clothes. But she'd felt . . . overshadowed. Dull. Stupid. *Young.* Compared to competent Beth, that was.

But did it really matter if she'd been outshone? There were men in the world who outshone Adam in some respects. Alice's husband, Daniel, was handsome in a clean-cut way and always dressed well. Suki could picture him as a hero in a film. Kate's husband, Leo, was dashing and full of life. Both men were kind and smiled often. But it was small, dishevelled Adam who made Suki's heart race. Perhaps she could make his heart race, too. If she didn't get back on that horse, she might never find out.

CHAPTER THIRTY-THREE

Ruby

Ruby had heard that Naomi had told everyone in the bookshop about the poison pen letters on Thursday. Now it was Saturday, so the whole of Churchwood probably knew about them by now and the talk in the shops and on the streets must be of little else. How brave she was!

But how cowardly of Ruby to fear writing to her parents in case they hurt her again. Nothing ventured, nothing gained, and who knew? She might be pleasantly surprised.

Ruby made a couple of false starts with her letter.

Dear Mum and Dad,
    It's been a long time since I last saw you and I've been thinking that the time has come to put that right.

No, that was too . . . gushing. Not by most people's standards, perhaps, but certainly by the Turner family's. She tried again.

Dear Mum and Dad,
    I hope this letter finds you safe and well. I'm pleased to report that all is fine here in Churchwood.

The poison pen letters meant that wasn't strictly true, but Ruby's parents didn't know Naomi and were unlikely to be interested in her troubles, particularly if they learned that Naomi was divorced. Naomi might have been the innocent party in the divorce, but Ruby suspected that might make little difference to her parents' judgemental inclinations.

Timmy is happy here and popular at school and in the village. He's grown up a lot over the past two years and I'm sure you'll be proud of how he's . . .

No, they wouldn't like to be told how they should feel. Ruby sighed and tried for a third time.

Dear Mum and Dad,
I hope this finds you safe and well. I'm pleased to report that all is fine here in Churchwood. Timmy is still happily settled at school and I'm working hard on the farm. It's been a while since we saw you, though, so I wonder if you'd like us to visit? We needn't stay long. Just a day or two. And we needn't get in your way since we can look around London for some of the time. We'll be able to bring some supplies from the farm to help out with meals.

Ruby read it over. It sounded humbler than she'd like, as though she was pleading with them. Begging, even. But she could swallow her pride if it hit the right tone for persuading them to agree to a visit. And once there, Timmy's sunny personality might be all that was needed to thaw their disapproval.

How should she sign off? With love? No, that wouldn't sound right. They might even begin to suspect she wanted something from them. Money for the wedding, perhaps. She signed off in her usual way: *Take care, Ruby.*

No kiss. The Turners weren't a kissing sort of family.

She wrote her parents' names and address on an envelope, added a stamp and decided to post the letter as soon as she got the chance.

Should she tell Timmy that she'd suggested a visit? Best not. If they put her off, she'd rather bear the disappointment herself than let Timmy feel rejected. Only if they agreed to a visit would she mention it.

CHAPTER THIRTY-FOUR

Beth

'Do I have your attention, Nurse Ellis?' Matron asked.

'Of course,' Beth assured her, though the truth was that her attention had wandered because she could see Nancy and Adam further down the ward, talking to Private Harris. Talking to each other, too?

'You were telling me that Corporal Anstey won't be having therapy today,' Beth continued.

'He had a bad night and isn't feeling well,' Matron explained. 'Overdoing things might set him back.'

'I understand. I'll encourage him to rest today.'

'Thank you.' Matron walked off again and Beth headed for Corporal Anstey.

Knowing he was keen to recover enough to go home and would be disappointed to learn that his therapy couldn't go ahead, she spoke to him gently. 'Doctor has decided bed rest will be better for you today, Corporal.'

'Bed rest? But I'll never get fit if I lounge in bed!'

'I know it's disappointing, but sometimes it can be counterproductive for patients to push themselves. It can set them back for days. If you rest today, you'll be in better shape to tackle therapy tomorrow.'

Seeing he looked disconsolate, Beth nodded towards his locker on which a letter had been placed. 'Is that a letter from Betty?'

The change of subject acted on him like a tonic. 'It is. She's sent a new photograph. See?' He picked up a small snapshot of a young woman with a pleasantly plump face and a nice smile.

'Lovely,' Beth said.

'She writes that she can't wait for me to get home. Three years we've been courting. I'm thinking of asking her to marry me.'

'Well then, instead of fretting about your therapy, you can lie here thinking about how to make your proposal romantic.'

'I'll do that, Nurse.'

Beth heard the sound of laughter. Nancy's laughter. 'I'll see you there, then,' Nancy told Adam.

See him where? And when?

Not knowing was frustrating.

CHAPTER THIRTY-FIVE

Naomi

'Naomi, I'm glad I've seen you,' Aggie Hamilton said when Naomi stepped out of the post office on Monday morning. Naomi's heartbeat quickened. Aggie was mother-in-law to Hannah, the young girl whose little baby, Rose, Naomi had taken in as a foundling temporarily. Aggie hadn't always been a nice person but she'd improved considerably since her son had threatened to disown her if she didn't accept Hannah and Rose. Now she was highly protective of both her daughter-in-law and granddaughter, and a great help to both of them. Naomi doubted that Aggie had written the letters but perhaps she knew who had.

It seemed not. 'I just want you to know how sorry I am to hear of your . . . troubles,' Aggie said. 'I've been thinking about those letters a lot but I've no idea who sent them.'

It was the same wherever Naomi went. She received plenty of sympathy but no information.

'I've nothing to report either, I'm afraid,' Alice had said earlier that morning.

Neither had Kate, Adam, May, Janet and even Bert.

'But it's still early days,' Bert said, when he called round to see her later that morning.

Perhaps it *was* too soon to expect the writer to have been exposed but Naomi was still disappointed that days had passed since she'd gone public about the letters and no one had shared even the slightest suspicion as to the culprit's identity. She had no wish to cast a cloud of gloom over her friends and household, though, so she smiled and said, 'Indeed. Early days.'

Bert wasn't fooled. He never was. Sighing, he sat down beside her and drew her to him so she could have a little cry. Another one!

No matter how much she reasoned with herself, Naomi just couldn't silence the doubts that whispered in her ear that there must be something unpleasant about her to inspire such malice.

'Going to the bookshop this afternoon?' Bert asked.

Naomi was tempted to invent a headache so she could stay at home but she refused to be so feeble. 'I am.'

'That's my girl.' Bert gave her a bracing kiss and walked to the door to leave. 'I've brought veg for your dinner. It's in the kitchen. Make sure you eat it. You need to stay strong, woman.'

Kind, practical Bert.

Naomi was welcomed with open arms at the bookshop – quite literally. She was hugged, stroked and generally comforted. But did one of those smiling faces mask ill will and perhaps gloating satisfaction, too, since a glance in the hall mirror before Naomi had set out had shown that she was looking old and haggard with strain.

'Let's not dwell on one person's nastiness,' she said. 'We're here to enjoy ourselves so let's do just that.'

She chatted, laughed, helped old Mrs Pike to the lavatory, cradled her goddaughter Rose and gave out books with gusto. But she felt as though she'd been draining her reserves of energy for weeks now and those reserves were almost depleted.

Kate called in briefly, doubtless in the hope of hearing good news, but one look at Naomi appeared to tell her that there was none. 'The viper is still masked, then,' she said.

'So far,' Naomi confirmed.

'They'll slip up one day, and I'll be waiting to throttle them when they do.' Kate was fiery by nature and fiercely protective of her friends. She wouldn't actually use violence, but she'd certainly give the viper a piece of her mind. Her gaze scanned the faces in the room suspiciously. Alice came over and the two young women hugged.

'No news, I hear,' Kate said then.

'Not yet,' Alice conceded. 'But now everyone knows about the letters they may remember clues that appeared to be insignificant at the time. They'll be watching out for new clues, too.'

A burst of laughter had their heads turning towards a corner of the bookshop. 'Do you know who I'd like the letter writer to be?' Alice asked.

'Who?' Kate wondered.

'Constance Pearce.' Marjorie's cousin sat surrounded by others like a queen entertaining her court. 'I don't like to take against people, but that woman . . . Do you know, I heard her saying that it was her opinion as a newcomer looking on the village with fresh eyes that Marjorie wasn't always treated with the respect and consideration she deserved from old friends.'

'One old friend in particular, I suppose,' Naomi said. 'I'm afraid I have been rather short with Marjorie recently.'

'With good reason, I'm sure,' Kate speculated.

But back in the days before Kate and Alice had even been born – the days when Naomi had lorded it over the village as compensation for her secret insecurities – Marjorie had stood as her loyal friend. Her *only* friend, if the society women who'd fluttered on the edges of Naomi's life were discounted. Naomi had tried to keep her friendship with Marjorie alive but the fact was that she much preferred the company of her newer friends. It was hardly surprising that Marjorie was feeling displaced and it was to Constance's credit that she should feel resentment on her cousin's behalf. Besides . . .

'I got off to a bad start with Constance, too,' Naomi admitted. 'I was almost rude to her. In fact, I think *I* might have taken offence in her shoes.'

Kate and Alice murmured protests but Naomi still felt guilty. Besides, there was something none of them could question. 'Whether we warm to Constance or not, she can't be the letter writer since the first letter arrived before she'd even set foot in Churchwood,' Naomi pointed out.

'Pity,' Kate said. 'We could have sent her packing and returned to normal.' Because Constance's guilt would have meant Churchwood's innocence.

Instead, Naomi was still left with the awful suspicion that the writer must be someone she'd considered a friend.

'The thing I don't like about Mrs Pearce,' Alice said, who disliked people only rarely, 'is that, even if she isn't the writer of the letters, she's enjoying the fact that they're upsetting you, Naomi.'

'She's spiteful,' Kate agreed. 'But shouldn't she be going home soon?'

'Apparently, the works on her house are taking longer than anticipated,' Naomi said, having overheard Constance talking about it. 'The plumber discovered wet rot, it seems, so she's waiting for another workman to deal with that.'

More laughter burst from Constance and her cronies. Should Naomi try harder to make up with her? So far, an offended Constance was proving a tough nut to crack.

No matter how much warmth Naomi tried to show, it was meeting with polite words and even smiles but with ice behind them. And in her current fragile state Naomi feared a rebuff if she tried to push in where she obviously wasn't wanted.

'I must go,' Kate said. She bent to kiss Naomi's cheek. 'Stay strong. You're going through a horrible time but it won't last for ever.'

Naomi certainly hoped it wouldn't. Her nerves were in tatters.

Kate hugged Alice again and left, and, after pressing Naomi's hand sympathetically, Alice went to answer a question someone had called out about a book. 'That detective in those Agatha Christie books. Hercules Parrot. He's from France, isn't he?'

'Belgium,' Alice corrected. 'And I think his name is Hercule Poirot.'

Naomi headed for the kitchen to put the kettle on. She wasn't on tea-making duty today but she wanted to give herself a few minutes alone. Not that they were peaceful minutes since she could hear Constance speaking.

'Marjorie and I would be delighted if you all came to tea. It won't be a grand tea since we're humble people with no airs and graces, unlike some.'

Unlike Naomi.

'We have no great wealth to parade but our invitation is heartfelt. Would tomorrow suit?'

'It's recipe club here at the bookshop tomorrow,' Elsie Fuller said.

'Yes, we usually come to the bookshop on Tuesdays,' Betty Oldroyd added.

'We wouldn't wish to compete with the *bookshop*,' Constance told them, making the bookshop sound a grubby little place. 'But a break from the boredom of routine can be quite stimulating, in my experience. *I've* never been the sort of person to let myself fall into a rut, but I know some people prefer to follow the same routine, week in and week out.'

'Perhaps we could miss the bookshop for once,' Elsie said, and Betty said, 'I suppose we do need more variety in our lives.'

Oh dear. Was this the beginning of trouble for the bookshop, too? If so, it would be Naomi's fault for antagonizing Constance Pearce and turning her into . . . Well, some sort of rival.

CHAPTER THIRTY-SIX

Suki

'You're sure that's all right?' Suki asked, when Mrs Harrington suggested she could go to the children's club if she liked.

'I'm not suggesting you should go if you don't want—'

'No! I'd love to go.'

'I'm sure Adam will be glad of the help. He runs himself ragged helping people, that man.'

'That's because he's a good person,' Suki said.

'Indeed.'

'Is there anything I can do here first?'

'I don't think so. I've already spoken to Victoria and she's on top of things.'

'Then thank you!'

Suki hastened to get ready, running up to her attic bedroom to throw off her black-and-white uniform. She paused in front of the narrow cupboard in which she kept her clothes but decided again to wear her old skirt and blouse. She could save her second-best dress for another time, perhaps if – hopefully, when – Adam asked her to walk out with him or take tea at the vicarage.

She ran most of the way to the bookshop but slowed down when she neared it, wanting to appear calm and collected, as befitted a young woman of eighteen years.

Was it mean and selfish to hope that Beth was far away at the hospital? Undoubtedly, especially considering Beth was Suki's friend. But there'd be more chance for Suki to shine in Beth's absence.

Reaching the door, Suki paused to take a deep breath and then stepped inside to see that not only was Beth there, but so too was the new nurse. Nancy. How attractive she was with that glossy dark hair and that infectious laugh! Suki's confidence began to crumple but she saw Beth approaching and forced a smile.

'How are you, Beth?'

'Fine, thank you.'

'And Naomi? Mrs Harrington? How is she coping?'

'Bravely,' Suki told her.

Beth nodded. 'She's admirable, but she must be deeply distressed inside.'

Suki realized Nancy was coming over, too. While Beth gave off a reliable, comforting air, Nancy brought sparks of energy. 'You're talking about that nasty letter writer, I assume,' she said. 'You'll send my best wishes to Mrs Harrington? And tell her that, once the sender is identified, I'll be at the front of the queue of people willing to run that person out of town.'

'I'll tell her,' Suki promised.

Then her eyes sought out Adam. He smiled and waved a welcome, and the three young women went over to join him.

'We're going on a nature walk today,' Nancy told Suki.

'How does that sound?' Adam asked.

'It sounds fun,' Suki answered, wishing she could take a moment first to steady the jangle of feelings that the presence of Beth and Nancy had stirred up in her.

But the children were eager to be gone so Adam divided them into four teams, each with an adult in charge. Suki

179

tried to take comfort in the thought that at least Adam considered her to be an adult, but as they all made their way to the woods behind Foxfield she feared she was going to struggle to keep up with the others in making the expedition fun. She wasn't in the right frame of mind for it.

Adam had given each adult a list of leaves to find and identify. Oak, sycamore, hornbeam, hawthorn, beech . . . Suki's team included none of the evacuee children. Which was a pity since she could have relied on Arthur or even Lewis to throw themselves into the challenge with gusto. She set her children searching but as the minutes passed she was conscious of the merry laughter coming from the other teams. Nancy's team seemed to be spending most of the time larking around, which the children appeared to love, racing each other, playing hide-and-seek . . . Beth's team and Adam's team seemed rather more focused but they were clearly having fun, too.

Suki's team . . . 'I need the lavatory,' one little girl announced, dancing from foot to foot.

Suki took her behind a bush and when she returned to her group a boy told her that his friend had said something mean to him and he was going to tell his mum about it.

'He started it,' the friend protested. 'He called me carrot-top.'

'Only after you called me speccy four-eyes for wearing specs.'

'Everyone calls you speccy four-eyes. It doesn't count.'

'Yes, it does. It's mean.'

'*I* need the lavatory now,' another girl said.

Suki took her behind a bush as well and then did her best to raise her team's spirits.

'Let's just concentrate on finding these leaves, shall we? Come on!' she urged. 'It's a challenge!'

But her voice sounded hollow even to her own ears and the boys didn't stop bickering, while one of the girls complained that she'd stung herself on some nettles and wanted to go home. Suki rubbed the stings with dock leaves, which were supposed to relieve them, and tried again to fire her team with zeal.

'Only five minutes left!' Suki heard Nancy declare. 'Quick, team, we've still got leaves to find!' Laughing and whooping, they raced around the woods.

By the time the challenge was finished, Suki was relieved that, even if her team members hadn't enjoyed themselves as much as others, they had at least found all the leaves.

But no. Somehow, she'd overlooked the hornbeam leaf. Nancy's team was two leaves short but they all shared comic downcast looks that had them laughing again. Clearly, they didn't care a hoot that they hadn't quite succeeded. Both Adam's team and Beth's team had found every leaf. Suki supposed she'd expected no less from highly competent Beth.

They headed back to the bookshop for biscuits and a drink. Then the children departed and the clearing-up began. 'I'll wash up the cups,' Adam said, rolling up his shirtsleeves. He never minded taking on what some men would regard as women's work. One of the many reasons Suki had fallen in love with him was because he valued women just as much as men.

'I'll dry them,' Suki said quickly.

He smiled at her. And for a moment Suki's breath caught in her throat. 'That would be helpful,' he said.

How lovely he was! She picked up a tea towel and set to work, picturing herself doing the same and similar jobs in the vicarage kitchen. Adam would help her and she'd help him in providing hospitality to anyone who came to the vicarage because they had business with Adam or needed his assistance. She'd join him in visiting the sick and frail of the parish, too.

She'd arrange flowers in the church. Polish the brass and silver. And when evening came she'd draw the curtains against the approaching darkness and add coals or logs to the fire. She'd cook and serve his favourite meals, and afterwards they'd sit cosily on the sofa, their arms wrapped around each other as they talked about their days and made plans for their happy future. Children, perhaps. A boy. A girl . . .

But the images faltered. Blurred. Because, despite being busy with the children and the search today, Suki had still been aware of her fellow adults and certain suspicions had taken root at the back of her mind.

CHAPTER THIRTY-SEVEN

Beth

Nancy burst into the nurses' sitting room where Beth was enjoying a much-needed cup of cocoa with Babs and Pauline. After starting work early and following it with the children's club Beth was tired, but Nancy's energy appeared to be undimmed. She struck a pose and asked, 'Well?'

She was wearing a new dress.

'You look lovely,' Beth told her while Babs and Pauline nodded agreement.

'This dress was May Janicki's idea. She suggested it at the fashion evening and did the measuring and cutting out for me. I'm doing the sewing, though. By hand, so it's taking an age, but I hope it's worth it. I only have the hem to sew now.'

'What's the dress made from?' Babs asked.

'An old plain navy dress of mine that had an iron burn on the bodice, plus a flowery curtain that May was cutting up.' May was often given old curtains and bedspreads as well as unwanted or damaged clothes since she was best placed to distribute the fabrics around the village.

With Nancy's dress, the short sleeves and skirt had been retained and May had used some of the flowery curtain to fashion a bodice in a lighter shade of blue and pink.

'May told me she likes to help nurses because her

husband – Marek, is it? – is fighting in the war and may need nurses to care for him one day,' Nancy explained. 'She knows Marek's nurses would probably be working miles from here but it's a symbolic thing.'

Pauline nodded thoughtfully. 'War makes a lot of people superstitious.'

'To be honest, I think May would have helped anyway because she's nice,' Nancy said. 'Now then, girls, is this dress the right length? I've pinned it up but I'd like your opinions before I sew it.'

'I think it's the perfect length,' Beth said, because it really was perfect.

Babs and Pauline nodded.

'Then I have an hour or two of sewing ahead of me. Thanks, girls! Oh, I almost forgot to show you this.'

She held up a large flower made from more of the navy fabric and then positioned it on her chest. 'I can pin it on for dances and things like that,' she said.

Babs looked excited. 'Does that mean you've heard there's going to be a dance somewhere near?'

'No, but it doesn't hurt to be prepared because there's bound to be a dance sooner or later, isn't there? They put on social events at the bookshop sometimes, apparently, with dancing included. And I've heard there's an American army base only a few miles away.'

'We've never been invited there,' Babs told her. 'And no way of getting there even if we were to be invited.'

'Oh, well.' Nancy was philosophical. 'There's a first time for everything, and what are obstacles for if not to be knocked out of our paths?'

The last words brought that creeping sense of foreboding back to Beth. Was she an obstacle in Nancy's path? Not that she was putting up much of a fight as an obstacle.

Nancy had shone brightly at the bookshop that afternoon and Beth . . . She'd felt cast into the shade. Not quite invisible but hardly Nancy's equal.

Nancy left the room only to return moments later. 'I've had an idea!' she announced.

'An idea about what?' Babs asked.

'About my new dress and where I can wear it.'

'I don't think there are any parties planned for the bookshop just now,' Pauline ventured.

'There aren't,' Nancy conceded. 'Not according to Alice. So I thought we could have our own party.'

'Here in the nurses' quarters?' Beth was surprised.

'Not in our quarters, but here in the hospital. A dance of some sort. For patients and staff alike. I'm going to speak to Matron about it. I heard she allowed a concert to be held here not so long ago to cheer the patients up, so why not a dance? I know not every patient can walk let alone dance on their feet, but they can still dance from their beds and wheelchairs, or simply enjoy the music and the atmosphere. What do you all think?'

'I think it's a great idea,' Babs said.

'If anyone can make it happen, it's you, Nancy,' Pauline said.

More nurses entered and when Nancy told them her idea they were full of enthusiasm.

'It'll give me a chance to wear my new shoes . . .'

'I haven't danced in ages . . .'

'I hope we can have some decent music. Like Glenn Miller . . .'

Beth smiled along with them but her mind wasn't on clothes or dancing or music. It was on the secret hope that, if Nancy became preoccupied with the dance, she'd have no time or inclination for the children's club.

185

Not that Nancy was her only rival. Beth had begun to suspect that Suki, too, had romantic feelings for Adam. She hadn't made those feelings obvious, but Beth had noticed yearning in the way Suki looked at Adam when she thought she was unobserved. She'd also shown a touching eagerness to please him. Was Adam aware of it? Possibly not, just as he might equally be unaware that Beth and perhaps Nancy also felt tenderly towards him, natural modesty blinding him to his own attractions.

Oh, heavens.

CHAPTER THIRTY-EIGHT

Naomi

Though she seemed determined to criticize Naomi and the bookshop – even if she wrapped her criticism up in fake smiles – Constance Pearce had appeared in the bookshop again. Perhaps it was only to recruit people to draw away from it, the way she'd drawn some of them away to a tea party yesterday when it could easily have taken place when the bookshop was closed.

Sure enough, Naomi heard her talking to another small group of ladies who'd gathered around her. 'Churchwood is a dear little place and I'll miss it when I leave. I wonder, though . . . The world beyond Churchwood is such an interesting place I'm surprised no one has thought to venture out to see more of it. Marjorie tells me she hasn't been further than Barton in years. I understand Mrs Harrington – Naomi – was often in London and elsewhere but Marjorie was never invited to accompany her since I suppose it couldn't have been convenient. How often have you dear ladies been away from the village?'

The answers came with a sense of wonder.

'Now you come to mention it, I haven't left Churchwood for two or three years . . .'

'I went as far as Bedford to see an ageing aunt before the war broke out, but Aunt Hilda is dead now and I haven't been anywhere since . . .'

'Barton is as far as I go. I have an old schoolfriend there . . .'

Constance clasped her hands together. 'It's just as I thought. And you've given me an idea. Why don't we go on a little trip somewhere? We needn't go far on our first adventure. We could go to St Albans on the bus, look around the cathedral and then have lunch in a cafe. If we enjoy ourselves, we can organize more outings. Bournemouth, where I live, is delightful.'

'I'm not sure I can afford to go gallivanting,' one of the women said. Joan Blackwell, Naomi thought, though she was trying not to stare.

'The last thing I want is for anyone to be excluded,' Constance assured her. 'Our trips won't set rich against poor or old friends against new friends. They'll be about bringing together everyone who wishes to come. A trip to St Albans will only incur a bus fare. And if a cafe lunch sounds too expensive, we'll take a picnic. What do you say?'

'Put like that . . .' Joan agreed. 'Perhaps Naomi would like to come with us.' Was she feeling disloyal?

'Let's ask,' Constance said. She caught Naomi's eye and beckoned her over. 'We're thinking of a little trip out,' she said.

Naomi wanted to tell her that she'd already heard the discussion but she didn't want to appear like an eavesdropper. 'How lovely.'

'It's just to St Albans to see the cathedral,' Constance said. Rather coolly, it seemed to Naomi. 'You're welcome to join us but no offence will be taken if you'd prefer to excuse yourself. I expect St Albans sounds dull to someone who's travelled regularly. Besides, you're always so busy!'

Was Constance suggesting again that Naomi had no time for her old friend Marjorie? 'If you let me know which day you fix for the trip, I'll see what I can do,' Naomi said.

'Of course,' Constance said with a chilly smile.

Feeling as though her presence was somehow bringing awkwardness to the group, Naomi retreated. But she remembered what Kate and Alice had said about Constance being spiteful and found herself agreeing with them.

'I'm so glad you're here, Connie.' Marjorie's voice still reached Naomi across the room. 'You're livening up the village. I didn't realize I was living such a small life before.'

'You always say such kind things to me,' Constance told her. 'Rest assured that there are more adventures to come now we've found each other. I can't wait for you to come to stay in Bournemouth. I expect you're desperate to get away from all the nastiness here.'

A nastiness to which she was contributing with her grudge. As far as Naomi was concerned, that was. So far, most people seemed unaware of the barbs she threw out every time she spoke to Naomi or even looked at her. Surely it wasn't kind of Constance to hold on to her grudge when Naomi was trying her best to make up for treating her so negligently when they'd first met? But maybe Naomi deserved it. After all, Constance wasn't the only person who disliked her. Naomi had made two enemies, it seemed, though one of them – the letter writer – had gone to ground, perhaps through fear of exposure now all the village was on the lookout for them.

Or so Naomi assumed, until she reached home and found another letter awaiting her.

CHAPTER THIRTY-NINE

Bert

IT'S PATHETIC, THE WAY YOU'RE GOING
AROUND FEELING SORRY FOR YOURSELF, BUT
YOU ALWAYS THINK THE WORLD REVOLVES
AROUND YOU. ARROGANT FOOL.

Reading the letter, Bert had never felt so angry in all his life.

He squeezed Naomi's shoulder with what he hoped was comfort. How tired she looked! How drained!

'If the letter writer has been watching me, they must be local,' Naomi pointed out.

It certainly looked that way. 'What it says . . . It's nonsense,' Bert insisted, but, despite the truth behind them, his words felt repetitive and weak. 'Every letter this person writes increases their risk of exposure,' he added. 'Someone may have seen the letter being posted to London.'

But those words felt feeble, too. Dozens of letters were posted in Churchwood every day and it would be the work of a moment to take an envelope from a bag and slip it into the pillar box without anyone seeing the address. Might Bert have a word with the postman? Ask him to look out for any letters that were sent to London? No, there were laws against interference with the post.

All Bert could do was increase his own vigilance. The market garden was busy but he vowed to get up early and work late so he could spend as much time as possible in the village. Watching . . . Listening . . .

CHAPTER FORTY

Ruby

Ruby had smiled at the postman when she'd taken the farm's letters from him but she'd let the smile drop after he'd moved on. None of the letters had been addressed to her.

Five days had passed since she'd written to her parents suggesting she visit them and they hadn't yet replied. Why was that? Because she'd taken them by surprise and they weren't sure how to reply? Or because it simply wasn't their way to write back to her letters quickly? Often, a month could pass before she heard from them. Once, almost two months had passed.

One thing was certain: they hadn't been overjoyed by her suggestion or they'd have rushed to encourage the visit. On the other hand, they hadn't rushed to refuse it, either.

However her letter had made them feel, Ruby was sure her best chance of making them care was to meet them face to face so they could see what an incredible boy Timmy was and what an excellent job she was doing of bringing him up. She was glad she hadn't mentioned the suggested visit to him, though. If her parents rejected her suggestion – rejected Ruby and Timmy, in fact – then he'd know nothing about it and could continue his happy life in blissful ignorance.

Not that she was giving up hope of being invited to visit. Not yet, anyway.

One of the letters was addressed to Pearl in her father's handwriting. She groaned when she read it. 'They're coming!'

'Here?' Ruby asked.

'Yes, here. They want to talk about my wedding. They can't stay here, though. Not on the farm.'

'Perhaps Naomi or Alice will put them up,' Ruby suggested. 'I can ask for you.'

Ruby had been wondering whether Pearl's parents were as bad as she made out. It looked as though she'd have the chance to find out.

CHAPTER FORTY-ONE

Suki

'I want to thank you both for the way you're continuing to run this house so efficiently while I'm . . . not at my best,' Mrs Harrington told Suki and Victoria.

'It's our pleasure,' Victoria answered, and Suki nodded.

'I appreciate your kindness and your discretion, too. Please don't think I ever take it for granted. I'm grateful, and I'm proud of you.'

Mrs Harrington was always generous with her praise. It never failed to warm Suki and just now she needed that warmth more than ever. Getting Adam to notice her as a woman had seemed difficult even before her last visit to the children's club. But now it was even more complicated because of what she'd come to suspect.

Which was that Beth loved Adam, too. The nurse wasn't the sort of girl who wore her heart on her sleeve, as the saying went, but the way she'd looked at Adam when she thought she was unobserved had given it away, as had the way she tensed slightly whenever he drew near. It wasn't mere attraction Beth felt, either. Knowing that her friend's emotions ran deep, Suki was sure that what Beth felt was love.

But Beth wasn't Suki's only rival, because Nancy found Adam attractive, too. Nancy had made no secret of her liking for him, but whether it was love or a passing fancy was hard to gauge since Suki didn't know Nancy well. It was enough to give Beth pain, though. Beth had tried hard to hide it, but Suki had still seen the suffering in her face when Nancy charmed Adam into laughter.

Three young women, all interested in the same young man! Suki's confidence wilted every time she thought of the situation but it was for Adam to choose between them. And how did he feel? It was even harder to gauge his feelings because Adam was kind to everyone. Short of slinking away to avoid the fight, Suki could only hope that he'd see something in her to match what she saw in him.

She returned to the children's club on Saturday, determined to do justice to herself.

'I'm so glad you're here!' Adam cried, when she arrived.

He was? That was wonderful, especially since she could see neither Beth nor Nancy there but only Alice. And Suki's romantic hopes were surely safe from any competition from happily married Alice.

Buoyed up by such a promising start, Suki smiled. 'It's a pleasure to be here.'

'I hope you won't mind holding the fort with Alice?' he asked then.

Holding the . . .

'Mrs Ingram over in Barton has received news of the death of her grandson in the fighting,' Adam explained. 'I got to know her well when I was a curate there and she's been asking for me.'

'I see. Well, of course you must go to her,' Suki said.

'Thank you.' He smiled and touched her shoulder in passing as he hastened to the door.

The touch sent an electric thrill through Suki, but the smile . . . It was a lovely, sweet smile, but did it hold any regret that he was unable to spend time with her today?

She was being ridiculous. Adam's thoughts and feelings had all been focused on a former parishioner who'd received devastating news. And rightly so. It would have been out of place for his mind to be on anyone else. No, Suki needed to wait for a more fitting occasion to show the best of herself to him. In the meantime, there was a club full of children to be entertained.

CHAPTER FORTY-TWO

Beth

'Matron agreed!' Nancy announced, bursting into the nurses' sitting room. 'We're going to have a tea dance on Friday. Dr Marwood will lend his gramophone and all his records, too.'

'That's wonderful!' Babs cried.

'Matron has her rules, though,' Nancy said. 'She made me write them down to avoid what she called any misunderstanding about what's allowed and what isn't.'

She cleared her throat and held up a notebook. 'Are you all listening?'

Everybody was.

'Firstly, we're to behave with decorum,' Nancy said. 'In other words, no rowdiness.'

'Shame!' Babs called, but she was joking.

Nancy continued. 'Rule two – though I don't think these rules are in any particular order – we're to treat patients with respect and consideration. That means we don't disturb the patients who need to rest or just prefer not to take part. And we don't let the patients who come along get overtired or carried away to the point of worsening their injuries.'

'Fair enough,' Pauline said.

'Thirdly, we have to keep the music down. Fourthly – and

take especial note of this, girls – we're to dress with decorum. Nothing racy will be allowed.'

'And I was planning on wearing a short skirt and feather boa!' Babs called.

Nancy grinned and then looked back at her notebook. 'What's next? Oh, yes. There's no money in the kitty so it really will have to be a tea dance. Meaning only tea to drink. And nothing to eat unless we can rustle up some biscuits from somewhere.'

'No wine? No sherry? No beer?' Pauline asked.

'Not a chance. We need to get everything ready and clear up afterwards, too. And finish exactly on time. Strict rules, you may think, but it's a dance!'

Nancy's enthusiasm was infectious. Beth saw excitement on every face, and no wonder. It would be fun, especially with Nancy organizing it.

'Will we all be able to attend?' Babs asked.

'I'm afraid not. Those of us who aren't on duty can attend in our free time, if we choose to do so. Those of us who are on duty but detailed to look after the patients who go to the dance can also attend but must wear uniform and keep a careful eye on the patients. And those of us who are on duty elsewhere in the hospital . . .'

'Can't attend at all,' Babs finished.

Beth imagined that every nurse would be crossing her fingers that she'd be able to attend somehow.

'What about people from the village?' Pauline asked.

'Matron wants to keep the dance small so it isn't too noisy and busy for the patients who need to rest. But we'll invite our volunteers. Alice and Adam.' Nancy's eyes brightened. 'I'm looking forward to a twirl around the room with Adam!'

Beth felt vaguely sick, picturing lovely, lively Nancy being twirled around the room by Adam. A dance was just the sort of occasion where Nancy would sparkle while Beth . . . She enjoyed dancing but very much doubted she'd be able to sparkle, even if she was allowed to attend.

She noticed Nurse Gibbs who'd returned to the hospital after taking some time away to come to terms with the death of her sweetheart. Lucy was clearly trying hard to focus on her work but it was obvious that it would be a long time before she was through the worst of her grief. 'I hope you get to go to the dance,' Beth told her, thinking it might do the nurse some good to set aside her troubles for an hour or two.

'You, too,' Lucy said.

CHAPTER FORTY-THREE

Ruby

It had come: the letter from her parents. Ruby stared down at her name on the envelope: *Miss* R. Turner, wondering if her mother had grimaced at the *Miss* bearing in mind that Ruby had a child, or if time and absence just might be beginning to soften her. There was one way to find out. Ruby tore open the envelope and pulled out the letter. Quite a short letter, but what had it to say?

> *Dear Ruby,*
>
> *Thank you for your letter. You can visit if you want, and you can bring Timothy with you but on the strict condition that you both remember that, no matter how you're living in that village, the boy is known here as your brother and that's the way it must stay. Write again to let us know when to expect you.*
>
> *Your mother*

It wasn't the most encouraging letter. Reading *Timothy* and *the boy* made Ruby wince. He was darling Timmy to her yet there wasn't even a hint that his grandparents had missed him and were excited at the prospect of seeing him again.

Ruby tried not to judge them prematurely, though. Her mother wrote letters rarely and couldn't express herself well in speech, let alone in writing. She was clearly worried the truth about Timmy's parentage might come out, too. Having passed Timmy off as her son rather than her grandson, it would appal her to be caught out in a lie.

Ruby preferred to think that it would be different when they met face to face after almost two years. They'd see then that Timmy was a fine boy.

'He's a delight,' his teacher, Mrs Gregson, had said and he seemed to be well liked throughout the village.

Ruby herself may not have been the sort of daughter they'd wanted, which was a girl who'd content herself with a plain, ordinary life instead of dyeing her hair film-star blonde, wearing cosmetics and dreaming of travelling to Paris, New York or even Hollywood one day. But no one could call her flighty now, even if she did still dye her hair and wear cosmetics.

No, this was a chance to put her relationship with her parents on a much better footing and thinking about it filled her with warmth.

CHAPTER FORTY-FOUR

Naomi

'We're going to St Albans on Saturday,' Constance told Naomi at the bookshop.

'Saturday? I'm afraid I'm needed in Churchwood. But I hope you have a lovely time.'

'I'm sure we will,' Constance said. She nudged Marjorie's arm and walked away.

'You didn't really think she'd make time to come?' Naomi heard Constance say.

'I suppose I didn't,' Marjorie admitted. 'Not any more.'

'Don't be disappointed, dear. Naomi Harrington may prefer to keep company with her newer friends, but I hope you enjoy keeping company with *your* new friend.'

'With you, Constance? Of course, I do.'

Naomi heard no more.

'Take no notice,' Alice said into Naomi's ear. 'That woman will be gone soon enough. She can't spin out the story of wet rot in her flat for ever.'

'I suppose she can't.' Naomi attempted a smile. It would be nice to be rid of Constance Pearce, but the letter writer . . . The letter writer would remain.

CHAPTER FORTY-FIVE

Bert

Bert stopped in the village to run a few errands after making some deliveries. Ten minutes later, he returned to his truck feeling thoughtful. Hmm . . .

There could be a perfectly innocent explanation for what had just happened in the post office and Bert's imagination might be making a ridiculously big leap towards suspicion. But in the absence of any other clues that might lead him to the letter writer, he decided to pursue it anyway. He was willing to put himself to endless trouble for the woman he loved.

He drove home, made himself a cup of tea and sat down in his favourite armchair, scooping Elizabeth on to his lap. 'Right, then,' he told her. 'Old Bert needs to do some thinking.'

Stroking Elizabeth's warm fur and feeling her purr beneath his fingers always helped to clear his mind.

Should he tell Naomi of his suspicions? No, not yet. They were too obscure at present – as insubstantial as an early-morning mist that would evaporate into nothing with the first rays of sunshine. Bert might have an inkling as to *how* the campaign had been waged, but as to *why* it had been waged he had no idea.

After a while he decided that a phone call or two might

be a good place to start. Bert had a telephone at home, which was lucky since it meant he could make his calls in private. The first led nowhere. The second added only a little to what he already knew. He needed to take a trip if he were to find out more. That would mean time away from the market garden at a busy time of year. 'Which means I'd better try to get ahead,' he told Elizabeth.

He worked for another few hours, ate some dinner and then worked again until darkness fell, making sure that all his plants had enough water to get them through a day or two. He got up early the next morning, too, putting in more work before calling at Foxfield.

He saw Naomi pretty well every day but today there must have been something particularly purposeful about him because she looked at him warily. 'Is everything all right?' she asked.

'Fine,' he told her. 'I just want to let you know I may be away for a day or two.'

'Oh? I have a feeling you're not going on market garden business.'

'I'm not. I've an idea about who may be responsible for those letters.'

'The poison pen letters?' Naomi gulped. 'Who?'

'I know you'll find this frustrating, but I don't want to name anyone until I'm certain,' Bert said.

'But I'm desperate to know!'

'Which I understand, beloved. Trust me, I'll be home just as soon as possible, hopefully with cast-iron information.'

'I could come with you.'

'Not this time, but you'll help enormously if you call round at my house to feed Elizabeth and spend a few minutes telling her she's the best cat in the world. I need you to tell everyone else I'm away on market garden business. I don't want this person to know that I may be on to them.'

'How *did* you get on to them?'

'All in good time, beloved. Meanwhile, just act normally.'

'That'll be easier said than done,' Naomi protested.

Bert knew she'd been struggling to act normally ever since the arrival of the first nasty letter and hadn't slept well in an age.

He drew her to him and kissed her. 'Just try, hmm?' he said and, dropping one last kiss on to her forehead, he left.

CHAPTER FORTY-SIX

Beth

Yes! Beth felt like Cinderella. She *could* go to the ball. Or rather the Stratton House tea dance. Whether Adam danced with her remained to be seen but Beth was determined to stay hopeful.

She had few clothes compared to many of the other nurses but she had a rather lovely blue satin dress that brought out the matching blue of her eyes. She'd worn it once since coming to Churchwood – at a bookshop concert – but she could wear it again. Perhaps she might also dress her hair so that—

On duty in Ward One, Beth became aware that Lucy Gibbs was passing by, trying but failing to look happy. Clearly, the death of her fiancé was still hitting her hard. 'Are you coming to the dance?' Beth asked her.

'Not this time. I'm on duty.'

'I'm sorry.'

Lucy shrugged. 'Can't be helped,' she said, and walked on.

But perhaps it could be helped. Beth wrestled with her conscience for a while and then went to see Matron. 'It seems a shame that Nurse Gibbs can't go to the dance,' she said.

'I haven't excluded her deliberately,' Matron told her. 'I put the nurses' names in a hat to keep the selection fair and she was one of the unlucky ones. It's a pity but I couldn't favour one nurse over others.'

'I understand,' Beth said. Then she heaved breath into her lungs. 'Perhaps I could swap places with her?'

'Perhaps you could,' Matron said, giving an approving nod. 'I suggest you tell her soon so she has a chance to prepare.'

'I'll tell her now,' Beth said. 'Thank you, Matron.'

'Are you sure?' Lucy asked, when Beth told her she was happy to swap places. 'I wouldn't want you to feel obliged to swap just because I'm . . . Because of what happened with my Christopher.'

Beth noticed that tears welled up in Lucy's eyes at the mention of her sweetheart. It confirmed that swapping places to give the girl an hour or two of pleasure was the right thing to do, even if it cost Beth dear in personal disappointment.

CHAPTER FORTY-SEVEN

Bert

'Wish me luck?' Bert asked Elizabeth as he prepared to set out. It was early but he'd already put in two hours' work in the market garden, eaten a large bowl of sustaining porridge and made a sandwich for later because who knew when he'd have a chance to eat while he was away from home?

Elizabeth got to her feet. She was used to Bert leaving the kitchen to work outside or go further afield on deliveries, but perhaps she'd picked up something in the atmosphere that suggested this departure was different. And serious.

He bent to caress her. 'Don't worry, Lizzie. I've arranged for you to be fed and cuddled so you shouldn't be too lonely without me.'

Straightening again, he slung his bag over his shoulder and left the house, heading into the village to catch the first bus of the day. He paused when he reached Foxfield and stared through the gateposts. Was Naomi still sleeping? He hoped so. 'If good fortune goes my way, I'll have information for you soon, my love,' he murmured. Then he blew her a kiss and walked on.

CHAPTER FORTY-EIGHT

Naomi

Bert's truck was parked in its usual place when Naomi called at the market garden to feed and fuss over Elizabeth. He must have taken the bus on his mystery mission. She wished she knew where he was but understood his reluctance to make accusations against anyone without evidence of their guilt. Bert had integrity.

She spent a little while in the familiar kitchen, touching surfaces and objects just to feel close to their absent owner. This would be her kitchen, too, once they were married. Not that she'd be quitting Foxfield. They hadn't worked out any particular plan but would probably share their time between both properties. At the beginning of their marriage, anyway.

Would Bert's quest be successful? She hoped so rather desperately. Naomi dreaded learning that the letter writer was someone she knew. How would she ever face them in the street or at the shops or – even worse – at social events? She had no answers to those questions, but not knowing the letter writer's identity was worse.

It was making her fragile and feeble. Once she could sleep again she'd be better placed for giving the bookshop a much-needed boost instead of standing by as Constance Pearce did her best to diminish it. Even that morning,

Naomi had heard her telling her ever-growing group of cronies what fun they were going to have on their little adventure to St Albans and how she hoped it would be the first of many such adventures. Seeing Naomi, her smile had turned triumphant. Or so Naomi had thought. Perhaps she was simply so exhausted and upset that she was losing all perspective.

She headed back to Foxfield and saw Alice approaching. 'You must say if it's inconvenient, but Pearl's parents are coming on Saturday,' Alice said. 'You offered to put them up, but do say if that feels too much at present. I'll be happy to put them up at The Linnets.'

'No, it'll be fine,' Naomi said. Even the thought of it was tiring but Naomi was determined to stop her backbone from crumbling still further. She had to be strong.

CHAPTER FORTY-NINE

Ruby

It felt strange to be back in London again after so long away – familiar and yet unfamiliar. After the quiet of Churchwood, St Pancras station seemed loud. Trains hissed as they released steam. Guards whistled to warn of departures. A newspaper vendor shouted, 'War latest!'

Other people called out, too. 'Porter!' and 'Wait for me, Bill!' and 'For goodness' sake, hurry up, Sylvia!'

Some people wore service uniforms – khaki, navy, air force blue and the green of the Women's Voluntary Service. And there were countless others in regular clothing.

'Cor!' Timmy said. 'So many people!'

'Stay close,' Ruby cautioned, holding his hand tightly.

They travelled to the Turner home in Bermondsey by bus, climbing to the top deck to make the journey an adventure for Timmy. Signs of the war were everywhere – in the two air raid wardens they saw, in the gaps where buildings had once stood, in the boarded-up windows of other buildings, in the piles of sandbags, in the gas masks that banged against people's legs as they hurried this way and that way.

They were heading east so missed many of London's landmarks such as Buckingham Palace, Trafalgar Square and the Houses of Parliament, but their route took in

Tower Bridge and the Tower of London. 'There, Timmy, see?' Ruby said, pointing. 'Do you remember them?'

'A bit. Is the Tower the place where they chop people's heads off?'

'They used to, but not for years and years, so I think we're safe.' Ruby wished she could be sure they were safe from enemy air raids and glanced up at the sky periodically in search of bombers, though the sirens would surely have sounded before German aircraft reached London. She'd coached Timmy in what to do should a siren sound. 'Grab your gas mask before anything else and stick close to me. I can't tell you where we'll go but we'll follow the crowd or ask for the nearest shelter. It might be in an underground station. Hundreds of people go down into the stations. They sing songs and have a jolly time as they wait until it's safe again.'

'What if I need the toilet?'

'Hopefully, the air raid won't last long. Or someone may have got buckets ready . . .'

Reaching Bermondsey, they made their way to Colin Street, which comprised rows of terraced houses that were soot-blackened and had doors opening straight on to the pavement. Ruby had spent more than twenty years living here and many of the streets and buildings they passed brought memories of her childhood. There was the house where three savage-looking dogs had lived. Two doors further on was the house of the woman who'd sung to herself when she walked. Opposite was the home of the Clough family, the roughest in all Bermondsey, or so people said. The Cloughs' neighbour had turned her nose up disapprovingly when Ruby had dyed her hair, though she'd have had a fit of apoplexy if she'd known Ruby had given birth outside marriage.

There were happier memories. The house of the woman who'd offered Ruby pearl drops from a paper bag. The house where a parrot lived, brought home from somewhere exotic by a sailor. The house where Peter Perry had lived. Three years older than Ruby, she'd had a crush on him when she was thirteen or so. What had happened to Peter Perry? Ruby had no idea.

Ruby knocked on the door of Number Six and took a deep breath as she waited for the knock to be answered.

CHAPTER FIFTY

Bert

It was late when Bert returned to Churchwood. He'd missed the last bus so he'd caught a taxi from St Albans train station and it had cost him dear. Not that he cared about that. All money spent in Naomi's best interests was money well spent as far as he was concerned – the travelling costs, the phone calls he'd needed to make and the dinner he'd eaten before catching the train on his journey back. He hadn't succeeded in his mission yet. In fact, he'd uncovered no concrete evidence at all. Even so, he felt the day's work had been useful and tomorrow's appointment might bring all the jigsaw pieces together.

At Bert's request the taxi driver dropped him off outside Foxfield. Once again, Bert looked up at the house and blew his beloved a kiss. Then he walked home, letting himself into the house and feeling pleased when Elizabeth got up from the hearth rug to miaow and pad towards him in welcome. Bert scooped her into his arms. 'That's a nice greeting. Have you been good while I've been out? I'm sure you've been fed well.'

A note stood on the kitchen table. He guessed it was from Naomi and, walking closer, he saw that he was right.

Dearest Bert,
    I hope you've arrived home safely from your mystery journey.

214

I've given Elizabeth some food and also spent some time with her so she doesn't feel abandoned. Perhaps you could call at Foxfield tomorrow to let me know what you've been about.

'Can't do that, beloved,' Bert muttered. 'But I hope to see you very soon.'

In case you're still away I'll come back to give Elizabeth more food and attention. I'm missing you, Bert. So very much.
    All my love,
    Naomi x

'I'm missing you, too,' Bert said into the ether. 'Have patience and all will be revealed in due course. At least, I hope so.'

He cradled Elizabeth for a little longer then returned her to the hearth rug and pulled a map book off a shelf of the dresser. Carrying it to the table, he sat down, found the page he needed and perused it.

'Hmm,' he said to Elizabeth. 'It looks as though neither a bus nor a train will get me where I need to be tomorrow. Not in good time, anyway. I'll have to use the truck. Don't look at me like that, old girl. I know petrol rationing means I shouldn't use the truck except on market garden business but I think this counts as an emergency. Besides, I've been conscientious up until now in sticking to the rules ever since war broke out, and helping Naomi could be seen as helping the war effort. After all, she's a big part of keeping up the morale of the entire village.'

Elizabeth didn't argue.

CHAPTER FIFTY-ONE

Naomi

Bert's truck was gone when Naomi arrived at the market garden. He must have returned home last night only to go out again this morning. Using her key to let herself into the kitchen, Naomi saw that her note had been replaced by one addressed to her.

Dearest Naomi,
   Thank you, darling woman, for looking after Elizabeth. My quest was . . . interesting, but I need to be away a little longer. Trust me when I say that I'll return as soon as possible.
   I love you, woman.
   Bert x

CHAPTER FIFTY-TWO

Beth

Matron addressed the nurses who were required to work later. 'I'll have no long faces because you're missing the dance. All being well, there'll be other dances for you to attend but right now your job is to cheer our patients up, not make them feel as though they're spoiling your fun.'

'Of course, Matron,' Beth said, and other nurses murmured agreement.

'Excellent. Now, I suggest you all get to work.' Matron clapped her hands to speed them on their way.

'Sorry you're missing the dance,' Corporal Peplow told Beth when she tidied his bedlinen.

'I don't mind at all,' Beth answered. It was a fib, but Matron was right about not making the patients feel guilty.

'You don't like dancing? A pretty thing like you?'

'I like dancing . . . sometimes,' Beth admitted. 'But it's also nice to be on duty when things are a little quieter. Now, Corporal, is there anything else I can do for you?'

Private Stokes had a different view. 'Dancing! A very silly way for a person to spend their time, if you ask me,' he grumbled.

'No one did ask you,' Corporal Peplow told him, sending Beth a look that was both sympathetic and comic.

Moving on, she wondered what was happening at the

217

dance. Had Adam arrived? Was he dancing with Nancy?

Life seemed to be giving Beth a hard lesson at the moment. It was showing her the difference between infatuation and love. When Oliver Lytton had let her down, there'd been tears and sobs. High drama, in fact, even though it was conducted in the privacy of her room. But her infatuation with Oliver had been spun around his exceptional good looks and smooth way with words. Around her own fantasies of the sort of man he was and the life they could lead together, too. Once reality had shone its bright, revealing light, fantasy had fallen away. Rapidly, giving way to dislike and even disgust.

It wasn't the same with Adam. Her journey to loving him had been gentler and slower, its foundations building strength and steadiness gradually because they included respect, regard and joyful affection as well as attraction – emotions that were less flamboyant than those she'd felt for Oliver but which ran much deeper and with much more intensity. Beth wasn't being at all dramatic when she acknowledged to herself that if Adam didn't return her love, she was likely to take a long time to recover.

Those were private thoughts, though. Private feelings. And Beth had a job to do. She took a deep breath and greeted her next patient with a smile.

She didn't need the clock to tell her when the dance ended. It was obvious in the way the hospital atmosphere lightened and fizzed as the patients who'd taken part were returned to their wards by their nurses. Beth caught laughter and chatter.

'What fun we had!'

'That was my best day since I was injured!'

'I could only dance in my wheelchair but next time I'll be on my feet.'

Alice came too, looking prettily flushed. 'I thought I'd distribute a few books before I left,' she said.

'Did you have a good time?' Beth asked her.

'A lovely time, thank you. I didn't dance much' – she touched her swollen stomach to indicate that she'd been thinking of her baby – 'but I managed a couple of the slower numbers. I'm sorry you had to miss out, Beth.'

'I'll have my chance another time,' Beth said.

Adam joined them. His colour was heightened and his hair even shaggier than usual. As one of the few fully able men present, he'd probably been called upon to dance non-stop. 'It all went well, I hear,' Beth said.

'It did. The patients seemed perked up by it and it was fun for the rest of us, too. But it could never have happened without you and others holding the fort on the wards while we partied.'

'There'll be other dances,' Beth said.

'And when the next one comes along, you must save a dance for me,' Adam said.

He was smiling and his brown eyes were soft. But oh, it was impossible to read anything in them except kindness.

It was hardly surprising that the talk in the nurses' quarters later was all about the dance. 'Did you see Larry Gibbons waving his arms about?' Pauline asked.

'It was lovely to see him enjoying himself,' Babs agreed.

'Little Tommy Tinkerton said he'd never danced with a girl before,' a nurse called Violet confided. 'He was blushing scarlet but said it was heavenly.'

'Adam made sure everyone had a good time,' Nancy said.

Babs nodded. 'He's such a sweet man. I think he danced with all of us. But he only danced with one person twice and that was you, Nancy.' Babs accompanied her words with a wink and a grin.

And Beth felt sick. The dance hadn't kept Nancy apart from Adam. It had brought her even closer to him.

But was Nancy actually in love with Adam? Beth still had no answer to that question. Her pleasure in his company was there for all to see. But love?

CHAPTER FIFTY-THREE

Naomi

Bert was still absent the following morning but there was no note for her. The note she'd written yesterday was still on the kitchen table where she'd left it, one corner secured under the teapot. He'd passed the night somewhere else.

Naomi spent some time with Elizabeth, returned home to deal with bookshop paperwork and then walked into the village. She saw Constance Pearce, Marjorie and three or four others up ahead of her, waiting for the bus that would take them on their adventure to St Albans. For a moment Naomi hesitated as awkwardness overcame her, but she squared her shoulders and walked on, ensuring she was displaying a smile.

'Naomi!' Molly Lloyd said. 'How nice to see you, but what a pity you're not coming with us today.'

Clearly, Molly was anxious to show that she still considered herself to be Naomi's friend. Elsie Fuller was in the group, too. 'Yes, such a pity.'

Not wanting to give Constance Pearce a chance to gloat, Naomi pantomimed confusion. 'Coming with you? Oh, of course! You're going on your little trip today.'

She glanced at Constance and saw a tightness in the woman's smile which suggested she hadn't appreciated having her adventure dismissed as a little trip that hadn't even warranted a place in Naomi's memory.

Naomi beamed a smile of her own. 'I hope you all have a lovely time. I'll have to ask you to excuse me now. I have business at the vicarage.'

She walked off across the village green, wondering if it had been petty of her to fight back like that. It was an easy question to answer. Of course it had been petty. But it had also been satisfying. Naomi was sick and tired of being at the mercy of the letter writer, an enemy she could neither see nor identify in any other way. Sick and tired, too, of being feeble while others – Bert especially – tried to unmask the letter writer on her behalf.

Constance Pearce was both visible and present. Naomi might not have been the best hostess the day the woman had come to lunch, and perhaps she'd been rather too impatient with Marjorie before then. But a little forgiveness once the letters had been made public . . . Surely it hadn't been unreasonable to hope for that? Instead, Constance's resentment had bedded down into spite, and as for Marjorie . . . Naomi had never had high expectations of weak-headed Marjorie, but to have her walking around looking smug while her cousin tried to undermine Naomi and the bookshop was more than a little hurtful.

At the vicarage she had a short chat with Mrs Harris, the woman who spent a few hours each week cleaning for Adam and trying to feed him, and dropped off a letter one of their outlying residents had sent, thanking everyone at the bookshop for their help during a recent illness. 'I thought Adam would like to see it,' she explained.

'I'm sure he would,' Mrs Harris agreed.

Naomi turned to leave and saw that the bus was arriving. Constance and her fellow adventurers would soon be on their way. Perhaps one day soon, Constance would get on a bus and leave Churchwood for good. But what about Naomi's other enemy? The letter writer?

Naomi's thoughts turned back to Bert. How was he getting on? Was he succeeding in his mission? Or had he met with failure?

Naomi hoped desperately that he was succeeding. Much as she dreaded coming face to face with her enemy, it might give her the chance to understand their grievance and perhaps even put it right. The chance to sleep again and, oh, what a difference that would make! She'd be much better able to deal with Constance. Best of all, Naomi would be able to plan her wedding with joy.

CHAPTER FIFTY-FOUR

Bert

Bert hadn't expected to spend the night away from Churchwood but circumstance had decided an overnight stay was necessary. Driving home the following morning, he thought over what had happened on his visit to the wilds of Bedfordshire. Fairfax Court had sounded rather grand and, turning up the drive towards the property, Bert had decided that it was grand indeed – not a palace, but certainly a mansion. There was a central porch held up by stone pillars, a row of long windows to each side and two more rows of windows above them.

Set in large, well-tended grounds, the house was pleasing on the eye but Bert felt no tug of envy. He could appreciate beauty without having to own it and he was happy with his lot in Churchwood, especially now Naomi was to share his life.

He parked the ancient truck, smiling at how incongruous it looked in such a lovely setting, and tugged on the doorbell. It was answered by a black-suited man Bert took to be a butler. 'Bert Makepiece. I'm expected,' Bert said.

But his host's health had apparently taken a turn for the worse and a doctor was with him. 'I'm sorry to hear that,' Bert told the butler, mastering his disappointment with a burst of kindness and compassion. 'Perhaps it'll be best if I come back another day.'

'No, no,' the butler told him. 'Sir John is adamant that he wants to see you today but he'll be grateful if you'd allow him a few hours of rest first.'

'Of course.'

'He asked me to show you to the library, where you can pass the time with a book.'

'I'll be glad to do just that,' Bert said. 'But would it be an inconvenience if I took a turn around the grounds first? I've been cooped up inside a truck and my legs need stretching.'

'It won't be an inconvenience at all. The library is at the back of the house and I'll leave a French window open for you. Please pull the bell by the fireplace when you'd like some refreshment and the housekeeper will bring it to you.'

'I'm grateful,' Bert said. He set off around the house, admiring lawns and flower beds and a rose garden. There was a walled kitchen garden, too, and Bert passed a pleasant half-hour talking to the gardener about the produce he was growing. But then he headed back to the house so no one would be wondering where he'd got to.

Stepping through the French window, he stared about him at the library – shelves and shelves of leather-bound books, a large mahogany desk with a chair behind it and leather-covered sofas arranged beside a large stone fireplace. Gradually, he registered details. The fine marble clock. Tall lamps with fringed shades. A globe on a side table. Crystal glasses and decanters on another table. And the books themselves – about natural history, gardens of the world, birds, other wildlife, historic kings and queens . . .

He smiled, imagining Alice, Kate and Naomi here. They'd go into raptures, though Bert doubted that everyone who came to the bookshop would find what they wanted in Thomas Carlyle's *The French Revolution* or John Milton's epic poem *Paradise Lost*. People like Ada Hayes and Phyllis Hutchings preferred books about romance featuring handsome dukes and sheikhs. Like *Sunset Kiss* and the *Count of Amarrin*.

He took a book titled *Wildflowers of Bedfordshire* from a shelf and settled down to read it, though descriptions of marsh orchids, dog violets and gentians couldn't hold his interest for long. His mind was too busy with imagining what was happening back in Churchwood and with the woman he loved.

He didn't ring the bell for refreshments, not wanting to be troublesome, but the housekeeper came to check that he was comfortable and insisted on bringing tea, accompanying it with a sandwich. Bert had to admit that both tea and sandwich were welcome.

It was mid-afternoon before the butler returned and said that Sir John was ready to see him now. Bert was led up a wide mahogany staircase covered in plush red carpet and brightly gleaming brass stair-rods. A door was opened. 'Mr Makepiece to see you, sir,' the butler announced to someone inside the room.

The butler retreated, making space for Bert to enter. Bert stepped inside and saw a huge four-poster bed with a man inside it, leaning back against at least six pillows. 'Thank you for seeing me, Sir John,' Bert said, moving forward to offer a hand. 'But do tell me if you're not up to talking.'

'No, no, I've kept you waiting long enough. I'll talk as best I can. Pull up a chair, do.'

There was a chair next to the bed. Perhaps it had recently been vacated by the doctor. Bert brought it closer, sat down and contemplated his host.

Sir John might once have been a fine figure of a man but

now he was shrunken, looking almost lost inside the enormous bed. His face was skeletal, his colour yellow with ill health. Yet, his faded blue eyes managed a twinkle. 'I look to be at death's door,' he said. 'That's because I'm knocking on it and soon it'll let me in.'

'I'm sorry,' Bert said.

'Don't be. I'm eighty-four years old. I've lived a good life and I've outlived most of my contemporaries. I'm at peace. Which isn't to say I don't enjoy some company still, and you look like a sensible man, Mr Makepiece.'

'I hope I am,' Bert said.

'No forelock tugging or fawning over his so-called betters from you, I suspect.'

'Your suspicions are well founded.'

'You're a revolutionary?'

'Not quite. But I believe the worth of a person owes nothing to money, status or grand titles but everything to how he treats other people. That should be as equals, in my opinion.'

'You'll be given no argument by me. Now, then. To business.'

A half-hour passed. 'Satisfied, Mr Makepiece?' Sir John asked.

'Perfectly satisfied,' Bert confirmed.

'Excellent. I'm glad to have given you what you wanted. In return, I hope I can prevail upon you to dine with me. It won't be a fine dinner. I have my meals brought to me here since I can't get out of bed any more. You could have that small table brought over so you can eat nearby.'

'I've no wish to impose,' Bert said.

'It'll be a favour, not an imposition. The only company I have these days is my doctor. A decent man, but he goes around with a face as long as a lamp post and nags me

227

constantly about my health. I need someone around me who'll talk cheerfully instead of gravely. Don't worry about driving home in the dark. My housekeeper can make up a bed for you here and you can leave first thing tomorrow so you'll still have most of your day at home. What do you say?'

Bert felt a pang. He wanted to be with Naomi so he could share his news but Sir John had helped him and it was only fair that he should be given help in return. 'I'll be delighted to stay,' Bert said.

'I'll need to sleep again before dinner but I'm sure you can amuse yourself for another couple of hours.'

'I'm sure of that, too,' Bert said.

He passed a companionable evening with Sir John. 'You'll forgive me if I don't see you tomorrow. Mornings are difficult for me now my health is failing. Mrs Parsons will look after you.'

Bert wanted to leave the moment he woke but he feared offending Mrs Parsons. He ate a solitary breakfast brought to him in what was described as the morning room. Then he got up to leave, sending best wishes and thanks to Sir John.

Driving home, he'd felt his spirits lift with every mile that took him closer to Churchwood. Minutes ago, Bert had reached a crossroads and remembered the white-painted signpost that had stood there before. Like so many others, it had been removed to foil enemy spies or an invasion. *Churchwood 5 miles*, it had said, pointing straight on. Now he passed the place where a milestone had announced, *Churchwood 2 miles*. This was familiar territory to him. He recognized an ancient oak tree that towered above a hedgerow, a family of scarecrows that stood in a field, a cottage with a horse in the paddock next to it . . .

Reaching the village outskirts, his spirits soared even higher. He'd head straight for Foxfield to tell Naomi he now knew the who and the why of those awful letters, but since he was approaching from the opposite side of the village, he'd keep an eye out for her as he drove in case she was out shopping or on bookshop business.

Hearing something that sounded like a far-off droning, he glanced in the truck's rear-view mirror and saw a motorbike in the distance behind him. He let a few moments pass and then looked in the mirror again. 'Young fool,' he muttered, for the motorcyclist was gaining on him, driving too fast for safety, especially considering the road ahead would soon curve on its way into Churchwood. It was an American soldier.

Only a fool would overtake just before a blind curve but Bert moved the truck closer to the kerb just in case this soldier was reckless enough to try it. The soldier did try it, taking a wide swing on to the opposite side of the road, and seemed to be in no hurry to move back – until a bus rounded the curve. The driver tooted his horn furiously. The motorcyclist tried to swerve out of its path but lost control. The bike went over, spilling its rider on to the ground. Obviously trying to avoid hitting him, the bus driver also swerved and he too lost control, the bus smashing into the window of a house and powering through into what had to be the sitting room.

Good grief! Bert braked hard and steered the truck to a halt. Then he jumped out and ran to help.

CHAPTER FIFTY-FIVE

Naomi

Naomi had been walking back across the village green when she'd heard the distant toot of a horn. Presumably the bus driver had been warning of his presence on the curving road as he left the village.

To Naomi's horror a screech of brakes had followed and then an ear-splitting bang that had stopped her heart temporarily. Oh, heavens! A bang of that magnitude must surely mean that the bus had crashed?

Praying that no one had been hurt, she set off after it as fast as her short legs could manage. Other people began to emerge from shops and houses. 'That wasn't a bomb, was it?' Jonah Kerrigan called out to her.

'I think the bus crashed,' Naomi called back.

Just past the curve in the road she came to a halt, shock jolting through her at the sight of what lay ahead.

A motorbike and its rider were sprawled on the road several yards apart from each other. As for the bus . . . its front half was embedded in a house, having smashed through the downstairs window and possibly the door as well. It was the house that belonged to Ted Newcross, a widower who lived alone. Had he been caught inside it? Naomi could only hope he'd been out or at the very back of the house, or, better still, in the garden.

Pulling her trembling wits together, Naomi rushed forward again – and realized Bert was rushing forward from the opposite direction, having pulled his truck to the kerb further on. He must have been on his way home. Relief at the sight of him weakened her limbs. Solid, steady Bert was the very best of men to have around in a crisis.

'You see to the motorcyclist while I start getting people off the bus,' he suggested.

Naomi could see anxious faces in a couple of the bus's windows. Pale, anxious faces, some bloodied and all with dishevelled hair. At that moment, the motorcyclist let out a groan. Bert was right. Naomi should see to him while Bert – and the others who were gathering to help – dealt with the bus passengers and driver.

She got down on the ground beside the American, who was groaning again. 'It's all right,' she assured him. 'Help is coming. Try to keep still until it arrives. You may do more damage to yourself if you move.'

'My leg!' he moaned. 'Have I still got it?'

'Yes, though it may be broken so keep it steady. Have you pain anywhere else?'

He opened his eyes at last and gave her a helpless look that suggested he was hurting everywhere. But Naomi was glad to see that, while he was clearly in pain, those eyes were focused and his words made sense. With luck he didn't have a significant head injury.

Naomi heard the sound of breaking glass. Bert and his team had smashed the bus's back window to make an escape route. The bus was a single decker and the only door was at the front, currently implanted in the house. There were cries of 'Careful!' and 'Watch out for broken glass!'

One by one, the passengers began to be lifted through the now-empty window. Dazed and tousled, they were welcomed into the comforting arms of more Churchwood residents.

'There's a woman with a broken arm,' Naomi heard one of them say, and another said, 'Elsie Fuller has cut her head.'

Presumably, it was the least badly injured who were being unloaded first. Naomi feared for those who'd been at the front of the bus, the driver especially.

She realized Suki had appeared and was staring at the bus in open-mouthed shock, her shopping basket dangling from her arm as though forgotten. Naomi called her over. 'Would you mind running back to Foxfield and asking Victoria to telephone to the American base to let them know that one of their men has been hurt?' she asked. 'It may be the quickest way of getting this soldier some help.'

Naomi had heard Bert asking for an ambulance to be called, but one ambulance might not be enough.

'Right,' Suki said. She gave the bus one last appalled glance and ran off.

Alice appeared next with her retired doctor father. 'My father is going to help the worst injured here until the ambulance comes. I'm going to open the bookshop so he can send the walking wounded there. I'll have tea ready for anyone in need of it, even if they just want to sit down and recuperate for a few minutes.'

'Good idea,' Naomi said, having every confidence that Alice would soon have help from Janet and May and maybe others, too.

Adam joined them. 'I'll start shepherding the walking wounded in that direction,' he said.

He walked over to a group of bewildered-looking passengers. 'This way, please.'

Victoria could have lost no time in telephoning the

American base because, even sooner than anticipated, a vehicle drove up at speed and American medics leaped out. Naomi got to her feet, feeling creaky and stiff, and stood aside while they assessed their patient and stretchered him into their vehicle. 'May we help with other casualties?' their doctor asked, but just then the ambulance arrived.

'It looks as though we have our own cavalry now,' Naomi said.

'If we're surplus to requirements, we'll get our soldier back to base for treatment.'

It took time to bring out the more severely injured, especially the driver who had to be stretchered out unconscious. 'He's breathing, though,' Bert told Naomi.

Finally, Ted Newcross, the owner of the house, was brought out. He could walk but was covered in dust and appeared to be in severe shock. 'I was putting the kettle on for tea,' he kept saying, as though that humdrum domestic detail should have made calamity impossible.

A woman ran up. Ted's daughter, Doris, who lived in Barton with her husband and their small son, Bobby. Seeing her father, relief rippled through her, but then she looked around and, growing frantic again, asked, 'Where's Bobby?'

'Bobby?' her father repeated.

'Where is he?'

Bewildered, her father simply looked back at the house.

'He's still in *there*?' Doris demanded, her voice rising to hysteria.

'Leave this to me,' Bert said.

He began to squeeze his large frame into the narrow space between the side of the bus and the house's front wall, kicking debris out of the way. Naomi's hand went to her mouth. Surely it wasn't safe for him? 'Take care!' she called, and then wrapped her arms around Doris who'd begun sobbing.

Bert was out of sight now. From within the house came a scrape followed by the thud of something falling. Then Bert's head reappeared in the narrow space. 'I need a torch. There's one in my truck if—'

'I've got one!' A neighbour of Ted's ran into his house and returned seconds later with a large torch. 'Use this!' he said, stretching his arm out to pass it to Bert and then jumping well clear of the now-fragile building.

Bert disappeared from sight again, Naomi calling after him, 'Please be careful, Bert!'

More sounds followed – scrapes, thuds, the pattering of loose debris . . . And, at last, a shout: 'Got him!'

'Thank God!' Naomi muttered and Bobby's mother sobbed again, this time with relief.

But then there came a trembling sound. A vibration. And without further warning, it seemed as though the whole house were crashing down – bricks, roof tiles and timbers collapsing on to Bert and Bobby.

CHAPTER FIFTY-SIX

Bert

Some sixth sense had warned Bert what was to happen. Whether it arose from a sudden moment of stillness, a faint vibration through the soles of his boots or something else, he hadn't known. Neither had he cared. What he'd felt hadn't been fear, exactly. It had been dread. He was on the brink of blissful happiness with Naomi. To have it snatched away . . .

There'd been no chance of escaping. But he'd decided to do everything he could to save the little 'un.

He'd clutched the boy close to his chest and braced his shoulders as the house came down on them. Blow after blow had struck him and knocked him to the ground. And still the blows had fallen, one of them stunning him momentarily as it landed on his head.

'It's all right,' he'd told the boy. 'It's all right.'

But it hadn't been all right. Now Bert lay with the boy under a weight of debris that crushed him and made it barely possible for him to breathe.

He tried to cry out so help could reach them sooner but his mouth and lungs filled with dust and he feared it might choke them to death.

Oh, Naomi! She was the love of his life and he'd give

anything to marry her. But his strength was draining rapidly. He could feel it slipping away. He'd had something important to tell her, too.

CHAPTER FIFTY-SEVEN

Naomi

There were shouts and screams. Someone grabbed Naomi from behind and pulled her back to safety as rubble smashed on to the pavement and even the road, while dust turned the air to a noxious grey cloud.

'Bert!' Naomi fought for freedom from whoever was holding her, driven by terror for her darling man and little Bobby and the urge to help them. But she was held fast.

'Wait!' her captor hissed in her ear. 'It isn't safe!'

But Bert and Bobby needed help *now*.

Finally breaking free, she rushed forward and began to claw at the rubble with her bare hands. 'Speak to me, Bert!' she implored. 'Call out! Let me know where you are.'

Bert was silent.

'You're hurting yourself, Mrs Harrington,' someone said.

It was true. She was ripping her nails and making her fingers bleed but Naomi cared not at all about that. She continued clawing, ignoring the choking, stinging dust and fearing that to pause for even a second might mean the difference between life and death. She sobbed with relief when others came to join in.

'Bert!' she called again and this time she thought she caught a distant answer.

'Hush!' she told everyone, but the only sounds were the laboured breathing of rescuers and the occasional creaks and clatters of settling debris. She must have imagined Bert's voice because she was so desperate to hear it. Wishful thinking.

'Back to work,' someone called, 'but let's be careful. We don't want to dislodge rubble that'll fall on the very people we're trying to help, do we?'

The clearing work resumed, buckets from neighbouring houses being filled with bricks, mortar, broken slates and bits of wood and metal, before being passed from person to person in a chain. 'Careful of glass and sharp edges!' someone called.

Naomi flinched as some rafters were lifted from the site and the movement made debris slide in an avalanche. She prayed that neither Bert nor Bobby was beneath it.

Her fingers reached softness suddenly and her heartbeat quickened. Could it be Bert's jumper? She scraped dust and dirt away and felt near despair when she realized it was only a curtain. She eased it aside and got back to work.

'Here!' someone called, and she struggled to her feet only to see the caller's head shake. False alarm.

Naomi sank back down on to knees that were bruised and bloody and continued to dig with her fingers. Shouts and instructions crowded the air around her. Occasionally, she looked up to see who was calling and what was being moved – a broken bed, a crushed light fitting, a chair that was missing two legs . . . But mostly she dug and dug and dug . . .

Her fingers found softness again. At least, it felt like softness, though it was hard to be sure, given that her fingers were scraped and torn and stinging. She dug deeper. Yes, there was softness. Filthy, gritty, but soft. She dug deeper still and tried to clear a space. *Please don't let it be more curtains or a cushion or bedding . . .*

What colour was it? The dust had turned everything to grey but one of the people around her changed position, letting more light reach it, and Naomi saw that it was green. Bert had been wearing a jumper that was green. She worked harder, faster and revealed that it was wool. Knitted wool. 'Here!' she cried, her voice croaky from the dust she must have inhaled. 'I think they're here!'

Men came to help. So, too, did Suki, who must have returned from her errand to Foxfield to support Naomi and Bert. She gave Naomi a small but encouraging smile.

The cleared space grew bigger. Big enough for them to realize that Bert was lying on his side with his back to them.

Questions rent the air. 'Have they found Bert?'

'Have they found Bobby?'

'Are they all right?'

'Are they . . .?'

Naomi closed her ears to that last question, clinging to hope that both Bert and Bobby had survived.

'Now, now, Naomi, you've done your bit,' someone said, trying to coax her away. 'Let the rest of us help now.'

Naomi drew back but only a little, watching and praying as careful hands cleared more space. 'Bert's breathing,' someone called to her.

Thank heavens for that!

'And he's got Bobby with him,' someone else called. 'The lad's breathing, too.'

Enough rubble had been cleared to show that the little boy was cradled in Bert's arms, peeping out and looking frightened, confused and filthy, but showing no obvious signs of being badly hurt. Bert had protected him well.

The rescuers continued to work and the side of Bert's

much-loved face came into view. Yes! He was indeed breathing, though shallowly, and there was blood on his temple. With a grimace of pain and a great deal of effort, he ground out, 'Save the boy.'

Debris was cleared from Bert's arms and Bobby was lifted out, the movements clearly costing Bert more pain.

'Bobby!' the child's mother cried, and the medic carried him over to her.

'Come to the ambulance,' he said. 'I don't think the boy is injured. I need to make sure, though . . .'

'You next,' Naomi told Bert, wanting him to cling to whatever strength he had left.

The clearing work continued. Bert's hand came free and Naomi clutched it, raining kisses down on it. But now she could see that a great slab of wall had come down on his lower body. Had it crushed him?

She swallowed. Hard.

'I love you, beloved woman,' Bert got out, grimacing.

'I love you, too, beloved man,' Naomi told him. 'I'm looking forward to marrying you, so you'd better not think I'm going to let you malinger over a few injuries. I want you to walk up the aisle with me for our blessing, and then lead me in the first dance at our reception.'

'I need to tell you something. About—'

But Bert gasped as the heavy rubble was lifted from him.

His hand went limp. His eyes closed. And he spoke no more.

CHAPTER FIFTY-EIGHT

Ruby

'Look, Mum!' Timmy sat up straight in his seat and pointed through the bus window.

'What is it, Tim?' Ruby followed the direction of his arm and gasped. She wasn't the only one. Other passengers were letting out shocked noises, too, and pressing closer to the windows, the better to take in the scene outside.

'What happened?' Ruby asked the conductor. 'Do you know?'

'Well, miss, what I was told at the depot was that an earlier bus went into that house you can see. Swerved to avoid a motorbike, so I heard.'

'When was this?'

'A few hours ago now.'

'No one was hurt, I hope?'

'I believe it was quite serious, but I don't have complete information so I won't mislead you with guesswork. Looks as though the bus has been towed away and now they're shoring up what remains of the house.'

Passing by, Ruby saw that there were men at work with poles and wooden planks. The entire downstairs appeared to have been hollowed out and much of the upstairs and roof had caved in on top. She recognized some of the men: Mr Miles the grocer, Mr Weeks, Adam Potts . . .

The bus followed the curve of the road into the centre of the village. 'Come on, Tim,' Ruby said. 'We need to get off.'

The bus decanted them opposite the village green. Ruby stood for a moment, eager to find someone to reassure her that no one had been hurt but unsure whether to venture into a shop or run back to the shattered house. Old Jonah Kerrigan emerged from the post office. 'Just heard the news, have you?' he asked, and Ruby supposed she must be pale with shock.

'We came past on the bus. I was told another bus crashed into the house but I don't know any more.'

'It's Ted Newcross's house but he's all right. Shocked, of course. Who wouldn't be? But not a scratch on him. His grandson is all right, too, though he has a few bruises. Bert managed to keep him safe. Wrapped the boy in his arms, Bert did, and took all the damage on himself.'

'Damage?' A wave of dismay rippled through Ruby. 'Bert's been hurt?'

'I hate to be the bearer of bad news but, yes, I'm afraid he has.'

'Not badly hurt, though?'

'You saw the house,' Jonah answered.

Ruby had seen it. And she shuddered at the thought of the rubble that must have rained down on Bert if he'd been caught beneath it. 'He isn't . . .' Ruby swallowed. She couldn't say it, especially not in front of Timmy who was looking wide-eyed with worry. Bert was like a granddad to him.

'He was unconscious but alive when he was taken off to hospital, but I don't know more than that,' Jonah said. 'The whole village is holding its breath for news but Alice and Nurse Beth are down at the bookshop so you might get more information out of them.'

'Thank you,' Ruby said, and nodded to Timmy to walk on.

The bookshop was busy. Standing on the threshold Ruby saw some people who looked like walking wounded, and others with solemn faces who appeared to be present just to give comfort to each other.

In the middle of it all, Alice, Beth and Alice's father, Dr Lovell, were helping the wounded and those who were crying, while May Janicki and Janet Collins were handing round cups of tea. Alice spotted her. 'Ruby!'

She gave Phyllis Hutchings a reassuring pat on her arm and came over. 'You've heard about the accident?'

'We have,' Ruby said. 'About Bert . . .?'

'Naomi's with him at the hospital. We're hoping she'll telephone Victoria at Foxfield to let us know what the doctors say. Victoria has promised to come over and share the news as soon as that happens.'

Ruby nodded. 'Naomi must be . . . frantic.'

'Indeed. But we have to stay hopeful.' Alice's worry showed in her face but she was outwardly calm and controlled. A good person in a crisis. Naomi would need the support of Alice and everyone else if the worst happened.

Beth came over, too. 'Not the best homecoming for you, Ruby. Or you, Timmy.'

'No, but you all seem to be pulling together,' Ruby said.

'Matron gave me permission to come and help. We've had a few minor injuries from people who were on the bus and a lot more people needing to be in company. Can I fetch you a cup of tea?'

'Thanks, but unless there's something I can do to help, I should get back to the farm.'

'How was your visit home?' Alice asked.

Ruby shrugged. This wasn't the time to talk about her own affairs. But then another thought struck her. 'Oh,

243

heavens! Pearl's parents are coming today, aren't they? They're expecting to stay at Foxfield.'

'Pearl tried to telephone them to ask them to postpone the visit but they'd already set out so they'll be staying at The Linnets instead,' Alice said. 'A little cottage may not suit them as well as Naomi's house but it's the best we can do.'

How kind of Alice. 'What about food?' Ruby asked.

'Victoria is preparing a meal and she'll bring it over to The Linnets later.'

'You've thought of everything,' Ruby said, relieved.

'We've tried. I think Kate is struggling with Pearl, though.'

'I imagine so,' Ruby acknowledged. Pearl hadn't wanted her parents to visit even in the best of circumstances. And these were far from being the best of circumstances with the village in a tizzy. 'If there's nothing I can do here, I'll get off home,' she said again, and then paused before adding, 'We're not on the phone, though, so if there's news . . .'

'We'll try to get it to you as soon as possible,' Alice promised.

Ruby took Timmy's hand and they headed back outside. 'I hope Bert doesn't die,' Timmy said. 'He's a nice man, isn't he?'

'A very nice man,' Ruby confirmed, feeling desperately sad for Bert, Naomi and all of Churchwood.

'Might it help if I keep thinking about him and hoping he'll get better?' Timmy asked. 'I know we don't go to church much, but it'll be a bit like the praying Adam does, won't it?'

'You go right ahead, Tim. Think about Bert and pray for him, too. I'll do the same. If anyone deserves to get well again, it's Bert. Now let's walk a little faster. We may be needed to pour oil on troubled waters at the farm.'

CHAPTER FIFTY-NINE

Beth

It was by chance that Beth glanced through one of the bookshop windows just as Victoria was hastening along Churchwood Way. Oh, heavens. Was this tragic news approaching? Moving to intercept her, Beth passed by Alice and whispered in her ear, 'Victoria's here.'

Alice was a calm and capable person but still she paled in a way that suggested she too feared the worst. They slipped outside to meet Victoria so they could hear what she had to say in private and decide what was best to be done about it.

Victoria must have understood the looks on their faces. 'Bert's still alive,' she reassured them quickly. 'I telephoned the hospital and managed to speak to Naomi. I hope I didn't make a nuisance of myself but I couldn't bear knowing nothing at all. He's had surgery to relieve pressure on his brain, apparently. At least, that's how Naomi explained it. Does that make sense, Beth?'

'It does,' Beth confirmed. 'The brain can swell after it's received a blow so it can push against the skull. Surgery can relieve that pressure so there's no permanent damage.'

Alice nodded, as though it made sense to her. Which it probably did, given that she was a doctor's daughter.

'So he's going to be fine?' Victoria said. 'I didn't like to ask Naomi.'

'Hopefully,' Beth told her.

'But not necessarily.'

Beth hated to disappoint Victoria but she couldn't lie. 'I'm afraid it depends if the surgery was done soon enough and successfully enough.' Sometimes surgery saved patients' lives. Sometimes it didn't. And sometimes it kept patients alive but with permanent damage to their brains.

'We must stay hopeful,' Alice insisted. 'We won't help Bert, Naomi or anyone else if we fall to pieces.'

'Of course,' Beth agreed. 'Is Naomi coming home now?'

Victoria shook her head. 'At the moment she's refusing to leave Bert's side.'

That sounded like Naomi.

'I said I'd telephone the hospital again later. We can work out what we can do to help once we know more.'

It was a sensible plan.

'In the meantime,' Victoria continued, 'I've made a casserole for Pearl's parents, Alice. All it needs is to go into your oven for a couple of hours. I've also made them a fruit flan. When should I drop them round?'

'Anytime,' Alice told her. 'My father is here at the bookshop but the cottage isn't locked.'

'Suki is hunting for more tea for you all,' Victoria said. 'Hopefully, she'll be here soon. I'll head off home now. Just in case there's a phone call from Naomi.'

'I'll tell my father the news,' Alice said.

Victoria set off to return to Foxfield, while Beth and Alice headed back to the bookshop. Beth was about to follow Alice through the door when she saw two figures approaching. One was Mr Miles, the grocer, who looked unsteady. He had a handkerchief wrapped around his hand as though it were injured. Supporting him was Adam.

Beth's heartbeat had quickened at the sight of Adam. She waited for the men to draw level. 'Another patient for you, Beth,' Adam said. 'Mr Miles has a deep cut that needs cleaning and possibly a stitch or two, though you'll know better than I what it needs.'

Adam's smile was self-deprecating. Beth loved his modesty. She loved the warmth in his eyes, too.

Alice must have heard them talking because she reappeared at the bookshop door. 'Come on in, Mr Miles,' she said. 'We'll soon have you shipshape again.'

Mr Miles went towards Alice, and Beth turned back to Adam. 'How are things at Mr Newcross's house?'

'I think it's as stable as we can make it for the moment. We need experts to assess what needs to be done in the way of repairs. A surveyor, a builder . . . Meanwhile, we're boarding it up to keep out curious children. I'm sure you don't want more patients.'

'Not if we can help it,' Beth agreed. 'How is Mr Newcross?'

'Still in shock. Luckily, his daughter has taken him to stay with her until his house is repaired. We're worried about his neighbours. The houses on each side of Mr Newcross's look stable enough, but who knows? It seems foolish to take chances so the Robertsons are going to stay with Mrs Robertson's brother in Barton and I've invited the Smiths to stay at the vicarage. I'll be going there now to help Mrs Harris to get a room ready for them.'

'That's kind of you,' Beth said, but Adam merely shrugged because kindness came naturally to him.

Beth told him about Victoria's telephone call.

'Poor Bert and poor Naomi,' he said. 'They're going to need all our support. Which brings me to something else I'd like to say. Thank you, Beth. It was a lucky day for Churchwood when you arrived in the village.'

'Churchwood is my home now,' Beth said. 'I feel part of it.'

'Me too,' Adam said.

For a moment neither of them spoke. She wondered if he was feeling the same pulse of attraction as she. The same fizz of potential for romance.

But then Wilf Phipps appeared at the bookshop door. 'I thought I heard your voice, Adam. How are things at Ted's house? I wish I could help.'

Wilf was growing frail. 'We've done as much as we can for the time being,' Adam assured him. 'I know you'd have helped if you could.'

Wilf nodded sadly. 'What a pickle,' he said. It was a pickle indeed.

A light footstep behind her had Beth turning. 'Hello, Suki. I see you got some tea.' Suki was holding a packet.

'I'd better get it inside.' She gestured towards the bookshop door.

Beth smiled at her and Adam did too. Then Adam said, 'I'd better get on.' He reached out and touched Beth's arm. 'Thanks again,' he said, and headed for the vicarage.

Beth watched him go only to realize she wasn't the only one who was watching him. Suki had stepped into the bookshop after Wilf, but lingered in the shadows just beyond the door, her gaze following Adam's retreat with unconcealed longing before she roused herself and continued inside.

Beth was no longer in any doubt. Suki loved Adam, too. Oh, dear.

Sighing, Beth replayed the moment of apparent intimacy *she'd* just shared with Adam. But was it the intimacy of early romance as far as Adam was concerned, or mere friendship? Beth had no way of knowing. But what was she doing, standing here thinking of her own hopes and desires when the cloud of tragedy hovered over the village? There was work to be done.

She returned to the bookshop and busied herself helping Dr Lovell clean and dress Mr Miles's hand wound. But a thought came into her mind and wouldn't shift. She'd called Churchwood her home and that was exactly how she felt about it. At the moment. But what if Adam didn't want her? If he married someone else?

Suki? Unlikely, in Beth's opinion, though she could be wrong. Suki was a lovely girl and full of potential but still so young. Nancy seemed a more likely candidate. Attractive, vivid, hard-working, funny – and a good person. It was all too easy to picture her sharing Adam's life. She'd be more outgoing than him. Full of liveliness when Adam was quiet and thoughtful at times. But the contrast could work, each bringing out the best in the other. Suki, Nancy, Beth. They couldn't all be made happy. Beth wouldn't begrudge his happiness if he chose another – she loved Adam and was fond of Suki and Nancy, too – but could she bear to stay in Churchwood where his presence would be a constant reminder of her disappointment? Could she live with the hurt?

Enough of that, though. This really wasn't the time nor the place for dwelling on her own problems.

CHAPTER SIXTY

Naomi

Naomi sat in the chair she'd been given and stared down at Bert's face. It was roughly hewn and lined with age but she couldn't have loved it more. She held his hand, too. His big, paw-like hand that was calloused from hard work but could touch her so gently.

How pale he was for such an outdoors type of man. He looked as though his skin had been turned to parchment.

Bending, she kissed his hand for what felt like the hundredth time. 'Don't leave me, Bert. Please don't leave me,' she begged.

A nurse put her head around the door.

'I'm staying here,' Naomi told her firmly.

The nurse nodded. Naomi had said the same thing many times over. Staying in the hospital outside of visiting hours might not be allowed but just now Naomi cared nothing for rules. She cared for Bert.

It wasn't as though she was disturbing any other patients. Bert was in a room of his own.

The nurse disappeared but returned minutes later, placing a tray beside Naomi. 'Tea and toast,' she said.

Naomi blinked back tears. Kindness was overwhelming. 'Thank you.'

The nurse left again, patting Naomi's shoulder in passing,

and Naomi picked up the teacup. The tea was welcome. She was less enthusiastic about the toast since her appetite had abandoned her, but it would help no one – least of all Bert – if she were to grow weak and perhaps even fall ill. She had to be strong for Bert's sake. Besides, it would be a poor repayment for the nurse's kindness if Naomi didn't eat it.

The toast tasted like nothing. An unwelcome foreign body in her mouth. But she chewed it and swallowed it down. How strange she felt. Utterly exhausted, yet fizzing with tension.

'Mr Makepiece received multiple injuries with varying degrees of severity,' a doctor had explained. 'His hips and legs are very badly bruised – I understand a slab of wall fell on them – but, miraculously, no bones were broken. Not even the small bones in his feet.'

'He'll be able to walk again?'

'Eventually. All being well.'

'But all isn't well, is it?' Naomi had asked. The doctor's expression was grave.

'It's the head injury that's causing us concern.'

'It only bled a little bit,' Naomi said.

'Perhaps so. A few stitches have taken care of the cut. It's the blow that caused damage. To the brain.'

Naomi had felt her strength draining away at that. 'But he was talking. After the accident, I mean. He was speaking normally. Well, not normally, exactly. He was in pain. But what he was saying . . . It made sense. His thoughts were clear.'

'Sometimes it happens that way,' the doctor had told her. 'A person can be lucid immediately after a blow to the head.'

He'd explained about the swelling and the surgery. 'Now

251

it's a case of waiting to see, firstly if Mr Makepiece survives, and secondly . . . Well, we'll come to that later, if necessary.'

To the possibility of brain damage. Permanent brain damage.

If Bert woke now, would he know her? Would he even know himself?

Whatever happened, Naomi would love him and care for him. But oh, it would be too cruel if the essence of Bert was gone – if they lost all the love and companionship they'd shared over the last years!

'When will he wake?'

The doctor had shrugged. 'It's impossible to say, I'm afraid.'

With that he had left her, and Naomi kissed Bert's hand again. 'Come back to me, darling man. My heart is breaking, and I need you. I can't imagine life without you.'

CHAPTER SIXTY-ONE

Ruby

'Thank goodness you're back!' Pearl declared as Ruby and Timmy entered the kitchen to find Pearl and Kate there.

'It's good to see you,' Kate confirmed. 'Though I'm afraid you've come back to a dreadful situation with Bert. Pearl was down in the village an hour or so ago but all she heard was that he'd been taken to hospital unconscious.'

'That's what I just heard,' Ruby said. Ernie opened the kitchen door and glared at them. 'Are any of you bothering to get back to work today?'

'When we're ready,' Kate told him. 'Which isn't now.'

He went off grumbling.

'I believe your parents are going to be staying with Alice tonight,' Ruby said to Pearl.

'Yes, and Victoria is going to take them something to eat. The plan is to give them time to settle in and eat in more civilized surroundings than this dump. I'm supposed to drive down in the cart to join them.'

'Fred isn't going with you?'

Kate answered for her. 'The idea is to ease them into Churchwood gently.'

She didn't need to explain that charmless Fred wouldn't help with that.

'Fred doesn't want to go anyway,' Pearl said, which was

no surprise to Ruby. Fred would hate having to be on his best behaviour in a house he probably considered to be grand. Not that The Linnets was large, but every house was grand compared to ramshackle Brimbles Farm.

'Do you think I should change my clothes before I go?' Pearl asked.

It was a sign of how very nervous she was that Pearl should be thinking of appearances. She was in her usual land girl outfit of none-too-clean breeches, limp shirt and a jumper that had holes in the elbows. She'd kicked off her boots and one of her big toes poked out from a hole in a sock.

'Getting changed might be a good idea,' Ruby said. 'To give your parents a good impression, I mean.'

'I agree,' Kate said. 'But really, Pearl, you can think about that later. Just now Ruby needs to sit down and have a cup of tea after her journey.'

'Eh? Oh, crikey. You're right. Sorry, Ruby. It's just . . .'

'I understand,' Ruby said. 'You were dreading your parents coming even when the village was ticking along as usual. Now it's in turmoil . . .'

'Mmm,' Pearl said, looking grateful for Ruby's sympathy.

Kate put the kettle on for tea. She had to be curious about Ruby's trip home but, as though she sensed it had been difficult, she asked nothing personal about it.

'How was London looking?' she asked Timmy instead, and he told her about the bombed and boarded-up buildings they'd seen, the numerous uniforms of service personnel and the war posters exhorting them to 'Dig for Victory' by growing their own fruit and vegetables, to 'Keep Mum' so careless talk wouldn't be heard by enemy spies, to salvage metal, paper and even animal bones to help with the war effort, and to urge women to 'Come into the Factories' to help the war effort still further.

254

At six o'clock, Pearl clomped her way upstairs.

When she returned a few minutes later she'd removed the green jumper but it was hard to gauge whether she'd put on a fresh blouse since all three of her blouses were limp from wear and creased from being stuffed into the closet. The breeches had also been removed and in their place Pearl wore a brown skirt that her mother had probably bought her years ago in a vain attempt to feminize her daughter. It was badly misshapen – doubtless from suffering the same poor treatment as the rest of Pearl's clothes – and the fawn socks and enormous brown lace-up shoes she wore beneath it didn't improve matters.

'I told you I'd look a fool,' she said.

'You look fine,' Ruby insisted.

'Yes, fine,' Kate agreed, though Ruby suspected they both knew they were stretching the truth.

'Good luck,' Kate and Ruby called as Pearl let herself out through the kitchen door to harness Pete, the ageing pony, to the cart, Kate having persuaded her that it might be wiser to greet her parents looking fresh and tidy instead of in a sweat from the long walk.

'I'd better shut the chickens up for the night.' Kate patted Ruby's arm in passing. 'When you're ready,' she said, meaning they'd talk about London when Ruby felt comfortable doing so.

Timmy went with Kate, flapping his arms in imitation of the chickens and making *cluck, cluck* sounds.

Alone, Ruby's thoughts drifted elsewhere, fixing first on Bert and Naomi. She pictured Bert lying pale and still in a bed while Naomi sat beside him, fretting with anxiety. The image made Ruby's heart feel flooded with sympathy.

She wasn't sure what she believed about a god. All that churchy kneeling and chanting wasn't for her, but when she'd mentioned this to Adam – who never pushed religion on to anyone – he'd replied with, 'Spirituality comes in all sorts of guises, Ruby. In quiet moments when we lie in bed, in the smile of loved ones, when we walk in fields and woods . . .'

This had struck a chord with her because there were moments in her life when she walked outside and felt thankful, though she couldn't have said who or what she was thanking.

Of course, there were other moments when she felt angry instead. The circumstances of Timmy's birth and the times when she'd seen unkindness dealt out to other children who were born out of wedlock had been among them. 'I don't mean to insult your god, Adam,' she'd said, 'but I've had to shift for myself for most of my life. I wasn't aware of him helping me.'

'You found the strength to shift for yourself, Ruby.'

Because God had given her that strength? Ruby had shaken her head. She'd felt untouched by inner peace or anything along those lines. All she remembered was struggle and hurt. And yet . . .

She'd rather liked Timmy's idea of thoughts or prayers or whatever else a person wished to call them. There could be no harm in them, anyway. She sent up a silent prayer for Bert and Naomi. 'If you know anything at all,' she told the deity, 'it's that these are good people who do good in the world. They deserve your blessing.'

Doubtless, preaching to God about what he should and shouldn't do wasn't a typical way of praying, but Ruby couldn't help herself.

Her thoughts turned next to her visit to London. Colin Street, where her parents lived . . .

*

Mrs Turner had opened the door to Ruby's knock. The past year had added more lines to her face, increasing the dour look that was her standard expression. 'You'd better come in,' she said.

They stepped into the room they called the front parlour though it was the only parlour the house boasted, the back room being a kitchen with a small wooden table where the family ate their meals. 'I assume you've eaten already,' Mrs Turner added.

It was just as well Kate had packed a picnic for them to eat on the train. Ruby was glad that a small slice of pie remained so she could slip it to Timmy later. 'Yes, but we'd love a cup of tea,' Ruby said.

'We don't usually have tea at this time but I suppose I can manage a pot.'

Ruby nodded to her father who glanced up from his paper to say, 'I hope the boy hasn't trodden dirt into the house.'

'I'm sure he hasn't,' Ruby told him. 'It's a dry day so there's no mud.'

Mrs Turner busied herself with the kettle and tea things and Mr Turner returned his attention to his newspaper. 'There's no sign of this war ending,' he said, which Ruby took to be a conversation opener.

She gestured Timmy to a chair and took one herself. 'It's a pity, isn't it? We have a military hospital not far from us in Churchwood and it's terrible to see the injuries some of the servicemen have suffered.'

'Mrs Pringle's youngest boy died at Tobruk,' Mrs Turner reported.

Clifford Pringle had once chased Ruby with a worm but she bore him no grudge. 'I'm sorry to hear that. How is Mrs Pringle coping?'

'Life is full of disappointments and at least he died doing his duty.'

Was her mother suggesting that Ruby hadn't done her duty because she'd chosen a different life from them and had a child when unmarried? Probably, but surely she was doing her duty now with her land girl work? 'We brought you some produce from the farm,' she said, beginning to empty a bag she'd brought. There were carrots and potatoes. Green beans and tomatoes. Ruby had scrubbed them all clean.

'Not on the table, please,' her mother said. 'Put them in the veg basket.'

Ruby did as she was told. Busy with the tea-making, her mother had barely glanced at the produce but, once she did, she'd see how fresh and luscious it was. The tea was brought to the table. 'It isn't as strong as I'd like,' she said.

'It's difficult with rationing, isn't it?' Ruby said.

The visit hadn't got off to the best start but one way or another Ruby had been determined to make it successful. Somehow.

Now, Ruby startled as Timmy rushed into the kitchen. 'I found an egg!' he announced, holding it up for her approval. 'Pearl must have missed it earlier when she collected the other eggs.'

'I think she's in a bit of a tizzy over her parents coming,' Ruby explained, and her thoughts wandered again, this time to how Pearl was getting on with them.

She soon had her answer. Pearl returned surprisingly early, freed Pete from his harness to turn him out into his field and then trudged into the kitchen. 'My mother took one look at me in this skirt and socks and announced she had a headache. She's lying down at Alice's. All I got from

my father was one of his tight-lipped grimaces. I've said
I'll collect them and bring them here in the morning. Isn't
that something to look forward to?'

CHAPTER SIXTY-TWO

Naomi

A visitor arrived. Alice. She scraped lightly on the door and put her head around. 'Tell me to leave if this is a bad time,' she said.

'No, come in,' Naomi invited, 'though I've no news to share because Bert's condition hasn't changed.' She'd sat with him all night.

'Bert's alive. That means there's hope,' Alice said. She pulled up another chair and began to unpack the bag she'd brought. 'I called at Foxfield and Victoria gave me these fresh clothes for you. I also called at Bert's market garden. There's a rota of people looking after Elizabeth and also the growing beds and greenhouse. William knows all about the orders so he's giving advice from school – he says he'll be in Churchwood just as soon as possible – and Kate and Pearl are helping with deliveries, both being drivers. You can imagine how Ernie Fletcher feels about that but, frankly, no one cares about his opinion any more.'

Alice brought another package from her bag. 'I thought it might be nice for Bert to have a few cuttings from home. Fragrant herbs he can smell even if he can't yet respond. There's lavender, mint, sage, rosemary . . . You might want to hold them beneath his nose so he breathes in the scents. You could touch them to his hands, too.'

'Good idea,' Naomi said. Then her face crumpled. 'Alice, I'm so afraid.'

Alice's arms moved around her and held her close. 'I know. We're all afraid. But, like I said, there's every reason to hope.'

Naomi cried for a while but then drew back. 'Sorry.'

'You've nothing to apologize for, but you do need to keep your strength up. Have you slept at all?'

'I've dozed a little.' And felt terribly guilty about it. What if Bert had stirred? What if he'd needed her?

'You can't go without sleep indefinitely,' Alice pointed out.

'I know.'

'But you're afraid to leave Bert. I understand that. Why don't I sit here while you sleep now? I know you won't go to a hotel but you could rest here. I can wake you instantly if there's any change?'

'I won't be able to sleep,' Naomi said, but Alice was so eager to help that Naomi hadn't the heart to keep resisting.

'Put this around you,' Alice said, producing a blanket from her bag.

Naomi settled in her chair, her head resting on a cushion. She wouldn't sleep, but if sitting like this would please a dear friend who was trying to help her . . .

When she woke Naomi was startled. 'What? What?' she said, flustered and unsure what she was actually asking.

'There's been no change,' Alice told her, and Naomi's heart began to return to a more normal rate. She looked at Bert. He was still dreadfully pale. Still unmoving.

'How long was I asleep?'

'A couple of hours. You needed it.'

Naomi dragged her hands across her worn and doubtless pasty face. She could feel that her hair was dishevelled.

Dirty. She needed a bath but she couldn't – wouldn't – leave Bert.

'I've brought you fresh clothes,' Alice said then. 'Some washing things, too. There's a bathroom just along the corridor. I checked with a nurse and she promised to turn a blind eye if you want to wash and change there.'

Naomi looked at Bert. What if something happened while she was gone?

'I'll call if you need to get back in a hurry,' Alice promised.

Naomi heaved herself up and went to the bathroom. It felt good to dip her hands into cool, clean water and splash it over her face. She washed thoroughly and changed into clean underwear, stockings and blouse. Then she brushed her hair in front of the mirror. She'd never looked older. More careworn. But appearances didn't matter just now.

She hastened back to Bert.

'No change,' Alice told her again. 'Now, eat this picnic Victoria packed for you.'

'I'll save it for later. The nurses have been giving me toast.'

'You need more than toast.' Alice uncovered a sandwich, a slice of fruit pie and an apple. 'Soup, too,' she said, taking out a thermos flask.

'How kind of Victoria. How kind of you as well.'

Carrying a bag made heavy with supplies for Naomi must have been difficult for Alice, but she was the sort of person who'd walk through fire to help a person in need. Again, the kindness had tears shimmering in Naomi's eyes but this time she managed to blink them back. She nibbled at the sandwich. 'Tasty,' she said, though she could have been eating cold ashes from the fire.

'How is everyone at home?' she asked.

'Worried about you and Bert, of course. Apart from

262

that . . . Well, Pearl's parents arrived yesterday and stayed at The Linnets.'

'I'm sorry I couldn't host them. To be honest, they went clean out of my mind.'

'It was no bother,' Alice assured her. 'I can't say I particularly warmed to them, but they'd had a long journey so perhaps they weren't at their best. I left them having breakfast with my father so I could come and see you. Mr Newcross is staying with his daughter. Both he and little Bobby are well physically, though I'm sure they're still shocked. Churchwood has been rallying round as always.'

'I hope everyone is going about their business as normal. The bookshop, the children's club . . . I'd hate to think people felt unable to go because of what's happened. Bert would hate it, too.'

'I'll pass that along,' Alice said.

Naomi was about to thank Alice when a doctor appeared. 'If you wouldn't mind?' he said, in a hint that they should leave, and for an agonizing few minutes they were forced to wait in the corridor while Bert was examined, Alice clutching Naomi's hand in support.

But the doctor's report was simple. 'No change.'

CHAPTER SIXTY-THREE

Ruby

'Well?' Kenny asked when they managed a stroll together on Sunday morning. Work on the farm didn't stop on Sundays but it was a little more relaxed. 'How were your parents?'

'Awful,' she admitted.

'Awful how?'

'Unwelcoming. Disapproving. And not just of me. Timmy couldn't have been sweeter to them but they just weren't interested. I'm always going to be the daughter who let them down and Timmy is always going to be the shameful family secret.' She'd stuck it out for two nights, hoping her parents would thaw in the face of Timmy's merry good manners, but she'd wasted her time.

'Did you ask if they'll be coming to the wedding?'

'I did,' Ruby told him, and her mind returned to that conversation.

Her parents had exchanged looks and Ruby had felt her spirits slide as though they'd mounted a hillside, reached the top and set off down the other side.

'This place you live,' her mother had begun.

'Churchwood,' Ruby had reminded them.

'It's quite some distance away.'

'Not so very far. Thirty miles or so. And I can probably

264

manage to get you a bed for the night so you don't have to travel back the same day.'

'There's your father's work, too.'

'We'll be marrying on a Saturday. Dad will only lose a few hours of work then and none at all on the Sunday.'

'It's quite an undertaking. We'll have to think about it.'

Ruby had left it there.

But when she'd prepared to set off home her mother had said, 'This wedding. Let's hope it goes well.'

Which meant they wouldn't be there to see whether it went well or not. It would be too much bother for them.

In Churchwood, Ruby had grown used to hugging people. She'd made no attempt to hug her parents, though, or even kiss their cheeks. 'Come along, Timmy,' she'd said. 'It's time we were leaving.'

'Humph,' Kenny said, when he'd heard the sorry tale. He wasn't comfortable talking about feelings but he was trying his best. 'I suppose you're no worse off than before,' he suggested.

Except that she'd allowed herself to hope for better and disappointment tasted bitter.

'I still love you,' Kenny reminded her.

'I know.' Ruby smiled at him.

Despite still feeling the sting of rejection, she decided to tell the rest of the household about the visit, too. Except for Ernie, of course, who wouldn't have been interested.

'Your parents are fools,' Kate declared staunchly.

'I'll say!' That was Pearl.

Kate hadn't finished yet. 'They're the ones who are missing out on having a lovely daughter and an utterly delightful grandson in their lives,' she said.

Kenny nodded agreement, wrapping an arm around Ruby. 'That's right.'

Even Vinnie had something to say. 'They sound like a pair of moaning minnies to me. You're better off without them.'

Ruby was grateful to them all. 'Let's hope you're more successful with your parents, Pearl,' she said.

'That would be expecting a miracle.' Pearl looked glum, but perhaps she was letting her parents' irritation at her refusal to conform to their image of femininity blind her to their love and desire to see her happy.

Whatever the rights and wrongs of Pearl's feelings, Ruby threw herself into making the visit of Pearl's parents as successful as possible.

'I don't know what all the fuss is about,' Kenny grumbled when Ruby announced that all work boots had to be left outside the kitchen door today so mud wouldn't be trodden all over the kitchen floor, which she intended to sweep and mop as best she could.

Luckily, Kenny complied with the order despite his protestations.

Ernie was a tougher nut to crack. 'It's my house and if I want to wear boots indoors then I will,' he said, scowling.

'Very well,' Ruby told him. 'But the more mess you make, the more time we'll spend clearing it up instead of working.'

'Your choice, Ernie,' Kate added.

It wasn't in Ernie's nature to concede defeat openly. He went out muttering surly curses but when he returned a little later he left his boots outside the door, revealing filthy socks. Ernie didn't excel at personal hygiene.

Vinnie also resisted the order about the boots. 'It's a farmhouse,' he pointed out. 'There's always mud on farms.'

'But it's best left in the fields,' Ruby had told him. 'Of course, if you'd rather I spent my time clearing up after you than making scones . . .'

'Scones?'

'Mmm.'

'I suppose I could leave my boots off . . .'

Pearl had told them last night that her parents had specified that they only wanted a light luncheon. As well as scones, sandwiches were planned – cucumber and tomato from Kate's kitchen garden, egg from the Brimbles Farm chickens, a little rationed cheese . . . Kate had also produced home-grown lettuces and radishes, as well as rhubarb for a fruit tart. It was to be a light meal but still as splendid as they could manage.

There was little they could do about the dilapidated house and the outside toilet but Ruby and Kate made sure they were clean and tried to disguise the shabbiness with jars and jugs of greenery brought in from around the farm. In an attempt to show Fred in a good light, they also placed some of his woodcarvings on the windowsills and fireplace. Meanwhile, the chipped and mismatched crockery was hidden away, and tea was to be served using china and silverware borrowed from Alice. Kate had fetched it that morning before Pearl's parents were up.

Fred spent most of the morning hiding out in the barn after whining that he was marrying Pearl, a farm labourer, instead of snooty Mr and Mrs Ambrose Grimes of The Hollies, and if he was good enough for Pearl then he couldn't care less what her parents thought of him. 'It isn't as though we're ever likely to see much of them considering we work here on the farm while they go to cocktail parties and such,' he argued.

Ruby knew that he was secretly terrified of being judged an unsuitable husband for Pearl. He was trying to lock that terror up inside himself but it was finding its way out in the form of crankiness.

He didn't possess a suit but he was nagged into the shirt and trousers he'd worn for Kate's wedding. Wheelchair or false legs? No one dared to ask that question for fear of Fred snapping back at them, but he supplied the answer anyway.

'I look like a drunken sailor on those legs.' He was still getting used to them, though he'd been warned that he'd always walk stiffly and lurch from side to side a little. 'I'm a cripple so they might as well get used to seeing me in my wheelchair. If they don't like it, they can lump it.'

Ruby winced when he talked of being a cripple. Kate, too. But there was nothing to gain by trying yet again to persuade him to be less brutal about his disability.

Pearl went off to fetch her parents in the trap and Kate and Ruby insisted that Fred, Kenny and Vinnie should be ready in the kitchen to welcome the arrivals. Fred spent the wait complaining that he was wasting time he could have spent carving something that might earn him a shilling or two. But, again, it was doubtless his nerves that were talking. Time and again he ran a finger around the inside of his shirt collar as though it were throttling him and swallowed hard as though his Adam's apple had doubled in size.

With the food prepared and the kettle filled with water for tea, Ruby stood at the side of the kitchen window as a lookout, ready to alert them all as soon as the cart came into sight. 'Oh, dear,' Ruby murmured, watching through the kitchen window as the cart drove into the farmyard.

Pearl was looking stiff and tight-lipped. Her usual outdoor complexion had given way to pallor, except for her large nose which looked even ruddier than normal in contrast. As for her parents, Mrs Grimes was wearing a smart coat and hat but sat with her handbag clutched on her lap as though she were trying to protect it from contamination.

Mr Grimes wore a suit and tie that looked more appropriate to a plush London office than a visit to a farm.

Pearl jumped down from the cart with so little ladylike grace that her mother winced and her father shook his head in disapproval.

'Do you want help in getting down, Mother?' Pearl asked.

'I think your father is the best person to assist me, thank you.'

'Snooty madam,' Ruby whispered to Kate, who was watching the scene unfold at her side.

Mr Grimes got down and turned to help his wife alight. Then they stood exchanging looks of distaste as they stared around the farmyard and up at the house.

'Pearl's forgotten to bring them inside!' Ruby said, as Pearl tugged Pete and the cart towards the barn. 'You'd better get out there, Kate.'

Kate squared her shoulders and stepped outside. She was wearing breeches and a shirt but they were clean and pressed in honour of the occasion. Not that Kate ever looked less than lovely, whatever she wore. Tall and slender, with gorgeous auburn hair which she wore in a braid down her back when she was working, she also had a beautiful face with clear, fresh skin, curving cheeks and clever, dark eyes. Surely the Grimeses would warm to her?

'It's a pity Leo can't be here,' Ruby had commented earlier, because Kate's dashing flight lieutenant husband would surely have impressed Pearl's parents.

'He can't get away from the base,' Kate had told her.

Now Kate approached the Grimeses alone, smiling and offering a hand. 'Welcome to Brimbles Farm. I'm Kate Kinsella, formerly Fletcher. My father owns the farm.'

Mrs Grimes studied Kate's hand — checking for dirt? and then shook it. Limply, Ruby suspected.

Mr Grimes gave it a more businesslike squeeze but there was no friendliness in his expression.

'I hope you've recovered after your journey?' Kate asked.

Ruby couldn't catch what Mr Grimes said in reply but it looked like, 'Humph.'

'Do come inside,' Kate invited, gesturing for them to go ahead of her to the kitchen door. 'I won't embarrass Pearl by saying this in front of her, but she's a much-valued member of our household. She works incredibly hard to put food on Britain's tables and we're all very fond of her, too.'

'Her name is Gertrude,' Mrs Grimes pointed out.

'Of course. But Pearl is her preferred nickname and it's an appropriate one since she's a treasure. You must be terribly proud of her.'

Ouch, Ruby thought. Kate knew the Grimeses were far from proud of Pearl but she was sticking up for her friend and Ruby determined to do the same.

Opening the kitchen door, she beamed her best smile. 'Hello, Mr and Mrs Grimes. I'm Ruby Turner, another land girl. I met your daughter during training and that was a lucky day for me, I can tell you. I was so pleased when we were posted here together. There's no one I'd rather work with than Pearl.'

'Gertrude,' Mrs Grimes corrected.

She hadn't looked over-impressed by Kate but she looked positively disgusted by Ruby and so did her husband. It was Ruby's dyed fair hair and bright-red lipstick that offended them, she supposed, and also her voice with its echoes of cockney London. They thought her common and far beneath them on the social scale.

The obvious contempt stung her. Kenny and Kate must have noticed it, too, because she heard swift intakes of breath from each of them. Kenny took a step forward but

Ruby put out a hand to hold him back while deterring Kate from interfering with a hard stare. If anyone was going to defend Ruby, it would be Ruby herself. For the moment, she was going to let the insult pass, since an outbreak of open hostilities would help no one, least of all Pearl.

That would change if they upset darling Timmy by looking down on him when he got home from the village where he was helping old Jonah Kerrigan to tidy his garden, but first she'd try to keep the peace.

There was no sign of Pearl. She was supposed to introduce her parents to Fred but, probably, she'd lost her nerve and was skulking in the barn. Ruby sent Kate a nod that encouraged her to take over again.

'May I introduce my brother, Fred? Pearl's fiancé?' Kate said.

Fred nodded a mute greeting. Doubtless, his nerves were suffering, too, but Ruby still gave his wheelchair a small kick to prompt him to do better.

The hint was lost on him. He glowered up at her. 'Why did you . . .?' Ruby glared back and the message finally got through. 'Oh,' he said. 'It's – um – a pleasure to meet you.' He sounded like a badly rehearsed actor regurgitating lines that had been drilled into him but which he was in danger of forgetting. He offered a hand which the Grimeses took turns at shaking with pursed lips. Fred hadn't made a good impression.

'And this is my fiancé, Kenny,' Ruby said.

'My eldest brother,' Kate explained.

Kenny stepped forward and shook the Grimses' hands but with a glower that suggested a threatening growl was just below the surface. Pearl's parents continued to look unimpressed and the introduction of Vinnie wasn't going to help.

271

'Afternoon,' he said, with an inane grin, and Ruby saw Mr Grimes's lips actually curl downwards.

Vinnie was hardly a fine specimen of humankind but he didn't deserve to be treated with disdain just for his existence.

'Your father?' Mr Grimes asked Kate.

'He's out on the farm. I'm sure you can appreciate that farms are busy places.'

Apparently not. Mr Grimes and his wife looked displeased by the neglect, though everyone else was relieved that Ernie wasn't there since he could only make a bad visit worse.

Where on earth was Pearl?

The kitchen door opened and there she was. At almost six feet in height, Pearl was hard to miss but just now she looked as though she wished she could make herself invisible. 'You've met everyone, then,' she said, obviously assuming that it hadn't gone well. Which it hadn't.

'It's lovely to meet your parents,' Kate said gamely, but Pearl's attention was on Fred.

If she was hoping to see a sign that he'd made some sort of connection with the Grimeses, she was doomed to be disappointed. Fred sat hunched in his wheelchair, looking down at his lap.

'I'll serve the lunch,' Ruby said, and everyone sat down at the table.

'You weren't wearing your engagement ring last night, Pearl,' Mrs Grimes said.

'I don't wear it when I'm working in case I lose it, and I don't always remember to put it back on.'

'May we see it now?'

Oh dear. Kate wasn't wearing her magnificent emerald and diamond engagement ring but she still wore a gold wedding band. Ruby was wearing her little garnet ring, which was modest in the extreme but still more likely to impress Pearl's parents than the ring Fred had given her.

'Most girls I know enjoy showing off their rings,' Mrs Grimes added.

Pearl dug in her pocket for her ring and slipped it on. 'Here,' she said, thrusting out her hand.

Mrs Grimes frowned and looked at her husband, who frowned too.

'Is that thing made of *wood*?'

'It is, and it's perfect considering Fred works with wood.' Pearl's tone was defensive.

'He makes beautiful woodcarvings,' Ruby said. 'Don't you, Fred?'

He only shrugged.

'All the carvings you see in this room are Fred's,' Kate said, her voice full of enthusiasm. 'They're beautiful, aren't they? Fred sells them locally and also through a gift shop in St Albans. It's a new venture so he's hoping more gift shops will sell them in the future.'

'Is this how you earn your living, young man?' Mr Grimes said to Fred. 'Is this how you expect to support my daughter?'

'I don't need supporting. I work,' Pearl protested.

'But after you're married . . .' her mother said.

'Kate is married and she still works,' Pearl pointed out.

Mr Grimes showed exasperation. 'Perhaps so, but there's a war on so life is a little different from usual. The normal conventions have relaxed. Even your sister is volunteering with the Women's Royal Voluntary Service. She's learning first aid, for one thing. But when peace comes, life will return to normal. I'm sure Mrs . . . Kinsella, did you say?' He looked at Kate, who nodded, before continuing with,

273

'I'm sure Mrs Kinsella's husband won't want her working on a farm once the war is over.'

'We haven't decided what will happen then,' Kate said. 'But my husband respects women as equals. He isn't the sort of man who'll force me into a situation because some outdated convention dictates it.'

Clearly, Mr Grimes *was* that sort of man. He scowled at Kate as though suspecting her of being some sort of rabid revolutionary and addressed Pearl again. 'There may be children to feed and educate. To accommodate, too.' He glanced around the shabby kitchen in distaste as though it was unthinkable that a grandchild of his should ever be brought up in such a hovel.

Pearl only sulked so her father turned back to Fred. 'We need to talk about your prospects, young man.'

Fred's eyes widened like those of a startled horse. 'I don't have any prospects,' he said, unhelpfully.

Mr Grimes ran a hand through his thinning hair and made an obvious effort to control his rising temper. 'My wife had a long journey on trains and buses yesterday. She isn't used to travelling in that way and it must have tired her.'

Taking the hint that refreshments were required, Ruby brought the teapot to the table and began to pour it into the cups that had been set out in readiness. Kate brought the plates of food and the salad bowl. Mrs Grimes glanced over them and sighed regretfully. 'Luncheon used to be my favourite meal of the day but it isn't the same with wartime rationing, is it?'

Ruby resisted the impulse to snatch the food back from these ungrateful people.

Matters didn't improve when Ernie walked in. 'Why did no one tell me that lunch was ready?' he complained.

Because they'd all hoped he'd stay far away, of course. Ruby had planned to set some food aside for him to eat once Pearl's parents had left.

He didn't bother removing his boots or washing his hands but sat at the table and crammed some food into his mouth without waiting until the guests had made their choices. He glanced at the Grimeses and then nodded towards Pearl. 'You're her folks, I suppose,' he said, chomping on his food. He didn't tell them they were welcome because as far as he was concerned visitors were never welcome.

He saw Ruby was offering him tea in a china cup. 'What's this? Where's my own cup?' he demanded. His usual cup was a dented metal mug.

He must have realized they'd borrowed the china for the Grimeses' sake because he rolled his eyes, took the cup and slurped some tea. Then he poked a finger at Mr Grimes. 'I'll say one thing for that girl of yours. She isn't a bad worker. Clumsy as an elephant, but not a bad worker.'

Not knowing that any praise from Ernie was earth-shatteringly rare, Pearl's parents looked both horrified and outraged.

Oblivious, Ernie turned to Kenny. 'That fence in Five Acre Field is coming down again. You need to get down there and see to it.'

The kitchen door opened again and Timmy appeared, fresh-faced from his walk home from the village. Timmy's urchin-like grin was broad. The sight of him had Ruby's heart swelling with love though she tensed at the thought of the trouble that might lie ahead.

He was a sweet-natured boy. A little rough around the edges, perhaps, but polite and friendly. He walked up to the table and said to the Grimeses, 'Sorry if I'm late. You must be Pearl's mum and dad. I'm Timmy.'

He offered a hand the way Ruby had taught him.

Mrs Grimes put her cup down and allowed him the merest touch of her fingertips. 'Timmy? I'm not sure I know who—'

'My son,' Ruby said, staring Mrs Grimes in the eye.

'Your son?' She glanced at Kenny in puzzlement and then, as though she'd made sense of the situation, back at Ruby. 'You're a widow. Did your husband lose his life in the war?'

'No,' Ruby said. 'I haven't been married before.'

'Haven't been . . . Oh.' Mrs Grimes was cold now. 'I see.'

She shot her husband a look that said, 'This is going from bad to worse.'

'Come and sit by me,' Ruby told Timmy, and she was glad when Kate offered him a plate with a reassuring smile while Kenny reached out to ruffle his hair.

'Now, about your wedding, Gertrude,' Mr Grimes said.

'You got my letter?' Pearl asked.

'You know we did. Why are you asking when I referred to it in my letter proposing this visit?'

Pearl flushed and looked down at her plate. Normally, Pearl's appetite was hearty. Thanks to her parents, it had almost deserted her, for she was rearranging her food rather than eating – until her mother chided the bad manners with, 'Gertrude, really!'

'What we suggest is that you don't rush into getting married,' Mr Grimes said.

Everyone at the table knew the reason for this change of attitude, except perhaps for Ernie who didn't care enough to give it any thought. Now Pearl's parents had met Fred and seen Brimbles Farm they were hoping she'd see sense and break the engagement off.

'I want to get married soon,' Pearl muttered.

'What was that?' her father asked. 'How many times do we have to tell you not to mumble?'

'I said I want to get married soon.'

The answer displeased both of her parents, who exchanged troubled looks. 'Your engagement is new,' her father pointed out. 'It would be wise to think about what it will mean before you race ahead with a wedding.'

'I want to get married now,' Pearl repeated, cowering under her father's hard glare.

His mouth tightened. 'If you're going to insist upon it, we should move forward with the arrangements we've already suggested: a ceremony at St Cuthbert's and a reception at the golf club.'

'But—'

'No buts, Pearl. It's for the best.' Mr Grimes turned to Ernie. 'You agree with me, don't you, Fletcher?'

'Eh?' Doubtless, Ernie had been thinking about the work that needed to be done around the farm instead of listening to a man waste his time by talking about weddings.

'You agree that a girl should obey her parents' wishes on marriage matters? Especially since those parents will be picking up the expenses.'

'Expenses?' The mention of money sharpened Ernie's attention. Ernie hated spending money.

'The costs of the wedding,' Mr Grimes explained. 'Flowers, dresses, catering, cars . . . Naturally, it falls to Mrs Grimes and I to bear those costs as the bride's parents. It will be easier for us – and less disruptive to your farm – if Pearl marries at her home church.'

Ernie's relief was obvious. He glowered at Pearl. 'Do as they say,' he instructed, and then looked at Ruby. 'What's for afters?'

She served the rhubarb tart.

Ernie scoffed his slice and then belched before announcing, 'Farm needs tending.'

With that he made his exit.

Mr and Mrs Grimes exchanged offended looks, doubtless sharing the view that etiquette and Ernie Fletcher were strangers to each other.

'Would anyone like more tea?' Ruby asked, to fill the awkward space Ernie had left behind.

No one did.

Ruby kicked Kenny under the table.

'Ow!' he complained. 'What was that for?'

'I don't know what you mean,' Ruby said sweetly. Then she looked at Kate who rolled her eyes at her brother.

'Oh,' Kenny said, as understanding dawned at last. 'I need to get back to work, too.' This had been agreed in advance to give Mr and Mrs Grimes more time to concentrate on Pearl and Fred.

He coughed but for a moment neither moved nor spoke again.

Ruby guessed he was rehearsing the words she'd taught him. Sure enough, he coughed again and said, 'It was a pleasure to meet you, Mr Grimes. And your missis, of course.' He was hardly word perfect but at least he was trying. 'Pearl is a much-valued member of our household,' he continued, 'and I'm happy she's going to marry my brother. That's Fred, in case you're wondering.'

'I think they know who Pearl is engaged to marry,' Ruby said.

'Right. Yes. Well, goodbye.' He looked at Vinnie and beckoned with his head.

Vinnie ignored him – until Ruby kicked him, too.

'That hurt!' he protested, but he followed Kenny outside.

'Are you sure you wouldn't like more tea?' Kate said,

with smoother charm than Ruby possessed. 'It'll be no trouble to make a fresh pot.'

'No, thank you,' Mrs Grimes said.

The much-valued member of the household sat with her arms folded over her middle and her lower lip jutting sulkily. Her fiancé sat with hunched shoulders and stared into space.

'Don't slouch, Gertrude,' Mrs Grimes said, with obvious exasperation.

Pearl sat up straighter and so did Fred but both looked thoroughly miserable. Ruby looked at Kate again, hoping Kate could think of something to say to the Grimeses that would lighten the atmosphere. But before Kate could speak, Mr Grimes said, 'My wife needs to rest,' he announced. 'Gertrude, you'll take us back to Mrs Irvine's house?'

Clearly, The Linnets was a thousand times more preferable to Brimbles Farm.

Pearl got to her feet looking dejected.

'Good day to you all,' Mr Grimes said then, helping his wife to her feet as though she were a flower in danger of losing its petals. 'Thank you for the meal.'

'Yes, thank you,' Mrs Grimes echoed faintly.

Kate showed them to the door. 'I hope we'll see you again soon,' she said.

'We're going to visit friends once my wife has rested, but we'll call at Churchwood on the way home on Thursday,' Mr Grimes answered. 'We'll expect to see Gertrude but there's no need for us to inconvenience the rest of you.'

In other words, they were giving Pearl a few days in which to think about her wedding, after which they expected her to fall in line with their wishes without requiring them to sully their feet and sensibilities with the mud and uncouthness of Brimbles Farm.

Pearl and her parents stepped into the farmyard. 'We need to talk,' Mr Grimes told her ominously, unaware that he could be heard inside the kitchen because the window was open – or not caring about it. 'This place . . . It's even worse than expected,' he said. 'As for this family . . . The vulgar father, the doltish older sons, the fool you want to marry . . . Why, he can barely string two words together.'

'That's because he knows you don't like him,' Pearl said.

'You can hardly expect us to like someone so ill educated and unpolished. I'm not even sure he's *clean*. And what are his prospects? Answer that, Gertrude.'

'We'll get by.'

'With his whittling?'

'It's good enough for me.'

'The fact that you believe so only proves you aren't thinking straight.'

'Didn't you even like Kate?'

'The daughter? There's something of the suffragette zeal about that young woman – and I don't intend that as a compliment – but at least she's shown good sense in marrying out of her family situation. Once the war ends I'm sure she'll be off to a better life elsewhere. You want to marry *into* that family.'

'I like Fred. I'm going to marry him.'

'You're of age and we can't stop you, but at least show some consideration for your mother and me by marrying from home.'

'Why? If you think so badly of the Fletchers, why do you want them to be seen by all your friends?'

'Don't be stupid, Gertrude. Isn't it obvious?'

'Not to me,' Pearl said.

But Ruby breathed in as understanding sank into her

280

brain. Into Kate's brain, too, judging from the sympathetic look she sent in Ruby's direction.

'If you don't get married from home, people will wonder why,' Mr Grimes said.

'Just tell them it was easier to get married from here,' Pearl told him.

'And tolerate the tittle-tattle that's sure to follow?'

'Tittle-tattle?' Pearl still hadn't understood.

'They'll think you're getting married out of sight for a reason.' Pearl's slow wits irritated her father more than ever. 'They'll think you have no choice but to get married because . . . well, because you've behaved like a common strumpet and got yourself into trouble.'

'You mean they'll think I'm *pregnant*?' Pearl finally said.

'Must you be so coarse?' Mrs Grimes said.

'But I'm not pregnant,' Pearl said.

'It's what people will think that matters. Just imagine your poor mother having to put up with tittle-tattle at her charity lunches, not to mention me having to put up with it at the golf club. You should think of your sister, too. Her reputation needs to be protected, even if you're careless of your own.'

'You've had your mind turned,' Mrs Grimes said. 'Perhaps it isn't surprising that you've lost sight of your morals when you're keeping company with that other girl. Ruby. A common name for a common girl. Not only an unmarried mother, but so . . . shameless about it.'

Kate smoothed a hand over Ruby's shoulder. 'What horrible people Pearl's parents are,' she said comfortingly.

Mr Grimes took up his wife's point. 'Shameless indeed. Parading that boy as though . . .' Mercifully, the words trailed off as Pearl and her parents reached the barn where Pete and the cart awaited them.

'Did I do something wrong?' Timmy asked, his eyes wide with bewilderment and hurt.

'No, you didn't,' Ruby told him, holding him close and feeling fiercely protective of him. 'Your manners were perfect.'

'I hate that man!' he declared, obviously meaning Mr Grimes.

'Let's just say we dislike him,' Ruby said, not wanting Timmy to hate anyone, no matter how appalling they were.

Pearl was right about her parents: they were awful and Ruby wouldn't want their money no matter how grand it could make her wedding.

CHAPTER SIXTY-FOUR

Naomi

The doctor's report was simple. 'No change.'

It was the same when Victoria visited in the morning and Adam in the afternoon. 'No change.'

Bert had been unconscious for two days.

'There's still plenty of hope,' they told Naomi in turn.

Between them they passed on the good wishes of Churchwood – from Mr Corbett, the cobbler, to Sykes, the Foxfield gardener, a taciturn sort of man who barely spoke two words together out loud.

William dashed in, too, since the hospital wasn't far from his school and he'd managed to borrow a bicycle. Bert's appearance obviously shocked him but he swallowed hard, making his Adam's apple bounce up and down in his thin throat.

'I'm going to Foxfield tomorrow,' he told Naomi. 'To look after the market garden. Don't worry, I've got the school's permission since it's nearly the end of term anyway.'

'Only if you're sure,' Naomi said, gratefully.

'I'm sure.' He left her with words of comfort. 'Bert's strong and he loves you. He wants to marry you so he'll fight.'

It was sweet of him to say it, so Naomi didn't point out that sometimes fighting wasn't enough. Not that she was giving up hope. On the contrary, she was clinging to it as though letting it go for even a moment would mean she'd drown.

It was Alice's father, Dr Lovell, who finally put his foot down with Naomi on Monday evening, after she'd spent two nights at Bert's bedside. 'Enough,' he said. 'You'll be no use to Bert or anyone else if you don't have some rest. Proper rest, I mean. Not a doze in a chair. I've booked you a room at the Belvedere, the hotel across the street. Go there. Have a decent meal, a bath and a sleep in the bed and come back tomorrow – after you've breakfasted.'

'I don't want to leave Bert.'

'But you must, and you'll be leaving him in safe hands. Mine. I may have retired but I was a doctor for many years. I'll know if there's even the smallest change in Bert's condition and I'll let you know immediately if that happens. Don't think I'm in danger of nodding off or becoming distracted. I didn't even bring a book with me because I'm going to sit at Bert's side, watching him all night long. Now go. Make your way to the Belvedere before you collapse.'

More tears shimmered in Naomi's eyes. Would they never end? 'I don't—'

'Go,' he said, pulling her gently but firmly from her chair and guiding her to the door.

He opened it to put her outside and then closed it again, shutting her out.

Naomi dithered for a moment but Archibald Lovell was right. She felt weak; in danger of crumpling down to the floor, in fact. She steadied herself by putting a hand flat to the wall and taking a deep breath. And then she tottered away, hoping she wasn't doing the wrong thing by trusting Dr Lovell.

*

'No change,' he reported in the morning. 'As far as Bert is concerned, that is. But you look a little better, Naomi.'

She still felt drained and sick with worry but she knew he was right. She wasn't as shaky on her feet.

Archibald Lovell went off and Naomi sat down with Bert. 'Will today be the day you open your eyes and come back to me?' she asked. 'I'm utterly bereft without you, my darling.'

But Bert stayed the same.

No change.

No change.

No change.

CHAPTER SIXTY-FIVE

Bert

Bert couldn't understand what was happening to him. He supposed he must be dreaming, though the word *nightmare* felt more appropriate. He couldn't move as much as a fingertip. It was as though he was lying in the ooze at the bottom of an ocean and the weight of the water above him was holding him fast. His eyes remained shut but now and then he was aware of lights shining on his lids from far above him.

There were voices, too. Indistinct murmurs that he couldn't quite hear. He didn't like this dream. He hoped he'd wake soon, especially since he had a feeling he had news to share. Important news, though for the life of him he couldn't remember what it was.

Perhaps there was no news. Just a twist of the dream to add to its unpleasantness. He felt the shadows closing in on him. Again. The shadows seemed to be closing in on him often.

In some ways they brought relief from the frustration of being imprisoned here. But in other ways they brought fear because he couldn't be sure they weren't closing in on him for ever.

CHAPTER SIXTY-SIX

Suki

Business as usual, Alice had instructed. So, too, had Victoria.

Suki wasn't the only one to believe that business quite as usual was impossible.

'It feels strange, so it does, to be going out to work while poor Bert and Naomi . . .' Mags, one of the evacuee women who lived at Foxfield, said. She was London-bred but her speech still bore the influence of her Irish parents.

There were murmurs of agreement from her fellow evacuees.

'I can understand that,' Victoria told them. 'I can be reached by telephone here but you have to wait until you get home to learn if there's news. But it won't help Bert and Naomi to let things fall apart and, besides, the children need the reassurance of structure to their days.'

'I can't argue with that,' Mags said. Two of the evacuee children were hers.

The women went off to work. A little later the older children went off to school and the younger children went off to Nearly School, a bookshop initiative that helped to prepare them for school as well as entertain them in the meantime.

Suki cleared up the breakfast things and then headed off to Mr Makepiece's market garden to feed his cat. Emotion rushed over her as she entered his house. There, open on the table, was the seed catalogue he must have been reading recently. Beside it, a notepad and pencil suggested he'd been writing a list of items he planned to order. Would he ever need those seeds now?

A row of cups hung on hooks from a shelf of the dresser with saucers behind them. Would he ever drink from one again?

And over by the hearth was his favourite armchair, the old cushions moulded to his body shape. Would he ever sit in that chair again?

Suki stood in sadness for a moment but then roused herself, knowing that moping wouldn't help. 'Good morning, Elizabeth,' she said, going over to the cat which lay on the hearth rug.

She fussed over the cat for a few minutes then fed her some food. Bert grew tomatoes for sale in his greenhouses but there were plants on his windowsills, too, probably placed conveniently for his own use. Suki watered them and also watered the tubs of flowers that stood outside the kitchen door.

There was nothing she needed to do for the growing beds and greenhouses since William had sent instructions to an army of volunteer helpers and would be coming to supervise them himself. Alice had taken fragrant herbs to the hospital which struck Suki as a wonderful idea. Keen to do something similar, she fetched some scissors and snipped off a few roses so they could be taken to the hospital along with the cards, notes and children's drawings that were arriving at Foxfield for him daily. He wasn't yet awake, but Naomi would read out the messages or describe them and Suki hoped the smell of the roses would reach him, reminding him of home and the fact that he had so much to live for. Even if he was unaware of them, Naomi might find comfort in their beauty and scent.

'You just missed Adam,' Victoria told her on her return to Foxfield.

What rotten luck. Suki's disappointment sent her spirits sliding downwards but Victoria lifted them up again by saying, 'He wondered if you might be able to help at the children's club later.'

Adam had asked for her! 'What did you tell him?'

'I said I thought you'd be glad to help but you'd let him know if you couldn't manage it. Was that all right?'

'It was fine,' Suki confirmed, relieved.

It felt wrong to be excited when Bert's life was in danger but she couldn't help small bursts of excitement from working through her worries now and then. Would anyone else be helping at the children's club today? Beth? Nancy?

Suki reached the bookshop to find Beth had arrived ahead of her and felt what had become the usual conflict of emotions: liking and admiration for Beth battling with jealousy and the fear of being outshone. At times like this it seemed impossible that Adam would ever choose Suki ahead of pretty and capable Beth. But surely Suki wouldn't feel such an overwhelming attraction to Adam if he felt nothing in return? No, that was stupid. Not all love was returned. There was even a name for it. Unrequited love. Yet Adam had asked especially for her and surely that counted for something?

'How are you all coping at Foxfield?' Beth asked, kindly.

'It's difficult,' Suki admitted. 'But we're trying to stay strong.'

Beth nodded. 'I was tempted to call in as I passed to ask if there was any news but I don't want to make a nuisance of myself when I know it's such a busy household.'

'I'm afraid there isn't any news,' Suki told her.

'Hopefully, there'll be good news soon.'

'Beth! Suki!' Adam said, smiling as he came in from the back garden. 'I'm so glad you could make it. I asked you both because I'm keen to make today's session a particularly good one for the children. The village is under a lot of strain just now, and the Foxfield children are suffering most of all. And here comes Nancy!'

'I got your message about coming to help if I was free, so here I am,' Nancy said.

'Wonderful!' Adam declared.

Suki kept her smile in place but it was disappointing to realize she hadn't been singled out for an invitation.

'It looks as though it's going to rain soon but if we start off in the garden, we can give the children some running-around games before we're driven indoors.'

'That sounds perfect,' Nancy said. 'If we exhaust them, they won't give us half as much bother.'

She was joking, of course, and she laughed to prove it, winning an appreciative smile from Adam. Nancy was like the sun appearing after rainclouds had drifted away. She was vivid and vibrant. Cheerful, too. And Suki felt cast into the shade by her.

Did Beth feel the same way? Perhaps, though it was difficult to tell because Beth was careful about what she allowed to show in her expression, either through the years of practice as a nurse or because nature had made her that way.

The children arrived in a lively burst of sound and energy. They played with the bats and balls in the garden. Then they came in for drinks and biscuits. The rain held off so they spent a few more minutes in the garden playing tag before returning so Adam could talk to them about how the planets moved around the sun, using potatoes to represent the planets. 'No throwing the potatoes or biting them,' he warned. 'Or I'll have no supper this week.'

Drawing of the planets followed, Saturn being the most popular one with its rings and Jupiter being the next most popular with its red spot. A few children had drawn Earth, including Victoria's Arthur who'd added an arrow beside which he'd written, *I live here.*

Suki threw herself into the entire session, determined to give the children the best possible time and, yes, to impress Adam, too. She was also watchful, trying to reach some sort of conclusion about how the four adults who were present felt about each other. Suki's own feelings were easy to define: she was in love with Adam.

She was pretty sure Beth was in love with him, too. It showed in a warm glow in Beth's eyes whenever he was near and Suki sensed that her friend's heartbeat quickened also.

As for confident Nancy, the nurse appeared to be making no secret of the fact that she liked Adam. She made him laugh, often and delightedly. She touched his arm with easy intimacy. And she exchanged wry looks with him as though humour was a bond they shared. But love? Suki didn't know Nancy well enough to judge.

And Adam? He sent Suki smiles at times. She read affection in his gaze. But it was clear from his soft looks that he also liked Beth and admired her, too, just as it was equally clear from his laughter that he found Nancy's liveliness a source of joy. What did all that mean? Suki felt the handicap of inexperience and unsophistication when it came to interpreting the depths of his feelings – for the nurses and for herself. He was a kind and gentle man. It would be easy to mistake a tender look for something more.

Knowing that two of them were likely to be disappointed

felt terribly sad. Beth was her friend. Nancy wasn't quite a friend, yet Suki couldn't dislike her. Nancy was nice – scrupulously fair and encouraging with the children, never shoving herself forward at anyone else's expense and generous with her praise of both Beth and Suki. How complicated adult emotions were!

There were cries of regret from the children when Adam announced that the time had come for them to go home. 'I was having so much fun!' Victoria's Arthur declared.

No one wanted to go home, it seemed. 'Sorry,' Adam told them, 'but your families will be expecting you. Goodbye, everyone, and see you next time.'

'Bye, Adam. And thanks!'

Cries of thanks and farewell rang out for Suki, Beth and Nancy, too.

Adam smiled after seeing the last child off the premises. 'That was wonderful,' he said. 'Thank you all so much for coming.'

'I hate to leave the clearing up to the rest of you but duty calls for me back at the hospital,' Nancy said.

'It's all right,' Beth told her. 'I'm not on duty tonight so I can help to clear up.'

Suki helped, too. Still eager to please, she took on the task of gathering up the bats and balls from the garden while Adam and Beth washed up the cups and glasses.

They were talking when Suki returned, having stored the equipment in the shed. 'Such a sweet little thing, Suki,' she heard Adam say, and it was like a knife to her heart.

He meant it kindly. Suki was in no doubt about that. But no man who was in love or even thinking about love would speak of his sweetheart as 'a sweet little thing' to her friend. It was the way he might speak of a child. Victoria's five-year-old Jenny, perhaps.

Something must have signalled her presence – maybe she'd let out a small gasp of dismay – because he turned to her. 'Thanks for putting the equipment away, Suki.'

She nodded, muttered something about it being no bother and grabbed a broom to sweep the floor, her real goal being to try to get a grip on the feelings that were crying out to her like wounded things. What a fool she'd been even to think he might fall in love with a naive girl like her, especially when he had his choice of two attractive and capable young nurses.

She swallowed, fighting to keep the tears at bay. She needed to leave. Urgently. She finished sweeping and returned the broom to its place. 'Bye, then!' she called out.

'Suki, wait!' Adam called, but she didn't wait.

She let herself out through the front door and was dismayed to hear footsteps approaching rapidly from behind her. It was Adam. 'Suki!' he called again and now he was much too close for her to pretend she hadn't heard him. She took a deep breath and turned. Adam was frowning. 'Are you all right?' he asked.

'I'm fine,' she said.

'Only you seem a little . . . distressed. Have I upset you somehow?'

'Why should you think that?' It was a stupid question but the best she could manage.

'I don't know,' he said. 'Perhaps you heard me talking about you with Beth. If that's the case, let me reassure you I said only nice things about you. I said you were sweet. That's nice, isn't it?'

Suki winced. Yes, it was nice – unless you wanted to be swept off your feet into romance with the speaker. Needing to answer, she nodded.

'So we're still friends?' he asked.

'Of course.'

'That's a relief.' He smiled again, this time sympathet-ically, as though attributing the sudden shift in her mood to another cause. 'Bert is hanging on. It's encouraging.'

'It is,' Suki agreed. 'I'd better get home now.'

'Thanks again for coming.'

Suki turned away and started walking back towards Foxfield. She managed to wave to Ralph Atkinson who lived next door to the bookshop, seeing him through a shimmering waterfall of tears, but then she broke into a run, unable to stop the tears from falling but wanting no one to see them. She neared Foxfield but, instead of passing through the gateposts, she ran a little way along Brimbles Lane and pushed her way between bushes and trees into the woods behind the house.

There, she sat on a fallen tree trunk and allowed the sobs to come freely. Adam didn't love her and, oh, it hurt so much!

In time the sobs ceased as sobs always do, but they left behind misery and physical pain in the region of her heart, as though it really had been lacerated by sharp glass. Her dream of a happy life with Adam was over. What was she to do?

No answer came back to her save for the obvious one. Somehow or other, Suki would have to learn to live with the heartache. And she'd have to do so with dignity, to avoid causing upset and worry to those around her – even her family, since they had enough worries at the moment given that Suki's sister Sally was increasingly unhappy in her job, working in service for a Mrs Nyse over in Barton. Suki had wanted to leave childhood behind and be treated as a woman. The time had come to act like one.

She thought of some of the women she knew and how

admirably they behaved in adversity. There was Mrs Harrington, desperately worried about Mr Makepiece but not for a moment losing her concern for other people. There was Victoria, taking on the care of two orphaned children with love and compassion, and May Janicki, doing the same with the refugee children. There was Ruby, standing up for Hannah Powell when the village was condemning her. And there were all the women who went about their days helping others when they'd been widowed or lived in fear of being widowed as a result of the war. Like the evacuee women from London. Like Alice Irvine. All were showing Suki the way forward.

She realized that time was passing and she needed to return home before her absence was questioned. She must look a fright, though – woebegone, with swollen red eyes. She was glad when a light pattering on the bushes around her alerted her to the fact that the rain that had threatened all afternoon had finally begun. She raised her face to the sky and felt cooling drops on her skin. With luck – and heaven knew she needed some luck after the crushing disappointment of the day – the rain would help to soften the swelling or at least disguise it.

The pattering increased to rattling as the shower gained strength. Getting up, Suki stood facing skywards for a moment longer and then headed back to Foxfield. She walked around the side of the house and entered through the kitchen door.

'Suki!' Victoria said. 'You're soaked.'

'I got caught in the rain on the way back from the bookshop.' Suki pushed her bedraggled hair from her face to avoid meeting Victoria's gaze. 'I'll run up and get changed.'

'Take a towel from the scullery,' Victoria advised.

Suki grabbed a towel, leaving her sodden shoes behind,

and ran up to her attic bedroom in her stockinged feet. There, she threw open her casement window and leaned outside to cool her face further. But, again, time was against her if she wasn't to arouse the suspicion that something was wrong.

Of course, she could always admit her heartbreak to Victoria or anyone else, knowing she'd receive sympathy and comfort, but her feelings rebelled against that idea. Foxfield already had troubles aplenty.

Stripping off her wet things, Suki put on dry clothes and brushed her hair. Her only other shoes were old but she pushed her feet into them and headed downstairs, pausing at the bathroom to wash her face, and then continuing into the kitchen. 'Sorry I came back from the children's club looking like a drowned rat,' she said. 'I hope I didn't drip water everywhere?'

'Nothing I couldn't mop up quickly,' Victoria told her. 'How was the club?'

'It was fun!'

A glance at the clock told Suki that an hour had passed since her heart had been broken. Now to survive the next hour . . .

CHAPTER SIXTY-SEVEN

Beth

It was difficult to know what to do. Beth had seen Suki's stricken face when Adam had called her a sweet little thing. He'd meant it kindly, of course, but to Suki, desperately in love with him, it must have signalled a death knell to her hopes by making it obvious that he saw her as a young girl still instead of a woman he might come to love.

Beth felt no sense of triumph now one of her rivals had come to grief. She felt Suki's pain instead and wished she could do something to ease it. But Suki had her pride and might prefer to keep her disappointment private. Was there a way in which Beth could deliver sympathy without disclosing that she knew about the emotional wound her young friend had received?

She settled on a large bouquet of flowers from Bert's market garden – blue delphiniums, white roses and pink dianthus – insisting on paying a fair price to William on Bert's behalf. Securing them with a ribbon she'd brought for the purpose, Beth called at Foxfield.

Victoria answered her knock on the front door. 'Goodness,' she said. 'What beautiful flowers. They're for Bert and Naomi?'

'Actually, no. I believe they've been inundated with flowers already.'

'Flowers, fruit, cards and letters,' Victoria confirmed.

Beth had contributed to the flowers Matron had sent on behalf of the hospital and also sent a card of her own. 'These flowers are for you and Suki. You're both under a terrible strain, yet you're holding the fort for Bert and Naomi so well.'

'It hasn't been easy,' Victoria admitted. 'I've noticed Suki looking rather wan and I imagine I don't look any better. Come in, Beth.'

They headed for the kitchen. 'Look, Suki,' Victoria said. 'Beth has brought flowers.'

Suki turned from the sink. She looked both panicked and mortified, obviously fearing that Beth somehow knew of her feelings for Adam and – worse – had told Victoria about them.

'The flowers are to show you and Victoria that your hard work in looking after things while Naomi and Bert are away has been noticed and appreciated,' Beth hastened to explain, and was relieved when the hot colour that had scorched Suki's cheeks receded.

'How nice of you,' Suki said.

'There's still no change in Bert's condition?' Beth asked.

'If only!' Victoria said.

Suki appeared to be getting a stronger grip on herself. 'I'll be going to the hospital tomorrow,' she said.

'Please give Naomi and Bert my love.'

'I will.'

'Well, I won't keep you from your work and I must get back to mine,' Beth said.

She turned to retrace her steps.

'The flowers are beautiful,' Suki called after her. 'Thank you.'

Beth hoped they would at least make Suki feel valued – a small drop of comfort amid the bleakness.

Walking back to the hospital, Beth reflected that it was a bleakness she might soon be sharing if Adam chose Nancy.

Beth was working in Ward Two when Adam arrived at the hospital. 'I called in at Foxfield and saw the bouquet you left for Victoria and Suki,' he told her.

'It was just a few flowers.'

'It was kind of you to recognize what they're going through.'

Beth shrugged. 'I only hope the flowers cheered them up a bit.'

'They did.'

'What's this about flowers?' Nancy was also on duty.

Adam told her what Beth had done.

'That was kind of you,' Nancy told Beth. 'Thoughtful.'

Beth couldn't doubt Nancy's sincerity. She always gave credit where credit was due. It was one of the qualities that made her so likable.

'Nurse!'

Nancy turned to Private Eddie Marshall, who beckoned her over.

'Me and Bobby here . . .' He gestured to the man in the next bed. 'We're having a competition to see who walks first.'

'Hmm. Well, don't be falling out over it and remember, you might both have leg injuries but no two injuries are identical.'

'True,' Eddie Marshall conceded, 'but a bit of competition will put some spice into our days and spur us on.'

'Then may the best man win,' Nancy said.

Was that her approach to life in general? A person did what they could to win the prizes they wanted, enjoyed it when they succeeded and took it on the chin when they were beaten? With so many older brothers at home, maybe Nancy had grown up knowing she wouldn't always be the winner in any competition and had learned to take a philosophical approach to life as a result. Did that mean she wouldn't suffer unduly if Adam didn't return her interest? It was impossible to gauge, especially as a cheerful exterior could hide a deep well of internal pain.

Certainly, Beth's own feelings ran deep. She'd suffer like poor Suki if Adam chose Nancy.

Lost in her thoughts just then, Beth didn't hear what Nancy said next to the patients but they both burst into laughter and, smiling, Adam raised an eyebrow at Beth as though saying, 'Isn't Nancy just wonderful?'

Beth answered with a smile of her own but it was accompanied by a private, painful squeeze of her heart.

CHAPTER SIXTY-EIGHT

Naomi

Naomi studied the doctor's face. He was staring down at Bert thoughtfully. 'Well?' she asked.

'He's holding on,' the doctor observed.

Naomi could see that for herself. She was more aware of Bert's breathing than her own, every breath he took meaning he was clinging to life. 'That's it,' she sometimes told him when they were alone. 'Breathe in, breathe out and let your body heal so you can come back to me, darling man.'

Five days had passed since the accident. 'Is he out of danger now?' she asked the doctor anxiously.

He sucked on his teeth as though he thought she was leaping ahead too quickly. 'I wouldn't say that, exactly. And even if he wakes . . .'

There was no way of knowing yet if his brain had been affected.

'What form would it take?' Naomi asked. 'The damage?'

'Memory loss is possible. People, places, the life Mr Makepiece led . . . A change in personality is possible, too. A shorter temper. More aggression. But it doesn't do to speculate. Let's . . .'

'Cross that bridge if we get to it,' Naomi finished for him. *If* they got to it.

She sank back into her chair. She'd never felt more

drained in all her life but she'd stay by Bert's side for as long as he needed her, leaving him only when absolutely necessary and only when a friend was there to take her place temporarily.

How lucky she was with her friends. She was being visited every day by at least one of them, and Archibald Lovell was insisting that every second night he'd stay at Bert's bedside while Naomi slept at the Belvedere. Clean clothes were being brought to her and food to eat. Food that she knew in her head was tasty and nutritious to keep her strong, though she'd lost both her appetite and sense of taste. Always it was accompanied by a flask so she'd have soup or tea to sustain her during the long hours of her vigil.

Again and again she thought what a fool she'd been to let the poison pen letters taint her enjoyment of life. Naomi knew now that the malice of one embittered person was insignificant compared to the love she received from those who cared about her and the love she had to give to those she cared about in return. Why hadn't she appreciated this before? Naomi didn't know.

She stared at Bert's unhandsome but much-loved face. How strange it felt to be here in this quiet little room while elsewhere – in Churchwood and around the world – life went on. 'Stay with me, Bert,' she urged. 'Please stay with me.'

CHAPTER SIXTY-NINE

Ruby

Mr and Mrs Grimes looked as though they'd had enough of what they'd probably call 'Pearl's nonsense'. They arrived at Brimbles Farm with the sort of tight expressions and brisk manners that announced that the time for foolish prevarication was in the past and now was the time to be serious.

Pearl had received a telegram from them the previous day. ARRIVING AT NOON TOMORROW ON BUS STOP PLEASE COLLECT FROM VILLAGE STOP NO REFRESHMENT REQUIRED STOP.

'Wonderful! They won't even take a cup of tea here,' Pearl had declared with dour sarcasm. She'd been subdued ever since their first visit but refused to talk about it.

'Their loss,' Ruby told her.

'I don't know what you think of this idea,' Kate said, 'but why don't I collect them from the bus stop and bring them back here to the farm? It'll save you from being alone with them and make it harder for them to bully you.'

'Safety in numbers,' Ruby agreed.

So Kate had driven the cart into the village and collected Mr and Mrs Grimes from the bus stop. The look Kate gave Ruby on her return suggested they hadn't been pleased but protecting Pearl was more important than her parents' sensitivities.

'Well, Gertrude,' Mr Grimes said, wasting no time on pleasantries and pausing long enough only to register who was present – Pearl, Ruby, Kate and Fred – and grimace at Pearl's filthy breeches and mud-spattered shirt, 'your mother and I trust that a little reflection has persuaded you to our way of thinking regarding the wedding. We'll speak to Reverend Lucas at St Cuthbert's and to the secretary of the golf club and let you know the date that's agreed. I imagine the banns of marriage will need to be read at the local church here as well as at St Cuthbert's but we can arrange that later. You'll need to come home for dress fittings, of course, and, naturally, your sister will be your bridesmaid.'

Mr Grimes looked satisfied with his speech. Or at least as satisfied as a man could look when he considered his daughter was throwing herself away on an unworthy man who lived in a hovel and depended for his living on whittling random bits of wood.

'That's settled,' he added. Then he turned to Pearl's mother. 'Come along, dear. I see no reason to linger here any longer.'

He made it sound as though he and his wife would need fumigating when they got home.

He'd just got to his feet and offered his arm to help Mrs Grimes do the same when Fred spoke.

'Now just one moment.' Only four words but he'd spoken them with a force that made everyone take notice.

More words followed. 'You've made it plain that you don't think much of me, but that's all right because I don't think much of you. For some reason I can't fathom, Pearl – yes, that's her name now, because neither of us like Gertrude, since it makes her sound like a sow – doesn't want to upset you. I don't see why, when she's spent all her life being upset by you two for not measuring up to your expectations of her, but that's the way it is. It doesn't mean you can bully her into the sort of wedding she doesn't want, though. The sort of wedding I don't want, either. You can keep your money and your fancy golf club. We'll pay for getting hitched ourselves here in Churchwood. Oh, I'm sure that means you'll turn your noses up at what we do – the *style* of the occasion, I suppose you'd call it if you want to be fancy – but the choice isn't yours to make. It's *our* choice. So there'll be no champagne or oysters or – what's that other stuff rich people seem to like? Caveat?'

'Caviar,' Kate told him.

'That's the stuff. I've never tried it but there'll be none of that either. We'll have home-made beer and a sandwich or two because if that's what my Pearl wants, that's what my girl will get.'

Mr Grimes stared at him in amazement as though a dog he'd been kicking into a corner for years had suddenly bared its teeth at him.

'You were right about one thing, though,' Fred continued. 'There's no point in you lingering here. I suggest you run off home and we'll let you know the wedding arrangements when we've made 'em. It's up to you whether you bother to come. I couldn't care less either way. Oh, and you can tell Pearl's sister that she isn't going to be a bridesmaid. Right, Pearl?'

'Right, Fred,' Pearl confirmed.

Mr and Mrs Grimes had puffed up in outrage like angry turkeys. 'Well!' Mr Grimes said. 'That speech proves just what an unsuitable match you are for our daughter.'

'It proves the opposite,' Pearl said, emboldened now.

'Perhaps I should return you to Churchwood now,' Kate suggested to Pearl's parents.

'Perhaps you should,' Mr Grimes barked.

They all turned as Timmy arrived home from school for his lunch. His grin swelled Ruby's heart with joy but Mr and Mrs Grimes only grimaced.

Mr Grimes ignored the boy as he stepped through the door. Following, Mrs Grimes drew her coat away from Timmy as she passed him, as though she feared he'd dirty it.

How awful they were, Ruby thought. But she simply gathered Timmy close as they closed the door behind them.

Pearl promptly threw herself at Fred. 'My hero!'

'Yes, well done, Fred,' Ruby agreed. 'I didn't know you had it in you.'

'A man of hidden talents, that's me,' Fred said, smirking.

'I'm glad you're getting the wedding you both want,' Ruby said.

'A wedding just like yours,' Pearl confirmed.

'Let me know if there's anything I can do to help,' Ruby said.

She warmed some soup for Timmy and then went out and stood by the outhouses, thinking over what had just happened. She straightened when Timmy came out to join her and stood, shifting from foot to foot in the way that meant he had something important to say.

Or something to ask. Not that he was a demanding sort of child. Far from it. But Ruby always encouraged him to talk about his thoughts and feelings because nothing mattered to her more than her son's happiness. Even so, she hoped he wasn't bringing troubles to her door.

'What is it, Tim?' she asked, smiling to give him the confidence to be open and honest with her, however upsetting or inconvenient the subject might be.

'I've been thinking,' Timmy announced.

'Yes?'

306

'About Granny and Granddad.'

Oh, no. Ruby's stomach clenched. How much had their coldness upset him?

'The thing is, they don't really matter,' he said. 'To us, I mean. They don't like us and we don't like them, so why don't we just leave them to get on with their lives and we can get on with ours? We'll be happier without them because we have other friends who *do* like us. Kenny, Pearl, Kate, Leo, Fred, Alice, Adam, Mrs Harrington, Mr Makepiece . . . All of Churchwood, apart from Ernie, who doesn't like anyone, and that horrible Mrs Nugent. I didn't like seeing my grandparents and I don't care if I never see them ever again.'

'What we have without them is enough. Is that what you're saying?'

His bright expression told Ruby she'd understood correctly. 'That's exactly what I'm saying. We shouldn't let them upset us for a single second because we have loads of much nicer people here. It's the same with Pearl's mum and dad. They're horrible. So horrible that they don't . . . don't . . . Oh, what's the word? De . . . De . . .'

'Deserve?' Ruby suggested.

'That's it. They don't *deserve* us to care about what they think.'

He was right. So what if Ruby's parents didn't come to her wedding? So what if she didn't have a special dress, fine food and a three-tiered cake? She was marrying the man she loved, who loved her in return, and there were plenty of other people to wish them happy. It was more than enough. It was wonderful.

'Have I ever told you that you're a wise boy, Timmy Turner?' she asked

'No.'

'Well, don't let it go to your head, but you've been very wise today and I'm grateful.' She kissed him and ruffled his hair. 'Back to school with you now.'

He grinned and headed outside, crossing the farmyard on light, carefree feet, and Ruby felt at peace for the first time in many years. She'd found her niche in Churchwood. She belonged here and she'd be happy here.

CHAPTER SEVENTY

Suki

It was unusual to see Victoria looking angry, but angry she was after calling in at the bookshop on her way home from the shops. 'Alice, May and Janet were doing a splendid job of keeping things going,' she said. 'But Constance Pearce! She came up to me with Marjorie and in that simpering way of hers asked for her best wishes to be sent to Naomi and Bert. She said she'd heard that it was to be business as usual while they were *indisposed* and I confirmed that it was. Obviously, we all – well, most of us – don't want the bookshop to fall apart in their absence, but what did I hear only moments later? Constance Pearce trying to revive her idea of day trips and afternoon teas *away* from the bookshop!'

She made a humphing sound before continuing. 'People are free to do as they wish, of course. There's nothing wrong with day trips and afternoon teas and no one is *obliged* to come to the bookshop. But I can't help feeling that Constance Pearce is motivated by spite. And just when we should all be pulling together.'

'At least no more poison pen letters have come,' Suki pointed out.

'That's something to be thankful for,' Victoria agreed.

'And most of Churchwood is on Mrs Harrington's side.'

'Indeed, yes. In fact, I have another bunch of goodwill

messages for her and Bert.' Victoria took several envelopes from her shopping basket. 'Also, strawberries from Edna Hall,' she said, holding up a small punnet of fruit, 'and lemon verbena soap from Phyllis Hutchings who said she'd been saving it for a special occasion but Naomi's need was more important. Also, a bottle of what Jonah Kerrigan called his home-made pick-me-up. I expect there's enough alcohol in there to make a person breathe fire but I'm sure he meant well.'

'I'll take everything with me today. I'll be on my way now you're back.'

'You'll—'

'Give Mrs Harrington and Mr Makepiece your love? Of course I will.'

Suki hadn't got into the way of calling them Naomi and Bert as most people did. Perhaps it was a sign that she was still young. The thought put her in mind of Adam, so she pushed it away.

It returned when she boarded the bus, though. She wasn't sleeping well and it was a strain pretending to be fine all the time when she'd never known disappointment like this before. It was utterly crushing. But she had to go on.

She'd seen Adam briefly and it had hurt, but at least she could take comfort from the fact that she'd been able to hide her feelings. Not for anything would she embarrass him – or humiliate herself – by letting him know that he'd dashed her hopes to the ground. No, she had to pretend to be all right and perhaps one day she *would* be all right again, even if that day didn't come soon.

She'd been grateful for Beth's gift of flowers. Had they really been for Victoria, too, or had Beth merely been exercising tact because she'd guessed how Suki felt about Adam's rejection and wanted to comfort her? Suki would have preferred no one to know about it, but better Beth than anyone else. Beth would keep her knowledge to herself.

Would Adam choose Beth over Nancy or Nancy over Beth? Time would tell.

The bus rounded the curve that led out of Churchwood and Suki leaned closer to her window to see what had become of Ted Newcross's house. Not very much, but it was early days. Boards had been put up outside it to keep children out, but it would probably be quite some time before enough resources were found to carry out repairs. At least the houses on each side of Mr Newcross's home had been declared safe for their occupiers' return.

Thinking of Mr Makepiece trapped beneath what had to be tons of rubble made Suki shiver. She hoped he hadn't been afraid before he lost consciousness.

Suki hadn't been to St Albans often and never by herself. She was nervous of getting lost but she managed to find the hospital. It was much bigger than the cottage hospital on the outskirts of Barton. Walking up the stone steps to the main entrance, she realized this was the first time she'd ever actually been inside a hospital. She'd rarely been anywhere, in fact. How unsophisticated. But enough of her own life. This visit was about Mr Makepiece and Mrs Harrington.

'Visiting isn't until three,' the receptionist informed her, but Suki had been warned and prepared for this response.

She told the receptionist she was here to see Mr Makepiece and saw the woman sigh. Clearly, Mrs Harrington had gained a reputation as a rule breaker.

Suki followed the directions she was given and knocked on a door. 'Come in,' she heard. Mrs Harrington's voice.

Suki opened the door and peeped into the room to be sure she was welcome. 'Suki!' Mrs Harrington said. 'How nice of you to come.'

Suki was shocked to see how worry had ravaged her poor employer. Anxiety had stripped weight from her and deepened the wrinkles in her face. Her hair was untidy, probably because it had been scraped back from her face when her mind was elsewhere, and her clothes were creased.

As for Mr Makepiece, Suki was even more shocked. The big, bustling man with the outdoor complexion was as pale as ivory. A shrunken man in the hospital bed. There were bruises and scratches on his arms and a bandage around his head.

But Suki was here to help, not hinder by letting herself crumple. 'I'm so sorry about what's happened,' she said. 'If I can be useful in any way, just say the word.'

'You're being useful already.'

'I didn't come empty-handed.' Suki took the notes and gifts from her bag. 'I've also brought some food for you and a change of underwear, stockings and blouse. Also, some roses from Mr Makepiece's garden.'

'How kind,' Mrs Harrington said. 'How kind you're all being.'

'It's because we care,' Suki said. 'Now, why don't you wash and change, and then eat some of this food? I'll stay beside Mr Makepiece.'

Mrs Harrington gave her beloved man a look that suggested she was reluctant to leave him.

'I won't move an inch from his bedside,' Suki promised.

Mrs Harrington left the room and Suki sat in the chair she'd just vacated. 'I don't know if you can hear me, Mr Makepiece, but it's Suki here. I want you to know that all of Churchwood is wishing you a speedy recovery. We miss you. We need you, too. The village isn't the same without you in it.'

She chatted about this and that, seeing no change in

his all-too-still face. But then he let out a sound. A groan? A cough? Halfway between the two? Had he done this before? Was it to be expected?

It happened again and, alarmed, Suki watched as his head thrashed from side to side. There was no doubt about it now. He was groaning.

'I'll fetch help,' Suki told him, and, jumping up, she ran to the door. There was a nurses' station at the end of the corridor. 'Help!' she called. 'I need some help!'

CHAPTER SEVENTY-ONE

Naomi

There was a commotion in the corridor outside the bath-room where Naomi had been washing and changing. A commotion about Bert? Throwing her hairbrush down, she raced for the door to see a nurse hastening into Bert's room. With her heart feeling as though it were falling from a cliff, Naomi set off in pursuit.

Bert's doctor was even faster on his feet. He reached the room just after she did, gliding past her with an 'Excuse me' to arrive at Bert's bedside.

Naomi remained by the door, grateful to have her arm taken by Suki, who squeezed it comfortingly.

The doctor leaned over Bert who was still moving rest-lessly and, by the look of it, painfully, too. His eyes remained closed but was he waking at last?

It seemed so. 'Mr Makepiece, this is Dr Gilbert speaking. I've been caring for you following an accident.'

Bert grimaced and appeared to be trying to work some ease into his neck. Another groan escaped his lips, clawing at Naomi's heart. She hated to see him hurting and while she'd waited so long for this moment, she was terrified of what it might reveal. The old Bert restored to her? Or a different Bert?

'Take your time, Mr Makepiece,' the doctor advised.

314

'Nurse?' He gestured to the bowl of water and the sponge that had been used for moistening Bert's lips.

The nurse soaked the sponge and applied it to Bert's mouth. And at last Bert's eyes began to flicker. Finally, they opened, though they held the dull, distant look of someone who was suffering. 'Welcome back, Mr Makepiece,' the doctor said. 'I'm—'

Bert nodded as though he knew who the doctor was but wasn't yet able to voice it. And surely that was a good sign?

The nod seemed to have cost Bert some pain. He raised a hand to his head and closed his eyes again, and Naomi felt another clutch of fear.

But after a moment his eyes reopened and he signalled for something.

'Drink?' the doctor suggested and Bert gave another small nod.

The nurse held a beaker and straw to his mouth. 'Slowly,' she advised.

Bert took a couple of sips and then sank back as though gathering his strength.

'Can you remember why you're here?' Dr Gilbert asked, and at last Bert got out a word.

'Bus.'

'That's right. A bus crashed and a house collapsed on you as you were rescuing a child.'

'Little Bobby came to no harm,' Naomi called to Bert, thinking that it was surely encouraging that his memory seemed to be intact. 'You saved him.'

'You're quite the hero, Mr Makepiece,' Dr Gilbert said.

Bert gestured for more water and took another couple of sips. Even then it took a minute or two before he had the strength to respond. 'I'm sure you're a decent man,' he told the doctor, his voice husky with disuse. 'I appreciate your care but, with all due respect, yours isn't the face I want to see right now.'

Naomi stepped closer.

'Now, *that*'s the face I want to see,' Bert said. 'It's the most beautiful face on earth to me, because the woman who lives inside it is beautiful.'

'Oh, Bert!' Naomi knew she must look haggard and old. 'You're talking nonsense, but I love you for it.' She took his hand and raised it to her lips.

'Nonsense, eh? Next thing, you'll be telling me I'm not a handsome devil.'

'I see your sense of humour is intact, Mr Makepiece,' the doctor said. 'But I need to examine you.'

'We shan't be long,' the nurse assured Naomi. It was a whisper but it told Naomi that she needed to leave the room.

She did so reluctantly, promising Bert, 'I'll be just outside.'

There was a bench in the corridor but Naomi was in no mood for resting. She paced up and down instead. Surely Bert was on the road to recovery now?

Suki also stayed on her feet, though she didn't pace. 'It must be a good sign that Mr Makepiece hasn't only woken, but also remembers what happened,' she said.

'I hope so,' Naomi replied.

She looked at Dr Gilbert anxiously when he left the room. 'I'm cautiously optimistic,' he said.

'Only cautiously? But Bert was talking just then,' Naomi pointed out. 'Making sense.'

'Which is encouraging. Head injuries are unpredictable, however. But take heart, Mrs Harrington. The signs are positive, though it'll be a long road to recovery. One step at a time.'

'I heard that,' Bert called from inside his room. 'I've no time for malingering. I've got to get my woman up the aisle as soon as possible. We should have got wed long ago.'

Dr Gilbert and Naomi went back in. 'Patience, Mr Makepiece,' Dr Gilbert urged.

Bert made a dismissive sound. 'Patience isn't one of my virtues.'

But for all his feisty talk Bert was clearly weak and exhausted. 'You need rest,' Dr Gilbert told him.

'Rest?' Bert scoffed. 'I've done nothing but rest for . . . however long it's been since that house fell down on me.'

But Naomi could see that he knew it made sense.

He beckoned her to lean towards him. 'I've remembered something I need to tell you first. The letter writer. I know who it is.'

For a moment Naomi was confused. Oh, of course. The poison pen letters. 'Never mind about those,' she said.

Oh, doubtless, the letter writer would need to be challenged eventually and there'd be unpleasantness involved. But at this moment her only concern was Bert's health.

He heaved breath into his lungs and began to speak, only to let out a gasp of pain. His eyes closed and his hand went slack in hers.

And Naomi knew fear all over again.

317

CHAPTER SEVENTY-TWO

Bert

Bert had never known pain like it. Pulsing against his skull, it brought waves of nausea with it. Dizziness, too, even as his eyes remained closed. He'd managed to open them to see his beloved by his side but was that to be his last-ever glimpse of her? Why, oh why, hadn't he married her already?

At least he'd remembered the name of the person who'd written the poison pen letters and passed it on. At least, he thought he'd passed it on. The pain had been overwhelming him at that point. Had it slurred his words and dragged them into tatters that made no sense? He wished he knew but it was hard to make sense of anything against so much pain. He felt a groan building but fought to contain it. If he was giving Naomi memories of their last moments together, he didn't want them to be of the sort of suffering that would grieve her. He wanted her to be happy, even if he couldn't be with her for much longer.

CHAPTER SEVENTY-THREE

Suki

'You look exhausted,' Victoria declared, when Suki arrived back at Foxfield from the hospital.

'I'm fine,' Suki said, but Victoria insisted on sitting her down and making her a cup of tea before she reported on the visit.

'Any news?' Victoria asked then, her pretty face wary with worry.

'Bert woke,' Suki told, and hope leaped into Victoria's eyes. 'But then he . . . But then he . . . he seemed to collapse again.'

Victoria was silent for a moment. 'But waking at all . . . even if not for long . . . That's a good thing. Was he lucid?'

'If you mean did he know who he was and what happened to him? Then yes.'

Victoria nodded. 'That leaves plenty of room for hope.'

Suki wondered if she should point out that the doctor was still worried. But it felt cruel to do so when morning might bring more encouraging news.

'And Naomi?' Victoria asked.

Suki felt a pull on her heart. 'She looked worn out. I managed to persuade her to drink a little soup and I left the rest of the food with her but I doubt she'll eat much of it.'

'I'll be visiting again tomorrow,' Victoria said. 'Hopefully, we'll have even more encouraging news then and I'll be able to persuade her to eat more.'

'I should tell others about Bert waking,' Suki said. 'Alice and Adam for two.'

'Drink your tea first.'

Suki finished her tea and then crossed the lane to The Linnets. Like Victoria, Alice looked thoughtful when she heard what had happened. 'Cautiously optimistic, the doctor said? It's a start.'

As long as that optimism hadn't been cancelled out by Bert's later collapse.

'Let's hope for more progress tomorrow,' Alice said. 'Thank you for taking the trouble to come over, Suki.'

'I knew you'd want to know.'

'Indeed. Don't worry about telling Adam. I'll do that.'

'It's no trouble for me to walk up to the vicarage,' Suki said, thinking of Alice's baby.

'The exercise will do me good,' Alice insisted. 'You go home and take it easy for a few minutes. Adam will circulate the news around the village and I'll be going to Stratton House in the morning so can pass on the news to Beth and everyone at Brimbles Farm.'

Suki nodded. 'That sounds ideal. I'll head home now.' She got to her feet and Alice accompanied her to the door.

There, Alice reached out and squeezed Suki's hand. 'Look after yourself, won't you?'

'I will,' Suki confirmed, but keeping busy would be better for her than moping.

She had another point to ponder, anyway. She'd heard what Bert had said about knowing the identity of the nasty letter writer. Who could it be?

CHAPTER SEVENTY-FOUR

Ruby

Ruby was feeling content but Pearl, it seemed, was not.

'What is it?' Ruby asked. 'You haven't changed your mind about your wedding, have you?'

'Course not.'

'So . . .?'

'I don't suppose . . . No. Forget it.'

'You don't suppose what, Pearl? Come on. Just say it.'

'You remember I said I want a wedding just like yours?'

Ruby nodded.

'I meant it literally.'

Ruby was puzzled. 'You want to marry Kenny?'

'Of course not! I want to marry Fred. But at the same time as you marry Kenny.'

Ruby worked it out. 'You want a double wedding?'

'If that's what they call it. But you won't want a clod-hopping carthorse like me trooping down the aisle with you. Who would?'

'I would,' Ruby said. 'But I'll need to speak to Kenny first.'

'I'll pay for special licences so we can marry soon, if that helps,' Pearl said. 'And I'll pay for food and drink for as many people as want to come.'

Kenny didn't need time to think about the suggestion.

'I don't care if we share our wedding with twenty couples if it means we don't have to wait any longer to get married,' he said.

A double wedding it was to be. But Ruby suggested that instead of special licences they should have the banns read in church in the traditional way. 'It'll mean waiting a few weeks before we can get married, but it'll also mean there's more chance of Naomi and Bert being able to come.'

'Good idea,' Pearl agreed.

Kenny sighed but couldn't argue.

CHAPTER SEVENTY-FIVE

Beth

Beth checked her pace when she saw Adam and Alice talking in the corridor outside Ward One. Was there news of Bert and Naomi? Beth was desperate to know but didn't wish to intrude.

She took a step backwards but then Adam glanced up and saw her. 'Beth! You've saved me from having to search for you.'

Beth joined them. 'Is there news?'

Adam told her about Bert waking – and the doctor's concerns for him.

'Head injuries can be tricky,' Beth agreed. 'How's Naomi coping?'

'She's exhausted. So I have a favour to ask. I'm going to the hospital to sit with Bert through the night so Naomi can get some sleep, but that means I won't be available for the children's club. Might you be able to help?'

'I'm sure I can,' Beth said.

Adam looked relieved. 'It's very kind of you. Would you mind asking Nancy if she might help, too? Not just today but any day.'

'Of course.' Beth clamped down on a feeling of jealousy. This was no time for self-interest.

'Thank you.' Adam touched Beth's arm. 'I must get off now.'

'Let us know if there's any change,' Alice called after him. Then she turned back to Beth. 'I'd happily stay at the hospital all night but no one will let me.'

'They're concerned about your condition.'

'I know. It's just frustrating that I can't do more.'

'I imagine we all feel that way,' Beth said.

Alice headed for Ward Two and, after collecting some bedpans from the sluice room, Beth returned to Ward One.

An hour passed before she had a chance to talk to Nancy.

'Of course, I'll help,' Nancy said, without a moment's hesitation.

'Adam will be at the hospital,' Beth pointed out.

'Then we'll have to do a good job in his absence, won't we?'

Nancy sounded determined to do just that. No wonder everyone liked her.

CHAPTER SEVENTY-SIX

Naomi

Naomi reached her hotel room and kicked off her shoes but didn't bother to remove her coat. She'd never felt more tired but knew she'd barely doze her way through the night, so she simply climbed on to the bed and sat back against the pillows, thinking over the day.

Bert had woken again that morning. In fact, he'd woken several times as the hours passed and each time she'd watched him fight through the pain to open his eyes. Talking was an effort for him. The first time he'd woken he'd clutched her hand and managed to say, 'I love you.'

It had brought tears to her eyes. 'And I love you, Bert,' she'd told him. 'More than words can say. But don't try to talk. There'll be plenty of time for talking when you're better. Just now you need to concentrate on getting well.'

'You talk,' he'd said.

And so she'd read out a note Suki had sent in.

Elizabeth is doing well. She's being thoroughly spoiled, in fact, though I'm sure she's missing you, Mr Makepiece. William has been keeping the market garden going splendidly and I've been watering your tomato plants. They've been ripening nicely. I took a few of the riper tomatoes back to Foxfield for the children to eat. I can't believe you'll mind that . . .

Bert had closed his eyes again but Naomi had seen a fleeting smile of satisfaction flicker across his face. Generous Bert was all too pleased to give his tomatoes to the evacuee children.

Naomi had read out a note William had sent in, too. 'All's well in the market garden. Kate came down and went out in the truck making deliveries for us. Pearl is going to come tomorrow to make some more. They both seem to enjoy annoying old Ernie by leaving the farm. I hope you'll teach me to drive the truck when you're home . . .'

Naomi jerked awake suddenly and looked around the darkened room in confusion and alarm. Bert. How was Bert? Awareness gradually filtered through her mind. She was in the hotel room and must have fallen asleep for . . . she didn't know how long. Stiff and fumbling, she got up from the bed and managed to switch on a lamp so she could read her watch. Two a.m. Goodness. She'd slept for hours. Panic loomed as she wondered if she'd missed news of Bert, but surely not? Adam had promised to telephone the hotel if there was any change. Just to be sure, she checked that no note had been pushed under her door by the hotel staff. Nothing.

Naomi rubbed her hands across her face. Her clothes had been pulled out of shape as she slept and they were uncomfortable now. Her appearance as well as her nerves was fraying around the edges.

Stripping off her clothes, she slipped on her nightdress and got into bed, hoping to rest some more. Come the morning, she'd bathe and dress in the clean clothes that had been brought for her, ready to face another day at the hospital. She needed to be strong for Bert's sake.

'It's been a quiet night,' Adam told her when she reached the hospital. 'Bert woke a couple of times but I read to him until he drifted off again.' He held up the book he'd brought. A P. G. Wodehouse comedy. 'I figured sleep is his best friend just now. After you, of course.'

'You're a good friend to him, too, Adam,' Naomi said. 'We're lucky having so many well-wishers in Churchwood.'

'That's because you deserve them,' Adam told her.

Movement in the bed had them both turning to Bert. He was surfacing again. His mouth tightened as though to hold in a groan and his eyes opened, flickered shut again and then opened more steadily. 'Good morning, Bert,' Adam said. 'I hope my reading didn't bore you last night. I'm off back to Churchwood now since I'm sure you'd prefer Naomi's company to mine.' He touched Bert's arm by way of farewell, kissed Naomi's cheek and left.

'Another day,' Bert got out as she moved to his bedside and kissed him.

Another day of survival. 'Another day closer to your recovery,' Naomi said.

Bert didn't comment on that. Instead, he said, 'I want to eat today.'

'You're hungry?' Naomi was encouraged – until she realized it wasn't appetite that was driving his wish but the hope of regaining some strength. Weight was dissipating from him daily.

'Is that all right?' Naomi asked Dr Gilbert when he came to examine Bert.

'I think it's fine to try some food. Something light. Soup, perhaps. Just sips to begin with, Mr Makepiece. No gulping.'

As if Bert was in a state to gulp anything.

'Adam brought me a flask of soup Victoria made from vegetables grown in your market garden. That means the best vegetables in the world. I haven't opened the flask yet so the soup should still be warm.'

Naomi poured some into a cup and held it to his mouth. He managed two sips. Three. Four. But then he needed to rest. 'It's a start,' Naomi said, as brightly as she could manage. Four sips was pitiful.

Kate arrived with more soup later. 'There's a second flask of tea, some sandwiches, two slices of pie and fresh fruit,' she said. 'There's also a little cake that Hannah Powell – Hannah Hamilton, I should say – made especially for you.' Hannah was the young mother of the foundling baby Naomi had taken in. 'She sends her love to both of you. She said she'll always be grateful for the help you gave her. She mentioned the pram wheel you mended for her, Bert. She says she feels the benefit of it every day.'

Kate was tall and had the energy of the supremely healthy, but she made herself appear smaller by sitting low in a chair with her legs tucked beneath her. She also spoke softly. 'News from Churchwood? I have a drawing here that Timmy did for you, Bert. It's of you in your market garden.' Kate held it so Bert could see it and he managed a smile. 'Timmy said the sun is shining in the garden because he thinks you're like sunshine. I've notes from Ruby and Pearl, too.'

The notes wished Bert well and mentioned their weddings. Kate told the story of how Fred had dismissed Pearl's parents and how the girls had agreed to a double wedding.

'Don't let them wait for us, if that's what they're thinking of doing,' Naomi said. 'We wouldn't want that, would we, Bert?'

'We would not,' Bert confirmed. 'Life goes on.'

Something about those words made Naomi shiver. It was as though Bert thought he was no longer part of life in Churchwood. Not that he appeared to be complaining about it. On the contrary, he was philosophical. Old life died so new life could flourish.

But Naomi wasn't ready to let him go. Not nearly.

Kate studied Bert's increasingly gaunt face. 'I must be tiring you both out with my chatter so I'll be on my way. Victoria is coming tomorrow, I believe, but I'll look in again soon. Naomi, do you have empty flasks and laundry for me to take back?'

Naomi handed them over and Kate left after kissing Bert's forehead and Naomi's cheek.

Alone with Bert again, Naomi let him rest for a while then suggested he try more soup. Another four sips went down him.

Hearing Dr Gilbert out in the corridor, she went out to tell him about the soup. 'It's a good sign, isn't it?' she asked, desperate for some reassurance.

'Let's hope so.'

'Forgive me, but you don't sound convinced,' Naomi said.

Dr Gilbert sighed. 'I can't lie to you, Mrs Harrington. My fear is that the progress Mr Makepiece is making is due to willpower rather than healing. The headaches aren't getting any better and neither is the dizziness that accompanies them. I'm sorry to have to say it, but I'm worried.'

CHAPTER SEVENTY-SEVEN

Bert

'I'm going to sit in a chair today,' Bert told Dr Gilbert when the doctor looked in on Sunday morning on his way to golf.

'I admire your pluck,' Dr Gilbert told him. 'However, it's too soon, what with the dizziness.'

'I need to try,' Bert insisted.

'Mr Makepiece, even talking exhausts you.'

Bert simply glared at him.

'Oh, very well! I know a stubborn man when I see one. But on your head be it.'

Bert tried. But failed. Even before he was being moved the world was spinning and making him feel sick. It didn't settle when he sat and breathed deeply to try to steady himself. 'Back to bed,' Dr Gilbert instructed.

Bert supposed he should be grateful for the doctor's forbearance since he didn't say, 'I told you so.'

But all Bert wanted to do was weep with frustration.

CHAPTER SEVENTY-EIGHT

Suki

Victoria had reported on Bert's ill-fated attempt to sit in a chair but Suki arrived at the hospital on Monday to hear that he was determined to try it again, just as soon as he could persuade Dr Gilbert to agree. 'If he could get out of bed without help, I'm sure he'd try it,' Naomi told Suki. 'As it is . . .'

Suki passed on more messages from Churchwood, including the fact that Ruby and Pearl had set a date for their wedding. 'It's going to be on Saturday the eighth of August at St Luke's, with the reception at the bookshop. They asked me to tell you that you're both invited and they hope you'll be their special guests.'

Suki smiled as she spoke but a glance at Bert's still-colourless face made her afraid that there was no way he'd be fit enough to attend, even though the date was almost four weeks away. Naomi's harried expression showed that she feared the same.

Suki also handed over fresh flasks, food and laundry and packed the previous day's supplies into her bag. 'Victoria made the soup,' Suki said, because Victoria made excellent soup.

'Like to try it?' Naomi asked Bert.

He tried some. But a very few sips were all he could manage.

'I'll sit with Mr Makepiece if you'd like to go and wash,' Suki told Mrs Harrington.

Alone with him, Suki wanted to ask him about the poison pen letter writer but was afraid of overtaxing him, especially since Mrs Harrington wished him to rest. She settled for saying, 'We've had no more poison pen letters,' hoping the news would boost his spirits.

He beckoned her closer. 'Someone needs to know who sent them,' he said.

He paused to draw in breath then spoke again. Just a few sentences. They didn't give her a full picture of the situation. Suki didn't learn what had aroused Bert's suspicions and how he'd gone about following up on those suspicions, but she did learn the identity of the letter writer and the reason for the letters.

Heading for home again, Suki reflected that, while she couldn't give Mr Makepiece strength and healing, there was something else she could do to bring him and Mrs Harrington some peace of mind.

She waited until after she'd cleared up the breakfast things the following morning. 'I'll do the shopping today,' she said. 'I may take a little longer than usual, though.'

'Oh?' Victoria said.

'I'll explain later. If all goes to plan.'

'Sounds mysterious,' Victoria said.

Suki headed for Miss Plym's house. Reaching it, she paused for a moment, held back by trepidation. She had no evidence of Mrs Pearce's guilt, after all, and Suki was in no doubt that the woman could turn nasty. But Suki was an adult now and she was equal to any nastiness Mrs Pearce could throw at her. She knocked on the door and heard voices inside.

'I'll go.' That was Mrs Pearce.

'Thank you, Connie.' That was Miss Plym.

'Good morning,' Suki said, when the door opened and Mrs Pearce stood in the space, looking bold and confident. 'I'd like to see Miss Plym, please.'

'I'm not sure if—'

'I know she's at home. I heard her talking.'

Mrs Pearce's eyebrows rose. Doubtless, she thought Suki was being impertinent. 'She may be at home but it doesn't follow that she's free – or willing – to invite *you* inside, young lady.'

'I'll be happy to speak to her here on the doorstep,' Suki replied, undaunted.

Miss Plym called from inside the house. 'Who is it, Connie?'

Mrs Pearce called back over her shoulder. 'It's that housemaid. The one who works for Naomi Harrington.' Her tone suggested that both Suki and Mrs Harrington were undesirables.

It strengthened Suki's resolve. 'Could I have a word, please, Miss Plym?' she shouted.

Miss Plym came into the hall. She looked both awkward and defiant, as though she'd find it embarrassing to exclude Suki but didn't want to set her will against her cousin's. Suki pretended to look over at one of her neighbours. 'Good morning, Mrs Oldroyd. Yes, I'm here to see Miss Plym. If she'll let me into her house.'

The pantomime worked. Miss Plym blushed puce. 'Suki, really! You're making me out to be inhospitable. Of course, you can come in.'

Mrs Pearce and Miss Plym led the way into the small sitting room with the ancient, sagging sofa that tended to eat a person up. Mrs Pearce sank her substantial frame into an armchair and stared at Suki as though to intimidate her. How had anyone fallen for her act of being a nice person? Suki might not know the full story of the letters yet but she was increasingly persuaded that Bert had been right about naming Constance Pearce as the writer of them.

Suki stared back and then glanced at Miss Plym. 'Am I allowed to sit down?'

Miss Plym's blush deepened, her thin hands twisting around each other in a way that showed how flustered she was. She wasn't used to a steely Suki. Nor, perhaps, to seeing the hardness at the core of her cousin. 'Perhaps the sofa?' she suggested, gesturing towards it.

Suki sat on the edge so as not to be consumed by it and Miss Plym took a dining chair.

'Naomi . . . Is she well?' Miss Plym asked.

'As well as can be expected,' Suki said. 'I don't have a message from her, if that's what you're wondering. I'm here about the poison pen letters she received.'

'Wicked things!' Miss Plym declared.

'Indeed,' Suki agreed. Then she looked at the other woman. 'Mr Makepiece believes you wrote them, Mrs Pearce.'

Outrage turned Constance Pearce's face bright red – but not before Suki had seen the flicker of a different emotion. One she rather thought could be identified as fear. 'That's a disgraceful accusation!' Mrs Pearce spat.

'A terrible thing to say!' Miss Plym agreed.

Suki said nothing but simply sat and let the allegation sink in.

Cunning crept into Mrs Pearce's features. 'When did he make this . . . this monstrous slander? Before or after his accident?'

'After, I believe,' Suki said.

'That explains it. The man has a head injury. He was delirious.' Mrs Pearce was triumphant now.

Miss Plym looked relieved. 'I knew you could never have sent those letters, Constance.'

'Thank you, Marjorie.' Mrs Pearce pressed her cousin's hand as though to reassure her that no damage had been done to their friendship.

'Actually, Miss Plym, Mr Makepiece didn't just name your cousin. He also suggested you should speak to your great-uncle about his will.'

The effect on Mrs Pearce was electric. 'Enough of your troublemaking, young lady. Marjorie, you'll oblige me by asking this young person to leave. I don't know if Naomi Harrington put her maid up to this appalling performance because she's jealous of our friendship, but I've never been so insulted in my life.'

'Oh, dear!' Miss Plym looked more flustered than ever. 'Perhaps you should leave, Suki. Mr Makepiece must have received a truly terrible blow to the head to suggest that poor Constance would ever do anything wrong.'

'I thought this might happen,' Suki told her. 'Which is why I took the liberty of contacting your great-uncle myself by telephone.'

'Marjorie, please!' Mrs Pearce cried. 'Can't you see my distress? This girl needs to leave and take her bitter accusations with her.'

Miss Plym looked torn by indecision.

'Your cousin has nothing to fear if she's done nothing wrong,' Suki pointed out.

'Well, I . . .'

'Marjorie! My nerves can't bear this,' Mrs Pearce pleaded but Miss Plym still wavered.

'You may be surprised – but pleased, I hope – to learn

335

that your great-uncle intends to leave you a substantial gift in his will,' Suki told her.

The woman's muddy-brown eyes widened. Her mouth opened and closed but words were too much for her just then.

'Apparently, Mrs Pearce tried to persuade him to leave the money to her instead,' Suki continued. 'But Sir John told me he couldn't bear the sight of her. He described her as – I think I'm remembering this right – a money-grabbing, blood-sucking, insincere parasite who'd sell her own young for a shilling.'

'Lies!' Constance declared. 'All lies! He's a sick, old man who's lost his mind.'

'You seem to be making a habit of suggesting that men have lost their minds, Mrs Pearce,' Suki said. 'First Mr Makepiece. Now Sir John.'

Mrs Pearce grabbed Miss Plym's skirt and sobbed into it. 'You're not actually listening to this nonsense are you, Marjorie? You know how much I value your friendship.'

'I suspect she's beginning to know how much you value her inheritance,' Suki said. 'That's why you wrote the letters, isn't it? To separate Miss Plym from her oldest – and truest – friend, Mrs Harrington, who you feared might see through your act. By upsetting Mrs Harrington you thought she'd be distracted so you could scoop Miss Plym out from under her influence. And by making Churchwood out to be a dull little place, you hoped to get Miss Plym away entirely. What did you have in mind? A house for both of you somewhere Miss Plym had no friends to look out for her and where she'd come to depend on you for company and advice? A house by the sea, perhaps? All paid for from Miss Plym's money.'

Miss Plym's eyes widened even more. Clearly, there'd been a conversation about just such a move.

336

'This is all nonsense, Marjorie,' Mrs Pearce insisted. 'Why, Mrs Harrington began receiving nasty letters before I even arrived in Churchwood. That proves I had nothing to do with them.'

'No, it doesn't,' Suki argued. 'All it proves is that you made thorough preparations for your plan by looking into Miss Plym's circumstances so you could decide the best way of getting her to yourself. I don't know whether you got a friend to make enquiries or paid someone to make them, but you sent the first letter before you arrived so no one would suspect you of writing it.'

Miss Plym looked as though she was struggling to keep up.

'There's one way of establishing the truth easily,' Suki told her. 'You could telephone your great-uncle yourself. He may be old and unwell, but he can speak and think clearly. He'll be only too glad to confirm that Mrs Pearce tried to influence him into leaving his money only to her. She didn't care about you then. Better still, go and visit him. He told me you'd be welcome at his house because you couldn't possibly be worse than that woman there.'

At last Miss Plym appeared to see the truth in what Suki was saying. 'Constance?' she asked wonderingly, tugging her skirt out of her cousin's reach.

'Our great-uncle took against me,' Mrs Pearce admitted. 'That's true, though I don't know the reason. I believe he must have misunderstood my concern for his welfare. Perhaps I was a little too pushy about ensuring he was properly looked after. But the letters . . . There's no proof that I sent them because I didn't send them.'

Yet somehow Mr Makepiece had seen or heard something to make him suspicious. What could it have been? Suki looked around the room and sensed the moment

Mrs Pearce tensed, though she tried to hide it. It was the moment Suki's gaze reached Mrs Pearce's handbag.

Suki let her gaze pass on as though it had found nothing of interest. Then she got to her feet. 'I'm going to do something rather naughty now, I'm afraid,' she said. 'I wouldn't normally dream of invading someone's privacy but in these circumstances needs must.' She walked to the window to lull Mrs Pearce into a false sense of security and then darted back to grab the handbag before Mrs Pearce could grab it herself.

'Leave my bag alone!' Mrs Pearce shrieked. 'You've no right to touch it.'

'I'm going to do more than touch it,' Suki said. 'I'm going to see what's inside it.'

Mrs Pearce managed to heave herself out of her chair but not before Suki had upended the bag and let the contents fall on to a side table. Among the usual purse, handkerchief and hair comb was a package. Suki picked it up and reached inside, bringing out four envelopes. Two were addressed to Mrs Harrington. The other two were addressed to a Mr Ralph Picksmith of Whitechapel, London. 'Mr Picksmith is your accomplice, I assume. You write the letters and send them to him to post.'

'Give them back! Those letters are nothing to do with you!' Mrs Pearce attempted to reclaim them but Suki was much lighter on her feet and danced across the room out of the older woman's reach.

She drew a sheet of paper from inside one of the envelopes that was addressed to Mrs Harrington and read it out loud. '*Do you know what people are saying about you? That you stick your nose in where it isn't wanted. Leave people alone.* Charming. I won't bother reading the second letter as your poison doesn't deserve another moment of my time. I'll take it with me, though. As evidence.'

'Marjorie. My dearest friend,' Mrs Pearce said. 'Nothing needs to change. I might have made a little error of judgement with these letters but I've had a lot on my mind and we enjoy each other's company so much! Let's leave all this unpleasantness behind and set up in a little house together somewhere new.'

'I don't enjoy your company, Constance,' Miss Plym told her. 'Not any more. I'd like you to leave.'

'You're upset. And I know it's my fault. But once you've calmed down, you'll see that—'

'I want you to leave now. Right now.'

'There's a bus in about twenty minutes,' Suki put in helpfully. 'It's time I was leaving, too.'

She turned to Miss Plym. 'I'm sorry I had to bring bad news to your door.'

Miss Plym didn't answer. She'd begun to cry.

Suki let herself out of the house and set off for Foxfield.

'Suki!' She turned at the sound of her name being called.

Miss Plym stood on her doorstep, wringing her thin hands. 'Do you think . . . Do you think Naomi will ever forgive me?'

'I don't know,' Suki told her. 'I can pass on your apologies, if you like. But I suggest you don't come to the house unless or until Mrs Harrington invites you.'

CHAPTER SEVENTY-NINE

Beth

'Suki!' Beth called, seeing Mrs Harrington's maid in the distance as she made her way towards the Churchwood shops.

Suki stopped and turned, then waited for Beth to draw level before they walked on together.

'I heard what you did,' Beth told her. 'About Constance Pearce, I mean. It was splendid of you to take her on. To vanquish her, too!'

'She deserved it,' Suki said.

'There's no doubt about that. Churchwood must be glad to see the back of such a nasty woman. Is Mrs Harrington aware of what you did?'

'Victoria told her.'

'It must have been a weight off Mrs Harrington's mind. Not that she doesn't have even weightier things on her mind at present, of course. Is Mr Makepiece any better?'

'I believe he's no worse.'

'These things can take time,' she said.

Suki nodded. She looked pale. Worried. But there was something else about her, too. A new sort of presence. Of dignity, as though she'd passed from girlhood to womanhood and found strength along the way.

'You'll send Mrs Harrington my regards again?' Beth

asked. 'I expect you're being overwhelmed by requests to pass on messages but I imagine many people are feeling as I am – wishing we could do something to help and frustrated because all we can do at present is keep hoping and praying and sending messages.'

'I will,' Suki said. 'I know she's grateful for the kindness everyone is showing.'

'It's no more than she deserves,' Beth said. 'And you, Suki. You deserve a medal for the courage you showed in challenging the awful Mrs Pearce.'

'I was glad to do it,' Suki told her, and Beth nodded.

'You're a remarkable young woman, Suki. I admire you and I expect many other people admire you, too.'

It wasn't quite the right thing to say. Suki's face twisted momentarily, doubtless because she was thinking that Adam didn't admire her the way she'd have liked, but she straightened her shoulders and raised her chin. 'Thank you, Beth.'

They'd reached the shops. Suki went into the baker's and Beth went into the grocer's, hoping to be able to buy a treat she could leave at Foxfield for the evacuee children, knowing how much they'd welcome it.

She managed to buy a packet of custard creams and called in at Foxfield on her way home, where they were gratefully received. Walking back to the hospital a few minutes later, her thoughts returned to Suki. She might be young but she was brave, not only in the way she'd gone into battle with Constance Pearce but also in the way she was managing her disappointment over Adam. There was no doubt that Suki believed she had no chance with him, yet she was conducting herself impeccably. Beth could learn from her.

CHAPTER EIGHTY

Naomi

'Good for her,' Bert managed to say when Naomi told him how Suki had run Constance Pearce out of town.

He also managed to stay out of bed for ten minutes.

'Pure willpower,' Dr Gilbert said again, and, indeed, Bert looked terribly, terribly ill.

CHAPTER EIGHTY-ONE

Bert

'I want to go home,' Bert told Dr Gilbert.

'I'm sure you do, Mr Makepiece. I'm doing everything I can to make that happen. In time.'

'I didn't express myself clearly enough,' Bert said. 'What I meant to say was that I'm going home whether you discharge me or not.'

'Now, now, let's not be hasty,' Dr Gilbert said. 'You've made some progress. You're eating a little and you've managed to sit up. For a while. But you're far from recovered. I try hard not to frighten my patients, Mr Makepiece, but since you seem set on discharging yourself I feel morally bound to warn you against it in the strongest terms. The brain is a delicate instrument and we don't fully understand its workings. I'm concerned about the headaches and dizziness you're suffering.'

Bert was worried about them, too. Deeply worried. But if his remaining days on earth were likely to be few, he didn't want to spend them in hospital. He wanted to spend them at home – in Churchwood, the place he loved, and with the woman he loved beside him, preferably as his bride. Could he hang on long enough to marry her? He'd keep trying to his last breath. And if the worst happened, Naomi wouldn't be alone in his hospital room. She'd be at home with the people who loved her all around her.

CHAPTER EIGHTY-TWO

Ruby

'Bert's agreed to stay in hospital for another week,' Alice told Kate, Ruby and Pearl.

'He hasn't had a setback?' Ruby asked.

'Not a setback. He just isn't nearly well enough to come home and never was.'

'How does Naomi feel about it?' Kate said.

'Relieved, because hospital is what Bert needs right now, even if he hates it.'

'He's still in danger?' Ruby ventured.

'Very much so.'

'Poor Bert. Poor Naomi, too,' Ruby said and the others nodded.

'They want you to go ahead with your wedding plans, though.'

Ruby grimaced. 'It doesn't feel right.'

'But they'll feel guilty if you don't go ahead,' Alice answered. 'Have you decided what you're wearing?'

'Just clothes we already have,' Ruby said.

'Our resident fashion expert, May, wants to help with your outfits if you're willing? In fact, here she comes right now . . .'

CHAPTER EIGHTY-THREE

Suki

It had been satisfying to confront awful Mrs Pearce and put an end to the cruel letters. The village had been abuzz with talk over it. Not that Mrs Pearce had stayed long enough to hear what was being said, since she'd left immediately after Suki had exposed her guilt. It was Miss Plym who'd been left behind to face the wrath and disgust of Churchwood.

'It wasn't my fault,' Suki had heard her pleading in the village. 'I wasn't to know I was nursing a viper in my bosom. Everyone knows I think the world of Naomi. Of Bert, too . . .'

'You're a silly woman, Marjorie,' Edna Hall had told her. 'Constance Pearce was living under your roof. Didn't it even occur to you that she was here for a purpose?'

Marjorie had run home crying.

Suki had found herself a minor celebrity. 'It was nothing,' she'd said. 'Mr Makepiece did all the hard work of investigating her. I simply tidied things up for him.'

The mention of Mr Makepiece always brought sober looks since he was still languishing in hospital.

'Even so,' people said, 'you did a good thing in getting rid of that woman.'

Suki was pleased to have helped but there was something else she needed to do which had nothing to do with Constance Pearce. It was entirely personal.

Suki needed to come face to face with Adam. Oh, she'd seen him briefly in passing but they were both so busy that they'd barely exchanged more than a few words and it had been easy for Suki to avoid his gaze. She needed to spend time with him. To talk to him properly. And to be sure that, despite her desolation, they could function normally together, without awkwardness – or rather without awkwardness for anyone except Suki herself. Perhaps one day her wounded heart would heal, but it would take time before she stopped hurting every time she saw him or even thought of him.

The best place to begin this new existence was the children's club, so to the bookshop she went. It was hard, though. Terribly hard. Bracing herself outside the door, she forced a beaming smile and entered. 'Hello!'

Immediately, she was surrounded by children clamouring for her attention.

'Come and see the hedgehog I made out of a fir cone . . .'

'Will you be my partner for dancing?'

'I fell over on the walk here, but I didn't cry . . .'

Attending to the children gave her a welcome few moments in which to quieten the beating of her heart. But at last she looked up, encountered Adam's gaze and managed not to shy away from it.

'How lovely to see you,' he said.

'It's always a pleasure to come to the children's club,' Suki told him brightly.

'I heard that you were the person who confronted Constance Pearce. It was brave of you.'

'I owed it to Mr Makepiece and Mrs Harrington,' Suki said, and then, uncomfortable with being treated as a heroine, she changed the subject. 'What are we doing today?'

'Rounders first, followed by another attempt to learn the

country dance we tried last time. Then singing and acting out a story.'

'It sounds wonderful. I think I'll be better at dancing than rounders after my first disastrous attempt at playing, but let's see.'

'Beth and Nancy are here, too,' he said, and Suki waved to both of them. Now that she was through the door and the first painful words and looks had been exchanged, she could feel herself gaining strength, as though she'd taken a cordial. Whatever she was feeling inside, on the outside she was going to cope.

The next hour passed quickly. It cost Suki a pang when Adam gave Beth a glowing look as he passed a rounders bat over, and again when he laughed with unbridled delight at something Nancy said. But deep breaths and determination got Suki through those moments with her smile intact.

She also realized that, now she no longer had her own hopes invested in Adam's future, she was able to watch him with much clearer eyes. She studied him with Beth and she studied him with Nancy. His smiles, his expressions, the way he looked when he glanced at them across the room without them being aware of it, or walked away after speaking to him.

It made her . . . thoughtful.

'It was nice to see you again, Suki,' Beth said, when the time came to go home.

There was sympathy in Beth's eyes and Suki was pretty sure that her friend was aware of her private suffering but sensitive enough to make no fuss about it.

'You did well with that country dancing,' Nancy told Suki. 'I didn't seem to know my left foot from my right today so it was lucky you were here to steer me in the right direction, otherwise I might have trampled over the children.'

Nancy gave one of her bright smiles and then said to Beth, 'Are you walking back to the hospital now?'

'I need to visit the shops first,' Beth said. 'You go on without me.'

'Right you are.'

Beth and Nancy set off in different directions. Suki said goodbye to Adam and then she left, too. 'Nancy, wait!' she called, chasing after her.

Nancy came to a halt and turned. 'Did I forget something?' she asked, smiling.

'No,' Suki told her. 'I just . . . I'd like a word.'

'Oh?'

'Perhaps you can guess what it's about?' she asked.

'No, but you look . . . purposeful, so I imagine you're about to enlighten me.'

Suki took a deep breath. 'I want to talk about Adam.'

'Really?' Nancy looked surprised, perhaps because she hadn't expected such boldness from Suki.

'Do you love him?' Suki asked. 'I know you *like* him, but do you *love* him?'

Nancy looked even more surprised. 'My, my. You don't hold back, do you?'

'Not when it's important,' Suki said.

'It's important because you want him for yourself, I suppose. Don't think I haven't noticed the way you look at him.'

Suki blushed, though Nancy hadn't spoken unkindly. 'The way I *used* to look at him, I think you mean. Not any longer.'

'Why's that?'

'Because I've realized I'm not the right person for him.'

Clearly, Nancy hadn't been expecting such a straightforward – and honest – answer. 'You must be disappointed,' she said, sounding genuinely sympathetic.

Suki shrugged. 'I'll survive.'

'Yes, I rather think you will, though that doesn't stop it from hurting.'

Suki shrugged again.

'I'm not sensing any encouragement from you,' Nancy said then, 'so I suspect you're here to tell me I'm not the right person for him either. But why does it matter to you if you're not a candidate for Adam's affections yourself?'

'Beth is my friend.'

'Ah.'

'I've watched Beth with Adam and I've watched you with Adam and I think Beth is the one who'll make him the happiest.'

'Isn't that for Adam to decide?'

'I think he *will* decide that eventually. But until then you're giving Beth pain.'

'Did she send you to talk to me?'

'Beth doesn't know anything about this conversation. I'll appreciate it if you keep it that way.'

'How self-sacrificing you are, Suki.'

'I'm just trying to be a good friend.' Suki paused. Was she making Nancy angry? It was hard to gauge. 'Look, I'm not suggesting that you're not every bit as pretty as Beth. Or every bit as kind and useful. But I think Adam and Beth are made for each other – if that doesn't sound too mawkish. If you make it plain to Adam that you're not interested in him except as a friend, he'll be free to focus on Beth and you'll save her the pain of not knowing where she stands with him. It won't change what happens in the end – at least, I don't think it will – but if you step aside, it'll shorten the uncertainty.'

'What if I'm in love with him? Won't I be causing myself pain?'

349

'Are you?' Suki asked. 'In love with him?'

'I don't think that's any of your business.'

'I can't argue with that,' Suki admitted. 'The thing is, you're not like Beth and you're not like me. We're quiet sort of people.'

'You weren't so quiet when you confronted Marjorie Plym's awful cousin – yes, I heard about that and I thought it was terrific of you – and you're not being so quiet now,' Nancy pointed out.

'I'm not finding this easy. But you really are different, Nancy. You're like the sun coming out on a dull day. You're bright. Fresh. Sparkling. You could have any man you wanted.'

Nancy laughed. 'I'm sure there are many men who can resist my charms easily.'

'Some, perhaps,' Suki conceded. But not many. 'Well . . .' Suki shrugged again. 'I won't take up any more of your time now, Nancy. Thank you for listening without getting angry at me. I'd have hated that.'

'You underestimate yourself, Suki. You're wasted as a housemaid.'

'I enjoy working for Mrs Harrington. She makes me feel useful. Appreciated.'

'There are other ways of being useful and appreciated.'

True. 'I hope this conversation won't make things awkward between us,' Suki said. 'I like you. I'd like to be your friend.'

'We'll have to see about that,' Nancy said, and Suki nodded, considering it a fair comment.

With a small and apologetic smile, Suki walked off.

Had she done some good for Beth? Or had she only made things worse?

CHAPTER EIGHTY-FOUR

Bert

Bert had allowed Dr Gilbert one week, and if willpower alone could have got him home after those seven days then he would have got there somehow. But willpower alone hadn't been enough.

Despite gritting his teeth in determination to overcome the pounding and spinning in his head, and despite the food he forced down himself, the pain and dizziness had been too much. Every movement of his head and every attempt to sit upright had the room swimming and nausea building in his throat.

But he'd persevered and now, after a second week, he was almost home. He still felt ill. He still felt ridiculously weak. But he wanted, *needed*, to be at home and physical suffering was a price he was willing to pay for that.

Naomi had suggested hiring an ambulance for the journey but Bert hadn't fancied being cooped up without a window beside him. He'd insisted on a taxi instead, though he'd given Naomi her way when it had come to swathing his now-feeble frame in pillows and blankets.

For the most part he'd let himself rest with his eyes closed but, sensing they were nearing Churchwood, he'd opened both his eyes and the window so he could breathe in the familiar air like a tonic to his soul. Summer sunshine had touched fields and trees and buildings with gold. He could hear a tractor at work. Hear also the hum of bees. Scents reached him, too: flowers and grass and rich, fertile soil.

'Nearly home,' he said.

'Yes.'

Bert glanced across at Naomi and saw that she had tears in her eyes. They triggered tears in his eyes also. Home truly was the best place on earth. He squeezed her hand, smiled and blinked the tears away.

But then he looked intently at Ted Newcross's house. It was strange to think that he'd almost lost his life under that rubble and might still succumb to the injuries he'd suffered, since Dr Gilbert had released him from the hospital only with dire warnings ringing in his ears. Bert couldn't regret saving the boy, though. He couldn't have lived with himself if he'd let a little 'un perish.

Would Bert live long enough to marry Naomi? That was the question that powered him onwards. It wasn't just a case of getting to St Luke's on Churchwood's village green. Naomi's divorce meant a church wedding wasn't possible. 'Horribly unjust when Naomi was the injured party,' Adam had agreed, but it was beyond his power to change the rules. Instead, they needed a civil ceremony in a register office to make the marriage legal, though Adam would bless them in church afterwards and it was this blessing, with all their friends present, that they regarded as the real wedding. In contrast, the civil ceremony would be a mere formality, but it occurred to Bert now that they should have arranged it for today, before they'd come home. It would have got that formality out of the way, but Bert hadn't been thinking straight. He'd been too focused on just getting through each day.

The taxi continued along Churchwood Way and Bert was pleased to see some familiar faces out on the street. Jonah Kerrigan, Edna Hall, Phyllis Hutchings . . . All of them waved and looked delighted to see him.

'Promise me you'll rest when we reach Foxfield,' Naomi said. 'No visitors until you've slept and only then if you're really up to it.'

Bert raised Naomi's hand to his lips and kissed it. 'I promise, beloved.'

He'd put her through enough worry already.

They turned through the Foxfield gateposts. 'As near to the door as you can get, please,' Naomi instructed the taxi driver.

He pulled up immediately outside it and Bert saw that the children had made a big, colourful banner saying, *Welcome home, Mr Makepiece and Mrs Harrington.* 'Now, that's nice,' he said, and another glance at Naomi showed that tears were welling in her eyes again. It was all he could do not to cry with her.

Someone must have been on the watch for their arrival because the door opened and Victoria, Suki and Dr Lovell emerged. 'Don't worry,' Victoria said. 'Everyone else is going to say welcome home a little later when you've settled in and rested.'

Much as Bert wanted to greet everyone, he was relieved. The journey had taxed his strength almost beyond endurance.

He'd always been a big man, while Dr Lovell's stature was a little below average, but Bert was glad of his friend's arm guiding him out of the taxi. 'Slowly does it!' Dr Lovell insisted.

Bert finally got his feet to the gravel drive and immediately Victoria took his other arm.

'I'll help *you*, Mrs Harrington,' Suki said, and Bert was pleased that his beloved was being looked after too.

The rest of the household might have been banished from the hall temporarily, but they'd left their mark in the form of more welcoming banners and drawings.

It was a slow process, getting up the stairs, though they were wide enough for Dr Lovell and Victoria to climb alongside him.

'You're coming back to Foxfield. It'll be easier to look after you there,' Naomi had said, and, much as he longed to see his own little house and market garden, he hadn't argued, knowing she was right.

He hadn't expected her to give him her own room but he should have done, for Naomi was always self-sacrificing.

'Into bed with you,' Dr Lovell said, when they arrived.

Getting ready for bed was easy since Bert had travelled in his pyjamas and slippers with an overcoat on top.

'Suki will bring tea,' Naomi said, following them into the room.

The kettle must already have been simmering because Suki appeared within a very few minutes, holding a tray with tea, soup and sandwiches. 'I heard about you trouncing Constance Pearce,' Bert told her. 'Well done.'

'You found out about her,' Suki said. 'Which means you did all the hard work. I don't know what that involved, though. What made you think she was the letter writer?'

'A small thing, really,' he explained. 'We were in the post office when she dropped her handbag. I hadn't warmed to the woman but good manners required me to help so I bent down to pick up the bag and some of the contents that had spilled out over the floor. Well! She almost shoved me out of the way, insisting she could manage. She stuffed the contents back into the bag and I saw they included a package. The sort of package that might contain envelopes. It got me thinking.'

He paused as though remembering, and then continued. 'Anyway, I took the train to Bournemouth and spoke to some of her neighbours. Apparently, there was nothing wrong with Constance's flat so that made me even more suspicious. And then I learned that she'd had a row with one of her neighbours – none of them seemed to like her – and announced that she wouldn't have to put up with the neighbour's yapping dog and the mean little flats for much longer because she'd be inheriting money from a great-uncle. Sir John Riley, no less. It was said to show off, of course, but it gave me someone to contact.'

'Sir John?'

'Indeed. I went to see him and he told me Constance had been trying to curry favour with him with a view to getting him to leave his property to her in his will.'

'That's what he told me when I telephoned him,' Suki said. 'He banished her from his house.'

'I wish I'd seen that,' Bert said, with a ghost of a grin on his face. 'I'd like to have seen you trounce Constance, too. What you did . . . It took courage.' He managed to wink at her.

'That girl is growing up,' he remarked when Suki left the room.

'She is, isn't she?' Naomi said. 'She isn't a young girl any more. She's a young woman.'

'Eat, Bert,' Dr Lovell urged and, to please them all, Bert did his best to sip some tea and soup. He ate a tiny bit of sandwich, too, but exhaustion was pressing down on him and he knew he could do no more.

'Sleep now,' Naomi said.

'You too,' he told her, his eyes already closing and his mind disappearing into a swirl of darkness.

He held out an arm to encourage her to embrace him but oblivion was already overtaking him.

CHAPTER EIGHTY-FIVE

Ruby

'I don't want to be a nuisance,' Ruby said when Naomi opened the door to Foxfield.

'You're never a nuisance, Ruby, but I didn't expect to see you on your wedding day. Come in.'

'Bert . . .?'

'He's sleeping. He sleeps most of the time.'

'Hopefully, it's doing him good.'

Naomi's sad smile tore at Ruby's heart. 'Let's hope so,' Naomi said.

She led the way into the drawing room which overlooked the back of the house. The French windows were open to the balmy summer's morning and Naomi gestured Ruby to look outside.

Ruby saw Bert in a wheelchair, padded out with cushions and swathed in blankets. Beside him, Dr Lovell sat in a garden chair.

'Bert would probably be better off sleeping in bed but he does love to be outside. The matron at Stratton House sent the wheelchair down. So kind of her. We're hoping to be able to use it to take Bert to see his market garden one day.'

'That'll perk him up,' Ruby said, but Naomi's smile remained sad. 'There's been no improvement?' Ruby asked gently.

'I think Bert's St Albans doctor would say any apparent

357

improvement is down to determination rather than healing,' Naomi told her. 'But he's still with us and I'm keeping hopeful that he's here to stay.'

Poor Naomi had lost weight and was looking wan. Were there more silver streaks in her hair or was that Ruby's imagination?

'I brought another drawing from Timmy,' Ruby said, handing it over. 'It's a picture of Bert feeding the robin in his garden.'

'It's lovely.'

'Don't feel you have to give it to Bert, though. I expect he's overwhelmed with drawings from the children who live here.'

'No, he'll love it. He's very fond of Timmy. Of you and Pearl, too. If you're here about your wedding . . .'

'It just doesn't feel right going ahead with it when Bert is so ill.'

'That's not how he feels at all. It isn't how I feel, either. We want you and Pearl to get married. We want you to have the most wonderful day. Even if we can't be there to share it, we'll take pleasure in knowing that there's still joy in Churchwood.'

Ruby felt tears well in her eyes. 'If you're sure . . .?'

'We're very sure. And Bert has asked for six bottles of his home-made wine to be sent to the bookshop to help with the party.'

'That's so kind!'

'We wish you, Pearl and your husbands very happy lives together. And we'll expect to hear all about the ceremony and the party.'

Not wanting to keep Naomi from Bert any longer, Ruby left, thinking that it was a tragedy that Bert and Naomi might never have their own wedding. But then she straightened her shoulders. Life did go on, and if it pleased them to think of Churchwood celebrating then she'd make sure they celebrated with gusto.

She walked back to the farm, deep in thought. She'd had a life of ups and downs so far – like most people, no doubt. As a child she'd been neither particularly happy nor particularly unhappy. Her parents hadn't made her feel loved or appreciated but set against this had been her natural drive and ambition which had convinced her that one day she'd be able to choose a different path that would suit her far better than the stilted dullness of home.

That ambition had been checked by the vile man who'd taken advantage of her, leaving her pregnant and face to face with degradation, fear and money pressures. But once again she'd found light in the shade, loving Timmy with a fierce passion she'd never felt before. There'd been more worries since then. Worries about him being sent away as an evacuee. Distress over the fact that he was miserable with the family who'd taken him in only to be unkind to him. Dread in case it became known that he was her son instead of her little brother. But she'd never stopped fighting to improve their lives, and now . . . Now real happiness beckoned.

Ruby loved Kenny despite his faults. He could be morose. He was unskilled when it came to mixing with people who weren't fellow farmers. He was clueless when it came to a knight-in-shining-armour sort of romance. But she loved him and he loved her. Best of all, he and Timmy loved each other, too.

All in all, Ruby felt as though she'd been steering a boat over threatening, choppy waters but was now coming into harbour safely. She wasn't a fool. She knew there'd be challenges ahead since challenges appeared in every life. But she – the city girl who'd once shuddered at the thought of wind-swept, rain-lashed countryside with mud underfoot and no access to the bright lights of shops and cinemas and bars – belonged in Churchwood now.

Oh, she wasn't the same as other people. She was the outspoken girl with the dyed-blonde hair and red lipstick, but no one was truly the same as anyone else and that didn't matter. A community was like a jigsaw puzzle. No two pieces were identical but, together, they made up a picture that was whole and satisfying.

Reaching the farm, she found Pearl in the kitchen, wearing the hideous men's brown dressing-gown that she favoured, her thin hair askew on top of her head. Kate had insisted that neither land girl should lift a finger in work today. 'I can't believe we're getting married in a few hours,' Pearl said.

'Feeling scared?'

'Terrified. I'm bound to trip up walking down the aisle or fluff my wedding vows.'

'No, you're not. You'll have your father walking you down the aisle and Fred will be waiting for you at the end.'

'He will, won't he?' Pearl's grin was full of wonder as Ruby passed her a cup of tea. 'Me, getting spliced! I still can't believe it.'

'You're going to be very happy with Fred.' Even if they did bicker all the time and neither of them could boil an egg. They'd muddle through in their own unique way.

'You'll be happy with Kenny,' Pearl said.

'I will,' Ruby agreed, 'Timmy will be happy, too.' She paused before adding, 'We're lucky, having this chance for happy marriages. Not everyone is so lucky.'

'You're thinking of Naomi and Bert?'

'No one deserves happiness more than them. Hopefully, there won't be a long delay before they can arrange their wedding. We must make today a tribute to them,' Ruby proposed.

Kate came in with eggs, freshly laid by the farm's chickens. 'I'll make lunch,' Ruby offered.

'You're supposed to be relaxing this morning.'

'Making lunch won't kill me, and perhaps it'll cheer Ernie up a little if he sees I'm busy.'

'It would take more than lunch to do that,' Kate said wryly.

Ruby set to work boiling eggs to eat with salad and Fred came out from his downstairs room. 'Why are you all making so much noise?' he demanded. 'I'm trying to have a nap.'

It was nerves that were keeping Fred from sleeping. He looked terrified. Kenny, too, looked apprehensive when he came in for the meal. 'It's just the thought of all those people watching me,' he explained.

'Keep your eyes on me. I'm your bride,' Ruby told him.

After lunch Ruby, Pearl and Kate prepared to set out for May's house, where they were to get ready. 'We'll see the rest of you at the church,' Kate said. 'And we'll expect you to be clean. That means scrubbing the earth from under your fingernails as well as washing your hair and giving yourselves an all-over body wash. Don't forget to brush your hair afterwards and pin flowers to your jackets. The flowers are in the pantry, keeping fresh. They've already been made into buttonholes and there are pins beside them. I don't want to hear any excuses about forgetting them. Make sure you arrive at the church early. I'll be waiting to check you all over.'

Ruby cupped Timmy's face in both of her hands. 'I'm

relying on you to keep these rascally men in order,' she told him.

Timmy grinned. 'I won't let you down, Mum.'

Mum. The word always made her heart soar. Ruby smiled and kissed him. 'I know you won't.'

May's refugee children – Rosa, Samuel and Zofia – were playing outside the house when the Brimbles Farm party approached. Seeing them coming, the children ran inside, shouting, 'They're here! They're here!'

May and Alice appeared at the door to welcome them inside.

'It's so good of you to let us get ready here, May,' Ruby said.

'It's become something of a tradition for brides to get ready here,' May said. 'Alice, Kate, now you two . . .'

May had a bathroom stocked with fluffy towels and was generous in the way she allowed the use of it while also turning her bedroom into a dressing room. Ruby and Pearl took turns to bathe and wash their hair.

Tea was drunk and teeth were brushed, then capes were whisked around their shoulders for hair-drying followed by cosmetics. 'No cosmetics for me, thanks,' Pearl said.

'Just a little powder,' May pleaded. 'Am I right, Ruby?'

Ruby was regarded as the Churchwood expert on all things cosmetic. 'You're right,' she confirmed and, begrudgingly, Pearl submitted to some powder being patted on to her cheeks to take the shine off them and on to her nose to reduce the redness.

'Lovely!' May declared.

'I don't know about that,' Pearl said, never confident about her appearance. But she glanced in the mirror and said, 'Humph,' which was taken to signal approval.

Ruby managed her own cosmetics, applying them with the ease of years of practice.

'Now for the dresses,' Alice announced.

Ruby's dress was pale pink, a sample May had made years before and kept in case it ever became useful. With little capped sleeves and a tiny waist, it suited Ruby to perfection, set off by a headdress of fresh pink roses and white baby's-breath.

Pearl's was a slender cream sheath adapted from Kate's wedding dress with a forest-green jacket on top that was shaped like a riding jacket. 'Land Girl colours!' Pearl declared, clearly thrilled with it. She, too, wore a headdress, but it was a riding hat covered in more of the forest-green fabric and sporting three long feathers and a natty little veil.

Ruby wore Alice's wedding shoes since both girls had small feet. Pearl's feet were too big for her to have borrowed shoes from any of the Churchwood women but May had taken the soles from some ancient work boots and stitched on straps made from still more of the forest-green material.

Rosa, Samuel and Zofia were whispering outside the door and doubtless peeping through the keyhole. 'We can hear you!' May called to them.

There was some giggling and May opened the door to let them in.

'You look beautiful,' Rosa told Ruby and Pearl.

'Pretty,' Zofia added.

Samuel looked as though he disdained such feminine descriptions but his wide eyes suggested that he was secretly impressed. The children had spoken little English when they'd arrived from Poland less than three years ago but now they spoke the language as though they'd been born here.

There was a flurry of last-minute activity and then they set out for the church. It was a fine day so they walked the short distance, May urging Pearl to be careful of her shoes.

Two men stood on the church steps waiting for them. One was Pearl's father and the other was Kate's handsome husband, Leo. Mr Grimes looked to be in a bad mood, though Ruby was in no doubt that Leo had done his best to mollify him. In fact, Ruby guessed that Mr Grimes was wishing his daughter were marrying the debonair flight lieutenant instead of the inarticulate whittler of wood.

Leo smiled. 'What beautiful brides!' he declared, kissing their cheeks in turn.

May smoothed a stray hair from Ruby's face and straightened Pearl's skirt. 'There's no need to hold it up as though you're going paddling in the sea, Pearl,' she chided. 'Just let it go and . . . glide along.'

'Me? Glide? I've never glided in my life.'

'Then it's time you started.'

'Ruby should go in first,' Pearl said. There was no need to add that she wanted to hide behind her.

But Ruby wanted to play fair. 'I'll be happy for you to go first, Pearl. It means you'll reach the end of the aisle sooner.'

'Ruby should go first,' May decided, settling the dispute. 'No one will see her if you go first, Pearl, since you're so much taller.'

With that May hurried into the church.

Leo offered his arm to Ruby and she took it with a grateful smile. Leo was to walk her down the aisle since her own father was absent.

'Come along, Gertrude,' Mr Grimes instructed, and Pearl took his arm with considerably less enthusiasm.

'Crikey, this is terrifying,' she said to no one in particular.

'Behave yourself, Gertrude,' her father scolded, but Ruby shared a grin with Pearl and saw that no one could dampen her friend's spirits today.

The organ began playing the first hymn inside the church. It was time to set off.

It seemed to Ruby as though the whole village had turned out, for every pew looked full of people who turned beams of goodwill on them as they processed down the aisle. Doubtless, there'd be a few absences. Mrs Nugent for one, but Ruby didn't bother looking for her crabby features among the crowd. She couldn't care less about Mrs Nugent and her meanness any more. The absences Ruby cared about were Naomi's and Bert's. She sent up a silent prayer for them but then straightened her shoulders, determined to enjoy this special day.

Adam awaited them at the end of the aisle, dressed in his robes and smiling sweetly. So did the grooms, Kenny and Fred, both looking a little sickly with nerves, and Fred self-conscious on his false legs. Beside them stood the best men – a proud Timmy for Kenny and an awkward Vinnie for Fred.

'You look beautiful,' Kenny whispered, when she reached him.

Pearl attempted a whisper when she reached Fred. 'Blimey, I made it without falling over,' she said, but so loudly that her voice carried through the church and everyone laughed. Apart from her father, who looked irritated.

Adam called everyone to order and the ceremony began. Kenny was mortified when he choked with nerves over his vows but Ruby forgave him and spoke her own vows confidently.

When it was Fred's turn, Pearl slapped him on the shoulder and said, 'Go on, then, Fred. Nice and loud.'

And when it was her turn she said, 'I will,' when asked if

365

she'd obey Fred, only to make everyone laugh again when she added, 'Of course, we all know I won't really obey you, Fred. I expect you to obey *me*.'

Then the ceremony was over. They were married!

'On behalf of our beautiful brides and their handsome husbands, I'd like to invite you all to the bookshop for one of our Churchwood parties!' Adam said.

Arm in arm with Kenny, Ruby walked back up the aisle with Pearl and Fred following. Outside, Kenny breathed out his tension. 'Phew! I'm glad I'm married to you, Ruby, but, heck, that was an ordeal. All those eyes on us!'

Timmy rushed up and circled his arms around Ruby's waist. 'Did I do a good job, Mum?'

Ruby looked to Kenny. 'You were the best of best men, son,' Kenny said.

Timmy's eyes sparkled. 'Thanks, Dad!'

Mum, Dad, son . . . Ruby felt a completeness she'd never felt before. Her parents might not have bothered to attend her wedding, but the day was all the better without them since they'd only have cast sourness over the occasion, just as Pearl's parents and sister had done, the sister being a younger version of the prissy mother, even down to the same sort of handbag.

No, Ruby might have disappointed her parents but she hadn't disappointed herself. On the contrary, she felt proud of the woman she'd become. She'd triumphed over her setbacks to bring up a son who was an absolute delight. She was useful to people. A good friend. And she had every intention of being a good and loving wife.

The disapproval of the past was behind her and she was free. So, too, was Pearl, judging from the sheer joy that was lighting up her plain but much-loved face.

They were both happy. So very happy, and they just

needed good news of Bert and Naomi to make that happiness complete.

'Party time!' Pearl said, and off to the bookshop they went, Ruby vowing to drink a toast to their precious, absent friends.

CHAPTER EIGHTY-SIX

Suki

Suki sat on one of the bookshop stairs, sipping from a glass of wine and, amid the chatter and laughter, taking a moment to herself. Waking up every day to the knowledge that Adam would never be hers was still causing her pain. It twisted inside her, sharp and lacerating, and watching him conduct the marriages of Ruby and Pearl today had been hard. Not that she begrudged the land girls their happiness. On the contrary, she was delighted to see them looking so full of joy.

She was also glad to feel she was being useful despite her heartache. She was throwing herself into her work back at Foxfield, determined that the house should be kept clean and sparkling for Mrs Harrington. She'd spent a little time pulling up weeds at Mr Makepiece's market garden under William's direction and she'd spent more time looking after the evacuee children. Even for today's weddings she'd helped to arrange greenery at the church and here at the bookshop.

'You look lovely, Suki,' Victoria had said when Suki came down from her room dressed for the wedding.

'So do you,' Suki had replied. Victoria was wearing a green dress that brought out the colour of her eyes, though Suki suspected that her radiance owed more to the fact that she was being accompanied by Sergeant Scarletti.

Letting everyone from Foxfield set out ahead of her, Suki had lingered to study her reflection in the hall mirror. She was wearing her best blue dress and had teased her hair into loose soft waves. Neither the dress nor the hairstyle were new but her face looked different somehow. Oh, it was the same old face she was used to, eyes, nose, cheeks and mouth all being in the same positions. But its expression seemed to be less naive than before. Wiser. More mature.

For a moment, thoughts of Adam made her breath catch in her throat. But she stared into her own reflected eyes and steadied herself, locking her distress into a private recess deep inside her so she could attend the wedding with a smile on her face and a determination to get on with her life.

So far she'd done nothing to make her think she'd let herself down. She took another sip of wine and looked towards Beth, who was sitting in the main room below. There was a quiet dignity about Beth. Suki's gaze shifted onwards to Nancy, who was standing on the opposite side of the room looking fresh and pretty in a dress that May had apparently helped her to make. It had a big flower on the bodice which looked fun – like Nancy herself. She was laughing and her eyes were sparkling merrily. But she hadn't looked at Suki once.

Someone put a record on the gramophone: Fred Astaire's 'Cheek to Cheek'. Tables and chairs were pushed to the side to make room for dancing and Suki suddenly realized that Nancy was looking up at her at last. And thinking . . . What? Angry thoughts? Resentful thoughts? Had Suki stirred up trouble and made an enemy?

She wasn't aware that she'd begun to hold her breath until Nancy looked away. But to Suki's horror Nancy headed straight for Adam. They spoke – Suki couldn't hear the words – but seconds later they were on the dance floor, dancing together.

Poor Beth! Another glance in her direction showed her stiffening at the sight of the merry couple and then breathing deeply to steady what were doubtless choppy emotions. Someone spoke to her – Mrs Lloyd – and brave Beth forced a smile and a reply.

But then the song came to an end and Suki watched as Nancy led Adam towards Beth and gestured for him to sit beside her. Leaving them – Beth with a look of surprise on her face – Nancy came upstairs and sat beside Suki. 'I thought about what you said,' she announced.

'Oh?'

'I decided you were right. Adam and Beth deserve their chance without me throwing a spanner in the works.'

'That's . . . good of you.' Suki was impressed. 'You're not too disappointed, I hope?'

'I like Adam. Very much. And when – *if* – I settle down with a man, I want him to have some of Adam's substance. As a person, I mean. I don't want to settle for a shallow sort of man. But I haven't known Adam for long and I haven't reached the stage of being in love with him. Besides, I don't think I'm the right sort of person for him. Oh, I'm sure he likes me and I make him laugh, but I've seen the way he looks at Beth and it's as though she's his . . . sanctuary. His soulmate. You're probably finding it harder than me to see them together. You've known Adam for longer and you're in love with him.'

'I'm coping,' Suki said. 'I won't pretend I'm not sad but I'm surprisingly calm.'

'That's because you've accepted the situation. You're no longer fighting it.'

'You didn't mind me . . . interfering? You don't hold it against me?'

'It's actually made me like you. Oh, I liked you well

370

enough before, but the way you stuck up for Beth . . . It shows what a good friend you can be. I'd like you to be my friend, too.'

'Really?'

'Really. It's going to be interesting getting to know you better. I suspect you have hidden depths, Suki.'

Had she? She'd know soon enough because she'd be leaving Churchwood before long. Who'd have thought it? Suki leaving the place and the people she loved so much!

She'd kept her plans to herself until that very morning, when she'd picked the post off the Foxfield doormat and taken it in to Mrs Harrington in the sitting room.

'Thank you, dear,' Mrs Harrington had said, but as Suki turned to leave she'd called her back. 'Sit down, Suki. I have a feeling there's something you want to tell me.'

Suki hadn't expected this. She'd blushed and blinked rapidly. 'It's nothing that can't wait,' she'd said.

'You don't want to be a worry to me. Is that what you're thinking?'

It was exactly what Suki had been thinking and she'd been cross with herself for not doing a better job of hiding the fact that she had something on her mind. With everything else Mrs Harrington was going through, the last thing she needed was to be worrying about her maid.

'I'm sorry if I've given the impression of being . . . out of sorts,' Suki had said.

'You haven't. In fact, you've made an admirable effort to appear cheerful. But I've known you for a long time now, and let's just say my instincts have been stirring.'

Oh, heck.

'Don't look so tortured, Suki. It's sweet of you to put me first but your happiness is important, too. So let me help you along. Are you thinking of handing in your notice?'

Suki's blush had deepened but she'd taken a steadying breath and conquered her awkwardness. 'If you'd asked me not so long ago if I'd ever want to leave Foxfield, the answer would have been no. When that Act of Parliament became law – the one calling women up to carry out war work of some kind or other – I dreaded the thought of being sent away. I loved it here. I still love it here. All the people . . . they're wonderful. You, especially.'

Mrs Harrington had smiled. 'But?' she'd prompted gently.

'I feel I need to test myself,' Suki had told her. 'To find out what I can do in the world. What I can achieve and how I can cope. Does that make sense?'

'It makes perfect sense. What sort of test do you have in mind?'

'I'd like to join one of the services and help with the war effort. The Women's Auxiliary Air Force, the Women's Royal Naval Service or the Auxiliary Territorial Service. I've made a few enquiries and found out how to apply. I'm not the best-educated person – you know I left school at fourteen – but I hope that at least the ATS will want me.'

'They'll be fools if they don't,' Naomi had said. 'I salute you, Suki, and wish you every success, but you're going to be sorely missed.'

'Actually, my sister Sal isn't happy working for Mrs Nyse in Barton. She'd love to take my place here, if you'll have her. She's a good girl. Hard-working and cheerful. And she'll be wonderful with the children.'

'I already like your sister, Suki, and if she's half as good a maid as you, she'll be marvellous. I'll miss you, though.'

Suki had felt the prickle of tears. 'I'll miss you, too. Dreadfully. You're the best employer anyone could have.'

There'd been tears in Mrs Harrington's eyes, too. 'Life is an adventure, Suki. Embrace it.'

'I will, and I hope you'll soon be on an adventure, too: marriage to Mr Makepiece.'

'Let's hope so, Suki.'

She really was going to miss Churchwood and all her friends but joining the services was what she needed just now. Oh, it would be hard work. Suki was in no doubt about that. It would challenge her physically, emotionally and every which way, but she'd meet those challenges with courage and the determination to cope. After all, Suki was a child no longer. She was a young woman. With a lot to offer.

CHAPTER EIGHTY-SEVEN

Beth

'Are you having a nice time?' Adam asked.

For a moment Beth was too flustered to answer. Why had Nancy brought him over? And why had she suggested that he should sit beside Beth for a chat? A chat about what? Having dazzled him on the dance floor just now, surely Nancy wasn't trying to demonstrate that Beth was a dull creature in comparison? That would be cruel and Beth had never considered Nancy to be cruel. Perhaps she was mistaken about that, though.

'It's a lovely wedding,' Beth finally said, which didn't quite answer the question but was honest. 'The brides and grooms look so happy.' And if Beth wasn't feeling as happy . . . well, she wouldn't let herself spoil other people's fun. She hesitated before saying, 'I saw you dancing. You looked as though you were enjoying it.'

'I was,' Adam admitted, but then he fell quiet.

Beth's gaze searched out Nancy, desperate to know if this was some sort of game of rivalry. There she was, on the stairs with Suki.

To Beth's astonishment, Nancy winked at her and Suki sent her an encouraging nod. And out of the confusion came glorious, blistering understanding. Nancy wasn't a rival. Not any more. She'd stepped aside and now she was trying to bring Beth and Adam together. So was Suki, despite her own heartache.

How utterly wonderful of them. How selfless, how kind people could be. Self-conscious suddenly with Adam beside her, Beth felt herself blushing. She looked down at her hands as they twisted in her lap. What next?

'I expect you're tired after dancing,' Beth said since she needed to say *something*, but Adam looked as though he'd barely heard her because he was wrestling with some sort of private issue.

At last, he spoke. 'I'm glad we have this chance to talk, Beth. We're both always so busy when we see each other at the hospital and the children's club. I'd like you to know that I enjoy your company. Very much.'

The words – and the apparent intensity behind them – had Beth's heart racing and agitation playing havoc with her head. Desperate to calm herself, she took a deep breath and looked at Adam. 'I enjoy yours.'

'You do?' The leap of pleasure in his brown eyes couldn't have warmed her more.

'Whenever I see you, Beth, it's as though joy fizzes in my heart like bubbles,' Adam said. 'I feel excited. But at the same time I feel . . . steadied. Warm and . . . *comfortable*, if that doesn't sound like a contradiction? I feel like I'm coming home.'

'It doesn't sound like a contradiction, because I feel the same way,' Beth admitted.

Adam's smile glowed. 'That's . . . that's wonderful.' He heaved a big sigh but then doubts appeared to set in. 'I'm not much of a prospect, though. I'm a country vicar and likely to stay that way. I'll never hold high office. I'll never be rich. In fact, I'll probably always be poor since I can never turn my back on a person in need. Someone like you could marry a doctor. You could . . .'

'Be blissfully happy with you, Adam.'

'Really?'

'I'm sure of it.'

He smiled again, wonder giving way to delighted acceptance. 'Do you think we might start spending more time together in future? By ourselves, I mean. Just as a beginning. I know it'll be difficult between your duties and mine but—'

'We'll manage.' Beth reached out and touched his hand. 'We'll make sure we manage.'

'Yes,' he said. 'We will.'

Beth glanced up at Nancy and Suki again. They grinned at her. And Beth smiled back. Friendship was . . . well, it was wonderful.

CHAPTER EIGHTY-EIGHT

Bert

'Can you hear that, Bert?' Naomi asked.

They were on the lawn at Foxfield, Bert in the wheel-chair and Naomi on a garden chair beside him. At their insistence, everyone else had gone to the wedding and this was, he realized, the first time they'd been properly alone since the accident.

They'd heard distant church bells earlier, signalling to the world that the weddings of Ruby and Pearl were now complete. 'Such a joyful sound,' Naomi had remarked, and Bert had agreed.

'I'm glad for them,' she'd added, though Bert had suspected that she was feeling as he did – that it was such a pity they hadn't managed to get married themselves.

Now music was reaching them, carried on the breeze. Dr Marwood from the hospital had lent the happy couples his gramophone and records. They'd heard Glenn Miller, Louis Armstrong, Bing Crosby . . . 'This is Paul Whiteman and his Orchestra,' Naomi said. '"Happy Feet".'

'You've made me happy,' Bert told her.

Naomi reached out and smoothed her hand over his. 'You've made me happy, too. So very happy.'

He smiled and then looked around the garden. At the towering trees in shades of green and copper. At the lush green lawn. At the beds of lupins, geraniums, holly-hocks . . . Bees were busy among them. Birds, too. Bert spotted blackbirds, a goldfinch and a jay. His ears picked up the sound of a woodpecker, too, though he couldn't see it. 'It's beautiful here,' he said, feeling the sun warm his face. 'It brings a man peace.'

Naomi smiled but then he said, 'It's time, my love,' and her face took on a look of dismay.

'Don't be afraid, beloved,' Bert urged her. 'Don't be afraid.'

CHAPTER EIGHTY-NINE

Naomi

'You didn't need to bring me tea in bed,' Naomi protested, when Victoria carried a tea tray into the room.

Before the arrival of the evacuee families Naomi had often enjoyed her first drink of the day in bed, but since then the household had been far too busy for pampering. Like everyone, Naomi had been required to get up and throw herself into each day.

'I want to look after you, after all you've been through,' Victoria insisted. 'We all want to look after you.'

How kind they were: Victoria, Suki, the evacuee families, Alice, Kate, Adam . . . Emotion welled up in Naomi at the thought of everything they'd done to support her over the poison pen letters and then – much more serious – Bert's accident. She was blessed to have such caring friends.

'Drink up,' Victoria advised, passing a cup and saucer to Naomi and placing the tray on the small cabinet next to the bed.

She opened the curtains and then the window. 'It's a lovely day out there,' she said, and smiled as she left the room.

It was a lovely day indeed. Sunny yet fresh. The open window let in air that tingled on Naomi's skin. It also let in

379

the sound of birdsong and the fragrance of summer-mown grass and flowers.

Naomi sat back against her pillows, reflecting on the twists and turns of life, from the traumatic to the joyful. For weeks life had held her in the grip of fear and uncertainty but now . . .

How frightened she'd been that day Bert had spoken to her in the garden. She'd dreaded the worst. But what he'd had to tell her was the best news possible. 'I didn't want to tell you before in case it was a false start that couldn't last, but I'm beginning to feel much better. The headaches have become a mild sort of nuisance instead of a pummelling and the dizzy spells aren't half as dizzying as before. I can feel my strength returning, too. It's as though I've drunk some brandy and I can feel the heat of it working through me.'

'Bert, that's wonderful!'

Naomi had cried countless tears in recent weeks but more tears had come into her eyes, this time drawn by jubilation and relief.

'Dr Gilbert will doubtless say I should take things easy and I will. But I can take things easy on a honeymoon with you, beloved. Let's get married just as soon as we can manage it. By special licence, if needed.'

Yesterday, they'd gone to a register office for a civil ceremony so technically they were man and wife already. But it was today's blessing here in the heart of Churchwood and the party to be held at Foxfield afterwards that mattered most.

Everyone was rallying round to make it a day to remember. Naomi drank her tea in bed but insisted on getting up for breakfast, to be thoroughly spoiled with fresh eggs. Neither Victoria nor Suki would let her lift a finger to help.

Instead, Naomi was ushered into the drawing room where the evacuee families waited to give her the cards and messages they'd made, including good-luck horseshoes cut from card, covered in silver foil and decorated with ribbons.

Then Alice and Kate arrived to take her off to May's house to get ready.

'There's no need for a fuss,' Naomi said, but for all the notice they took of her, she might as well have been talking to the birds in the garden.

'It's become Churchwood tradition for brides to get ready at May's house,' Alice insisted.

Naomi was nervous when she climbed the stairs to May's bedroom. May had measured her for a new dress but Naomi hadn't seen it yet since she'd been blindfolded for the trying-on session. She really hoped these young things had kept her age at the forefront of their minds. Her sagging skin and body, too.

She needn't have worried. The dress was beautiful, a sky-blue crêpe affair that fell to cocktail length and had a matching bolero jacket that May had trimmed with silver-beaded braid. The headdress was a small hat that was decorated with more of the sparkling braid and several navy feathers. 'Oh, May! You've done me proud!' Naomi declared.

Kate drove her to the church in the Brimbles Farm truck, which had been cleaned and decked out with flowers for the occasion. Apparently, Ernie had scowled and said, 'Not another waste-of-time wedding!' but no one had taken any notice.

Naomi arrived at St Luke's church to find Alice's father waiting on the steps. 'I know I offered to walk you down the aisle, Naomi,' he said, 'but I think you deserve a handsome young soldier beside you instead.'

He beckoned behind him and Alice's husband, Daniel, stepped out from the shadows of the porch. Trimly built, with cleanly cut good looks and fresh skin, he looked at Naomi with softness in his dark-brown eyes. 'Some might say it's a coincidence that I've been granted leave just in time for your wedding, but I prefer to think it's because the stars have lined up in kindness. You look lovely, Naomi.' So saying, he kissed her cheek.

'I couldn't be more pleased to see you,' Naomi told him. 'I don't know how Alice managed to keep your leave a secret from me.'

'With great difficulty, I think.'

Alice had popped into the church but now she emerged with a Pied Piper line of children comprising all the young evacuees from Foxfield; Ruby's boy, Timmy; and May's refugees, Rosa, Samuel and Zofia. They were all to follow Naomi down the aisle as bridesmaids and pageboys. It hadn't been possible to provide new clothes for them, but all were wearing their Sunday best and carrying a single flower plucked from Naomi's garden.

'You deserve this, Naomi,' Alice said. 'You deserve to be happy.'

She kissed Naomi's cheek and then Daniel's, and slipped inside the church with Kate, May and her father.

'Shall we?' Daniel offered Naomi his arm, and they too stepped into the church.

Naomi was touched to see how many people had turned out to wish her and Bert well. She'd speak to them all later, but just now there were two other people who deserved her attention. The first was Bert, of course, the love of her life. The second was Bert's best man, William, who'd become as dear to her as a son.

Bert beamed at Naomi as she walked slowly down the

aisle. 'You take my breath away, woman,' he whispered when she reached him.

She laughed. 'You're looking pretty dapper yourself. New suit?'

'The first in thirty years,' he confirmed. 'It isn't as though I've used my clothing coupons for anything else. I'll be back in my scarecrow clothes tomorrow, though.'

Naomi smiled. 'I wouldn't expect anything else.'

She realized then that Adam was waiting to begin the ceremony. Embarrassed, she glanced around but saw only smiles of tolerance and amusement.

Bert chuckled. 'Come on, then, woman. Let's get wed.'

The blessing began and Naomi was torn between wanting to remember every single second and floating in a daze of joy. Who would have guessed just a few years ago that she'd finally be free from cold-hearted Alexander, a man who'd reduced her self-esteem to pulp, and be facing bliss with a true gem of a man? Certainly not Naomi, but here she was.

The reception party was everything she could have wished for, too, the generosity of her friends astonishing her as ever. There was food and drink aplenty, a cake magicked into being by Janet with ingredients contributed by numerous well-wishers. Congratulations rang out and there was dancing in true Churchwood tradition.

Bert drew Naomi aside momentarily. 'Well, beloved. It's been a long and difficult road but we got here in the end.'

'We did,' Naomi agreed. 'We kept each other going through the dark times and we've been blessed to have the goodwill of so many friends.'

The Foxfield garden was filled with smiling, laughing faces. Alice and Daniel were holding each other lovingly as Daniel stroked the curve of their forthcoming child.

Kate and Leo were dancing enthusiastically. Duty had prevented Leo from attending the service but he'd rolled up on a motorbike not long ago.

Victoria's Paul hadn't made it to the wedding either, but he'd sent a telegram, sending his best wishes to the happy couple. Now Victoria was dancing with Arthur, Jenny and the other evacuees. May and her refugees danced with them. William was there too, swinging Suki around and making her giggle, while Beth danced in Adam's arms. As Naomi watched, Beth stepped back and gestured Adam to give young Hannah a turn. 'I'll be delighted,' he said, bowing at a glowing Hannah.

Naomi's gaze moved on to Ruby, who was trying – and failing – to teach rhythmless Kenny to dance, and to Pearl, laughing at Fred's dancing efforts and telling him he was even more of a clumsy elephant than she was.

How dear they all were. How precious. And how desperately Naomi hoped that they and their loved ones would come through the war unscathed. It was impossible to predict the future, but whatever challenges lay ahead for them, Churchwood's bookshop and togetherness would help them through.

Even Marjorie was present. She'd written a letter, explaining that Constance had deceived her and begging for forgiveness. Naomi's friendship was worth more than every penny of the inheritance she was to receive from Sir John, she'd insisted. She'd haunted the Foxfield gateposts, too, as though afraid to step on to the drive in case she was driven away. Eventually, Naomi had taken pity on her and Marjorie had sobbed in relief.

'Right, woman,' Bert said to Naomi. 'It's time *we* were dancing. I want to hold you in my arms and savour the moment you became my wife.'

'But you're not fully well, Bert.'

'I'm well enough for this. You'll need to brace yourself for squashed toes, but know that they'll be squashed in the good cause of a man celebrating with the bride of his dreams.'

'Put like that . . .' she said.

He led her on to the dance floor to cheers and applause. And as Naomi smiled up at Bert's craggy face, she reflected that it had taken forty-seven years to reach this moment but here she finally was. Happy, with a man she loved truly, and who loved her truly in return. She vowed to treasure every second of their life together.

Acknowledgements

My books are written mostly in my kitchen with only the kettle for company, but many people are involved in bringing them out into the world. They include the fabulous team at Transworld – my editor Lara Stevenson; my copy editor, Eleanor Updegraff; proofreader Clare Hubbard; production editor, Vivien Thompson; managing editorial coordinator, Holly Reed, and all involved in design, production, sales and marketing. You're all amazing.

They also include my wonderful agent, Kate Nash, and all at the Kate Nash Literary Agency. You're all amazing, too.

My lovely readers also deserve a massive thank you. Without you my books would remain between me and my kettle. Whether you buy my books or borrow them from the library, I value each and every one of you and am truly grateful for all your kind messages and reviews.

I must also thank my friends and family for putting up with me and giving me so much support. You're stars!

About the Author

Lesley Eames is an author of historical sagas, her preferred writing place being the kitchen due to its proximity to the kettle. Lesley loves tea, as do many of her characters. Having previously written sagas set around the time of the First World War and into the Roaring Twenties, she has ventured into the Second World War period with *The Wartime Bookshop* series.

Originally from the northwest of England (Manchester), Lesley's home is now Hertfordshire, where *The Wartime Bookshop*'s fictional village of Churchwood is set. Along her journey as a writer, Lesley has been thrilled to have had ninety short stories published and to have enjoyed success in competitions in genres as varied as crime writing and writing for children. She is particularly honoured to have won the Festival of Romance New Talent Award, the Romantic Novelists' Association's Elizabeth Goudge Trophy and to have been twice shortlisted in the UK Romantic Novel Awards (RONAs).

Learn more by visiting her website:
www.lesleyeames.com
Or follow her on Facebook:
www.facebook.com/LesleyEamesWriter

Don't miss the other books in *The Wartime Bookshop* series . . .

The Wartime Bookshop
Book 1 in *The Wartime Bookshop* series

Alice is nursing an injured hand and a broken heart when
she moves to the village of Churchwood at the start of WWII.
She is desperate to be independent but worries that her
injuries will make that impossible.

Kate lives with her family on Brimbles Farm, where
her father and brothers treat her no better than a servant. With
no mother or sisters, and shunned by the locals,
Kate longs for a friend of her own.

Naomi is looked up to for owning the best house
in the village. But privately, she carries the hurts of
childlessness, a husband who has little time for her
and some deep-rooted insecurities.

**With war raging overseas, and difficulties to overcome at
home, friendship is needed now more than ever. Can the war
effort and a shared love of books bring these women – and
the community of Churchwood – together?**

AVAILABLE NOW

Land Girls at the Wartime Bookshop
Book 2 in *The Wartime Bookshop* series

The residents of Churchwood have never needed their bookshop, or its community, more. But when the bookshop comes under threat at the worst possible time, can Alice, Kate and Naomi pull together to keep spirits high?

Kate has always found life on Brimbles Farm difficult, but now she is struggling more than ever to find time for the things that matter to her – particularly helping to save the village bookshop and seeing handsome pilot Leo Kinsella. Can two Land Girls help? Or will they be more trouble than they're worth?

Naomi has found new friends and purpose through the bookshop and is devastated when its future is threatened. But when she begins to suspect her husband of being unfaithful, she finds her attention divided. With old insecurities rearing up, she needs to uncover the truth.

Alice has a lot on her plate. Can she fight to save the bookshop while also looking for a job and worrying about her fiancé Daniel away fighting in the war?

AVAILABLE NOW

Christmas at the Wartime Bookshop
Book 3 in *The Wartime Bookshop* series

Alice, Kate and Naomi want to keep the magic of Christmas alive in their village of Churchwood, but a thief in the area and a new family that shuns the local community are only the first of the problems they face . . .

Naomi is fighting to free herself from Alexander Harrington – the man who married her for her money then kept a secret family behind her back. But will she be able to achieve the independence she craves?

Alice's dreams came true when she married sweetheart Daniel. Now he has returned to the fighting, but Alice is delighted to discover that she's carrying his child. Will the family make it through the war unscathed?

While **Kate**'s life on Brimbles Farm has never been easy, she now has help from land girls Pearl and Ruby. But what will it mean for them all when Kate's brother returns from the war with terrible injuries? And why has pilot Leo, the man she loves, stopped writing?

As ever, the Wartime Bookshop is a source of community and comfort. But disaster is about to strike . . .

AVAILABLE NOW

Evacuees at the Wartime Bookshop
Book 4 in *The Wartime Bookshop* series

January, 1942

Victoria is on her way to Churchwood in Hertfordshire, looking for a life away from the dangers of wartime London for herself and two orphaned children. But the village residents are already dealing with their own problems . . .

Alice is working hard to get the village bookshop back up and running after the previous premises were destroyed. The new building is in urgent need of repair and a builder has been hired, but where is he and where is the money he was paid?

Kate is struggling to work out the next steps in her relationship with pilot Leo. Injured in the fighting, he has returned to convalesce with his parents, but they are rich and elegant, and Kate suspects they want their son's sweetheart to be the same – not a country bumpkin like her with barely a penny to her name.

Meanwhile, **Naomi** shows kindness to Victoria and her evacuees, but is she biting off more than she can chew, especially when she is confronted with a surprising intruder . . .

With so much trouble and uncertainty in the village, can Victoria and her little family find the safe haven they crave?

AVAILABLE NOW

Don't miss Lesley's brand-new
Second World War series . . .

THE WARTIME
NEWSPAPER GIRLS

Coming soon!